MW00445406

DON'T TURN AROUND

Also by Harry Dolan

The Good Killer
The Man in the Crooked Hat
The Last Dead Girl
Very Bad Men
Bad Things Happen

DON'T TURN AROUND

A THRILLER

HARRY DOLAN

Atlantic Monthly Press

New York

FIRST EDITION

Published simultaneously in Canada
Printed in the United States of America

First Grove Atlantic hardcover edition: April 2024

Library of Congress Cataloging-in-Publication data is available for this title.

ISBN 978-0-8021-6282-3
eISBN 978-0-8021-6283-0

Atlantic Monthly Press
an imprint of Grove Atlantic
154 West 14th Street
New York, NY 10011

Distributed by Publishers Group West

groveatlantic.com

24 25 26 27   10 9 8 7 6 5 4 3 2 1

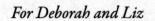

For Deborah and Liz

DON'T
TURN
AROUND

1

Later on, when the police questioned her, Katy Summerlin would say she went out to look at the full moon.

Her father was teaching at Seagate College that year, in a small town in upstate New York called Alexander. They lived in a rented farmhouse, and Katy's bedroom was tucked away in a corner of the ground floor. It had a tall casement window on the south wall, with sixteen panes of old glass.

Katy woke in the night to the moon shining through, the shape of it wavy in the glass. She sat up. It was warm in the room. The alarm clock read 1:06.

She drank from a bottle of water at her bedside.

She didn't feel tired.

She had snuck out once before, a few weeks earlier, on the night of her eleventh birthday. Because you should be daring on your birthday. That time she didn't go far. Into the backyard to gaze up at the stars. Lots of them, out in the country.

Now she crossed the room, smooth boards beneath her bare feet. She worked the latch of the casement window and swung it open. The hinges were quiet.

Cooler out there. She moved her desk chair over and stepped onto the seat. Then onto the sill, and then she was out, landing soft on the grass, knees bent.

For a moment she listened and didn't move. Her parents' bedroom was on the second floor. Her mother was out of town, but her father would be sleeping up there. Katy stood and looked up at their bedroom window. She waited for it to open, for her father to call down.

Nothing happened.

She walked to the middle of the yard. It had rained in the evening and the grass was still damp. She waded through it, farther on, through a scattering of dandelions. Flecks of yellow in the moonlight.

At the edge of the yard stood a trellis arch. Katy passed under it. There were flagstones in the grass. They made a path that led down to a stream. She followed them.

Nighttime sounds surrounded her. She hadn't noticed them before. Far-off crickets. Something scurrying in the brush on her left. The stream should be coming up on her right. The flagstones ran out and she was walking through grass again. It was rougher here and longer. Maybe she should have worn shoes.

When she came to the stream, she stopped to look at the sky. She found a bright star that she thought was Arcturus. Then Ursa Major, the Big Dipper.

She turned to look back. Thought about how far she'd come. She couldn't see the house from here.

She listened to the murmur of the stream. The water was clear. Katy could make out rounded stones at the bottom.

Might as well go a little farther, she thought. She was daring after all.

She walked along parallel to the stream. Away on her left were the silhouettes of trees, and somewhere beyond them a road.

The crickets chirped. The water flowed. She didn't stop or turn back.

A breeze brushed cool through her hair. A dark shape loomed up ahead. A tall oak tree with a great spreading canopy. The wind stirred its leaves in slow motion.

There was something else: a patch of white on the ground. White and gray. Vague shapes. They came into focus as she drew closer.

Someone was sleeping in the grass. A girl. Older than Katy. Maybe a student from the college. She wore a white blouse with white buttons and long sleeves. A gray skirt. She lay on her back with her head tipped toward her left shoulder, and strands of her long, dark hair fell across her face, obscuring her eyes. Her arms were spread straight out on either side. It looked like an uncomfortable position to be in.

Not how anyone would choose to sleep.

Katy knew this, but she knelt in the grass anyway. Reached out for the girl's shoulder as if she might wake her. That's when she saw the rope and the knots.

Thin rope like clothesline. Three lengths of it on either side, knotted under the girl's armpits and at her elbows and wrists. The rope secured her to a long wooden pole that lay underneath her. It held her arms outspread.

Katy felt her own heart beating. It occurred to her that she should be afraid. It should be beating faster.

But she was still taking things in: The black ribbon tied loosely around the girl's throat. The girl's hands, open, palms up. Blades of grass between the slender fingers.

The white blouse was untucked from the skirt, and its three lowest buttons were undone. Katy could see the girl's pale stomach in the moonlight.

There was something written there. In red, but not in blood. The lines were too crisp and smooth. They looked like they were drawn with a marker.

They formed a single word:

MERKURY

Neat red letters on the girl's flawless skin. Katy found herself wanting to touch them.

Before her fingers made contact, she stopped herself. Let her hand hover in the air. The water of the stream flowed beside her. The branches of the oak hissed softly in the wind. The noise of the crickets faded.

She heard a rustling behind her—something moving through the grass and the old leaves that littered the ground. It didn't sound like footsteps. Not at first.

The rustling stopped, and she knew someone was there. She heard him take in a slow breath.

Then she heard his voice.

"Don't turn around," he said.

2

EIGHTEEN YEARS LATER

It's not a shack, the place where she's living.

If it were in a more desirable location you might get away with calling it a bungalow. It's a one-story house: a sitting room, a kitchen, a bedroom, a bath. It's at the end of a long gravel driveway that connects it to an unpaved road in rural Ohio.

The front steps are broken concrete, and the vinyl siding is blistered along the south wall, where it gets the most sun. The white paint on the trim is cracked and peeling. There's a leak in the roof.

So you could be forgiven for calling it a shack.

Kate Summerlin steps out the front door in the early afternoon, locks up out of habit, and walks down the driveway to the road. It's warm, but the sky is gray.

Two miles east, there's a farm with a barn and a stable and a fenced-in paddock. She makes it there in half an hour. Sometimes there are horses in the paddock, but not today.

She turns around at the fence and walks back at an easy pace, and when she reaches the house she has company. There's a blue Ford Explorer in the driveway and a familiar figure sitting on her front steps: a Black woman in her early fifties, tall and slender, with braided hair. Police Chief Vera Landen from Alexander, New York.

"You've traveled a long way," Kate says.

Landen gets up on her feet, moving with a casual grace.

"I tried calling you," she says.

She called more than once. Kate deleted the messages.

"It wasn't easy finding you," Landen says. "No one knew where you'd gone. Not even your father."

"That's the way I wanted it."

"Eventually I went to Lee Tennick," Landen says. "He suggested I look for you here."

Kate frowns. "I don't talk to Lee Tennick."

"No."

"I definitely don't confide in Lee Tennick."

"You don't have to," Landen says. "As long as other people do." She gestures toward the house. "You've been doing some work. You went into town for supplies."

By "town" she means Bradner, Ohio. A single stoplight on Main Street and half a dozen storefronts. One of them is an Ace Hardware.

As a matter of fact, Kate hasn't done any work yet, but she intends to fix the roof. She bought shingles and roofing nails and a sheet of plywood.

Chief Landen is still talking. "Someone saw you in town and recognized you," she says. "They told somebody, who told somebody else, and eventually it got to Tennick. You know how it goes."

Kate knows. Lee Tennick has ways of finding things out.

"Once I knew the town, it wasn't hard to find your address," Landen says. "I started asking around at restaurants. You had a pizza delivered last week."

The woman shrugs as if to say, *And here we are*. She's been drawing things out, putting off the subject she has come here to talk about, but now she gets to the point.

"He's done it again," she says. "Merkury. You must have seen the news."

Kate saw it. Of course she did.

"The victim was male," Landen says. "That's unusual for Merkury, but not unheard of. His name was Bryan Cayhill. He was a student at Seagate College."

"I know," Kate says. She has read these details online and she knows why they're significant. The very first victim—the girl Kate found by the stream under the oak tree—was a student from Seagate too. Merkury has never gone back to that area, until now.

Landen presses on. "Bryan was found near water. A pond this time. The night he was killed, the moon was full. Or just about. Not that there's any pattern there. Merkury has never let himself be limited by the phases of the moon."

Kate crosses her arms and gives Landen a meaningful look.

"We're gonna talk about the moon?" she says. "Is that why you came all this way?"

"No."

"You must not have anything," Kate says. "If you had something, you wouldn't need to talk to me."

Landen shifts her weight from one foot to the other. "I'd talk to you either way, Kate. You're the only witness we have."

It's strange hearing Landen say her name. Kate can't imagine calling her Vera, even though they've known each other for almost two decades, ever since the night Kate found the body of Merkury's first victim.

Kate uncrosses her arms, tries to relax.

"You know I didn't see him," she says.

Landen shrugs. "You heard his voice. You were in his presence. And you're alive."

"I don't have anything new to tell you. I never do."

"I have to ask anyway. What did he say to you?"

"You know what he said."

"Remind me."

Kate sighs. "He told me not to turn around."

"His exact words?"

"Quote, Don't turn around, unquote."

"And what did you say to him?"

"Nothing. I froze."

"Did he have an accent?"

"I heard him utter three words—"

"I understand that."

"—when I was eleven."

"I understand that too."

"He had no accent that I can recall."

"And you never got a look at him," Landen says. "Not even out of the corner of your eye?"

"No."

"You've said he held a gun on you."

"Yes."

"How do you know, if you didn't see it?"

"We've been over all of this. Many times."

"Then one more won't hurt. How did you know he had a gun?"

"I felt the muzzle against the back of my head."

"You're sure it was a muzzle?"

"Maybe it was a toothbrush."

Landen lets that pass. "Why didn't he shoot you?"

"I have no idea."

"Could he have known you?"

"I don't know how you expect me to answer that question."

"What sort of mood was he in?"

"Are you serious?"

"Was he angry? Calm? Nervous?"

Kate puts on a thoughtful expression. "When he held the gun to my head, I kind of thought he might be angry."

Landen smiles, but her heart isn't in it. "I need something to work with. Please. How old would you say he was?"

"I don't know."

"Take a guess."

"In his twenties."

"What are you basing that on?"

"Nothing at all."

"What was your impression of him? What sort of vibe did he give off?"

"Did you really just say 'vibe'?"

"What did he smell like?"

Vera Landen has asked her hundreds of questions over the years, but never that one. Kate tries to take it seriously, tries to remember, but nothing comes to her.

"I'm sorry," she says.

Landen looks at the ground and nods. "And when he took the gun away from your head, what did you think?"

"I thought he had stepped back, and he was going to shoot me."

Another nod. "How long was it before you realized he had walked away?"

"I don't know. It seemed like a long time, but maybe it was only a minute."

"You didn't turn around, even then?"

"No."

"You didn't catch a glimpse of him? Even from the back, from a distance?"

"I didn't look for him. I ran home and told my father what had happened."

Landen nods one more time, resigned but undefeated. Kate knows what's coming next.

"All right," Landen says. "Let's try it again. This time we'll start from when you climbed out your bedroom window."

* * *

In the evening, after Landen has gone, it starts to rain.

Kate is in the sitting room in an overstuffed armchair, her feet propped up on packets of shingles. There's a footlocker by the chair, and on it an untouched bowl of soup. It came out of a can and it's cold now and she wasn't hungry to begin with.

Her box of roofing nails sits beside the bowl. The plywood she bought is leaning against a wall. She'll need a dry day to work on the roof, and there haven't been any lately.

She looks up at the ceiling. There's no water coming through here. The leak is in the bedroom. She can hear a steady drip into the tin bucket on the floor at the foot of the bed.

The wind picks up outside and rattles the window sashes. Kate rises from the chair and crosses to a small bookcase. She wants something to read. The shelves are stuffed with paperbacks: Robert Crais, Karin Slaughter, Ann Rule, Michael Connelly, Joe McGinniss. She spots two hardcovers with black spines and her name on them in red. They have three-word titles: *The First Secret* and *The Absent Daughter*.

They're true-crime accounts, each about a murdered woman. That's Kate's brand.

She opens one of them to the title page and reads the inscription: *To Uncle Jim with all good wishes*. It makes her cringe a little. She was just starting out then and never knew what to write.

Her uncle Jim—James Rafferty—is her mother's brother. He lives in a suburb of Toledo and sells commercial real estate. This house belongs to him. It's been in the Rafferty family for generations, and in years past Uncle Jim used it as a hunting cabin. These days he would rather play golf.

He's letting Kate stay here. She told him she wanted someplace remote to write. The truth is she had five chapters of a new manuscript when she came here, and she hasn't added a word.

She closes the book she's holding and returns it to the shelf. Grabs a copy of *Fallen* by Karin Slaughter. Kate has read it before, but it's worth diving into again.

It works for a while, distracts her as the rain comes down. But after forty pages her mind begins to wander. She catches herself reading the same paragraph for the third time. She tosses the book onto the footlocker.

Her cellphone rings.

It's in the kitchen charging. She lets it ring. It stops eventually, only to start again.

She can guess who it is. Her literary agent has been leaving voicemails every few days.

By the time Kate reaches the kitchen the ringing has gone silent, but after a few seconds it resumes. She unplugs the phone from the charger.

"Hello, Audrey."

"You sound tired. Did I wake you?"

"No."

"What time is it there?"

"I'm in Ohio, Audrey."

"I know."

"It's the same time zone as Manhattan."

"Are you sure? It sounds like you're on the moon. How's your beau? I can never remember his name."

"Devin."

"Of course. How is he?"

"He's not my beau anymore."

"Well I'm sorry to hear that, I truly am." Audrey pauses for a beat and then asks, "How's the book?"

There it is. The real reason for the call.

"It's coming along," Kate says. A writer's lie.

"How far though? Would you say you're committed?"

"Committed?"

There's another pause, and a hint of hesitation in Audrey's voice. "The reason I ask—and I hate to do this to you—but I think you might want to change course. The chapters you sent me are great. More than great. I love them. Love love love."

"Audrey—"

"But I've sent them around to a few people and the news is mixed."

Kate leans against the kitchen counter. "I asked you not to send them—"

"I used my judgment, darling. That's why you have me. The sales of your last book were soft."

"I know."

"Not terrible, but soft," Audrey says. "The trend is in the wrong direction. So I needed to gauge people's interest in the new one. Don't get me wrong, they like it, they want to see the finished manuscript. But nobody's offering a contract at this point."

"That's fine with me."

"It's not though. You want to have a contract in place, and an advance. Trust me. That's why I thought we might want to change course. Especially given the news . . . You've heard the news?"

Kate closes her eyes. "I've heard it."

"This latest killing," Audrey says, "Bryan Cayhill. It's awful."

"Look, just don't—"

"I'm sorry. I know how you feel about these things but I have to say, as tragic as it is, it's an opportunity for you. Because it's Merkury. You never wanted to write about the girl you found, the first victim, and I respected your decision. But now you should reconsider. You could write about both of them—"

"I don't want to do that."

"Listen. You could tie them together. They both happened in the same town. You've got a personal connection to the story. There would be interest, no question. I could get you an advance. Probably more than I got you for the last book."

"I don't care about the money."

There's quiet on the line for a few seconds, followed by Audrey's voice again, calm and patient. "Then it's good you've got me. I'll be the heartless one. I'll care about the money. But you should write the book. I think you know it, deep down. You could do something with it, something great. You could—"

Kate doesn't hear the rest. She thumbs the red button to end the call and drops the phone on the counter. When it rings again she silences it.

The rain has tapered off, but there's still a steady drip coming from the bedroom. Closer at hand, there's a sink full of dirty dishes. Kate collects her soup bowl from the sitting room and adds it to the pile.

She should clean up now, but she doesn't have the spirit for it.

Outside, it's dark. The sun went down an hour ago. Kate opens the back door of the house and stands in the doorway, staring across the yard into the gloom of the woods. Audrey is right about one thing: someone needs to start caring about money. Kate knows the balance in her bank account, knows it's getting smaller every week. There's nothing coming in.

That's one of the reasons she came here. She let the lease expire on her apartment in Columbus. Sold some things and put the rest into storage. But even that won't be enough. Though her expenses are lower now, she still has some.

She's been playing with the idea of staying here. Her uncle has told her the house is hers for as long as she wants it. She could get a job in town. There was a help wanted sign at the hardware store. She could go ahead with her plan to fix the roof. She's never fixed one before, but how hard could it be?

She leans against the doorjamb and feels like crying. She knows it's no good. Yesterday she might have believed that she had a future here, that she could find, not happiness, but maybe contentment.

But now, after Chief Landen's visit, things have changed. The house already feels different, even though Landen never set foot inside. She's gone, but an echo of her stayed behind. It's not even her; it's what she brought with her.

Merkury. Kate doesn't remember what he smelled like, but he's here in the smell of the rain and the wet grass. She's never going to escape him.

There's no point in trying. No point in staying here.

Kate steps back into the kitchen. Closes the door and turns the dead-bolt. She makes sure the front door is locked, and the windows too. All she brought with her was a couple of suitcases and the footlocker. She fills them up so she'll be ready to leave in the morning.

She brushes her teeth and climbs into bed. She's too cold without the blanket and too warm with it. She throws it aside. Switches off the bedside lamp, but the dark unnerves her. It didn't before. She gets up and turns on the bathroom light and leaves the door open a few inches.

She can't hear the rain on the roof anymore, and there's only an occasional drop from the ceiling. A hollow *plup* in the tin bucket.

Kate's last thoughts before she drifts off to sleep are of Vera Landen. Her endless questions. The same ones over and over, as if she expects Kate's answers to change. Landen may not be getting anywhere with the Merkury investigation, but she's not stupid. There's a keen intelligence behind her eyes.

Kate wonders if the woman ever suspects the truth: that for all these years, Kate has been lying to her.

3

The sky is the key, every time.

Lee Tennick is not a professional photographer, but he has a good eye. He knows that a clear sky is no blessing when you're shooting landscapes. You want clouds. But not a solid mass of them.

It's better if they're small, with bits of blue sky in between. Or long and feathery like strands of cotton. You want them to have texture and depth, so there's something to see when the light hits them.

Tennick can't complain today. The sun is starting to go down. He gets the red oak where he wants it in his frame. Not centered. A bit to the left. There's dark blue sky behind the tree, and darker blue clouds, and as you move down toward the horizon there's a touch of orange.

He'll boost the colors later. Editing is what makes the difference between good and great.

In the foreground there's yellow crime-scene tape, strung between wooden stakes that have been driven into the ground. This is where Bryan Cayhill's body was discovered.

The tape is twisted in a way Tennick doesn't like. He steps out from behind his tripod and tries to adjust it so it hangs the way he wants. It's stubborn. Ultimately he has to pull up one of the stakes and move it about six inches.

Then it's perfect.

He clicks the shutter a dozen times, altering his framing in subtle ways between each shot. Then he picks up the tripod and moves it back so he can take in both the tree and the pond nearby. There's a wedge of a cloud like a battleship over the pond, with a fleet of smaller ones trailing behind it, and all of them are mirrored in the water below.

Sometimes it comes down to luck. If he had gotten here twenty minutes later, he would have missed this.

Click.

He stays until the last of the orange is gone from the sky. Gets everything he could want. Then he stows his equipment and drives back into town to pick up something to eat.

It's a village, technically—Alexander, New York. Southeast of Syracuse, northeast of Binghamton. Population around four thousand, plus twenty-five hundred students at Seagate College.

Route 12B runs through the middle of it, with a crosshatch of streets on either side. Downtown is modest, but there's an inn and a bookstore and maybe a dozen other businesses. One of the standouts is a restored movie theater from the 1930s. Tennick used to have an apartment above a drugstore, but he gave it up. Now he lives in Alexander for only about six months of the year. The rest of the time, he travels.

He's got an old Winnebago and he drives it wherever it suits him. Along the way he stops in towns where people have gone missing, on back roads where bodies have been found—anywhere a famous crime has taken place. And "famous" is a flexible term. Some of the locations he visits are familiar only to a select few. True-crime junkies. But those are his people.

They're the ones who follow his Instagram account and read his blog. He started out posting pictures of old crime scenes. Then he added photos of law enforcement officers, witnesses, relatives of the dead. He wrote about cold cases and interviewed some of the people involved. Eventually he bought some microphones and recording equipment, and now he puts out a podcast episode every week.

Merkury is an obsession of his. At the time of the first killing, Tennick was a senior at Seagate College and a reporter for the student newspaper. He had a friend who worked as a dispatcher for the Alexander police department, and the friend tipped him off when the cops rolled out on a homicide one night near the end of the spring semester.

When he drove out to Bird River Road there was nothing to see but a trio of patrol cars parked at the roadside. One of the officers told him to move along. So Tennick moved along—half a mile down the road. There he left his car behind and walked back under the cover of the woods until he heard voices and saw the lights that the police chief had set up while she waited for the medical examiner.

The M.E. hadn't yet arrived. The chief, Vera Landen, was standing at a distance from the body of the victim. Landen was dressed in khaki trousers and a flannel shirt and military-style boots, her hair in two braids pinned up to make a crown at the back of her head.

Tennick kept well away from the lights. He leaned against a tree twenty yards from the scene and opened his bag. Found his zoom lens and twisted it onto the body of his camera.

He was grateful for the steady *chirp* of the crickets. He figured the noise would cover whatever small sounds he made.

He zoomed in on the body. The angle wasn't perfect, but the girl's face was turned toward him. He thought he recognized her from one of his classes. Melissa something. Melissa Cornelle.

The light was good enough. He could have taken a shot. But he had some measure of decency. He zoomed back a bit until he had both the police chief and the body in the frame. Then he pressed the shutter.

The chief moved then, and Tennick thought she had heard him. But she crossed in front of the body and walked a dozen feet to where two people waited. One of them was a child—a girl with a blanket draped over her shoulders like a cloak. A man stood beside her, holding her hand. Probably her father.

Chief Landen crouched down so she would be at the girl's level. They had a conversation Tennick couldn't hear. He took a shot of the trio together, but it wasn't the best. The chief had her back to the camera and was blocking part of the girl's face. He got a better shot later, when the chief stepped away.

That was when the M.E. arrived, and the girl and her father were left on their own. Tennick got some photos of the two of them, the father looking concerned, putting his arm around the girl, pulling her close.

One of the last shots Tennick took was a close-up of the girl, locks of curly hair framing her face, staring off at nothing in particular. This was the photograph that would, in time, spread everywhere on the internet. Katy Summerlin, the girl who found the body. And met the killer.

It was the shot that would make Lee Tennick's reputation.

There's only one place in Alexander where you can get decent Chinese food, and it's on Main Street across from the police station.

Tennick phones in his order and waits by the curb in his car. Traffic is sparse at this hour, but some people are out enjoying the mild October evening. There are students making their way to a bar called Ptolemy's. They walk in packs and cross the streets carelessly. There are families on the town square with their dogs, or standing in line for ice cream at the Dairy Queen.

Tennick checks the time on his phone and judges that his lo mein must be ready. When he steps out of his car, he glances across the street and sees a woman walking on the sidewalk. She has the look of a young professor from Seagate: moderately tall and casually stylish. She's wearing blue jeans and a black turtleneck. A leather handbag hangs from her shoulder. Her mouth is wide and her nose belongs on a Greek statue. Her auburn hair would fall in curls around her face if she hadn't tied it back.

She's not a professor. Tennick knows her.

She scans the street and catches sight of him and scowls.

Kate doesn't want to talk to Lee Tennick, but here he comes.

He does that fake jog that people do and bounds up onto the sidewalk. He doesn't get too close or try to shake her hand, which means he's wiser than she thought.

"Did you just get here?" he says.

She doesn't answer him.

"I wondered if you would come," he says. "I guess you couldn't resist. We should talk. I could tell you some things. About Bryan Cayhill. Show you where he was found."

She shakes her head. "No."

His eyes take on a wounded look.

"You don't have to like me, Kate," he says. "But we could help each other."

"I don't want to help you, Lee."

He gives her the eyes again, like a dog that's been swatted with a rolled-up magazine.

"I'll help you then," he says. "You don't have to give me anything."

She reaches into her bag for her car keys. "I'll manage on my own."

Two frat boys come up the sidewalk and pass between them, oblivious, talking loudly about someone named Manny. Will he show tonight? Absolutely. It's going to be epic.

When they've moved on, Tennick holds his palms out in a gesture of surrender.

"Have it your way, Kate," he says. "But maybe we'll talk another time." He points his thumb across the street at the Chinese restaurant. "I have to get my food. But I'll be seeing you. I'm sure of it."

Kate could use something to eat too, and she wouldn't mind Chinese, but she's not going to linger here. She's driven five hundred miles since this morning, and there are only a few more to go. She stopped to walk around the town, to see if it would feel familiar after all the time that's passed. It doesn't, not really. And now she needs to go on to her father's house.

She finds her car where she left it on the street and drives north through Alexander and out into the rural dark. Her headlights catch the sign for Bird River Road and she makes the turn. Gray fields stretch out on either side of her.

Farther on, there's a light on a pole at the end of her father's driveway. Set back from the road is a farmhouse with a garage and an old barn standing off to one side. The walls of the barn lean and the roof bows, but it hasn't fallen over yet.

Kate parks near the garage, cuts her engine, and slips the latch of her seatbelt. She can see lights on in the house, but she's not eager to go in. She has stayed away from here for a long time.

Her parents took her away the summer after she found Melissa Cornelle. Her mother insisted on it. Her father quit his job at Seagate and took a series of visiting positions at small colleges. They hopped around the country, finally landing at Oberlin in Ohio, where her father got tenure in the English department. But years later, after Kate left home and after her mother died, her father was drawn back to Seagate. He returned to the same house they had left, renting it for a year and then arranging to buy it from the owner.

It must have changed in the intervening years, but Kate would have been hard-pressed to identify the differences. She remembers the white-washed porch, the casement windows, the stone chimney rising from the roof. The main difference she sees is an old RV, white and silver, parked near the barn.

Her father is home, she's sure. She climbs onto the porch and knocks on the door. While she's waiting, she hears a car approaching along the driveway and turns to see headlights. The lights swing to the left and the car parks itself next to the RV.

The driver's door opens and Kate stares in disbelief. Lee Tennick steps out and raises his hand in a wave.

Kate's father seems amused by the situation.

"He's my tenant," Arthur Summerlin says.

He's got her sitting in the kitchen and he's making her breakfast even though it's eight o'clock at night.

"But you know who he is?" Kate says.

"Of course I do."

"And what he did."

He shrugs his shoulders. "That was years ago."

There's bacon sizzling in a skillet on the stove. Kate watches her father crack eggs into a mixing bowl. Watches him add milk and measure out Bisquick. He stirs the batter with a whisk and digs out a second skillet.

The first pancake is, as always, experimental: too light on one side, too dark on the other. Kate's father keeps it for himself. The second is perfect. He puts it on a plate for her, dresses it with butter and maple syrup. Tops it with two strips of bacon forming an X. It's a performance on his part—her favorite childhood meal. His way of welcoming her.

After they eat, Kate starts to clear the dishes, but her father tells her to leave them.

"I'm glad you're here," he says, "but I'm not sure why you came."

"You're not?" she says. She doesn't want to say the name Merkury, and she knows he won't say it. But it's there, between them.

"Best to leave all that alone," he says. "Don't you think?"

She doesn't exactly disagree, but it's nothing she wants to talk about. She changes the subject.

"Why is Lee Tennick living out in the yard?"

"He seems harmless," her father says.

"I wonder."

"And he's paying me three hundred dollars a month."

"Do you need the money?"

"It's nice to have. He pays me every month, even when he takes the RV on the road. When he's here I barely notice him. We leave each other alone. I don't see the downside."

Kate lets the subject drop. She asks her father about the classes he's teaching, and he goes on for half an hour about the students in his creative writing course. When their talk runs out, they clear the table. He loads the dishes into the dishwasher and heads upstairs.

Kate takes her suitcases to her old room. It's painted a different color than she remembers, and the bed is not the one she used to sleep in. There's a writing desk and a night table that look like they were bought secondhand.

She finds towels in the linen closet, takes a shower, puts on a T-shirt and sweatpants, and tries to sleep. Something keeps her awake, maybe the sugar from her pancake dinner. She lies staring at the ceiling, listening to the quiet house.

Someone has a fire going outside and the smell is not unpleasant. It grows stronger when she opens her window. She climbs out and walks through the yard to the front of the house.

Lee Tennick is in a camp chair by the side of his RV. He's got pine logs burning in a circle of rocks. When he sees her, he goes to the barn and brings out a second chair.

"This is a night for marshmallows," he says.

He disappears into the RV and comes back with a bag of marshmallows and two long metal skewers. When Kate declines the one he offers her, he sets it on top of a milk crate beside the remnants of his Chinese takeout. He impales a marshmallow on the end of the other and scoots his chair closer to the fire.

He's patient, browning the marshmallow evenly all the way around, not letting it burn. The look of concentration on his face makes him seem young, though he's older than Kate by a decade.

He's a thin man, gangly, all sharp elbows and knees. He's wearing steel-framed glasses perched on the bridge of his prominent nose. His hair is dirty blond and cropped short. When he sits back and pops the roasted marshmallow into his mouth, he looks far happier than he deserves to be.

"I'll make you one," he says to Kate.

"No thanks," she says.

"They're good though."

She watches the fire and ignores him.

"You don't like me," he says.

"No."

"Do you think that's fair?"

She laughs. "You don't want to talk to me about fairness."

He makes himself busy beside her. Extracting another marshmallow from the bag. Easing it onto the skewer. When he's got it over the fire, he says:

"I never wrote anything that wasn't true."

Kate watches him rolling the marshmallow back and forth over the flame.

"You wrote that my father was questioned by the police about the killing of Melissa Cornelle."

"He was," Tennick says.

"And that Melissa took one of his classes when she was a sophomore."

"She did."

"And that she had a history of having crushes on her professors."

"That's what her friends told me."

"So obviously he was fucking her and he killed her."

Tennick shakes his head. "I never said that."

"There are idiots on the internet who are still saying it. Where do you suppose they got the idea?"

Kate can feel her anger in the muscles of her shoulders. She makes an effort to relax: leans back in her chair, wiggles her toes in the grass. Tennick is staring at the fire.

"I might approach the story differently," he says, "if I had it to do over again."

Kate isn't ready to let him off the hook. "The night Melissa died, you crept around in the woods to get to the crime scene. You snapped a picture of the eleven-year-old who found the body. Me. And when the student newspaper refused to print it—when every decent paper around here refused to print it—you posted it on your blog. With my name."

The marshmallow begins to smoke and blacken, Tennick lets it burn.

"I'm sorry," he says.

"Oh, you're sorry."

His voice turns soft. "I am. I was young and arrogant. I had no judgment. You deserved better than you got from me. I don't expect you to forgive me, but I apologize."

He drops the skewer on the ground and turns to her. "What I said before, about helping you, I meant that. If you're going to write about Merkury—, I know the families of the victims. I've interviewed them myself. I've got hundreds of hours of audio. I'll let you have access."

She flicks her finger on the arm of her chair, brushing the idea away. "Who said I'm going to write about Merkury?"

"You have to." He leans toward her. "I've been thinking about this, waiting for you to show up. You write the book and we'll collaborate on the podcast. There's an audience for it—"

"I'm not doing a podcast."

"Just think about it," Tennick says. "I could do it on my own, but it wouldn't be the same. People will want to hear what you have to say. Not to be crass, but advertisers will love it. We'll split the ad money—that's only fair. Fifty-fifty."

Kate has been looking away from him, but now she meets his eyes. They're dark brown behind the lenses of his glasses. She stares into them until he bows his head.

"I shouldn't have mentioned the ad money," he says.

"No."

He takes off the glasses and rubs his face. "This happens to me sometimes. I get too eager. I get ahead of myself."

The fire pops, sending up a stream of sparks.

"You should have stopped with the apology," Kate says. "Or with the part about helping me. You sounded almost human then."

He composes himself, puts his glasses back on. "Forget that I talked about money. We could give the money to charity."

But Kate is already out of her chair. "Yup. Almost human."

She walks toward the house, and hears him call after her.

"Or we could do it without any ads."

She holds up a hand and keeps walking. "Good night, Lee."

4

The next morning Kate rises at eight o'clock and drives out to the place where Bryan Cayhill's body was found.

The reports she has read were vague about the location—a pond northwest of Alexander. But she doesn't need Tennick's help to find it. There are only two possibilities, and it turns out to be the first one she tries.

Weatherstone Pond is long and narrow at its northern end and widens out as you go south. You can access it from Portage Road, and there's a turnoff that leads to a small gravel lot edged with railroad ties.

The turnoff is blocked by a pair of sawhorses labeled ALEXANDER POLICE. Kate leaves her car on the side of the road and walks down a long slope to the water.

The scene is cordoned off with yellow tape, but she doesn't need to get close. There's an oak tree on the other side of the tape—just as there was at the place where Kate found Melissa Cornelle. The tree was a crucial part of Merkury's M.O. The police worked it out early on, and their theory was confirmed when Merkury claimed his second victim a few months later.

Kate could have confirmed it for them sooner, if she had been willing to tell them the truth about the night she found Melissa.

She remembers:

Kneeling by the body under the oak. Hearing the voice of the man behind her.

"Don't turn around."

She wasn't afraid. Or maybe she was numb to the fear. She went along with what he said. Kept her eyes on the girl lying in the grass.

"You shouldn't be here," he said. "Why would you come out here at this time of night?"

Katy lifted her shoulders and let them fall. "I woke up," she said.

As explanations went, it wasn't much. But he didn't ask for more. He was silent, but she could sense him, just as she could sense the branches of the tree above her, moving with the wind.

The ground felt strange beneath her, solid and not solid. She was dressed in the flannel pajamas she had worn to bed, and she could feel the cool damp of the grass on her knees.

She looked at the girl's outspread arms, bound to the wooden pole that lay under her. And then at the girl's face: the smooth, pale skin, the parted lips. The locks of dark hair falling over her eyes. Katy asked a question that came to her. It seemed important.

"What's her name?"

He didn't answer right away, and she thought she might have made him angry. But when he spoke, his voice was soft.

"Melissa."

"Is she dead?" Katy asked.

"I'm afraid she is."

"Were you with her when she died?"

"Yes."

"How did it happen?"

He took a few seconds to respond. A dozen feet away, the water of the stream flowed over a fallen branch. Katy listened to its rhythm.

"Someone smothered her," he said.

"Did you see who it was?"

He let out a breath that sounded almost like a laugh.

"You can ask me," he said. "We don't have to tiptoe around it."

So she asked him: "Did you smother her?"

"Yes."

"Why?"

"That's a big question."

"Oh."

"But I'm not sure it matters."

Katy frowned—and realized he couldn't see her frowning. She looked at the skin of the girl's stomach and at the red word written there. *MERKURY.* She pointed to it.

"What does that mean?" she asked.

"Nothing. I wouldn't worry about it. Can I tell you something else?"

A polite request. He waited for her to respond.

"Okay," she said.

"I was going to hang her in the tree. Not the way you might be thinking. Not by the neck. I was going to use the pole. I was going to make kind of a Y out of rope. That's the reason I wasn't here when you came. I had to go back to my van for more rope. A longer piece, and heavier. I couldn't carry everything at once. Anyway, I thought I'd make a Y and tie two ends of it to the ends of the pole, and the other end I would toss over a limb of the tree. I would haul her up that way."

"Why?" Katy asked.

"I guess I wanted to see."

"See what?"

"I wanted to see what she would look like. I thought she would look beautiful."

Katy looked at the girl's face and said, "But she must have been beautiful before."

"She was. I liked her skin. And her hair."

Katy had been resting her hands on her thighs, but now her right hand reached out. Almost involuntarily. She drew it back, embarrassed.

"You can do it," he said behind her. "It's just the two of us here."

"Do what?"

"You know. You can touch her. There's no harm in it."

She shouldn't, Katy thought. But she wanted to. She lifted her right hand and brushed her fingers over the skin of the girl's stomach. It wasn't warm, but it didn't feel cold either.

"Touch her hair," he said.

Katy had to lean forward to reach it. She wound a dark lock of it around her fingers and gently pulled her hand away, letting it fall.

"This seems wrong," she said.

"Which part?" he asked her.

"All of it. I thought she was alive when I saw her at first. She shouldn't be dead."

Katy heard him take a step closer to her.

"That's true," he said. "She shouldn't. She was talking and moving around just a while ago. No time at all. Now she's gone, and there's nothing that could bring her back. It's ridiculous, if you think about it. All the same elements are here. Flesh and blood and bone. But it's not the same. It shouldn't be so easy for the life to go out of someone. It shouldn't be possible, but it is."

He fell silent. Katy could sense him behind her. She imagined him holding a coil of rope in one hand. The other hand resting in his pocket.

"Are you going to do it?" she said.

"What?" he asked.

"Put her in the tree."

He took a moment to reply. "No. I think I'd better not."

She sensed him moving and braced herself. Waited. Then it happened. She felt a touch on the back of her head. She had the wild thought that it was a gun.

"You're very brave," he told her.

It was only his fingers. They wove themselves gently into her hair.

"I'm glad you were here," he said.

She felt his hand withdraw.

"I'm leaving now," he said. "Don't turn. Don't look. I'm trusting you."

Kate is looking up at the tree when she hears a sound that startles her.

She spins around, then feels foolish. Her mind has been wandering. She's lost track of her surroundings.

It was only the slamming of a car door.

After a moment she sees Lee Tennick walking down the slope of the hill toward her. He's got a cup of takeout coffee in each hand.

Kate lets him come to her and accepts the cup he offers. He's got packets of sugar and cream in his pockets, but she drinks it black. He's different from the way he was last night. Subdued. He's quiet until she asks him a question.

"They found Bryan Cayhill hanging from the tree?"

He nods. "You can see the limb there. The rope scraped off some of the bark."

"Did you see him?"

"I got here as they were taking him down."

"How did you know to come?"

"One of the cops tipped me off."

"How close did you get?"

"Not close." Tennick points back the way he came. "I had to watch from up on the hill."

"Take any pictures?"

He shakes his head. "Chief Landen takes a hard line on cameras at her crime scenes."

"Uh-huh."

"Also the light was poor . . . Why does he hang them in trees? Have you thought about that?"

"Not really," Kate says.

"Is he showing off? Trying to shock us? Demanding our attention?"

"Maybe he likes the way they look." She drinks from her coffee. Turns in a slow circle. "Would you say this is a secluded spot?"

Tennick rubs his chin. "Yes and no. You can be sure that no one passing on the road is going to see you down here, especially at night. But there's no telling who might pull into the parking lot up there. Students come here sometimes."

"Do they?"

"Sure. To drink, light a fire, make out. It was students who found the body."

Kate's eyes narrow. "That wasn't in the news stories I've read."

"The college has kept it out of the papers so far. But people around here know. It was three students."

"They came here to drink?"

"The way I heard it, they came to make a movie. They were taking a film class, or one of them was anyway. She was the director."

"I thought Cayhill was found at night."

"That's right."

"What kind of movie were they making in the dark?"

A smile passes across Tennick's face, but there's no pleasure in it.

"It was a horror movie," he says. "I guess they got more than they bargained for."

5

The leaves are changing colors, and from a distance Seagate College looks like a picture postcard. It's centered on a hill, which the locals call the Hill, with the academic buildings at the top—all stone facades and arched windows—and the more modern dormitories at the bottom.

Kate leaves her car in the visitors' parking lot and takes a pleasant stroll past the dorms and the student union. From there she finds a set of granite steps that wind their way up the Hill to the main quad.

She's been here before, long ago, but the only building she remembers is Corwin Hall, because her mother brought her there to visit her father's office in the English department. Corwin Hall faces off against the Hollister Library, and in between there's a wide green lawn spotted with old trees and crisscrossed by paved walkways.

There's movement all around, students heading to their afternoon classes. Some of them gather in groups of three or four, sitting on the grass in the sun. An idyllic scene, Kate thinks. Nothing to suggest that one of their classmates was murdered a week ago—except for some flyers taped up on lampposts. Kate sees the same two again and again: one announcing an upcoming memorial service for Bryan Cayhill, the other advising students not to walk alone at night.

Kate takes a seat on a bench and checks the time on her phone. She's early. Tennick gave her the names of the students who found Cayhill's body: Travis Pollard, Clay McKellar, and Lavana Khatri. He gave her their phone numbers too. "I've tried contacting them," he said. "Maybe you'll have better luck."

She left voicemails for all three and got a call back from Clay McKellar about an hour later. He needed some convincing but he agreed to meet. "After my chemistry exam," he said.

The chemistry department is in Trimble Hall. Kate spots Clay among a flock of students coming down the steps a few minutes after three o'clock. She recognizes him from some of the photos on his Instagram account.

Kate rises from the bench to catch his attention, and Clay crosses the lawn with a backpack slung over his shoulder. He's a few inches shy of six feet tall and his red hair is unruly. He's wearing jeans and hiking boots and a gray sweater.

After introductions and some small talk, he sits with Kate on the bench and turns shy.

"This is weird," he says.

Kate nods. "I know."

"I think I might be . . . naive. Is that the word?"

"What do you mean?"

"I talked to the police, about Bryan. And it was the first time I ever had anything to do with, you know, the law. I never even got stopped for speeding."

"I understand," Kate says. "You've been thrown into the deep end."

"Right, and I feel like I might drown," Clay says. "I don't know if I should talk to you."

"Well, you don't have to. Let's start there. I can't make you, and I wouldn't if I could."

"I mean, it's already been too much. I don't want to be part of this. Would you have to use my name?"

"We could talk about that," says Kate. "I could use your first name, or a pseudonym. But can I be honest with you?"

"Please."

"Your name is probably going to get out there, sooner or later. You're part of the story. You can try to keep it at a distance. But it won't go away."

Clay takes that in. He's sitting sideways on the bench. His brown eyes look troubled.

"I guess you would know," he says. "You're Kate Summerlin. Katy."

"Yes."

"So we went through the same thing. We both found a dead body."

Kate nods.

Clay leans closer to her. "It's crazy, right? I'm still, like, processing it. When it happened to you, did you know it was real?"

"Real?"

"I thought it was fake. That night at the pond, when we found Bryan, I thought they were messing with me—Lavana and Travis. Like it was part of the movie and they didn't tell me. But I should have known better. Lavana wasn't even filming. And the two of them were as freaked out as I was."

Clay looks out across the quad, then back at Kate.

"I keep thinking I'll see him," he says. "Bryan. Like he'll walk up to me and tell me it was a prank. What a relief that would be."

He's fidgeting, hugging himself as if he's cold. Kate tries to put him at ease.

"Tell me about the movie you're making."

Clay's face brightens. "It's cool. But it's not a *movie* movie. It's a short film. A few scenes. It's a slasher movie pared down to its essence. That's how Lavana describes it. It's a chase. There's a killer, that's Travis. And Lavana plays his victim.

"What part do you play?" Kate asks.

"There are only two characters," Clay says. "Which is good, because I'm not much of an actor. I help out wherever Lavana needs me. She's the director, and she does a lot of the camera work. But when she's in the shot, I work the camera. And I help with sound and lighting and props. It's just the three of us, so I pitch in wherever I'm needed."

"How long have you been filming?"

"We've worked on it maybe ten different nights. Starting about a month ago."

"And it's set at Weatherstone Pond?"

"Not all of it," Clay says. "We use different locations. A lot of the action is just two people running around in the woods at night. But we shot at the pond one other time."

"That other time—did you see anything out of the ordinary?"

"Like a body in a tree?"

"Like someone lurking around."

Clay's eyes narrow. "You think *he* was there? Merkury?"

"I think he must have gone there at least once before he brought Bryan there," Kate says. "To scope things out."

"I never saw anybody."

"What about on campus? Have you seen anyone new in the last few weeks? Someone older, who might have been paying more attention to students than he should have been?"

"No. Do you really think . . ."

Kate shrugs. "I think he must have chosen Bryan Cayhill somehow, for some reason."

"That's scary to imagine."

"Were you a friend of Bryan's?"

Clay looks thoughtful. "We weren't friends, but I knew who he was. You see the same people over and over at a college this size. He and I were in some classes together, our first year. We must have talked, if only to say hello. I can't remember his voice though."

Clay brings one foot up onto the bench and wraps his hands around his knee.

"I can't picture what Bryan looked like either," he says. "You know, when he was alive. I keep seeing him the way he looked at the end."

It's after sunset when Kate returns to her father's house.

She spent more than two hours with Clay McKellar, talking about the movie and his life at Seagate and what it was like, moment by moment, when he and his friends found the body. They covered Clay's dealings with the police afterward, and Kate even managed to get a couple of stories about his childhood. She's got most of it saved as a voice recording on her phone—something Clay agreed to readily, once he was comfortable.

There's more on the recording than Kate will ever use in the book, if she writes the book, but she's glad to have it. It makes her feel like she's accomplishing something.

After the interview she walked back to her car and sat for a long time writing in her notebook. Now she has a roadmap: people she needs to talk to, what she needs to ask them.

So her mood is good when she makes the turn into her father's driveway. But it sours when she sees what's waiting for her.

Her father's Volvo is parked by the house, and Lee Tennick's Honda Civic is in its usual place by his RV. But there's another car parked behind the Civic. A gray Lexus. It belongs to someone Kate hasn't seen since she left her apartment in Columbus and exiled herself to her uncle's hunting cabin.

Eight weeks. No, nine. That's how long it's been since she's seen Devin Falko.

But there he is, sitting at the kitchen table with a smile on his face when she walks in. There's a glass of lemonade in front of him. Her father is bustling around, cooking. Kate smells roasted chicken.

"You're just in time for dinner," Arthur Summerlin says. "And we have a guest."

Kate walks past him, through the kitchen, toward the back of the house. She beckons for Devin to follow her. "He's not staying," she says over her shoulder to her father.

She goes out the back door and into the yard. It's gray dark out there, only the brightest stars beginning to show in the sky. She keeps on until she comes to the trellis at the edge of the lawn. Devin joins her there.

"Kate," he says.

She shakes her head. "I don't believe this—"

"I'm glad to see you."

"I don't want you here."

"Yes, I'm getting that impression."

"Who told you where to find me?"

Devin waits a beat before he answers. He's calm, and he's left a respectful distance between them. He's one of those men who have a charming resting face: a strong chin, a hint of dimples. He's tall and broad-shouldered, and his hair is dark with a hint of curl. He wears it longer than most men do. These are some of the things that attracted her to him.

"Give me some credit, Kate," he says. "There's another killing, a Merkury killing, and it's here where you lived as a child, where your father lives. It's not a big leap to guess you might come here. I know something about how you think."

"Then you ought to know you're the last person I'd want to see."

He shakes his head slowly. "No, I don't. There are still some things I can't figure out about Kate Summerlin."

"Maybe you're not as smart as you think you are," Kate says. "I don't want to talk to you."

"That's the part I'm having trouble understanding."

"What is there to understand? You hit me."

Devin lets out a long breath. "Is that what happened, Kate?"

"Are you denying it?"

"No," he says patiently. "But is that all we can say about what happened?"

Kate can feel her fists clenching. She closes her eyes.

"Go away," she says.

"Maybe we could say there was a misunderstanding. Maybe we could say I acted on reflex."

"Is that your excuse?"

"I'm not making excuses. I'm trying to talk to you."

Kate opens her eyes, locks them on his. "I want you gone. I don't trust you anymore. Or your reflexes."

His charming face looks sad. "I can go. But you need to deal with this."

"Don't tell me what I need."

"Or it's going to happen again, and keep happening."

"Are you threatening me?"

Devin spreads his arms. "Now you're deliberately misunderstanding me. Something that could be solved if you were willing to have a real conversation. About why you push away people who love you."

"I don't need your kind of love."

His voice, when he speaks again, sounds weary. "Everyone needs love, Kate," he says. "I'm staying at the inn in town. Room 302. When you're ready, you can find me there."

He turns away from her and heads back the way they came. She follows at a distance. Halfway across the yard she realizes he's making for the back door.

"Go around the house," she says. "Not through."

He changes course and she watches him all the way to his car. Sees him drive out and turn onto Bird River Road.

Lee Tennick watches too. He's sitting in one of his camp chairs with a bottle of beer. He raises the bottle to her.

Kate ignores him and goes back inside the house. Her father has made mashed potatoes and roasted broccoli and he's cutting into the chicken.

"Your friend is gone?"

"He's not my friend."

"Seemed nice enough," her father says. "A little old for you."

"We're not together anymore," says Kate.

He pries a drumstick from the chicken. "That's too bad. Or maybe not. It's dicey, isn't it: dating your therapist? They're not supposed to do that, are they?"

"He's *a* therapist, not *my* therapist."

Her father moves to the kitchen island to fix their plates. He dishes up mashed potatoes and slices of chicken. Kate is standing by the table. She can feel herself trembling. She wonders if he can see it.

He stops what he's doing and his face turns serious.

"I hope I haven't failed you, Kate."

"What are you talking about?" she says.

"Your mother and I, we were at a bit of a loss. We sent you to talk to that lady doctor, after . . . you know."

"I remember."

"But you didn't like her and we let you stop going. Maybe we should have found someone else."

Kate shrugs. "I'm fine, Dad."

"Then you grew up, and your mother died, and I always thought, 'Kate's got a good head on her shoulders.' I never asked if you sought out anyone on your own . . . I mean, a professional . . . to talk about what happened. Did you?"

"No."

Her father goes back to what he was doing. Spoons broccoli onto both plates.

"Well, maybe it's not the worst idea," he says. "Maybe it would do you good. If you were to talk to someone now."

Kate feels a rush of heat run through her cheeks. She looks down at her right hand. It seems steady. Her father takes the plates from the island to bring them to the table. Devin's glass is still there, half full of lemonade.

Kate picks up the glass and draws her arm back. Then sweeps it forward. And watches the glass shatter against the wall.

6

Friday morning, Kate sleeps in.

She wakes at ten thirty feeling listless, throws off the covers, and reaches for her notebook on the bedside table. Her plan for today was to try to talk to the other students who found the body: Lavana Khatri and Travis Pollard.

Now she's not sure. Seeing Devin has made her anxious. Maybe it would be best to get in her car and drive.

Not back to Ohio. Not to any particular destination.

She checks her phone and there's a text from Lavana Khatri agreeing to talk, saying she's available around noon. Kate leaves the phone behind and wanders through the house to the kitchen. Her father is nowhere to be seen. She makes coffee and drinks a cup standing at the counter.

She makes up her mind to pack and go. All she needs is to choose a direction. She works it out in the shower. South. Why not?

She's toweling off in her bedroom when her cellphone chimes. Another text. Travis Pollard. He's available today too.

Kate consults her weather app and sees there's a chance of a storm later on. She doesn't like driving in the rain.

Better to stick around. She can always leave tomorrow.

A funny thing about interviewing people: most of them fall right into the role. You ask them questions; they give you answers. But there are some who don't play the game. They have their own agenda, or they want to test you.

With those people, Kate has found, you have to be willing to adapt. Sometimes you let them have their way.

"Tell me a secret," Lavana Khatri says.

Kate smiles. "That's a big ask."

"You want me to talk to you, and for that I need to trust you. We trust people who show us trust. Don't you think?"

"Sure."

"So tell me a secret. About you. Or even better, about Merkury."

They're in Lavana's dorm room, a small space, carefully organized. The bed is made. Kate is sitting at the foot of it. Lavana is in a swivel chair at her desk.

"This stays between us?" Kate says.

"Of course."

The thing about secrets, Kate thinks, is that you can make them up. They don't have to be true. You can stay in control.

Sometimes they can be half true.

"We moved away, my family," she says. "After Melissa Cornelle, after Merkury. We lived in different places, but usually in a house with a yard. If there was a tree in back, I would imagine him there, hiding."

"You thought Merkury followed you?" Lavana asks.

"I thought he would be able to find me. Sometimes at night I would go out and lean my back against that tree. I'd stay there for as long as I could, just to prove . . ."

"To prove what?"

"That I was brave."

Lavana Khatri has silky black hair drawn back in a ponytail. She has a face that looks severe when she concentrates. But now she smiles and it lights up.

"Thank you for telling me," she says.

And that's enough to put her at ease, to get her talking. Kate lets the conversation ramble. She gets some background: Lavana's parents are from Bangalore, but she was born in Raleigh, North Carolina. Lavana tells Kate about her experience at Seagate, and about what it's like to be a woman trying to break into filmmaking.

Kate steers her toward the night when she and her friends found Bryan Cayhill's body: what she saw and how it made her feel. But things take an interesting turn when they talk about her movie.

Lavana has some of it edited together. She has a laptop and a high-end monitor on her desk. She shows Kate the opening sequence.

It's dark and moody and the camera work is good. We're in a forest and there are random shots of trees. Then a slow pan across the side of a wooden shack. We come around a corner and see a figure in silhouette from behind. It's Lavana, with her hair set free of its ponytail. She's standing with her arms at her sides. There's a set of handcuffs dangling from her left wrist.

"Did you shoot that near Weatherstone Pond?" Kate asks.

"No," Lavana says. "We were in the woods south of campus."

"What's that building?" Kate asks.

Lavana looks pleased. "It's good, right? Clay found it. It's sort of an oversized tool shed. Not really used anymore. The lock was broken a long time ago, I think, and no one ever bothered to replace it. There's some junk inside. A workbench and a vise. A rusty lawnmower. Some shelves with bottles of motor oil and paint thinner on them."

"What about tools? Anything with a long handle? Rakes or shovels . . ."

"I remember a shovel. Why?"

Kate stares at the monitor. The video has begun to play over again on a loop.

"I'm thinking about the pole," she says. "The one Bryan Cayhill's arms were tied to. It had to come from somewhere. Did you tell the police about this shed?"

"Naturally," Lavana says. "They wanted to know everywhere we shot, like Merkury might have been following us around."

She taps the track pad on her laptop to stop the video.

"There's something else too," she says. "This is weird. We shot in and around that shed for five nights. On the third night, I left a lens behind. I swear I left it on the workbench. But when we came back, it had moved. Somebody put it up on one of the shelves."

When Kate leaves Lavana Khatri, it's two in the afternoon. By two thirty she's talking with Travis Pollard.

It's a different experience. Lavana wanted to hear a secret. Travis wants to show Kate he's in charge. It starts when he shakes her hand. His grip is too firm and lingers too long.

He leads her through his off-campus apartment, past a pair of roommates playing *Call of Duty* on a huge flat-screen TV, to a balcony with two plastic lawn chairs and a small patio table.

"I grew up on a farm," he tells her.

He looks the part, Kate thinks. He's six feet tall and solidly put together. Put him in overalls in a hayfield with a scythe and he would not seem out of place. But what he is, really, is Hollywood's idea of a farmer: handsome and golden-haired, with a three-day stubble on his face. His teeth have had the benefit of orthodontia. His biceps may have gotten their start doing farmwork, but since then they've spent some time in a gym.

"What I mean is, I've seen death before," he says. "Chickens torn apart by foxes. Calves that were stillborn. My father had to shoot a horse once. It had a broken leg and there was nothing else to do. I saw it. The shooting was the easy part. Afterward we had to drag it up a ramp onto a trailer. We couldn't leave it where it was."

"Did you bury it?" Kate asks.

Travis gives her an indulgent smile. "I guess that would have been the sentimental thing to do," he says. "We drove it to the rendering plant."

He's slouching in his chair, wearing shorts and a white T-shirt and sneakers. There's something irritating about it, the way he's taking up space. His legs are stretched out in front of him, one ankle crossed over the other. His feet are almost touching Kate's.

"So when you found Bryan Cayhill's body," she says, "it was like finding a dead horse."

The smile goes away from his lips, but it's still there in his eyes. "You're making me sound callous. I was as creeped out as Lavana and Clay were at the time. It was disturbing. But I'm not gonna carry it around for the rest of my life. Does that make me a bad person?"

"No."

"But you don't approve. You think I should be haunted."

Kate shakes her head. "I don't think there's any right way to react to something like that."

Travis looks her over. She knows what it is to be looked over by men. He's not even trying to be subtle about it.

"I wonder," he says.

She feels herself frowning. "What do you wonder?"

"I wonder what it did to you. You were what, nine years old? And you found a dead girl in the woods."

Tension in her shoulders. Kate makes an effort to relax them. She keeps her voice even.

"I was eleven," she says.

"Either way, you were young. It must have messed you up."

There it is. Arrogance. She has a sudden urge to kick him in the shin.

"We're not talking about me," she says.

"There's the obvious thing. You write about murders now."

"How about we stick to Bryan Cayhill," Kate says. "Did you know him?"

Travis looks off at the horizon. There's a mass of dark clouds hanging low in the sky.

"A little," he says.

"How much is 'a little'?"

"I saw him around. We had econ classes together. We played pool a few times."

"Who won?"

A hint of a smirk. "It could go either way."

"Would you say he was accomplished?" Kate asks.

"At pool?"

"At anything. Most of Merkury's victims had some kind of talent. Melissa Cornelle played the violin. She'd been invited to audition for the Boston Symphony Orchestra."

Travis wrinkles his nose. "I don't think Bryan played any instruments."

"What was he good at?"

"He was on the football team. Wide receiver. If you're impressed by that sort of thing."

"You aren't impressed?"

"I play ice hockey."

"And you act."

He shrugs. "That's more of a favor for Lavana."

"You hadn't acted before?"

He looks away, pretending to be the modest farm boy. "High school productions, back home in Vermont," he says. "And one or two things here. I played Caliban in *The Tempest*."

"He's a monster, isn't he?" Kate says.

She's mocking him. He doesn't like it. But he makes himself grin.

"Or he's misunderstood," he says. "Lavana saw me in that play and asked me to be in her movie."

"What's it been like? You never acted on film before."

"It's been all right."

"I gather the story is simple. 'A chase' is how Clay McKellar described it. Two people running around in the woods."

"That almost makes it sound exciting. But the filming itself can be boring. Doing the same thing over and over. Waiting for the lighting and the camera to get set up."

Kate raises her eyebrows. "Did you ever do anything to relieve the boredom?"

"Like what?" Travis asks.

"Lavana said she left a lens behind one night, in the shed where you filmed. When she came back, someone had moved it. Maybe you played a prank on her."

"That's a pretty lame prank."

"So you didn't move it?"

"No. Why does it matter?"

"It doesn't, necessarily. But it's likely that Merkury watches his victims before he kills them. That's what the police believe. He may even break into their houses. Some family members have reported seeing things moved around from one place to another. Small possessions. Things you'd hardly notice."

Travis frowns. "What would that mean—that Merkury was stalking us?"

"Possibly."

"Then why did he end up killing Bryan Cayhill?"

"It could be he watches more than one potential victim at a time. And there were three of you. He would have needed to get one of you alone. Maybe Bryan was an easier target. Did you ever see anyone else in the woods while you were filming?"

"No."

"What about at Weatherstone Pond?" Kate says. "I've heard it's a hangout spot. Had you been there before?"

"A few times."

"Did you ever see anyone there that you didn't know? Someone older. Someone who maybe kept his distance, hung around on the fringes?"

Travis is quiet for a few seconds, watching her.

"No," he says, and she can see that he's changed. He's more thoughtful. He uncrosses his legs and sits up straight in his chair. "Are you trying to write about Merkury or catch him?"

He has a self-important look, as if he's hit upon a revelation. Kate has a pen in her handbag. She could take it out now. She could stab it into his thigh.

"I'm a writer," she says. "I'm just asking questions."

He should let it go. But he doesn't.

"I wonder what it's like to be you," he says. "You must think about him every day."

"No. I don't."

"Come on," Travis says. "You'd have to. You must wonder if you'll ever run into him again. And if you did, how would you know, if you never saw his face? You must be afraid all the time."

His expression is all sympathy now. No telling if it's real or fake. To Kate, it doesn't matter. She reaches into her bag. Closes her hand around the pen. She could do it. He wouldn't expect it.

She releases the pen and rises from her chair.

"I think I've got enough for now," she says.

Travis gets to his feet too. "You don't have to go. I didn't mean to upset you."

"If there's anything else I need, I'll be in touch."

He follows her out through the apartment. She can hear him behind her.

"Wait. I shouldn't have said what I said. It was too personal. I can see that."

Travis's roommates are still playing *Call of Duty*. The stutter of gunfire is loud and relentless.

Kate gets to the door and the deadbolt is engaged. She fumbles with the lever. Travis is there, close. Too close. If he puts a hand on her, she really will stab him.

She works the lock and slips out into the corridor, pulling the door shut behind her. Then she's down a set of stairs and through another door into the open air. He doesn't try to come after her.

7

When Kate was thirteen, her father got a job at Wofford College in South Carolina.

They lived in a ranch house in Spartanburg and her mother kept a garden in the backyard, growing tomatoes and cucumbers and green peppers. There was a thick old sycamore in a corner of the yard that shed its bark in long strips that littered the ground.

Kate was enrolled in the public middle school, a tan brick building with harsh fluorescent lighting. She'd never been shy, but moving from town to town had been hard on her. She was slow to make friends.

She had come to understand that her history followed her. Anyone who searched her name on the internet could find out about her link to Melissa Cornelle. Kate compensated by lying low, fading into the background. She was wary of kids who tried to strike up a conversation with her. She wondered about their motives.

She had a lab partner in science class, a girl named Jessica Penn, who was always asking about the places she had lived. Jessica seemed nice. She was the kind of girl who went sailing and rode horses. She had a group of friends who ate lunch with her in the cafeteria. Kate would have liked to join them, but she had trouble trusting in groups.

One afternoon they were learning about acids and bases and how to use litmus paper. There was a thud against one of the classroom windows: a small bird had flown into the glass. Jessica went to investigate and Kate joined her at the window. She looked out to see a brown wren lying in the grass. It wasn't moving.

At the end of the day Kate went outside and found it in the same place. It had a white throat and white streaks above its eyes. Spots on its wings. She crouched down, but didn't touch it. She knew it had died.

It was beautiful though.

The next morning when she went to her locker, someone had written on the door in black marker: *K.S. loves dead things.* When Kate looked inside, she found the wren lying on the cover of her science book.

At lunchtime she sat as far away from Jessica and her friends as she could. They didn't stare at her, or point, but she saw them smiling among themselves. She saw them laughing.

That night Kate went to bed and couldn't sleep. At one in the morning she got up and sat at the desk in her bedroom, tore a page from a notepad. She found a pencil and wrote six words: *Jessica Penn. Mean. Rotten. Fake friend.*

She didn't need to climb out her window. She knew she could make it out the back door without waking her parents. The night was warm, the air heavy, as she walked out to the sycamore tree. She circled around it, trailing her palm over the peeling bark.

Watching out for *him.*

He wasn't there, of course. He was never really there. But to Kate it was still their place. She folded the note and hid it under a rock at the base of the tree.

Nothing happened for several weeks, but when Kate went back to school after Thanksgiving break, Jessica Penn was absent. Someone in science class said she would be staying home for a while. She had fallen from a horse and broken her leg.

A few nights later, Kate went out to the tree again. She bent down and reached for the rock, and then thought better of it. She didn't want to know if the note was still there.

She's not a child anymore.

She's twenty-nine years old. She's been supporting herself since she graduated from college. She's written two books and part of a third. She has friends back in Ohio. She's had lovers.

She's not a child.

She's not afraid of the boogeyman.

That evening she's sitting on her bed reading over the notes she's made about Lavana Khatri and Travis Pollard when her father knocks on her door to call her to dinner. He has fried steaks and made roasted potatoes and a cucumber salad. She goes out and fixes a plate and takes it back to her bedroom. She doesn't want to talk to him.

She eats at her writing desk. Only a few bites. The food is fine, but it's not what she wants.

At a little after eight o'clock she opens her window and climbs out.

No stars to be seen and the grass is wet. It rained in the afternoon and there was even some thunder, but nothing like the storm she'd been expecting. The rain tapered down to drizzle in the evening and now even that is gone.

Kate walks around to the front of the house. Lee Tennick is sitting by his RV with a fire going. He offers her a beer and she takes it. She tells him about her conversations with Lavana and Travis, about the shed in the woods and the mysterious moving camera lens.

"It might not mean anything," Tennick says. "Maybe someone else uses that shed, or just hangs out there. Some dude who wants to get away from his wife. Who knows?"

Kate can't disagree. There's such a thing as coincidence. And with Merkury, nothing has ever really made sense.

"There's no pattern," she says.

Tennick drinks from his beer and rests the bottle on his knee.

"Patterns are overrated," he says.

"I'm serious. Start with the numbers. He's been active eighteen years now, but there have only been twelve victims. Why not more?"

"You might as well ask, Why not less?"

"And there's no consistent interval. He's gone as long as four years in between, but he's also killed two in the same year."

"He might have been out of commission for those four years," Tennick says. "Chief Landen thinks he may have served time in prison."

"She's guessing," Kate says.

"We're all guessing. About a lot of things."

There's more to say about Merkury and his inconsistencies.

"The victimology—" Kate begins.

"I know," says Tennick.

"—is all over the place. He starts with a young woman in college. You would think he'd stick with that. But how old was the second woman?"

"Thirty-three," Tennick says.

"Right. And the third victim was a man. There've been three men now, with Bryan Cayhill, and nine women. The ages range from twenty-one to fifty-two. They've mostly been in the Northeast: New York, Pennsylvania, Massachusetts. But there was one in Missouri. What was he doing in Missouri?"

Tennick sets his beer bottle on the ground. Picks up a stick to poke at the fire.

"That was in Parkville, outside of Kansas City," he says. "I've been there. It's kind of a tourist town. People go antiquing."

"I don't think he was antiquing," Kate says. "Honestly, what do the victims have in common?"

There's no response from Tennick, not at first. He's shifting the logs in the fire, to no particular purpose that she can see.

"Well, they've all been smothered or strangled," he says eventually, "and their bodies put on display in a very distinctive way."

He says it flatly, with no trace of sarcasm. It's the simple truth. Undeniable. And useless.

"There should be more," Kate says. "I told Travis Pollard that they were all accomplished people. They were all good at something."

"Everybody's good at *something*," Tennick says. He's got the fire arranged to his liking now. He drops the stick and leans back in his chair.

"You're thinking like a profiler," he says. "Profilers have to look for patterns, and most of the time they find them. If they didn't, no one would pay them any mind. But if you can't find a pattern with Merkury, maybe it's because there is no pattern. Maybe we just have to admit we don't know why he does what he does."

It's midnight and Kate is awake.

She stayed with Tennick for a second beer, hashing out all the things they didn't know about Merkury. Then she came inside and tried to find a book to read, but her father's collection is mostly highbrow stuff: Colson Whitehead, Jonathan Franzen, Isabel Allende. She settled on John Irving—*The Fourth Hand*—but it didn't hold her interest. She fell asleep for a while, but now she's up again. Alert. Restless.

She's thinking about Travis Pollard, the way he looked at her, studied her. The way he thought he had worked out something about her.

I wonder what it's like to be you.

You must be afraid all the time.

She doesn't like him. She told Tennick as much when they were talking earlier. He wanted to know why, but she didn't feel like explaining.

"There's something off about him," she said. And then a question occurred to her. "Does he have an alibi?"

Tennick gave her a curious look. "For the Bryan Cayhill killing?"

"Yes."

"He's way too young to be Merkury."

"He could be a copycat," Kate said. "Did the police even consider him? Do you know?"

He looked offended by the question. Of course he knew. Lee Tennick had his sources.

"The cops checked alibis for all three of them," he said. "On the night Bryan was killed, Lavana and Clay were in her dorm room editing some of their footage. Other students saw them. They were showing off scenes from their movie. It was overcast that night, and they hadn't planned to go out and film, but the clouds moved on and the moon came out and they called Travis. Arranged to pick him up at a bar downtown. He'd been there for hours with his roommates. That's confirmed by a bartender and other patrons. When they met up with him at the bar, it was after midnight. Bryan Cayhill was already dead at Weatherstone Pond."

So Travis is in the clear, but Kate still doesn't like him.

She gets out of bed and sees her dinner on the desk, mostly uneaten. She tries cutting off a piece of steak, but it's dried out now. Unappealing. She takes the plate to the kitchen and leaves it on the counter. It joins some pans and her father's plate. He went to bed and left them for the morning.

On the counter there's a pad her father uses to make grocery lists. Kate peels off a blank sheet, grabs a pen, and slips them both in her pocket.

The only sound in the house is the clock ticking on the wall.

She finds her running shoes and puts them on, and then she's out through the back door, locking up with her key. The moon is riding high, but it's only a blur behind a veil of clouds.

Cutting across the yard at a jog, she passes through the trellis arch and heads down to the stream. The grass is wet but she doesn't slip. She hasn't been this way in eighteen years. Nothing much has changed. Even the sounds are the same: crickets and burbling water.

After a few minutes she sees the oak tree and slows to a walk.

The tree is different.

One of the limbs has broken off and fallen to the ground. It's not a clean cut, so it must have been lightning or rot. Kate bends down to examine it with the light from her phone.

Rot.

She pockets the phone. Circles the tree once, stepping over the fallen limb. Then circles it a second time, her fingertips skimming the bark of the trunk.

Dead leaves crackle beneath her feet.

She walks to the stream and crouches down to touch the water. With her back to the tree, she listens. There's nothing here. Nothing to be afraid of.

Before she heads back to the house, she takes the paper and pen from her pocket and writes his name: *Travis Pollard.*

Smug.

Arrogant.

She folds the paper. Pries up a rock from the bank of the stream. Leaves the note underneath it at the foot of the tree.

She takes her time going back. The ground is flat until she gets close to the house, then it rises away from the stream. The trellis arch looms up ahead of her. She passes under it and here's the yard. The house.

She slides her key into the lock of the back door and suddenly there's a tingling on the nape of her neck. She turns. Surveys the empty yard. There are trees out there in the distance. He could be behind one of them.

She's not going to check.

But she walks to the center of the yard and stands with her arms outstretched, waiting.

A minute passes.

Two.

She lets her arms fall to her sides.

"I didn't think so," she says aloud.

She lets herself into the house and locks the door behind her. Leaves her wet shoes on the mat. She knows she won't be able to fall asleep anytime soon, so she steps into the kitchen, thinking she'll load the dishwasher and run it. The overhead light is on, the way she left it.

Her father's plate from dinner is on the counter by the sink. Hers is there too. But not her steak knife.

The knife should be there. That's where she left it. On her plate.

But it's not.

It's on the kitchen table.

8

When Kate breezes through the lobby of the Seagate Inn, it's going on four in the morning. There's no clerk behind the check-in desk, which is just as well. She doesn't want to have to explain herself.

She takes the elevator to the third floor and taps on the door of room 302. When tapping doesn't work, she pounds. Devin Falko comes to the door barely awake, wearing nothing but boxer shorts.

"I'm not crazy," Kate says, pushing past him into the room.

He lets the door fall shut. Rubs his face. "What's going on?"

"He was in the house, Dev. He walked right in."

Climbed in, to be perfectly accurate. The doors had been locked, but she had left the window in her room open a few inches to let in some air.

"Who are we talking about?" Devin asks.

She kicks her shoes off and paces on the carpet.

"Him," she says. "Don't be dense. He moved my steak knife."

Devin shakes his head. "I'm not following you. Maybe start again."

So she tells him from the beginning, about going out for a jog and coming back to find the knife had been moved. Waking her father to find out if he had done it, and of course he hadn't. Going through the same thing with Lee Tennick, who opened the door of his RV in a robe and was the only one to recognize the seriousness of what had happened.

"So I called 911," Kate says. "What was I supposed to do? And try explaining something like that to a stranger without sounding like a loon."

Vera Landen herself came out to take the report, with two of her officers to search the house and the grounds. They bagged the knife and dusted the window for fingerprints. They took prints from Kate and her father and Tennick for purposes of elimination. "We're treating this seriously," Landen said.

"But you should have seen the look she gave me," Kate tells Devin. "Like she was sad for me."

Devin runs his fingers through his hair. "Okay. Let's breathe for a minute. Let's take time to assess. You're safe, right? Nobody's hurt."

He's calm and reasonable, just the way Landen was.

Kate makes a fist and punches him in the sternum.

"Don't patronize me," she says. "Don't try to minimize what happened."

"I'm not."

She punches him again and he takes hold of her wrist, so she hits him with her other hand.

"Stop," he says. When she doesn't, he grabs her other wrist. His grip is hard.

She struggles, but he won't let go.

"You're hurting me," she says.

He holds on long enough to make a point and then releases her.

"What do you want, Kate?"

She rolls her eyes at him. "You know what I want."

"If you need to talk this through—"

"Dense, dense, dense," she says.

She can still feel his grip on her, even though it isn't there. She lays a hand on his chest, gently this time.

He lets out a sigh. She feels the movement under her palm.

"That won't solve anything," he says.

"That's where you and I disagree."

"You think it'll make you feel better—"

"Oh, someone's catching on."

"—but it won't."

"I'll be the one to make that judgment."

He steps back from her. "We're not having sex."

"Not at this rate, we aren't," she says. "Take off my clothes."

"No."

She peels her shirt off, pulling it up over her head. "I'll do it myself," she says.

Her bra follows, then her jeans and underwear.

Finally her socks. She throws them at him and falls back onto the bed.

"We're not," Devin says.

"I think we are."

They do. It's warm in the room and the Seagate Inn has soft sheets. At first he wants to be sweet about it, kissing her stomach, her breasts, her lips, tracing the fingers of his right hand along her cheek and down to her shoulder. But she hurries him along, gets his boxer shorts off. She wants him inside. She has always liked the weight of him on top of her, the strength of his arms.

You think it'll make you feel better—

It does. She digs her fingers into his back and wraps her legs around him.

When it happens, every bit of tension inside of her rushes out in a moan. He covers her mouth with his hand before the moan can rise up into a scream. Because he knows her.

For a time she lies under him and the world is empty of everything else. Then she opens her eyes and his hand is gone from her mouth and she's breathing deep. He's lying on his side, propped on one elbow, looking down at her.

"Switch," she says.

The shake of his head is almost imperceptible. "No."

"*Switch.*"

"Why?"

"Because we're still going."

Devin rolls onto his back and Kate straddles him. He lies still at first, gray eyes watching her. She's the one who's moving. She falls into a rhythm that she can hear in the creaking of the bed. His hands find her hips and he begins to move with her.

She braces one arm against the headboard. Places her palm over his heart.

"Don't," he says.

She arches an eyebrow. "What?"

"Just don't."

"Don't what?" she says, moving her hand from his heart to his throat. "This?"

"Easy," he says.

"Or what? You're gonna hit me?"

He pushes up into her. Their rhythm intensifies. She tips her head back, laughing.

"I think you like it," she says.

Her fingers are loose on his throat. She tightens them a little.

"No," he says.

"You do. You like it."

She moves her other hand down from the headboard to his shoulder.

"Stop," he says.

"I'm not doing anything."

"There have to be limits," he says. "You get one. One is all you get."

She makes a pouty face, but moves her hand back to the headboard. The other remains on his throat. She leans down to whisper in his ear.

"I'll be nice. I promise."

*   *   *

Kate gets up from the bed after and turns the heat down in the room. Cracks a window and feels the night air on her skin. Devin is lying on his back with his right arm covering his brow. On his left arm there's a series of old scars below the crook of his elbow. She stands over him, touching the scars with her fingertips. Watching his chest rise and fall.

She gathers her clothes and puts them on. By the time she slips out the door he's on his side, asleep, his arms wrapped around a pillow.

9

There's a chapel at the top of the Hill behind the Hollister Library. That's where they hold the memorial service for Bryan Cayhill on Saturday afternoon.

It's an eclectic affair, the college's chaplain starting things off with a reading from the book of Psalms. Then a succession of students sharing reminiscences: A player from the football team talks about a low point in his life, when he was going to quit the game, and quit school altogether, until Bryan convinced him to stay. A young woman says Bryan taught her to play guitar, and confesses that they shared a love of Ed Sheeran songs. Others follow suit, relating stories about how Bryan helped them, or about how friendly he was, always making people laugh.

The chapel is filled to capacity, with some people standing in the aisles or behind the last row of pews. Kate is among them, along with her father and Lee Tennick.

Bryan's mother and father are seated down front. Kate gets a look at them when they step up to the microphone to thank everyone for coming. They're a dignified pair, slim and attractive, well groomed and well dressed. Bryan's mother thanks each of the speakers by name. His father reads a Rudyard Kipling poem, breaking down at the end until his wife puts an arm around him.

Then the organist in the choir loft plays the opening chords of "Amazing Grace," and everyone rises to join in.

Lee Tennick has always been an introvert. Which is ironic, since he earns his living by talking to people.

He spends most of the service waiting for it to be over. He wants to be free of the crowd. When they're done with their singing, he watches them spill out the doors and onto the grass of the quad. He stays behind until everyone is gone and sits for a few minutes in the quiet of the chapel.

By the time he steps outside into the sunlight, more than half the crowd has drifted away. The rest are lingering in small groups. Kate is with her father. He's introducing her to some of his colleagues from the English department. Looking toward the library, Tennick spots Lavana Khatri and Travis Pollard on a bench together. A pale kid with red hair joins them: Clay McKellar. He's dressed in a jacket and tie, though he doesn't seem at ease in them.

Tennick watches the three of them talking to each other. He can't hear what they're saying. He waits until they go their separate ways, then hustles to catch up with Clay.

He intercepts the kid as he's heading around the side of the library. Tennick touches his arm, and Clay stops and turns, confused.

"Sad day," Tennick says.

Clay mumbles his agreement.

Tennick nods back toward the chapel. "Nice ceremony, I thought."

"Do I know you?" Clay asks.

"I'm Lee. Lee Tennick."

An awkward handshake follows.

"You called me last week," Clay says. "You wanted to talk about Bryan. For a podcast."

Tennick nods.

"I don't feel like talking about him," Clay says.

Tennick gives him a sympathetic smile. "That's fine. I just wanted to see how you're doing. If you're okay."

Clay thinks it over. As if no one else has asked him.

"I guess I'm okay," he says.

"Good. Have you been drinking?"

The question throws him off. "No."

It's a lie. Tennick is close enough to smell the alcohol on his breath.

"It's all right," Tennick says. "Seriously. It's understandable. You've been through a trauma."

Kate endures her father's friends for as long as she can. They ask about the books she's written and what she's working on now. She keeps her answers general and breaks away at the first opportunity.

She winds up standing by herself, scanning around for familiar faces. She sees Lee Tennick in the distance talking to a young man. It takes her a moment to realize that it's Clay McKellar.

Tennick lays a hand on Clay's shoulder. The gesture seems almost tender.

Kate is trying to decide whether she should walk over to them when she hears a voice beside her.

"We meet again."

She turns, startled, and sees Travis Pollard. She didn't notice his approach. She steps away from him reflexively.

"I didn't mean to scare you," he says.

"You didn't scare me."

He looks skeptical. "Well, I'm sorry. About yesterday too. I wish you had stuck around. I like talking to you."

He hasn't moved, but it feels like he's leaning in close to her. He's wearing a dark gray suit that looks worn at the lapels, and he hasn't bothered with a tie.

"I had somewhere to be yesterday," Kate says, and regrets it right away. It's obviously a lie, and it makes her seem weak.

Travis doesn't call her on it. He turns around casually, looking up at the sky. There are a few wispy clouds above the golden spire of the chapel.

"Beautiful day," he says.

Now he's making small talk. Kate searches for an excuse to get away from him. She spots Mr. and Mrs. Cayhill on the chapel steps, talking to the chaplain. Travis sees them too.

"You have to wonder how they're feeling right now," he says. "Do they want to be here, or is this a chore, something they have to get through? The college felt obligated to put on this service and to invite them, and they probably felt obligated to attend. Everybody's intentions are good. But is this really helping them or is it making their lives worse?"

It's a perceptive question, and Kate is surprised to hear it coming from Travis. She doesn't want to think well of him.

She doesn't have to, not for long. With the next words out of his mouth, he's back to irritating her.

"You want to talk to them, don't you? The Cayhills. That's why you're here."

"No," she says.

"Sure it is. You need them if you're going to write about Bryan. But how do you approach them? If you do it wrong, you're screwed. You come across as a scavenger. Picking at their grief."

He's right. If she goes ahead with the book, she's going to need the Cayhills, and one of the reasons she came here today was to get a look at them. It's always a delicate problem: how to deal with the parents.

"You should probably keep your distance for now," Travis says. "Let them have their space."

It's sound advice, but she doesn't like getting it. Not from him.

"I know that," she says. "Give me some credit."

A tinge of anger in her voice. Travis picks up on it and backs away from her.

"I've upset you again," he says. "I should leave you alone."

"There's an idea."

Now he smiles. Gives her a little nod to say goodbye. She watches him walk away, strolling in the sunshine until he disappears around the side of the chapel.

Kate drove here with her father, and he's still talking with his friends. She sits on the library steps to wait for him. Tries to put the Cayhills out of her mind. But things don't always go the way you expect. Mr. Cayhill comes to her.

She's staring at the ground, lost in her own thoughts, and doesn't see him until he's practically in front of her.

"You don't need to get up," he says, but she's already rising. Up close, he's shorter than she thought, only a couple of inches taller than she is. His shoes are leather and unscuffed. His suit and overcoat fit him flawlessly. There are no diamonds on the watch on his wrist, but she's sure it's not because he can't afford diamonds. It's because diamonds would be gauche. He's a man who doesn't need to put his wealth on display.

"You're the writer," he says.

"Kate Summerlin," she tells him.

"Martin Cayhill."

His hands are in his pockets. He doesn't bring them out to shake.

"I know about your past," he says. "And I don't judge anyone for what they feel they need to do to make money. But if you intend to write about my son—"

"I haven't made up my mind yet," she begins.

He grimaces as if her interruption is distasteful. "If you do," he says, "you'll get no cooperation from me or my wife or anyone we know. I can't stop you from publishing. But whatever you may choose to publish will be reviewed by my attorneys with an eye toward suing you for libel if you give us any grounds at all."

"Mr. Cayhill—"

He stops her with a look. "Please. I've said what I wanted to say. Let's leave it there."

She nods once. "I'm sorry about your son."

He turns without acknowledging her and walks back to his wife.

10

Kate drives back to the house with her father. He's quiet in the passenger seat until she makes the turn onto Bird River Road.

"I know you went out last night," he says, "after the police left."

She doesn't respond.

"I know you were gone for hours. Am I supposed to mind my own business?"

"Yes," she says.

He doesn't call her for dinner that night. She zones out in her room until around seven thirty, when she hears Lee Tennick's car in the driveway. When she walks out to meet him, he's climbing the steps of his RV.

"What are you up to?" she asks him.

He holds up a bag of Chinese takeout.

"I'm starving," he says, and beckons her in.

The RV is surprisingly tidy inside. Tennick brings out plates and bowls and silverware and they sit at a two-top Formica table. He's got Hunan chicken and hot-and-sour soup. He shares it out evenly.

"I saw you with Clay McKellar," Kate says. "Do you know him?"

Tennick blows on his soup. Tastes it.

"Not before today."

"You two looked friendly," Kate says.

"I'm a friendly person."

"And then I lost track of you. Where did you go?"

He looks up at her. "Where is this interrogation coming from?"

She studies his face. She has never given any thought to Lee Tennick's sexuality.

"I'm wondering if you tried to make a move on a college kid," she says.

He turns his attention back to his soup. After a time, he says: "The kid is twenty-one. Just FYI."

"Uh-huh."

"He's a sensitive soul. He's been having a hard time, dealing with what he saw. I would think you'd be sympathetic."

"So were you—sympathetic?"

He laughs. "Your innuendo is far too subtle, Kate. Are you asking me if I screwed him?"

"Did you?"

"No. We went into the library together. It's easy to find an out-of-the-way place in a library. I let him cry on my shoulder. He's been holding his feelings in. Bryan Cayhill was only the second dead person he ever saw. The first was his grandfather, and he had some warning about that one. Clay hasn't had an easy time at Seagate. Lavana and Travis are among the few friends he's made. Helping out with the movie was his way of trying to fit in."

Tennick's voice has a gentle quality Kate hasn't heard from him before. She doesn't know whether to trust it.

"What's your angle?" she asks him. "Are you trying to cozy up to Clay so he'll talk to you?"

Tennick reaches behind him to open a small refrigerator. Brings out two bottles of beer and passes her one. Kate thinks he's avoiding her question, but after he's had a drink, he says:

"That was the idea I had, at first. But I don't know, there's something about him. I feel like we made a connection."

"Really?" she says. "A connection?"

He's looking down at his bottle, as if there's something fascinating to read on the label. After a few seconds he looks up at her with a smile that's half sad and half bitter.

"You said it yourself. Sometimes I'm almost human."

On Sunday morning it rains, and Kate sleeps until almost eleven. She takes a drive in the afternoon, winding around on back roads, and when Devin phones her she doesn't answer. When she arrives back at the house, Tennick comes out of his RV and follows her onto the porch.

"Listen to this," he says, "and tell me if you think I should be worried."

He holds up his cellphone and plays her a voicemail on speaker.

"It's me. You said I should call if I needed to talk. Don't know if you meant it. It's . . . I don't know what time it is. I've got all the curtains closed, but I can see daylight peeking through. So this is not a midnight drunk dial . . . Can't be if it's not midnight, right? . . . This can't go on. I thought I'd get over it. 'You're being paranoid,' I said, but I don't know. I saw what I saw. You can't unsee something, right? . . . God, I'm tired. I think there's something wrong with me. Heard something scratching on the door. Did I open the door? No, I did not. Not opening any doors . . . Anyway . . . That's where I'm at."

When it ends, Kate says, "That's Clay McKellar?"

Tennick nods.

"He's been drinking, obviously," she adds.

"Yes. But hold on. There's another."

He taps the phone and Clay's voice comes on again, a little steadier this time.

"I called you before. Don't remember exactly what I said. Pretty sure it was goofy . . . You probably think I'm nuts now. But I feel better. I slept for

a while . . . If the rain stops, I'm going out for a walk. Don't worry about me. I'm okay . . . Talk to you later."

"That's it," Tennick says. "The first message came in this morning at 9:22. The second at 2:05. I was recording audio for a podcast, so I had my phone in silent mode all day. Checked it about an hour ago."

"You tried calling him back?"

Another nod. "Texted him too. No reply."

"Maybe he did what he said. Went for a walk."

"Maybe." Tennick sounds unconvinced.

"Do you know where he lives?" Kate asks him.

"I can find out."

The movie theater in downtown Alexander is called the Odeon, and next door is a three-story building of weathered red brick. There's a coffee shop on the ground floor and apartments up above.

They climb a poorly lit stairway and pass down a narrow hall. Clay McKellar's door is like the others: dingy gray with peeling paint. Tennick knocks while Kate hangs back.

No answer. Tennick knocks again and calls out Clay's name.

Down the hall Kate spots movement on the stairs. There's something orange and furry coming down from the third floor. Its steps are cautious, as if it's unsure of its footing. It's roughly the size of a watermelon.

Kate touches Tennick's arm and points it out to him. "That's a cat, right?"

Tennick glances at it and frowns. Knocks on the door again.

The cat descends to the landing and ambles along the hall, stopping at the first door it comes to. It plants itself there, looking up expectantly, and raises a paw to scratch the door.

It keeps scratching until the door opens. A young woman's voice says, "Okay, come on."

The cat changes its mind and stays in the hall. The woman steps out and reaches for it. It wriggles away from her.

Kate says, "Hi. Do you know Clay McKellar?"

The woman gets her hands on the cat and lifts it. "A little," she says.

"Have you seen him today?"

"I saw him go out this afternoon," the woman says. "Maybe around two thirty?"

The cat squirms in her arms, but she keeps hold of it.

"Thanks," Kate says. "What's her name?"

"She's a he. Milo."

"He's a wanderer, is he?"

"Milo cannot be contained."

On cue, Milo twists in the woman's arms, but she manages a twist of her own, twirling gracefully into her apartment before he can break free. Pushing the door shut with her foot.

At Clay's door, Tennick has given up on knocking. He takes out his wallet and extracts a credit card.

"You heard her," Kate says. "He went out."

"That was hours ago," says Tennick. "He might have come back."

He tries to slide the card between the door and the jamb.

"I don't think that works," Kate says. "Have you done it before?"

"I've seen it done."

"In real life or in the movies?"

He ignores her and keeps at it with the card.

"Come on," she says. "There might be another way."

There's an alley between the movie theater and Clay's building, and a fire escape that could take them up to his window.

Tennick reaches up and tries to catch the bottom rung of the steel ladder. It's beyond him, even when he jumps.

"It'll have to be you," he says to Kate.

Before she can object, he has his fingers interlaced and he's crouching down to make her a step.

She looks down the alley to the street to see if anyone's watching.

"Relax," he says wryly. "I saw this done in a movie once."

She settles her left foot onto his hands and bounces on her other leg to build momentum. When she launches herself up, he lifts at the same time. Her aim is slightly off, but she manages to catch the rung with one hand and keep her grip as Tennick eases her down to the ground. The ladder slides down with her, squealing the whole way.

Then it's an easy climb to the second floor, with Tennick following. From the platform outside Clay McKellar's window they can see into his living room. Nothing looks amiss. There's no sign of Clay.

"He could be passed out in the bedroom," Tennick says. "Or the bathroom."

"Or he could have gone out," Kate counters. "And doesn't feel like answering his phone."

Tennick reaches for the window sash and tries to raise it. But it's locked.

"We're not breaking in," Kate says.

"I never said we were."

"You were thinking it. Look, we know Clay was drunk. Suppose Milo the cat scratched on his door and it spooked him. He was already on edge after finding Bryan Cayhill. That's all this is. Then he got some rest and felt better and went out. There's nothing to worry about."

Tennick leans against the railing of the fire escape. "Do you believe that?"

"Mostly," Kate says.

"Yeah."

"Almost entirely."

"Right," Tennick says. "I'd like it better if I saw him."

* * *

They go looking. Cruising through the town in Kate's car. They start on Main and branch out onto some of the residential streets. They travel south on Route 12B a mile past the football stadium and then swing back and drive to the top of the Hill. There are students out walking in the fading afternoon, but none of them are Clay.

The sun has gone down when Kate makes her way out to Bird River Road, but when she reaches her father's house, Tennick tells her to keep going.

He doesn't have to tell her where.

She drives north and west and comes to Portage Road. The turnoff to Weatherstone Pond is still blocked by sawhorses. She parks on the roadside and they walk down to the water. Clay's not there. Not on the shore of the pond, and not hanging from the oak tree.

On the walk back to the car, Tennick dials Clay's number again. He shakes his head when the call goes to voicemail.

"There's one other place we could try," Kate says.

The woods south of campus. That's as much as Kate knows.

She calls Lavana Khatri, explains the situation, and arranges to pick her up outside her dorm. Lavana climbs into the back seat and directs Kate to a trailhead down the road from the college gymnasium.

There's a patch of dirt and grass where they can leave the car. Kate takes a flashlight from her glove compartment.

They're only a few dozen yards into the woods when the shed comes into view, a dark shape among the trees. The door sags on rusted hinges. It's standing a few inches open.

"It's always like that," Lavana says.

Tennick draws the door open and Kate shines her light in. There's a workbench and a cast-iron vise. Their shadows flow across the wall.

Kate steps inside, Tennick and Lavana behind her. Here's a rusted lawnmower, here's a wrench lying on the concrete floor. Kate shines the light into the dark corners.

Clay isn't here.

Lavana lets out a breath she's been holding. A nervous laugh.

"You had me worried," she says.

Kate moves closer to the workbench. The flashlight reveals dark spots on the floor.

Under the bench is the blade of a shovel with the handle broken off.

"Son of a bitch," Tennick says.

He backs out through the doorway, Lavana stepping aside to give him room. Kate follows him, aiming the flashlight here and there: up into the trees, along the ground, across the side of the shed. Tennick rounds the back corner of the building and is briefly out of her sight. When the light touches him again, he's standing over Clay McKellar's body.

Clay is lying in a swathe of fallen leaves near the back wall of the shed. He's dressed for a hike: boots and jeans, a light jacket over a gray sweatshirt. His arms are spread wide, and the wooden handle of the shovel is lying underneath him. His eyes are open, staring blankly at the trees and the dark sky.

11

Kate doesn't know how many interview rooms there are in the police station in Alexander, but the one where they put her is cozy and clean, with walls painted a pleasant blue. There's no one-way mirror, just a window with a view of the parking lot. An overhead light shines down on a polished wooden table flanked by four office chairs.

An old, tired cop brings her a bottle of water and some magazines. He pulls the door shut when he leaves.

She waits. Two hours at least. There's no clock and they took her phone when they drove her here from the crime scene. She's not under arrest. She thinks she could walk out the door if she wanted, but what would be the point? She feels like screaming. Or laying her arms on the table and putting her head down. She doesn't do either.

She's standing by the window, fiddling with the lock, when the door finally opens and Vera Landen walks in. She's wearing a red flannel shirt with gray trousers and black boots. Her badge is on a lanyard around her neck.

She sees Kate at the window and says, "You're not leaving, are you?"

It might be a joke but Landen isn't smiling. She looks far sterner than she did when she came to see Kate at the cabin in Ohio.

She takes a seat, and Kate joins her at the table.

"How did Clay die?" Kate asks. "Was he smothered?"

Landen swivels sideways in her chair. "Why would you think so?"

"I didn't see any wounds on the body. Though I guess he could have been hit on the back of the head. I saw blood on the floor of the shed, or something that could have been blood . . ."

Landen sighs. "I don't know what this is, this girl-detective thing you're doing. But I'd like you to stop."

Kate feels a prickle of heat on the skin of her face. Not embarrassment. More like anger.

"I'm not a girl anymore," she says.

"I know," Landen says. "You're not. Let me lay things out for you. We're opening a homicide investigation into the death of Clay McKellar. So to start I'm going to need you to tell me, step-by-step, how you came to be in that particular spot in the woods tonight."

It's almost one in the morning when Landen tells her she can go. Kate picks up her cellphone from the desk sergeant, and a patrolman drives her back to the trailhead so she can retrieve her car.

The night is quiet and cold. Kate drives north past the campus and into downtown Alexander once again. The traffic lights are blinking red and amber. Instead of heading for home, she finds a place to park near the Seagate Inn and rides the elevator to the third floor.

Devin Falko is awake and dressed when she knocks on the door of his room. He lets her in and she tells him about the day she's had, right up to the interview with Vera Landen.

"You think it was Merkury," Devin says. "He's the one who killed this kid—Clay."

"That's how it looks," says Kate.

"But he didn't do his thing. With the rope, and the tree."

"Maybe something interrupted him."

"Is that what Landen thinks?" Devin asks.

He's sitting at the desk by the window. Kate is cross-legged on the hotel bed.

"Landen's not saying what she thinks," Kate says. "But who else would it be?"

Devin picks at a thread on his sweater. He looks thoughtful.

"What about Tennick?"

"What about him?" Kate asks.

"You said he just met the kid on Saturday. He went to a lot of trouble, searching for someone he barely knew."

"So did I," Kate says.

"Tennick started things off though," Devin says. "Whose idea was it to search the shed in the woods?"

"It was mine."

Devin smiles. "Well, there goes my big theory."

It hadn't occurred to Kate that Tennick might be a suspect, and she finds the suggestion unconvincing. She believes he was genuinely worried when they set out to look for Clay. If he knew Clay was dead all along, he hid it well. She puts the idea out of her mind and tries to relax. She's tempted to lie down, but she feels too keyed up to sleep.

"What made you think of it?" Devin asks her.

"Think of what?"

"That shed. Why did you decide to look there?"

It was a hunch, Kate thinks. But that's an unsatisfying answer.

"We were afraid something bad might have happened to Clay, and the shed seemed like a place where something bad might happen."

Devin nods. He's resting his elbows on the arms of his chair, and his hands are touching at the fingertips. It's a pose Kate doesn't like. She imagines it's how he sits when he's with his patients.

"How are you feeling?" he asks her.

"Don't," she says.

"What? It's a reasonable question. This is the second time you've discovered a body in the woods. That's an ordeal. Something you need to work through."

Kate stares at him for a moment, then slides herself off the bed. She stands in front of him and tangles her fingers in his hair.

"There's only one thing I want from you," she says. "And it's not therapy."

Vera Landen never asked for any of this.

Well, that's not exactly true. There was a time, as a young patrol cop in Rochester, when she envied the homicide detectives in the department. She thought they were doing the real work, the important work. Finding justice for the dead. What could be more noble?

Then she became a detective herself, at a time when the murder rate in Rochester was more than triple the average in New York State and in the country as a whole. The victims were mostly young men, killed over nothing, over drug deals and turf wars. And there was precious little justice to be found, and even less nobility.

She had her fill of it long ago. Traded it for a job as chief of police in a college town. She thought it would be a more peaceable life, and it has been, overall. Melissa Cornelle was murdered during Landen's second year as chief in Alexander, but afterward there was a blessedly long stretch of time when the worst Landen had to deal with was whatever mischief drunken frat boys got up to.

Now she has two more dead kids, Bryan Cayhill and Clay McKellar, in the space of a couple of weeks. She's had another night of making calls no one wants to make and giving orders no one wants to give.

By three in the morning, she feels justified in taking a break. She has contacted Clay's mother to notify her of her son's death. She has called in the county medical examiner, who has removed Clay's body from the woods. Her officers have secured the scene and will safeguard it until the morning, when a team of forensic specialists from the state police are scheduled to come in and process the shed and the surrounding area.

Landen wants to be on hand when the forensic team arrives, but until then there's nothing much she can do. If she's going to be of any use tomorrow, she needs a shower and a few hours of sleep. She tells the watch commander to call her if he needs her, finds her SUV in the parking lot, and heads off for home.

She has driven less than two blocks when she sees something that makes her slow down and pull over to the curb.

Kate leaves Devin sleeping in the dark and rides the elevator down to the lobby. As she's walking to her car, a blue SUV pulls up beside her. The driver lowers the passenger window.

It's Vera Landen.

"I thought you went home," she says.

"I'm going now," Kate tells her.

"It's very late."

"I know what time it is."

Landen looks past Kate at the Seagate Inn. She seems to be deliberating over something. After a second she comes to a decision.

"Get in," she says. "We need to talk."

"Haven't we talked enough?" Kate asks.

"Apparently not."

Landen presses a button to unlock the passenger door and Kate climbs in. She listens to the idling engine until Landen says, "Do you think it's wise, what you're doing?"

"I've been staying out after dark for a long time," Kate says.

"You're misunderstanding me. I tried to tell you this earlier, but maybe I need to be clearer. I don't think you should be here, involved in this."

"I think I'm involved whether I want to be or not," Kate says. "What would you suggest I do?"

Landen sighs and drums her fingers on the steering wheel. "Keep your eyes open, for one thing. Be aware of your surroundings. How long have you known Devin Falko?"

The question surprises Kate. She looks at the entrance of the inn, then back at Landen.

"How do you know about Devin?"

Landen gestures at the street. "This is my town. It's my business to know who comes and goes."

"Are you trying to tell me you keep track of everyone?"

"No. Just the important ones. Like the people you associate with. How did you meet Mr. Falko?"

Kate folds her arms, a stubborn pose, as if she's not going to answer. But she does.

"He came to one of my readings, at a bookstore in Columbus, when my first book was published. Four years ago."

"That's when you started dating?" Landen asks.

"He asked me out for a drink after the event."

"Did he know about you—about your past?"

"About Melissa Cornelle? Everybody knew," Kate says. "My publisher made sure of it. It was good publicity. Why are we talking about this?"

Landen turns her head to look at Kate directly. "Devin Falko is forty-six years old. He got his Ph.D. in psychology from the University of Pennsylvania, and he taught for ten years before he started his therapy practice."

"These are all things I know," Kate says.

"Do you know he spent a year as a visiting professor at Seagate?"

Landen says it so coolly that Kate wonders if she's making it up.

"When?" Kate says.

"When Melissa Cornelle was a sophomore."

"She was killed when she was a senior."

"That's right. And at the time, Devin Falko was teaching at Bingham-ton University. A ninety-minute drive away."

Kate feels a twist of doubt inside her, like a physical pain in her stom-ach. She tries to will it away.

"That doesn't mean anything," she says. "Are you sure he even knew Melissa?"

Landen shrugs. "No, not yet. And there are eleven other victims I would have to connect him to. Twelve if you count Clay McKellar. But I'm telling you this so you can use your own judgment. It might be best to stay away from Devin Falko. He doesn't feel right to me."

The pain in Kate's stomach eases, and she laughs. "Jesus. You almost had me scared. I'm supposed to go by your *feelings*?"

Landen gives her a disappointed look. "No, but you could use some common sense. When I found you last week hiding out in that house in Ohio, Devin wasn't there, was he?"

Kate shakes her head. "We broke up."

"When?"

"Two months ago. A little more."

"And ten days ago, Bryan Cayhill was hung up in a tree," Landen says. "Now you're here, and Devin is here. You're walking out of his hotel in the middle of the night. I can't prove a single thing. But maybe he killed Bryan, and maybe it got him just what he wanted."

12

On Monday the sun is defiantly bright. It's sixty degrees, a perfect autumn day. Kate sleeps until eleven, and when she goes to the kitchen to make breakfast the house feels empty. Her father is out. He has a class and office hours at the college.

She turns the television on around noon, and the cable news channels are shuffling between an active shooter at an office park in Reno, Nevada, and a suicide bombing in Berlin. Clay McKellar's death isn't on their radar. It gets less than a minute of coverage on the local CBS affiliate out of Syracuse.

Kate checks her messages and finds a text from Lee Tennick: Survived the Inquisition. How about you? She tells him she's okay. There's another text from Devin: How are you feeling? She leaves that one unanswered.

At one o'clock she locks up the house and drives out with no clear destination in mind. She ends up on campus in the visitors' parking lot. From there it's a five-minute walk to Lavana Khatri's dorm. Kate calls Lavana on the way and asks if she has time to talk. The girl comes down from her room and they walk to the student union and get coffee.

Lavana had an easier time the night before at the police station than Kate did. They made her wait for an hour and questioned her for thirty minutes and drove her back to campus. She's still coming to grips with finding Clay—it doesn't seem real, she says—but today she has a fresh set of worries.

"I told my parents what happened last night. And they already knew about Bryan Cayhill. Now they've decided this place is too dangerous."

"You can't really blame them," Kate says.

"They want me to come back home and go to Duke."

"Does Duke have a good film program?"

"That's not the point," Lavana says. "My father wanted me to go to Duke in the first place. He wanted me to study medicine. He thinks I'm flighty, but he holds out hope that I'll come around."

She sips her coffee and adds: "I'm in my senior year. If I switched to pre-med, it would be like starting over. And anyway, I don't want to."

"What will you do?"

"We came to a truce. I'll stay here, but I won't go out alone at night. I definitely won't be filming in the woods. Have you talked to Travis?"

"No," Kate says.

"He's in the same situation. His parents want him home. But the last thing he wants is to go back to the family farm."

Lavana sets her coffee down, and her face takes on a determined look. "I'll make the best of things. If I can't film, I'll keep editing what I have. And I might try revising my script. I've got friends in the theater department who could build me a set that looks like the interior of that shed. I'm thinking about a new scene—a conversation between the killer and the victim. That could be interesting, don't you think?"

Kate walks Lavana Khatri back to her dorm from the student union, then starts to return to her car. But she changes her mind and reverses direction.

It's a mile and a half from the Seagate campus to downtown Alexander. Kate covers the distance at a stroll, with a breeze at her back. She leaves Main Street and walks east along Summit Avenue and stops in front of the Odeon. The marquee advertises an Orson Welles retrospective. This week they're showing *The Third Man*.

Clay McKellar's building is next to the theater, and Kate would like to get access to his apartment. She only talked to him once, and now she'll never have a chance again. She thinks that being in the place where he lived, in the midst of his possessions, might help her understand him.

She has talked her way into places like this before, but in this case she doesn't know who to talk to. She spends some time in the alley looking up at the building, then goes inside the Odeon and buys a ticket for the three fifteen show.

The theater is almost empty. Kate is one of six people in the audience, and the others are down in front. *The Third Man* is one of her favorites, and it's easy to be swept along by the beauty of the images. When Orson Welles appears, it's the handsome, young Orson Welles, even if the character he's playing is despicable. There's a moment she always looks for, when Harry Lime finds out that the authorities who are supposed to believe he's dead have dug up his grave and learned the truth. You don't need any words then: you see everything in Orson Welles's face. The rogue has been found out, and he knows it, and in the next instant his confidence returns. He believes he can still get away with it.

The story rolls along to its end, to that final slow shot: Alida Valli walking along the street toward the camera. Joseph Cotten waiting for her. He's fallen in love with her but he knows it's hopeless. She walks past him without even looking, and neither one says a word.

When the house lights come up, there's a trio of students who hustle out, talking about getting pizza. And there's an older couple, a man and a woman, who take their time—his arm around her shoulders. As they pass in front of the screen, Kate recognizes them. It's Martin Cayhill and his wife, Bryan's parents.

Outside, the sun's still up, but the sky is dimmer than before. The Cayhills walk east along the sidewalk, passing in front of Clay McKellar's building. Kate follows them at a distance. Two blocks on, the character of the street changes. Brick facades give way to aluminum siding. There are two-story houses on small lots. One of them has a picket fence in front. The Cayhills pass through a gate in the fence, go up onto the porch of the house, and disappear inside.

Kate stops on the sidewalk half a block away, thinking she should turn back, but curiosity gets the better of her. It can't hurt to walk by and get a closer look. But when she reaches the fence, Martin Cayhill comes out onto the porch with a bottle of iced tea.

He spots her and calls out: "Miss Summerlin."

There's nothing to do but wave and open the gate. Cayhill perches himself on the half-wall that surrounds the porch and waits for her.

As she reaches the steps, she says, "I'm sorry. I saw you at the movie theater and I wondered . . . I didn't know you were staying in town."

Cayhill waves her up. "I'm glad you're here," he says. "I was rude to you on Saturday. I wanted to apologize."

"That's not necessary."

"It's been a difficult time. And I meant what I said: I have no desire to see my son's death written up in a book. But it didn't need to be said then, or in that way."

Kate is on the porch with him now and doesn't know what to do. She leans against a post. Says, "I understand."

An awkward silence follows, and she can't think how to break it. Cayhill seems to sense her distress. He takes pity on her.

"This is where my son lived," he tells her. "He stayed in a dormitory his first year, but he didn't like it. So I bought this house for him."

He says it casually, as if anyone faced with the same problem would do the same thing.

"Oh," Kate says.

Cayhill smiles. "You think I've got too much money for my own good."

"No."

"You do. You're probably right. But here we are. My wife and I have been staying here. The first few days after Bryan died, we couldn't bear to set foot in the place, but now . . . now we're packing Bryan's things. We'll be putting the house on the market and heading back home to Connecticut."

"Did Bryan live alone here?" Kate asks. "Or did he have roommates?"

"No roommates. He wanted a place of his own."

"Do you think he was happy here?"

Cayhill stares off at the street. "I don't know," he says. "Bryan was an only child. If he had brothers and sisters, they might be able to tell me something about his inner life. He had friends, of course, but it's not the same. In many ways he was a mystery to me, especially after his mother died."

He turns back toward Kate, and she glances at the front door of the house.

"Mrs. Cayhill—" she begins.

"Is the second Mrs. Cayhill," he says. "We married when Bryan was in high school. Before that, I raised him by myself for years." He makes a pained face. "That's not true. There were nannies, tutors. For much of his life, my son was raised by servants. I couldn't say if he was happy. Now I suppose I'll never know."

He's sitting on the half-wall with his shoulders hunched. He looks tired.

"I've told you more than I intended," he says. "I don't suppose we can keep this off the record?"

"We can," Kate says gently. "I don't have a recorder running, and I left my notebook at home. This conversation is already beginning to slip my mind."

Cayhill smiles and straightens his back. Fixes his eyes on Kate's. "You're not what I expected. You haven't pressed me at all. Haven't tried to persuade me to talk. But maybe that's the way you operate. You're giving me the soft sell."

Kate returns his smile. He's right. There are things she wants from him. She'd like some time inside the house before they clear everything away. She'd like access to Bryan's email accounts and to the texts on his phone. These things could help her.

"Do you want the truth?" she says.

"Yes."

"The truth is there's a standard pitch I make, to the parents of children who've died. I tell them that we're partners. 'Your daughter can't speak for herself now,' I say. 'So we have to speak for her. We have to tell her story, so she won't be forgotten.' And I could say the same to you about your son. But we both know that's nonsense. If I write about Merkury and his victims, it will be because I hope to gain something by it. I hope to advance my career. If I find a publisher for the book, it will be because they hope to sell copies and make money. None of it will do Bryan any good. He's beyond that now. There's no reason you should want to talk to me."

Lee Tennick sleeps on and off through the morning and part of the afternoon. He wakes around two with a dream fresh in his memory. He was in a room at the Alexander police station—like the one they had him in last night, but smaller and darker. Vera Landen was there, and he played her one of the messages Clay McKellar had left for him. The first one; the bad one.

You said I should call if I needed to talk. Don't know if you meant it.

"Did you mean it?" Landen asked.

"Of course I meant it," he said.

God, I'm tired. I think there's something wrong with me. Heard something scratching on the door. Did I open the door? No, I did not. Not opening any doors.

"He was a strange kid, right?" Landen said in the dream.

"No," said Tennick. "He was just afraid."

She gave him a dubious look and stood up from the table. She left the room without opening the door, because in the dream there was no door. There were only shadowy corners—like the one Clay McKellar stepped out of.

His skin was a translucent white, and his eyes didn't seem to blink anymore, but otherwise he looked fine and whole.

"Thank god," Tennick said.

"What are you thankful for?" Clay asked him.

"You're alive."

Clay chuckled. "Sure doesn't feel like it," he said, taking the seat Landen had vacated. There was a leaf on his shoulder, red and dry. It drifted down onto the table.

Tennick reached for it, but Clay snatched it up first.

"Big help you turned out to be," he said.

Tennick brews himself a cup of tea and tries not to think about the dream. When the tea fails him, he tries a bottle of beer, but the beer tastes sour.

He picks up his cellphone from its charger and makes some calls.

He has a friend in the admissions department at Seagate who digs out Clay's file and provides a phone number for Clay's mother in a town called Spearman in northern Texas. The first time Tennick calls, he gets no answer, not even a prompt to leave a voicemail message. Twenty minutes later, his friend from admissions calls him back. She's been reading Clay's application essay and it's a sad tale—about a father who ran off to Houston and died in a fire on an oil rig, about a mother who worked two jobs to take care of Clay and his younger sister.

"You be kind to that poor woman, Lee," his friend says.

Tennick promises he will.

When he tries the number again, he gets through after more than a dozen rings. Clay's mother apologizes to him. She was lying down, trying to get some rest.

The police have been in contact with her, and she knows what happened to Clay. Tennick offers his condolences and asks if she'll be traveling to New York. She doesn't give him a solid answer, tells him she's still making plans. She has her daughter to think of; she doesn't want the girl to miss too many days of school.

Tennick gets the sense that money is the problem and offers to arrange for Clay's body to be transported to Spearman, to a funeral home of her choosing.

"The expense would be covered," he says.

The line goes quiet for several seconds. Then she says, "You were a friend of Clay's?"

"I only met him recently," Tennick says. "But yes, I was his friend."

"Well it's nice of you to offer, but our family has always paid its own way."

Her voice is close to breaking. Her pride is holding it together.

"I'm sorry, ma'am," he says. "I wasn't clear. The college would cover the cost. It's standard in cases like this."

A few more quiet seconds tick by. Then: "Oh . . . I suppose that would be all right. Thank you."

She gives him the name of a funeral home, and he offers her his cell-phone number. Says she should call if she needs anything, anything at all.

He's ready to say goodbye when she asks, "Do you know what the police told me? That another boy was murdered earlier this month, and Clay and his friends found the body."

"I know."

"Clay never told me. Why wouldn't he tell me something like that?"

"He probably didn't want to worry you."

"They say the same person might have killed Clay."

"That's right."

"Well, what's the world coming to, Mr. Tennick? That's what I would dearly like to know."

It's after six and the sun has gone down when Kate returns to her father's house.

She hasn't spoken to him much since the night he asked her whether it might be a good idea if she talked to someone—

a professional
about what happened

—and she threw the glass against the wall. She retreated to her room afterward and when she went into the kitchen the next morning the shattered glass had been swept away. Her father hasn't mentioned it since.

She doesn't particularly want to talk to him now, but she's used to seeing him around this time every day, puttering in the kitchen, cooking dinner. He's not there, or anywhere in the house. And when she checks, his car is not in the garage.

She raps on the door of Lee Tennick's RV, and after a moment Tennick comes out.

"Kate," he says.

"Have you seen my father?"

"No. Why?"

"He should be home by now."

"Well, he's a grown man," Tennick says.

There's something in his tone, like he's making a private joke.

Kate says, "Do you know where he is?"

"No."

"I don't believe you."

"I'm not lying."

In Kate's experience, people who claim they're not lying are almost always lying.

"I'm not dumb, Lee," she says. "It's no accident that you're here, that you've literally parked yourself on my father's property. You're keeping an eye on him. I thought at first it was for your own odd purposes, but now I wonder if you're watching him for someone else."

"I needed a place to put the RV," Tennick says. "That's all."

"You haven't asked who," Kate says. "Who I think you're watching him for."

Tennick spreads his arms. "Why don't you tell me."

"The cops. Vera Landen. I think you told her that Devin was here in town. And now she thinks he might be Merkury."

The idea seems to take Tennick by surprise. He leans back against the RV and slips his hands in his pockets.

"That's interesting," he says.

"That's not the word I'd use," says Kate.

"There's a certain logic, if you want to see it. You must have wondered if Merkury ever gives any thought to you. He knows who you are. Anyone with a computer can look up the name of the girl who found Melissa Cornelle. With a little effort, he could track you down whenever he wanted. There are killers who try to involve themselves in police investigations. It's not a stretch to imagine that a killer might insinuate himself into the life of someone who was a witness to one of his crimes."

Kate gives him a wide-eyed look. "Gosh, Lee. I never thought of that. Here's me, living a footloose and carefree life. Maybe I should look over my shoulder more."

Tennick ignores her sarcasm. "What did Devin have to say when you told him what Landen thinks?"

Kate shakes her head. "I haven't told him."

"Why not?" Tennick says. "You could have a good laugh about it. Unless you think it might be true."

She can feel herself getting angry. "You still haven't answered me," she says. "Did you tell Landen that Devin was here?"

He sighs. "No, Kate. I didn't."

"Then who did?"

He seems to hesitate. "I don't know. Maybe your father."

"Why would he tell her?" Kate asks. "I don't think he even talks to her."

Tennick shrugs and turns his face away from her. "It's not for me to say."

He looks uncomfortable, Kate thinks. Like he's about to blush.

"What's going on, Lee?" she says. "What are you hiding from me?"

She has to wait, but finally he turns back to her.

"I think they talk fairly often," he says. "They've been seeing each other."

13

The next morning Kate lies in bed staring at the ceiling. Weak light comes through the window. The days are starting later as autumn wears on.

There are fine cracks in the paint on the ceiling and strands of cobwebs casting wispy shadows. They're nothing much to see, but you can get lost in them if you're not careful.

She did that once. Got lost. It happened in the days after that night under the oak—when the white of her bedroom ceiling reminded her of Melissa Cornelle. Her white blouse and its white buttons. Her pale skin.

Eleven-year-old Kate would lie awake on those mornings, not wanting to get out of bed. Her mother would try to coax her.

"Up, up, up," she would say.

"Don't want to," Kate would answer.

"You have to though. Get up, take a bath, brush your teeth. I'll make you eggs."

"I'm not hungry."

"Even so, you have to eat," her mother would say, sitting on the edge of the bed. "Get up and eat and deal with the world. These are things everybody has to do."

"Not me."

"Yes, even you. There's no way around it. But I promise you, it will get easier. We're leaving here, very soon. As soon as your father gives his exams and grades his papers. When all that's done, we're off. Somewhere better. I promise. Now take a deep breath."

That was her mother's trick for getting out of bed. Take a deep breath and hold it. Now your body thinks there's trouble. It needs to get away from where it is.

Twenty-nine-year-old Kate holds her breath and focuses on the ceiling as the seconds pass slowly by. After a minute she's feeling the strain. She throws off the covers and sits up. Swings her legs around and, when she's on her feet, lets her breath out in a rush.

She showers and brushes her teeth and gets dressed. There's coffee in the kitchen. Kate pours a cup and takes it onto the porch. Sits in a wicker chair with her bare feet on the railing.

Tennick's car is in the driveway. He took Kate for a drive last night, to a house on a rural road on the northeast edge of town. Vera Landen's house: a Dutch colonial with a horseshoe driveway in front lit by carriage lamps.

Kate's father's Volvo was parked under one of the lamps.

"You've seen him here before?" Kate asked Tennick.

He nodded. "It's hardly a scandal. They're both unattached. They can do what they like."

He found a place to turn around and they headed back home. Halfway there he said:

"Makes you wonder."

"What?" Kate asked.

"About when it started, your father and Landen. Did they get together after he moved back here, or did they have a thing years ago when you were a kid?"

Kate watched the road stretch out before them, rough and gray in the glow of the headlights.

"So you're suggesting my father had an affair with her while my mother was alive."

"Could be," Tennick said.

"You'd think he would have been too busy sleeping with his students, like Melissa Cornelle."

Tennick steered the car with one hand, the other resting on the gear shift.

"We've been over this," he said. "I never claimed your father slept with Melissa."

"Right."

He waited a beat. "Though technically he could have done both."

Kate leaned her head back and closed her eyes. "How about if we *don't* wonder about this?"

She finishes her coffee and sets the cup on the railing of the porch. She's thinking about going inside when a car slows on Bird River Road and makes the turn into the driveway. It creeps along on the gravel and eases to a stop twenty feet from the house.

The car is a decade old, a Ford Fusion with a scrape in the paint along the driver's side. The man who climbs out looks to be around fifty. His hair is streaked with gray, and he's wearing eyeglasses with black plastic frames. He's decked out in a navy blue suit, white shirt, and paisley tie. The kind of clothes you might wear to church.

Kate doesn't know him, but she knows why he's here.

The world is full of people who have suffered loss, and when you write about the missing and the dead, some of those people seek you out. They want to tell you their story, or they're looking for someone to take up their cause.

Usually they have a photograph. This man does. It's on his cellphone.

He walks to the porch and says, "You're Miss Summerlin."

"Yes."

"I'm Samuel Wyler," he says, holding up the phone. "This is my daughter, Jenny. She disappeared at the beginning of September."

Kate invites him up to sit and takes the phone, handling it like a sacred object. Jenny is a pretty girl, brown-haired with a round face and lively eyes. The image is a formal portrait, the kind that gets published in a high school yearbook.

"How old is she?" Kate asks, handing the phone back.

"She turned nineteen this past spring."

"Tell me about her."

She's a smart girl, Mr. Wyler says, though not the kind who ever liked to sit still in school. She's friendly and popular, but not wild the way some girls are today.

"Her mother passed when she was fourteen," Mr. Wyler explains. "And I've tried to raise her right. Tried to steer her toward the right kind of friends and teach her self-respect and self-control. I don't approve of parents who let their children run around till all hours of the night."

Jenny could have gone to college if she applied herself, her father says. But she wanted to work. A friend got her a job in one of the dining halls at Seagate College. Her plan was to get her foot in the door, maybe move on to an office job. She's always been a good worker.

"She saved her money, bought a secondhand car. I think she was on the right track. Then on a Tuesday night, September seventh, she packed an overnight bag. She was supposed to stay with a friend who lived about nine miles away. She drove out around seven fifteen. I haven't seen her since."

"She never reached her friend's house?" Kate says.

"No."

"And you were on good terms with her. She wasn't upset. Angry. Never talked about leaving?"

"Nothing like that."

Kate nods. "In a case like this, she's nineteen, old enough to live on her own, go where she wants without anyone's permission. The first thought is, she left home of her own free will."

Mr. Wyler regards her with patient eyes. "That's what the police said. But why wouldn't she tell me she was going? Why wouldn't she call me once she got settled in a new place?"

"I don't know," Kate says. "People have their reasons. They don't always make sense. Especially when they're young. I'm not sure what you hope I can do for you."

Mr. Wyler breathes in through his nose and raises his chin the way some people do when they're trying to ward off tears.

"That's fair," he says. "I don't know what I'm hoping for, except that I want to find my daughter. The police won't help. They said I should hire a private investigator, but I don't have the money for that. I've got nothing to offer you, but there's one thing I know: I can't give up on my girl."

14

"There are only a couple of ways this can go," Lee Tennick says.

They're on the porch together and there's a drizzle of rain coming down. It started after Samuel Wyler drove away. Kate has been telling Tennick about Jenny.

"Option one: Jenny left on her own," he says. "And now she's having a good time, enjoying her independence. She's not thinking about her father, because she's nineteen, and nineteen-year-olds can be callous. Or option two: somebody took her. In that case, the odds are she's dead."

"I know," Kate says.

"If it's option one, the thrill will wear off eventually. It'll stop being fun and turn into a grind, because life is a grind. Then she'll probably come home to dad. She'll want someone to take care of her."

"And if it's option two?"

"If she's dead and no one has found her body by now, then it might never be found. The chances of you discovering what happened to her are vanishingly small. If her body does turn up, the police will open a case file. Either they'll solve it or the case will go cold. If it goes cold, she'll turn into one of those victims people talk about online. 'What happened to Jenny Wyler?' I don't know why you'd want to get involved."

Kate knows. She knew the moment she said yes to Samuel Wyler. He was holding his phone, looking at the image of his daughter, but Kate was picturing Clay McKellar—the nothingness in his face when she saw him in the woods. She doesn't want to think about him, or about Merkury. She needs something else to focus on.

"I told him I'd try," Kate says to Tennick. "I told him he shouldn't expect too much."

Samuel Wyler lives in a town called Earlville, seven miles south of Alexander.

Kate drives there in the afternoon. The Wyler house is on a tree-lined street, the lawn covered with leaves. She walks to the front door, which is flanked by two milk cans painted sky blue. Mr. Wyler told her there would be a key hidden under one of them. She finds it and lets herself in and shuts the door behind her.

The first thing that strikes her is the staleness of the air. It smells of old smoke.

Next are the colors: beige paint on the walls, gray carpet in the living room. The sofa and chairs are a darker shade of gray. The end tables are made of oak and stained a muddy brown.

The brown carries over to the kitchen cabinets. The appliances are white. Nothing new or modern. The dishes drying in the rack look like garage-sale finds.

The bedrooms are down a short hallway. The first one Kate comes to is obviously Mr. Wyler's. The bed is disheveled, and the closet is full of men's clothes.

Mr. Wyler himself is working a shift at the Dollar General, where he's the assistant manager. Which is why Kate is here now. She wants time alone in the house.

Jenny's bedroom is at the end of the hall. Her bed is covered with an antique white bedspread embroidered with vines and flowers. The walls are pale blue instead of beige, and they bear hopeful signs of rebellion against the drabness of the other rooms. There's a framed print of a Georgia O'Keeffe painting. A poster of Machu Picchu.

The rebellion doesn't seem to have reached the closet. Jenny's clothes look like hand-me-downs. They're nothing you would expect a nineteen-year-old to wear.

It's the same in the dresser. Jenny's underwear and bras are white and utilitarian. Her jeans are out of fashion. There's not a single designer label in sight.

Kate makes a thorough search of the drawers, hoping she might find a diary or journal. She checks between the mattress and the box spring too. There's nothing—no clue to Jenny's state of mind.

There's no computer in the room. Jenny's father said she didn't own one. She owned a tablet and a cellphone and took them both with her on the day she disappeared.

Before Kate leaves the room, she has a look under the bed. There's dust and an old pair of sneakers and something she almost misses: a lone earring. The post looks like gold, and the stone could be a diamond.

Jenny's other jewelry is in a bowl on top of the dresser. A silver necklace, beaded bracelets of agate and sodalite. A few pairs of earrings, all of them lower-end, nothing to match the one from under the bed.

Kate slips the gold earring into her pocket and takes a final walk through the house to be sure she hasn't left anything out of place. The rain is falling harder now. Kate can hear it on the roof.

When she opens the front door the sound intensifies. The fresh air hits her and she breathes it in. She locks up and returns the key to its place under the milk can.

She's glad to be out. It's a relief.

Jenny walked out this door on the seventh of September around seven fifteen p.m. It would have been daylight still. Maybe it was raining, or maybe it was clear.

Either way, she would have stepped out into cleaner air, into a brighter world.

Maybe she felt the same relief.

When Kate leaves Earlville, she drives north to County Highway 62, following the route Jenny Wyler would have taken to reach her friend's house on the night she disappeared. She stays on 62 until she comes to a town called Lebanon and makes a left onto Billings Hill Road.

It's about nine miles altogether, and Kate covers it in fifteen minutes. An easy trip, even in the rain. No sharp curves, no obvious hazards. If Jenny had run off the road, she would have ended up in a farmer's field.

The end of the line is a two-story house clad in cedar shingles, with a slate roof and rusted rain gutters. Jenny's friend Colleen Rosewood lives here with her mother and sister and niece. Colleen is the only one home. She's a soft-spoken young woman with red hair and plump cheeks. She's wearing a wool sweater over a yellow sundress.

"I don't know what to think," she says.

She's sitting with Kate at the kitchen table. The front door stands open, though the screen door is closed. Colleen wants to be able to watch the road. The school bus should be dropping off her niece soon.

"I mean, I hope Jenny's fine, off having adventures somewhere. That would be cool. But I don't know why she'd go without telling me."

"Did she ever talk about doing that?" Kate asks. "Going off, having adventures?"

One corner of Colleen's mouth turns up in a smile. "When you live out here, you talk a lot about leaving."

"Where would she go if she left?"

The smile fades. "I don't know. Her family moved here from Chicago ten years ago. But Jenny was nine at the time. I don't think she knows anyone back there. Whenever she talked about leaving here, it was never about a specific destination. It was always about getting in a car and driving, and seeing where you ended up. Like a road trip in a movie."

"Did you ever take a road trip, the two of you?"

"We drove to Boston once to see my cousin. We've gone to concerts in Syracuse. We went to Gettysburg, but that was a high school field trip."

Colleen goes silent, rubbing a palm along the sleeve of her sweater. Outside, the rain is tapering off.

"This isn't helping you, is it?" she says.

"Anything you can tell me might help."

"But let's be real. No one's heard from Jenny for six weeks. That's not normal. If she was okay—"

"She could still be okay," Kate says.

"I want to believe that's true. But then I think about those students at Seagate. Bryan Cayhill and the other one . . ."

"Clay McKellar."

"They say it's Merkury. We grew up hearing about him. But just as a scary story. I never took it seriously. Do you think Jenny—"

"No," Kate says. "This doesn't fit with Merkury." She hesitates. "I don't want to be morbid, but if it was him, there'd be a body. He'd put it on display. And he would have taken Jenny and left her car behind. But the car hasn't been found. I think that's a reason for hope."

"Is it?"

"Look at it this way. If Jenny was abducted—by anyone—it would have happened as she drove between her house and yours. That's a small window of opportunity. How would it play out? Suppose her car broke down and someone passing by took advantage of the situation: he grabbed her or tricked her into his car. Fine. But then her car should have been left behind, and it wasn't. If you were going to do it right, you would need to plan it out, and you would need at least two people. They'd have to watch her beforehand and follow her. Find a way to get her to stop on a public road, in daylight, where there could be witnesses. They would have to abduct her and then split up, with one of them driving her car away from the scene. It's too elaborate. I don't see it happening."

It's hard for Kate to tell if Colleen is convinced. She's still fussing with the sleeve of her sweater, looking out at the road. Kate is almost convinced herself, but not quite. There are other ways it could have happened. Jenny might have picked up a hitchhiker, and he might have overpowered her and taken her away in her own car. Or she might never have intended to come to Colleen's house. She might have run off, to somewhere unknown—and something might have happened to her once she got there.

But this is all speculation. Not worth sharing. Kate spends a few minutes more with Colleen, asking about Jenny's personality, her likes and dislikes. When the school bus finally appears at the end of the driveway, she thanks Colleen for the talk and follows her outside. The rain has dwindled down to nothing. Kate hangs back by her car while Colleen walks out to meet her niece, a girl in a red coat with a blue backpack. Maybe seven years old.

As she watches them, Kate realizes how anxious Colleen was before, how subdued. She's different now, talking and laughing with the girl as she leads her by the hand into the house. She was living in a world where friends vanish without any explanation. Now she's in a place where children make it home from school safe and sound.

15

Devin Falko has been spending his day helping people wrestle with their demons.

That's the way he likes to think of it. If you were boring, you would say he's engaging in cognitive behavioral therapy to help his clients understand how their thoughts and patterns of behavior impact the way they perceive themselves and the world.

It's more exciting if you put it in terms of demons.

He normally conducts sessions in person, but more and more of his clients are growing comfortable talking over video online. Which is fortunate, because they're all in Ohio and he's stuck in a hotel room in upstate New York.

He's got his laptop open on the desk by the window, and the rain that's been falling for most of the day has decided to stop. He's conducting a session with Paul Hannigan, thirty-nine years old, a mechanical engineer. Paul is talking about his girlfriend, Ashley. Again.

Devin has been working with him for seven weeks. When they started, Paul was trying to decide if he and Ashley would be compatible in the long run and if he should ask her to marry him. Since then, he's made up his mind and bought a ring, but he keeps finding reasons to put off the proposal.

"She's like a rabbit," Paul says. "I have to be careful. If I move too soon or do the wrong thing, she'll run."

Paul is the son of an abusive alcoholic. He spent his childhood worrying, trying not to make mistakes, because he was afraid of how his father would react. Devin has discussed this with him before, and he could bring it up again, but it's been a long day and he feels in danger of falling asleep.

"That's an interesting metaphor," Devin says. "But it doesn't really apply, does it? If you're trying to catch a rabbit, you don't care what the rabbit thinks or wants, do you?"

"No."

"But Ashley is a person, and she could say no to you. No matter how you ask her, or when."

Paul laughs nervously. "I know. That's what I'm afraid of."

"Right. Let's try an exercise. Think about asking her—where you're going to do it, the words you're going to use. How it's going to feel. And when the fear hits you, don't shy away from it. Let it happen and keep going."

They go through it together, step-by-step. Twice. Once with Ashley saying yes, once with her saying no. They talk about how Paul's life will go on in either case.

Paul seems more optimistic afterward, though there's no telling if it will last. Sometimes the demons win. Either way, his fifty minutes are up. Devin tells him they'll talk again next week, signs off from the session, and closes the laptop.

He swivels his chair around to face the bed, and the faint squeal it makes is the only sound in the room. Normally he would be tempted to check his phone for messages or put on music to fill the silence, but Devin tries to practice mindfulness and he knows he can endure whatever discomfort he's feeling without doing those things.

He swivels back to the desk and opens the top drawer. There's a pen and a pad inside. He takes them to the bed and, lying on his stomach, begins to write down the thoughts that come into his head.

I am in room 302 of the Seagate Inn. I have been here for six days.

I've seen Kate three times. I want to see her again.

I don't know when I'll see her again.

I texted her yesterday. She did not reply. This is frustrating.

I could text her again or call her or drive to her father's house. These are all options.

The next thought that comes to him makes him smirk.

I need to be careful. Kate is like a rabbit. If you make the wrong move, she runs.

Case in point: The last time we were together back in Ohio, we were making love and she put both her hands on my throat and squeezed.

I was taken by surprise, even though she had done something similar before, many times. But those other times were far milder. One hand, not much pressure, almost playful.

She was playing at harming me.

I couldn't help thinking the gesture was connected to the trauma she suffered as a child.

Stumbling upon a dead body.

To use clinical terms: That shit will fuck you up.

Not that I'm trying to analyze her. As she has often told me, I am not her therapist.

But come on.

Anyway, it's not so playful when you use two hands the way she did. She squeezed, hard. And she's not weak.

So I hit her. Pushed her off, if you want to split hairs. But yeah, I hit her. Sue me.

She ran away. Like a rabbit.

I have to be careful now. I need to get her back. I've got too many years invested in her. Am I supposed to throw it all away over a misunderstanding?

No.

Devin sets the pen aside. Turns onto his back. He's trembling, but not so you could see it on the outside. He can feel it though. It's real.

He knows what he should do. A visualization exercise. Picture an open field, or the sun rising over the ocean. Something calm.

"Clouds over a mountaintop," he says out loud. "You're such a hack."

He sits up suddenly and reaches for the pen and pad.

So you need her? You've invested in her? What does this language say?

Fuck you.

Sounds a little controlling. Sounds like you think you're entitled to her.

Fuck you. I've been patient.

That's nice of you.

She's not going to find anyone more patient than me.

Uh-huh.

I deserve

The thought remains unfinished. Devin has filled three pages on the notepad. He peels them off, tears them up, and tosses the pieces into the wastebasket by the desk.

"Clouds over a mountaintop," he says again. "Mist rising from the surface of a pond."

He picks up his phone from the table beside the bed. It's after five p.m. He checks his messages. There's nothing from Kate.

He brushes his teeth and changes into a fresh shirt. Finds his keycard and exits the room. Down in the parking lot his Lexus is waiting. He aims it north. When he comes to Bird River Road, he makes the turn, but he passes the Summerlin house without stopping. From the road he can see that Kate's car isn't there.

In the western sky the sun hovers over the treetops. Devin loses track of time and distance. He takes random turns until he doesn't know what road he's on. His gas is running low. He drifts to a stop beside a cornfield and cuts his engine.

He lets the window down beside him and feels the cold air. Takes out his phone and calls Kate and listens to the ringtone on the line. She doesn't answer. There's no point in leaving a message.

In the faltering light he drops the phone on the passenger seat. He rolls up the sleeve of his shirt to expose his left forearm. On the pale skin below the crook of his elbow there's a hash of fine white scars.

The first time she saw them, Kate asked him what they were.

"Damage," he said.

They're mementos of his freshman year in college, when the pace of his classes and the volume of the work he was expected to do often overwhelmed him. Whenever it got to be too much, he brought out a razor blade, cleaned it with rubbing alcohol, and sliced a line in his skin.

Not too deep. Just enough to draw blood.

Sophomore year, after a political science exam he was sure he had failed, he got carried away. The bleeding wouldn't stop. His roommate made him go to the student health center. The doctor who treated him insisted that he talk to someone.

The someone turned out to be a psychologist. Dr. Park.

He was a young Asian guy who sat behind his desk with a tennis ball, bouncing it off the walls while he talked. He didn't deliver the lecture that Devin expected.

"What you're doing isn't uncommon," he said. "We'll talk about *why* you do it, but the bottom line is, I can't stop you. Nobody can. You've been getting away with it, and you could probably go on getting away with it. So you have to decide if you want to stop."

Devin remembers sitting in Dr. Park's office, the yellow ball rebounding off the wall, onto the floor, and back into Park's hand. He remembers trying to guess what he would need to say simply to get out of the room.

"Yes," he said. "I want to stop."

Dr. Park nodded approvingly. "We can talk about strategies. There are things you can do when you feel the impulse to cut yourself. Alternative behaviors. Would you say you're under a lot of stress? Is that what brings it on?"

Devin found himself wanting to snatch the yellow ball from the air. Instead he kept perfectly still.

"Sometimes it gets so bad," he said, "I feel like screaming."

Dr. Park caught the ball and held it. "That's not the worst idea. Have you tried it?"

The question made Devin laugh. "People would think I'm crazy."

Dr. Park looked pointedly at his bandaged arm. "I don't think you're crazy," he said. "And screaming probably isn't the answer in the long term. But it could work as a temporary fix. If you're worried about people hearing, go someplace private. Do you have a car?"

"Yeah."

"There you go. Scream in the car."

In the car, on the roadside, Devin checks his phone, as if Kate might have called or texted in the last couple of minutes without his realizing. But of course there's nothing.

He knows he should drive back to the inn. Maybe pack and head home to Columbus. Stop chasing her. Let her come to him.

If she doesn't though, what then?

He reaches across to the glove compartment and pops it open. He has a folding knife in there: a black carbon steel blade with an aluminum handle.

He shouldn't have it. That was one of Dr. Park's first pieces of advice. *Best not to keep sharp things within reach.*

Devin has never used the knife. It's there in case of an emergency. What if he were in an accident and had to cut himself free of his seatbelt?

He unfolds it and studies the curve of the blade.

It's a fine instrument.

He lays the edge of the blade against the skin of his left arm. Lightly. He's in control.

He keeps it there for a time, the black blade touching his white scars. Then he folds it and puts it away.

He steps out of the car and walks around to the passenger side. Far above him, a hawk wheels in the sky.

Devin puts his hands on top of his head, stares out into the field, and screams.

16

Samuel Wyler provided Kate with a short list of his daughter's friends. Kate added to it after talking to Colleen Rosewood. The name at the top is Diana Perez.

She's twenty years old and has lived in Earlville since her family moved there when she was four. She works at Seagate College in the main dining hall—the same place where Jenny Wyler worked before she disappeared.

Diana is on a break from the dinner shift when Kate talks to her. It's twilight and turning colder, but they're outside near a loading dock at the back of the building. They're standing on concrete, but the view isn't bad: there's a grove of young pine trees lined in even ranks, like soldiers preparing to advance up the Hill.

Diana has strong opinions about Jenny's father.

"You've been in his house?" she asks Kate.

"I was there today."

"There's something weird there. Right? It's not just me."

"No, it's not you. The house is . . . stuffy."

"That's part of it," Diana says. "The atmosphere. The smell. It's like the same air has been there for years, and it never changes. But there's more.

It's like nothing moves in that house. You go in, and you feel wrong. You wouldn't be surprised to learn the whole outside world had vanished, and you're stuck in there. I think it might be haunted."

Kate can't help smiling.

"I'm serious," Diana says. "If you told me it was built over an old graveyard, I wouldn't doubt you. It would make sense. I never liked going there."

She's a small woman, a shade over five feet, dressed in a white blouse, black capri pants, and a black apron. She has sleek dark hair in a pixie cut, brown eyes, beautiful skin.

"Mr. Wyler is like his house," she says. "He's not right. It's like he comes from a different time."

"What time?" Kate asks.

Diana ponders the question. "A stricter time. A time when people let you know if you failed to meet their moral standards."

Kate recalls her first impression of Samuel Wyler: thinking he was dressed for church.

"Is he a religious man?"

"If he is, he's not the kind who quotes the Bible," Diana says. "But he likes rules, and he enjoyed making his daughter follow them."

"What were his rules, exactly?"

Diana has a ready answer. "Modesty. Chastity. Temperance."

"Are those his words?"

"They're mine, but they're the right ones. He wanted to control what Jenny wore, where she went, who she saw. Heaven forbid she should go to a party. There might be alcohol. Can't have that."

"How did Jenny feel about all this?" Kate asks.

Diana doesn't respond. She's distracted. Another woman has come out for a break. She's older, with gray hair and tortoiseshell glasses. She leans against the brick wall of the building and lights a cigarette.

Diana waves a hand in the air as if she's waving away the smell of the smoke.

"She's not supposed to do that," she says. Raising her voice, she adds: "This is a smoke-free campus."

The other woman acts as if she didn't hear. Kate tries to set things back on track.

"Did Jenny get along with her father?"

Diana gives the woman a last, dark look and turns back to Kate.

"They didn't fight, if that's what you mean. Jenny learned to follow the rules. She had to. Her father had ways of enforcing them."

"Was he violent?" Kate asks.

"I don't know. Jenny claimed he wasn't. I guess he didn't need to be. If you live under someone's roof, if you're dependent on them, you get used to doing what you're told. If you don't—" She shrugs. "Mr. Wyler knew how to talk to Jenny, how to manipulate her. He could make her life miserable without having to hit her."

Kate remembers something Samuel Wyler said about his daughter: *I've tried to raise her right. Tried to steer her toward the right kind of friends and teach her self-respect and self-control.* It's easy now to take a different meaning from those words.

"Sounds like Jenny was in a bad situation," Kate says. "Do you think it was bad enough for her to want to leave?"

"I always thought she'd leave eventually," says Diana.

"Do you think that's what happened?"

"I hope so."

"You have to wonder though," Kate says. "Why now, and why like this? Without telling anyone. Did something change in her life?"

"What do you mean?"

"I don't know. Did she have a boyfriend? Someone to run away with?"

Diana smiles. "No."

"A girlfriend?"

"Perish the thought. Her father would have had a fit."

"Colleen Rosewood said Jenny talked about taking a road trip. Could that be what she's doing?"

Diana Perez crosses her arms as if she's beginning to feel the cold. "I wouldn't put too much stock in Colleen," she says. "Is she still looking after her niece?"

"Yes."

"I've known Colleen since elementary school. She's a genius, if you judge by grades. Straight A's. But she's a glorified nanny, and I'm not sure she even gets paid for it. At some point her niece will grow up and won't need her anymore, but by then there'll be someone else to take care of. Maybe her mom will get cancer. And Colleen will never leave that house, never have a life of her own . . . I hope she's right about Jenny though. I could see her on a road trip."

The sky is turning deep blue, verging on black. Kate feels the wind blowing down off the Hill. The gray-haired woman drops her cigarette and crushes it under her shoe before heading back inside. As she passes, she clears her throat meaningfully.

"That's my cue to go in," Diana says to Kate. "She's not above squealing on you if your break runs longer than fifteen minutes."

On Tuesday evening, Lee Tennick spends two hours at Ptolemy's Pub, drinking beer and eating chicken wings. Sitting across from him is Officer Ralph Beckham of the Alexander P.D.

Beckham is the model of a small-town cop: solid in build, ruddy in complexion, with the scarred hands of a man who knows how to handle himself in a fight. He's somewhere around fifty and his hair has turned gray. He wears it in a buzz cut and keeps his face closely shaved.

Tennick likes him, though he'd be here even if he didn't. He makes it his business to keep Beckham happy, buying him drinks and listening to his stories, and in return Beckham makes sure Tennick is up-to-date on all the department's current cases—including the Merkury investigation.

They've known each other for more than a decade, and Tennick considers Beckham a friend. He knows that Beckham married his high school sweetheart and is still with her after thirty years, that they have two children together, a boy and a girl, both of them grown and moved away. He also knows that Beckham is friendly with one of the bartenders at Ptolemy's—a cute blonde named Tracey who's easy to talk to. In fact, he once admitted to having a crush on her, though he swore he would never act on it.

Beckham is drinking Scotch and soda, and when his glass gets low Tracey brings him another without needing to be asked. She brings Tennick another beer at the same time.

Beckham thanks her and she responds with a pretty smile and a pat on his shoulder. After she's gone, he turns his attention back to Tennick and says, "Where was I?"

"Traffic stop," Tennick says. "Back road, late at night."

There's nothing new on Merkury, so Beckham has been telling stories about his early days on the job.

"Right," Beckham says. "It's one in the morning and I'm on patrol east of the college and I come up behind this guy driving an old Cadillac. The first thing he does is slow down. The limit out there is fifty-five, and he's going forty. Like he's nervous. When he slows down I see one of his brake lights is out. So I stay behind him to see what he does, and he keeps crawling along, and finally I light him up and give him the siren. For a second I think he's gonna bolt, but he pulls over. I do too, and I approach him with a flashlight and go into the routine.

"'Do you know why I pulled you over, sir?'

"He shakes his head, facing forward. Doesn't look at me. He's got his hands on the steering wheel in a white-knuckle grip, and I can see he's sweating. Now he's making *me* nervous.

"I say, 'Where are you headed tonight?' And he says, 'Nowhere. Home.' And I say, 'Which one—nowhere or home?' And he's flustered. He doesn't answer me.

"He's a big guy," Beckham says. "Maybe ten years older than me. I was in my twenties then. I can't figure out what's wrong with him. He doesn't seem drunk. I say, 'Do you have any weapons in the car?' And he says, 'Like a gun?' And I say, 'Any weapon at all.' And his face scrunches up like it's a hard question. Finally he shakes his head.

"The engine of the Cadillac is rumbling loud in my ears. I know something's not right, but I don't know what the hell it is, so I say, 'Do you mind if I search your vehicle, sir?'

"He doesn't like the idea. 'Wouldn't you need a warrant?' he says.

"'Not if you give me permission,' I tell him.

"'So I can say no.'

"'That's your right.'

"'Then I guess I say no,' he says.

"At this point I want to drag him out of the car and cuff him on the ground. But there's no cause I can point to, except for him being antsy. The engine is so loud I can feel it in my skull. I'm resigned to writing him up for the broken brake light and letting him go, and that's when I hear it: a scream. It's faint against the rumble of the engine, but it's real.

"'Sir,' I say. 'I want you to turn off the engine and hand me the key. Move very slowly.'

"'Shit,' he says.

"There's another scream. It's coming from the trunk.

"'Shit, shit, shit,' he says.

"I'm ready to put a bullet in the son of a bitch," Beckham says. "But I get him out of the car and cuffed and kneeling by the side of the road. He barely wanted to talk before, but now he's babbling. 'It's gonna look bad, but I can explain. I didn't mean it. I didn't mean to do it.' And I open the trunk."

Beckham takes a pause. For drama. Tennick obliges him.

"What did you find in the trunk?"

"A goddamn dog," Beckham says. "Terrier mix. He ran over it and thought it was dead. It was his kids' dog and he couldn't bear to tell them, so he was going to bury it and act like it ran away. He had a shovel and everything."

"What did you do?" Tennick asks.

"The dog kept whining and howling and he wanted to take it to a vet, but there was nothing open. I called a guy I knew who was willing to meet us at his office. We drove there, but the dog was too far gone. The back half of it was crushed. Had to put it to sleep. I let the driver off. Told him to get his brake light fixed. Stupid bastard never realized how close I came to shooting him."

When Tennick leaves Ptolemy's Pub, he knows there's something he needs to do—and that he doesn't want to do it.

He stops at a liquor store on his way home and picks up a fifth of vodka. The beer he had at Ptolemy's didn't do much for him, but the vodka is a different story. He drinks it from the bottle, sitting in a camp chair outside his RV, and it takes him to a lovely place. The stars are out. There's sweetness in the air and music on the wind. It's cold, but that's nothing a fire wouldn't fix.

He has wood in the barn and newspapers in the RV to use for kindling. It would be a chore to get them, but he's willing to make the sacrifice. He has just about resolved to do it when Kate's car rolls up the driveway.

She kills the headlights and the engine and comes over to sit in his second camp chair.

"Long day?" Tennick asks.

She nods.

"You're probably tired," he says.

"Yes, I am."

"Too tired to go for a drive."

She gives him a curious look. "Why? Where do you want to go?"

"Say you're too tired, and that's the end of it."

The look gets curiouser. "Are you drunk, Lee?"

"I'm getting there," he says. "I figure I'm too far gone to drive myself. So if you won't drive me, it will have to wait."

"What will have to wait?"

"Nothing. An unpleasant bit of work. Put it out of your mind. I'll do it tomorrow."

Kate extends her legs out in front of her and crosses one ankle over the other.

"All right," she says.

They sit in silence. Tennick takes a pull from the vodka bottle. He thinks again about lighting a fire, but the idea doesn't hold the appeal it held before.

"Shit," he says. "Might as well be tonight. I need to go to Clay McKellar's apartment and rifle through the poor kid's stuff."

Kate turns to him and frowns. "I thought we had this settled, Lee. It's not a good idea to break into Clay's apartment."

He puts the bottle on the ground and gets to his feet.

"That's the hell of it. I don't have to break in. I have a key."

It's a ten-minute drive into town, with Tennick brooding in the passenger seat. Kate parks in the lot behind the movie theater.

The coffee shop in Clay McKellar's building is still open, but the crowd looks thin. Kate climbs the stairs to the second floor with Tennick behind her. He may be drunk, but he seems steady when they come to Clay's door. He draws a key from his pocket and turns it in the lock and they're inside.

He explained before they left: Clay's mother asked him to sort through her son's things, ship anything personal to her, and dispose of the rest. Chief Landen provided the key.

The apartment is a sad place, cheaply furnished, smelling vaguely of sweat. Tennick sits himself down at Clay's desk and starts looking through the drawers. Kate attends to the kitchen, washing the dishes in the sink, pouring out a carton of sour milk from the refrigerator.

She fills a trash bag with food no one is going to want. They brought some cardboard boxes with them, though not enough. She fills one with the best of Clay's dishes and pans. The Salvation Army might take them. Might take some of the furniture too.

An hour passes quickly and Kate fills all their boxes with items to donate. She empties the bedroom closet and sets aside some sweaters that look handmade, thinking Clay's family might want them. The rest of the clothes go into plastic bags.

Tennick has kept busy too. He's filled a laundry basket with framed photographs, papers, a fountain pen, a wristwatch, a Bluetooth speaker. He's separated Clay's textbooks from the more personal ones. *The Catcher in the Rye* will be going back to Clay's mother. *To Kill a Mockingbird* and *The Great Gatsby* too.

"It's enough for now," Tennick says. "I'll come back and finish tomorrow."

They make three trips, carrying things to the car. The last time they go down the stairs, they meet Clay's neighbor coming up. Kate nods to her as she passes, but Tennick stops to talk.

"We were here the other day," he says.

"I remember," the neighbor says. "You were looking for Clay. It's terrible what happened to him."

Tennick agrees with her and adds: "I know this will sound strange, but was your cat out in the hall Saturday night or early Sunday morning?"

"Milo?" she says. "I don't let him wander at night. And I slept in Sunday morning. Why?"

Tennick shrugs. "It's nothing. Clay left me a strange message. He said something was scratching on his door."

"Well, it wasn't Milo," the neighbor says. "Maybe it was a mouse."

Kate thinks the night is over, but Tennick doesn't want to go home. Down in the parking lot he says to her, "Let's have a drink."

"It's late, Lee," she says.

"We'll drink to Clay. He deserves to have someone drink to him."

She senses it will be useless to resist. Says, "Okay. Where do you want to go?"

Tennick pulls a small bottle from a pocket of his coat. Bourbon. Maker's Mark.

"Did you bring that with you?" Kate asks him.

"I found it in Clay's desk," he says.

They walk around the block, passing the bottle between them. Tennick holds it longer and hits it harder. When they circle back to the movie theater, Kate decides to lead him east, away from downtown. A few blocks on, she comes to a familiar picket fence. She goes through the gate and climbs onto the porch where she talked to Martin Cayhill.

The house is dark. Kate imagines that Cayhill and his wife have gone home. They were only staying temporarily.

Tennick has joined her. He offers her the bottle but she shakes her head.

"Have you been here before?" she asks him.

"No. Who lives here?"

"I guess I know something you don't," she says. "Bryan Cayhill lived here."

Tennick has another drink from the bottle, then pushes the doorbell with his knuckle.

Kate hears it chiming inside. "What are you doing?" she asks him.

No lights come on in the house. No one comes to the door.

"I guess he's not home," Tennick says.

He steps down from the porch, stumbling a little, and walks around to the side yard. Kate goes after him.

"Let's head back, Lee."

"No, no," he says. "We should go in. This is a night for snooping around in dead kids' houses."

The picket fence from the front of the house gives way to a taller privacy fence in the back. The back lawn is dotted with wet leaves. Tennick stands in the middle of it and points up at a second-floor window that's partway open.

"There's your way in," he says.

"If we could fly," says Kate.

"I think we could climb it," Tennick says.

There's a portico over the back door, with a small peaked roof to keep off the rain. There are trash cans and recycling bins stored against the back wall of the house.

"All you need is one trash can and one bin," Tennick says. "Turn the bin upside down and use it to climb onto the can. From there you climb onto that little roof, and then you can reach the window. Easy-peasy." He winks at her. "I saw it done in a movie."

"You're in no condition to climb," Kate says. "There's nothing to see in the house anyway. The Cayhills were here cleaning it out, getting it ready to sell."

Tennick makes a noncommittal sound with his mouth closed. He twists the cap off the bourbon bottle and twists it on again. Kate is looking up at the window.

"I wonder if that's how Merkury got in," she says. "Through a window. Or did he convince Bryan to let him in?"

Tennick laughs softly at her.

"I guess *I* know something *you* don't know," he says.

"What?"

"Merkury didn't take him from his house."

"No?"

"No. Bryan was a runner, and he liked to go at night. Sometimes he ran down to the campus and back, and sometimes he ran out to Portage Road."

Portage Road led to Weatherstone Pond, where Bryan's body was found.

"How do you know this?" Kate asks.

Tennick waves the bottle in the air. "Sources," he says. "Methods. A cop named Ralph Beckham who likes to talk. Bryan wore a Fitbit to keep track of his runs. The police pulled the data from it. They know where he went the night he died. They know when he met up with Merkury, because he stopped for a brief time. When he started moving again, he was going much faster, because Merkury had him in a vehicle. They know exactly when he arrived at the pond."

Tennick slips the bottle into his coat pocket.

"It's maddening, if you think about it," he says. "Technology can tell you all that, but it can't tell you who killed Bryan Cayhill."

Tennick has more to say, on the walk back to the car, about how maddening everything is. He falls quiet on the drive home and Kate is unsurprised to find he's sleeping when she pulls into the driveway. She shakes him awake and guides him by the arm to his RV.

She unloads the car herself, carrying the bags and boxes into the barn. The remnants of Clay McKellar's life.

Once she's in the house, she checks her cellphone and finds a missed call from Devin Falko. But it's not him she's thinking about as she gets ready for bed. It's not Clay either. She's thinking about the missing girl, Jenny Wyler, and her friends Colleen Rosewood and Diana Perez.

Colleen seemed convinced that Jenny had been abducted. But Diana, intentionally or not, made a strong case for believing that Jenny might have run away to escape a bad homelife with her father.

In fact, Diana didn't seem overly concerned about Jenny's disappearance. If she was mourning the loss of a friend, she didn't show it.

The more Kate thinks about it, the more she wonders if Diana knows something she's not telling.

17

On Wednesday and Thursday Kate spends time in Earlville. She's working through her list of Jenny Wyler's friends and getting no closer to determining what happened to her.

By midmorning Thursday she has collected an impressive number of random facts and written them in her notebook:

Jenny's favorite color: blue.

Favorite singer: Phoebe Bridgers.

Jenny is fair at tennis, a good swimmer, played on her high school's softball team.

Was in the Girl Scouts, but dropped out.

Knows how to play chess.

A good kisser.

That information came from the one boy on the list, who based his judgment on a single incident in tenth grade.

Jenny likes drawing birds and butterflies.

Came close to getting a tattoo once, but backed out for fear of her father's reaction.

Picks apples in the fall and makes apple pie.

Misses going shopping with her mom.

There's more. Eight pages' worth. None of it seems likely to help Kate find Jenny Wyler.

Kate knows what the main problem is: she's not a detective, she's an author. She's used to writing about women after it's already known what became of them. Finding missing people is not her job.

At eleven fifteen a.m. on Thursday, she's coming out of the Bargain Basket Thrift Shop on Greene Street, where one of Jenny's friends works. Kate pauses in the parking lot to jot down a few facts before she forgets them. Chief among them: *Jenny is a lousy bowler, but enthusiastic.*

When she reaches her car, there's a flyer tucked under her windshield wiper. It's a black-and-white image of a cocker spaniel. *Missing. Answers to Sparky. If found, please call . . .*

Kate's first thought is that Jenny Wyler is not a missing dog. Her second thought: What could it hurt?

Back at her father's house, she composes a flyer on her laptop. She has the image of Jenny that Samuel Wyler showed her, because she asked him to text it to her. She's lacking basic facts like height and weight, and when she calls Mr. Wyler she gets no answer. But she tries Colleen Rosewood and Colleen comes through: Jenny is five feet six inches tall, 130 pounds.

Kate keeps the description short, makes the photo nice and large. Types *Missing Since September 7th* at the top and *Contact Kate Summerlin if you have information* at the bottom. She includes her email address.

She runs off a hundred flyers on her father's color printer and borrows a roll of packing tape from his junk drawer. Then it's back to Earlville, where she leaves behind more than sixty, taping them to lampposts and power poles. The rest she takes to the Seagate campus, where Jenny worked.

The sky is getting dark as Kate winds things up, taping flyers to the backs of benches on the main quad. Lights are glowing in the windows

of the academic buildings. Kate catches sight of Lavana Khatri coming
out of Trimble Hall. Travis Pollard is with her. Lavana walks with him
to the library and when they come to the entrance they hug briefly and
part ways. Travis goes into the library and Lavana heads across the edge
of the quad toward the granite steps that will take her down to the bottom of the Hill.

Kate follows her at a distance.

The steps are well lighted and though Lavana is alone she seems
unafraid. Kate is aware of her own footsteps on the granite, and Lavana
must hear them too, but she doesn't turn around. As she nears the bottom, there's another student coming up: a boy wearing a black hoodie
that obscures his face. His hands are stuffed in his pockets. Kate holds
her breath as he passes Lavana, but nothing happens. He doesn't lunge
at her. He doesn't spirit her away.

As the boy passes Kate, he smiles at her from under his hood. He
makes a show of shivering.

"Cold night," he says.

Lavana has reached the bottom of the steps. Kate hurries to catch up
and calls her name.

The girl spins around, her eyes wide. Then she lets out a nervous laugh
and puts a hand over her heart.

"Oh my god, you scared me!"

"I'm sorry," Kate says.

"I didn't expect to see you," Lavana says. "What are you doing here?
Were you looking for me?"

Kate still has one of her flyers. "I've been posting these," she says,
holding it out.

Lavana takes the flyer and reads the name. "'Jenny Wyler.' Who is
she?"

"She's missing," Kate says. "I told her father I'd try to find her."

"I don't recognize the name, but she looks familiar," Lavana says. "Is
she a student here?"

"No. She used to work in the dining hall."

"Maybe I saw her there," Lavana says, handing the flyer back. "You don't think about it, but I guess it's happening all the time."

"What?" Kate says.

"People going missing, people dying."

Lavana's voice is soft and she looks young, her black hair loose and mussed by the wind.

Kate feels protective of her. "You shouldn't be out alone at night," she says.

That gets her a smile and a head shake.

"The cold will probably get me before anything else does," Lavana says. "Come on."

The student union is close by. They walk to the south entrance and step into the vestibule, where it's warm.

"This is better," Lavana says. "I'm glad I ran into you. I wanted to ask you something."

"Go ahead," Kate says.

"The girl you found when you were a kid," Lavana says. "Do you still think about her?"

"Sure."

"Once in a while? Or every day?"

The answer is "every day," but Kate says, "Probably somewhere in between."

Lavana bows her head. "I still think about Bryan all the time. Clay too now."

"You'll have to wait for some time to pass," Kate tells her. "I think it'll get better for you."

It's the right thing to say, even if it doesn't turn out to be true. Lavana looks up. She seems hopeful.

"Thank you," she says, leaning against the wall of the vestibule. "I hope it was okay to ask. I know it's personal."

"It's okay."

"Travis thinks you're mad at him, because he asked you personal questions."

Hearing Travis's name shouldn't bother her, Kate thinks. But it does. It brings a series of images to her mind. There's his mouth, falling so easily into a smirk. The way his eyes looked her over the first time she met him.

She has a flash of the oak tree by the stream. The rock on the ground by its roots. The note she hid under the rock.

Travis Pollard.

Smug.

Arrogant.

Kate remembers what he said to her: *You found a dead girl in the woods. It must have messed you up . . . You must be afraid all the time.*

"It wasn't so much that he asked me personal questions," she says to Lavana. "It was more that he made personal comments about things that were none of his concern. Things he knows nothing about."

"Oh," Lavana says. She seems uncomfortable. Embarrassed.

"But I'm not mad at him."

Lie, lie, lie.

"And I'm not mad at you."

True.

"Cool," Lavana says.

There's an awkward pause. Kate focuses on the sound of the heating system, the warm air coming into the vestibule through a vent in the floor. Then Lavana abruptly pushes herself away from the wall and fishes her phone from her pocket.

"I almost forgot. I have something to show you."

She swipes and pokes at the screen, calling up a video.

"I've been editing the movie. You have to see this. It's not the whole thing, but it's part of the ending."

She turns her phone sideways and holds it up for Kate. Taps the play button.

And there's Lavana herself running through the woods at night. Long shots, medium shots, close-ups, all cut together. There's Travis, playing the killer, dressed in ragged clothes, chasing her through the same woods. You can hear him tearing through the undergrowth. Now the camera cuts to his legs, his feet in black boots.

Here's Lavana again. A close-up on her face. She looks terrified. There's a wound on her forehead, a trickle of blood.

It goes on, cutting between Lavana and Travis. You can't tell how close he is to catching her, but it feels like he's closing in. There's a musical score underneath the action. Discordant violin and piano. It works. It heightens the fear.

Then the final shots: Lavana breathing hard, with her back against a tree. She's clutching a broken branch, long as a walking stick, one end sharp like a spear.

Then Travis again, charging through the woods. Lavana, spinning out suddenly from behind the tree, planting one end of the spear on the ground, holding it down with her foot. Aiming the pointed end just so.

Close-up on Travis's face when he impales himself. The sound drops out when he screams.

A shot of him on the ground, lying on his side. You can see that the spear pierced his stomach. You can see the sharp end coming out of his back.

It's well done. Hitchcockian. Edited so skillfully that you think you saw him stabbed even though you didn't.

"What do you think?" Lavana asks.

"It's good," Kate says. "It's great."

When they step outside, it seems even colder than before. The moon is close to full, but it's veiled behind thin clouds. Kate walks with Lavana to her dorm, and along the way the wind plucks leaves from the trees and sends them floating to the ground.

The entryway is lit up bright and the door is locked. Lavana swipes a card and there's a click and she pushes the door inward. Kate says good night and turns away, heading for the lot where she parked her car. But before she takes a dozen steps, Lavana calls her back.

"Let me see that picture again," she says.

Kate is puzzled for a moment, then remembers the flyer. She tucked it in her coat pocket while they were talking. She brings it out and unfolds it.

Lavana holds it in the light, studying the image of Jenny Wyler.

"This might sound weird," she says.

"What?" Kate asks.

"I could be wrong, but I think I saw her with Bryan Cayhill once."

18

On Friday night at eight o'clock, Kate is sitting with Lee Tennick in a pub in Syracuse, an hour's drive from Alexander.

Her hair is pinned up and mostly covered by a knitted cap. She's wearing a scarf around her neck and a pair of drugstore sunglasses with amber-tinted lenses.

Tennick looks at her over his menu and says, "I know I was skeptical before, but I was wrong—"

"Shut up, Lee."

"You are completely inconspicuous."

On Thursday night, after Lavana's revelation about Jenny Wyler and Bryan Cayhill, Kate sent a text to Jenny's friend Diana Perez asking if they could talk again. A few minutes later she received a reply: the dinner shift was in full swing, but Diana could take a break in half an hour.

Kate waited for her at the spot where they had spoken before behind the dining hall. She kept her eye on the steel door near the loading dock, but when it finally opened the person who came out wasn't Diana. It was her coworker, the gray-haired woman with the tortoiseshell glasses. She leaned against the brick wall and lit a cigarette.

Diana appeared five minutes later, with a blue fleece coat over her white-and-black uniform.

"I thought of something else to ask you," Kate said. "Did Jenny know Bryan Cayhill?"

Diana made a show of being surprised.

"The guy who died?" she said.

"Yes, the guy who died."

"Where would you get that idea?"

Kate tilted her head to one side. "You're not saying no."

Diana smiled, but there was no humor in it. "Jenny didn't know him. Or if she did, she never told me."

Over by the wall, the gray-haired woman flicked ash from her cigarette. She was watching them. Listening in.

"You're doing this wrong," Kate said to Diana. "I just suggested that your friend, who vanished six weeks ago, knew a boy who was found hanging dead from a tree. That should be alarming. You should be worried for your friend."

"Of course I'm worried. I don't know where you got the idea that I'm not worried."

Kate took a step closer to her. "You're not though. And I can only think of one reason. You know she's okay. Did you help her leave?"

Diana lifted her shoulders and let them fall. "I don't know where you're getting this."

"Poor Colleen Rosewood is afraid Jenny's dead," Kate said. "She doesn't know the truth, does she? But you do. Are you hiding Jenny somewhere?"

Diana's expression went blank. "I don't have to talk to you."

"You're doing it again," Kate said. "Not saying no."

Diana leaned forward slightly and said: "We're done. You're not a cop. You don't get to interrogate me. Even if I knew where Jenny was, I would never tell you."

She waited a beat before turning away, then strode past the gray-haired woman and went in through the steel door.

Kate didn't try to follow. She looked up at the moon and turned in a slow circle with her hands in her pockets. When she came around to face the building again, the gray-haired woman was walking toward her.

"You're the little girl who found Melissa Cornelle."

"I was," Kate said.

"That was awful. I remember . . . But I guess you turned out okay."

"I guess I did."

The woman took a drag on her cigarette, held the smoke in, and let it out.

"I never really talked to Jenny Wyler when she worked here. But she seemed like a sweet girl. What's your interest in finding her?"

Kate kept her answer simple. "I'd like to know she's safe."

"Well, I don't know what happened to her or where she is," the woman said. "But I know *that one*"—she nodded at the door where Diana had gone in—"goes to Syracuse almost every weekend. She has friends who live there. If she were helping someone hide . . ." She let the implication hang in the air and drew on her cigarette again.

"Do you know the names of these friends?" Kate asked.

The woman shook her head. "But I know where they hang out. She's always talking about it. Must be where the cool people go. A place called Faegan's."

"Completely inconspicuous," Lee Tennick says. "Who notices a woman wearing sunglasses inside at night?"

Kate ignores him. The glasses might be overkill, but she doesn't want Diana Perez spotting her and tipping off Jenny Wyler. Assuming either one of them shows up here tonight.

Which they haven't yet.

The place is filling up though. Faegan's Pub on a Friday night. It's a young, lively crowd, mostly students from Syracuse University. They're lined up at the bar on the south wall, and they're in the booths that run down the center of the main room and at the tables that fill the rest of the space. Kate and Tennick are at a corner table in the front, where they can see everyone who comes in.

She orders a salad with grilled salmon, and he gets a burger and fries. They make the food last. When nine thirty rolls around, Kate is convinced she's on a fool's errand. Jenny's not going to come here. Kate takes off her sunglasses and brings out her phone. There's another missed call from Devin Falko. He's been calling her once a day.

"If you spend your time looking at your phone," Tennick says, "people will think we're an unhappy couple."

She's saved from having to respond when the waitress comes to clear away their plates. Tennick asks for another Diet Coke. He hasn't had a beer all night. In fact, Kate hasn't seen him with a drink since their visit to Clay McKellar's apartment.

At ten o'clock he's still nursing his Diet Coke. The check is on the table between them. Kate is about to reach for it when the door of the pub opens and Diana and Jenny walk in.

They're accompanied by two young men, one taller with the build of a football player, one shorter and more intellectual-looking. Both students from the university, Kate assumes.

The four of them find a table in the middle of the room, and in a stroke of luck Diana sits with her back to Kate. Jenny Wyler sits across from her friend.

She looks happy, healthy. Perfectly fine. But there have been some changes. She's not the same as she was in the picture her father showed Kate.

Her brown hair has been cut and styled. She's wearing lipstick and eyeliner. Her jeans hug her hips, and she's wearing heels and a low-cut blouse. Very different from the plain, modest wardrobe Kate remembers from the girl's closet.

She's a pretty nineteen-year-old out with her friends on a Friday night. Maybe that's the whole story. She left home to get out from under her father's thumb.

"You found her," Tennick says. "Now what?"

Kate isn't sure. She would like to talk to Jenny, but not here, not in this crowd, not in front of Diana.

"Let's wait and see," she says.

Jenny and her friends are in Faegan's for almost ninety minutes. In that time they order wings and nachos and quesadillas. Jenny drinks what looks like iced tea. The other three split two pitchers of beer.

Tennick orders a plate of nachos for himself.

"We can't just sit here," he says.

At 11:25, when Jenny and Diana and their college boys get up to leave, Tennick says, "We're tailing them, right? Like private eyes."

Kate drops some cash on the table. "Yup. Like private eyes."

Faegan's is on Crouse Avenue, one block north of the Syracuse University campus.

It's a cold night, but the sidewalks are full of students. Jenny and her friends walk north on Crouse. They cross over to the other side of the street, not bothering to wait for a crosswalk, confident that the traffic will yield to them.

At Adams Street, they split up. Diana and the football player set off east on Adams. Jenny and the other boy continue north.

"Do you think she's going home with him?" Tennick asks.

"I guess we'll see," Kate says.

They've been following the group from the opposite side of the street, but now they jog across. Jenny and her college boy are walking side by side, not quite touching. They encounter a woman heading south, walking a golden retriever. Jenny stops to pet the dog.

Now they're moving again, past a Chase bank and a parking lot. The boy, without breaking stride, looks back over his shoulder.

"Uh-oh," Tennick says under his breath. "Have we been made?"

The boy leans close to Jenny, as if he's telling her something. She doesn't look back.

"Possibly," says Kate.

Up ahead there's a building that looks like a temple. It has four tall columns on its front face and wide stone steps that lead up to a pair of red doors. The columns are flanked by long vertical banners that announce the building's name: Hotel Skyler.

Jenny and the boy walk up the steps and enter through the red doors.

Kate quickens her pace, with Tennick right behind her. She climbs the steps and pushes through the doors and into the lobby of the hotel. It's a grand space with polished hardwood floors and high ceilings. There's a large, curved breakfast bar and a fireplace and clusters of sleek armchairs.

Off to the right, a clerk stands behind a reception desk. Off to the left, Jenny Wyler and the boy are waiting in front of a stained-glass window.

The boy looks nervous. He's doughy and red-haired and he's wearing glasses with round silver frames. He's five-seven or five-eight and trying to look taller. He starts out beside Jenny, then steps in front of her as if he's her bodyguard.

She laughs and pushes him gently out of the way.

"You must be Kate Summerlin," she says.

19

"What's going on?" Kate asks. "Help me understand."

She and Jenny have taken off their coats, and they're sitting by the fireplace. Tennick has led the boy aside; they're talking quietly by the breakfast bar. The hotel lobby is otherwise empty, apart from the clerk and occasional guests coming in or going out.

"You first," Jenny says. "Why were you following me?"

"I'm concerned about you."

"Diana told me you were looking for me and I should watch out. Then I spotted you at Faegan's. You looked in my direction a few too many times. Did my father send you?"

Kate answers carefully. "He doesn't know I'm here, but I've talked to him. He's worried something happened to you."

"He's always worried," Jenny says. "Are you gonna tell him where I am?"

"Not if you don't want me to. But don't you think you should let him know you're all right? He can't force you to go back."

"No. That's not the way he operates. He would shame me instead."

"Is that why you didn't tell him you were leaving?"

Jenny lets out a sigh. "I just wanted to go. Is that a sin?"

Kate tips her head in the direction of the boy with the glasses. "Were you afraid he wouldn't approve of your boyfriend?"

Jenny's amusement shows in her eyes. "Ian? He's not my boyfriend. I met him three weeks ago. You make a lot of assumptions."

"I'm trying to make sense of this situation. This hotel, for instance. Seems expensive. Are you working?"

"I'm not staying here," Jenny says. "Do you think I would let you follow me to where I'm staying?"

"You didn't answer me. Do you have a job?"

"That's a nosy question."

"Because you have a new wardrobe, and apparently it didn't come from Ian."

"Nosy."

Kate leans forward in her chair. "I like your earrings."

She didn't notice them in Faegan's but up close they're quite lovely. The hooks are gold, and the dangling blue stones look like they could be sapphires.

"Were they a gift?" she asks.

Jenny brings her hand up to touch one of them, but offers no reply.

Kate's handbag is on the floor at her feet. She opens it and unzips one of the compartments. Brings out the gold earring she found at the Wyler house.

"Is this yours?" she asks.

Jenny barely looks at it. "No."

"That's strange. It was in your old room, under your bed."

"You were in my room?"

"I'm nosy."

Jenny wavers. Kate can see her thinking.

"I guess it is mine. I forgot I'd lost it."

Kate holds the earring up like she's seeing it for the first time. "It's beautiful," she says. "A cut above your other jewelry—at least the stuff you left at home. I took it to a jeweler. The diamond is real."

She's lying about the jeweler. She's only guessing that it's real.

"What?" Jenny says. "I'm not allowed to own nice things?"

"You're allowed," Kate says. "And I'm allowed to wonder where they came from. How well did you know Bryan Cayhill?"

Kate is expecting a denial, but Jenny says, "Well enough. We were friendly."

"When did you meet him?"

"Last spring."

"Did you date him?"

Jenny holds the palm of her right hand out toward the fireplace. "It's interesting how your mind works. It falls into certain grooves."

"Why don't you tell me how it went."

The girl lets the heat of the fire warm her hand for a moment, then draws it back. "I shouldn't have said we were friendly. That makes it sound more casual than it was. We were friends. It started out—we saw each other when I was working in the dining hall. We would talk. Then we would meet after I got off work, and the conversations lasted longer."

"What did you talk about?" Kate asks.

A sly smile plays across Jenny's face. "We talked about being orphans."

"But you're not an orphan. Neither was he."

"Our mothers both died though, and we were left with our fathers. They were both lousy, but in different ways. Mine was too much, Bryan's was too little. He felt . . . unseen."

"Unseen?"

"He missed his mother. She was the one who really knew him. His father was a poor substitute. It's sad. Bryan's family was rich. He could have anything he wanted. But he felt neglected."

"Did that bother you?" Kate asks. "That he was rich and you weren't?"

"Why would it?"

Kate holds up the diamond earring again. "Did he give you this? And the pair you're wearing?"

"What does it matter?" Jenny says.

"I'm trying to understand your relationship. When was the last time you saw him?"

"I don't see how that matters either."

"Did he ever visit you here?"

"In Syracuse? No."

Kate lets a few seconds pass. Jenny sits across from her impassively.

"What are you not telling me?" Kate asks.

"I told you all there is," Jenny says. "Or all you're entitled to know. We were friends."

"I think there's more."

"Like what?"

"Like Bryan's dead. He was murdered."

"By a serial killer."

"That's what everyone's saying."

Jenny narrows her eyes in confusion and lays a hand over her heart.

"Do you think I killed him?"

"No," Kate says. "I don't know what happened."

"She's smart," Kate says on the drive back to Alexander. "I'm not sure what I expected. Maybe someone . . . less confident."

"I can tell you this," Tennick says. "Ian is taken with her. She's got him wrapped around her little finger."

"Are they sleeping together?"

"I don't think so. But he wants to."

Kate lets a mile pass by. Thinking.

"Maybe she's nothing more than what she seems."

"And what's that?" Tennick asks.

"An innocent from a small town who moved to the city. But it bothers me that she knew Bryan Cayhill."

"A lot of people knew Bryan Cayhill."

"That's true."

"Maybe his death had nothing to do with her."

Kate finds it hard to believe, but she can't say why. She holds tight to the wheel and stares out at the road ahead.

When Jenny and Ian leave the Hotel Skyler, it's a seven-minute walk to her apartment.

They arrive outside the building after midnight, and Ian draws Jenny toward him on the sidewalk and kisses her. She likes him because he's eager but not rough. She pulls away and tells him he can come in with her.

She turns her key in the lock and she's glad to be home, though it still feels strange to think of this place as home. There's not much here: a thrift-store table and chairs, a sofa someone left out on the street. No dresser in the bedroom and no bedframe, only a mattress lying on the floor.

Jenny drops her keys on the table and slips out of her coat. Asks Ian if he wants something to drink, but before she can reach for glasses in the cupboard they're making out again. They move out of the kitchen, through the living room, into the bedroom. She lets him unbutton her shirt and take it off. Her bra too. He's sweet. He touches her so delicately, with his fingertips.

When he tries to unbutton her jeans, she moves his hand away and he gets the message. He kisses her with no less enthusiasm. Runs his fingers through her hair, down the back of her neck, between her shoulder blades.

This is new to her. Jenny has kissed other boys before Ian Gardner, but only in stolen moments that were over too soon. She likes being kissed, and she likes being touched, and most of all she likes not having to care if her father finds out.

She pulls away from Ian for a moment, long enough to light a candle. She doesn't have a stereo, but he finds some music on his phone, plays an album by a group called Birds of Chicago. He drops the phone onto the mattress and the two of them follow it down.

It's sweet and he's gentle, turning her over and kissing the skin of her back, between her shoulder blades and along her spine. She gets lost in the feeling of it, and in the music, and when he sits up suddenly on the mattress she doesn't know why.

"Did you hear that?" he says.

"What?" she asks him.

"That noise. Sounded like someone knocking on the door."

He reaches for his phone and pauses the music. They wait in the quiet of the apartment.

Then the noise comes again, but it's not a knocking. More like a ramming.

Loud and harsh and persistent.

Like someone trying to force their way in.

20

That night Kate has a dream about her mother.

Her father is there too, and they're in a restaurant in Oberlin, Ohio, celebrating. Kate has driven up from Columbus to share some good news: her agent has sold her first book to an editor at Grove Atlantic.

Her mother is effusive. She takes Kate's face in her hands and says, "This is yours, remember this. You worked for it, you earned it. I'm so proud." And she is. She smiles broadly and Kate can see tears welling in her eyes.

Kate's father congratulates her too, but he's restrained and oddly formal. "I hope the book does well for you," he says, almost as if he's talking to an acquaintance.

At the end of the meal, in the dream as in real life, Kate's father excuses himself to go to the restroom. Her mother puts a hand on her shoulder and speaks to her softly.

"He's proud of you," she says.

"I know," says Kate.

"He's jealous too. He's written novels but they never went anywhere. It's an ego thing. He teaches creative writing but he's never had a book published. So now he sees you and your success . . ." Her mother trails off, and before long her father is back at the table.

In real life, her father paid the bill and they left the restaurant soon after. But in the dream her mother has more to say.

"Your father is an ordinary man. You can't expect too much from him."

Kate's father looks away, as if he hasn't heard.

"You deserved better parents," her mother says. "You got a raw deal. You should never have been an orphan."

"But I'm not an orphan," Kate says.

"We're proud of you. That's the main thing. Remember."

"I'm not an orphan," Kate says again.

She turns to look at her father, but his chair is empty. She feels a sudden catch in her breathing, and a spasm runs through her body. Before she can turn back to her mother, she's awake.

The house is quiet, but Kate can hear the wind outside. She closes her eyes, even though she knows she's not going back to sleep anytime soon.

The dream bothers her.

It's not hard to guess what brought it on. She remembers asking Jenny Wyler what she talked about with Bryan Cayhill, and the answer Jenny gave about their lost mothers.

We talked about being orphans.

Kate lost her mother too. And she came very close to becoming an orphan.

About six weeks after Kate's first book came out, her mother and father attended an anniversary party for one of her father's colleagues in Westlake, a suburb of Cleveland. On the drive back it began to rain, and when they were only seven miles from home a white van passed them recklessly, cutting in ahead of them too soon. Kate's mother, who was driving, hit the brakes and lost control, swerving off the road and crashing head-on into a tree.

She was killed instantly.

The white van fled the scene, and its driver was never identified.

Kate's father suffered a broken leg, a broken collarbone, and several fractured ribs. His face, when Kate saw him in the hospital the next day, was a mass of bruises, his eyes swollen, his front teeth knocked out. She sat by his bed, holding his hand, and wept.

Her uncle Jim came into town with his family to help Kate with the funeral arrangements for her mother, but Kate was the one who made all the decisions, choosing the casket, the flowers, the hymns to be sung at the service. When the day came, Kate's father was still recovering in the hospital, and Kate was the one who delivered her mother's eulogy.

She had written it over three days, trying to choose the right details to represent her mother's life. She talked about the cakes her mother baked for birthdays, the vegetables she grew in her garden, the music she liked to listen to, how she used to laugh on the telephone talking to her friends. Kate tried to paint a picture of how her mother had shaped her life: the books she had read to her as a child, the example she had set for her.

"My mother was the reason I became a writer," she said, "because she was a writer too. She kept journals and she wrote letters, honest-to-god letters, in ink, on paper."

When Kate spoke the words of the eulogy in the church, they seemed too little and too soon over. Her voice, in her own ears, sounded weak. But when people came up to her after, on the church steps, they told her the words had been lovely. Kate thanked them, but she felt numb.

That's one thing she remembers about that day: the numbness of it. The slow drive from the church to the cemetery. Then the wait while the crowd from the funeral service reassembled at the graveside. Then the people who wanted to talk to her after her mother was in the ground: aunts, uncles, cousins, her mother's and father's many friends.

But that's not all Kate remembers.

When all the others had drifted away, she was left at the grave with her uncle Jim and his wife and their children. There was no gravestone yet, only a flimsy metal marker with stick-on letters that spelled out SUSAN RAFFERTY SUMMERLIN.

The plan was to return to Kate's parents' house, where a small group would gather for a meal. Kate asked her uncle and his family if they would go on ahead without her. She wanted a few minutes alone.

When they were gone she stood in the spring sunshine, the smell of new-mown grass in the air. She heard birds calling to each other in the trees by the cemetery fence.

She said, "I love you, Mom." Then thought there should be more. But nothing came to her.

The birds kept up their singing.

Kate's cellphone pinged to let her know she had received a text. She checked it, thinking it might be from her uncle, but it wasn't. There was no name, only a number she didn't recognize. The message was three words.

Don't turn around.

The world seemed to tip off-balance as she stared at her phone. She looked up and scanned her surroundings, thinking someone must be playing a cruel joke. Her mother's grave was at the top of a small rise, and the funeral director's black car was parked off in the distance. The director was there, speaking to the cemetery caretaker.

Kate's own car was somewhat closer, on the side of one of the narrow lanes that wound among the graves. But she could see a third car, a blue sedan, parked far off in the shade of a maple tree.

Her phone pinged again.

I'm not in that car. You really shouldn't keep looking. You don't want to see me.

Kate felt a sensation like tiny bugs crawling over the skin of her arms and up to her shoulders and the nape of her neck.

She typed a reply: This isn't funny.

Three dots appeared, to show that the person on the other end was composing a message. Then it came through.

No, Kate. I'm not trying to be funny.

The bugs changed course and began to crawl down her spine.

It was him. She knew it was, even though she didn't want to believe it. She tapped her thumbs over the keyboard on the screen: What do you want?

The three dots appeared again, and she waited.

Just to have a conversation. Like people. I saw you at the church. I heard what you said about your mother. It was beautiful. You've grown into an admirable woman.

A hollow feeling came over her, and before she could decide how she wanted to reply, another line came through.

You probably don't want to hear that from me.

Kate stared at the screen, then typed three words: No, I don't.

But you need to hear it. And this too: you need to let her go. Her death is a blessing for you.

The hollow feeling faded, replaced by anger. But he had more to tell her.

I know it's hard to see it that way. But you've been living in the shadow of your mother. We all do. Now you can come out into the light. This is a good thing.

Kate's hands trembled as she tapped the screen: I can't believe you'd say that.

You can get mad at me if you like. But I'm right. Someday you'll understand.

A white moth flitted through the grass at Kate's feet. She looked down into the grave at her mother's casket, and a terrible possibility occurred to her.

She tapped out a new message: Did you do this?

The reply came after a few seconds: Did I do what?

The accident. Was it you?

What are you asking? Did I kill your mother? Don't put that one on me.

The anger that had made her tremble turned a shade cooler, and she typed on the phone with steady hands: If I find out you did, I swear to god, I'll see you dead. I'll cut your heart out myself.

Kate watched the moth alight on a blade of grass, and waited.

That's my brave girl. I understand why you're upset, but you're wrong. I'm not responsible for what happened to your mother. The world is full of misfortunes, Kate. Don't you know? Time and chance. It wasn't me. I wouldn't do that to you.

The three dots appeared again and lingered for a long time. Then:

Can I tell you something? Maybe this won't comfort you, but it's true, and you should hear it. I lost my mother too. She was old. Older than yours. She had—well, it doesn't matter what she had. Ailments. More than one. They sapped her energy. Ate away at her mind. It was pneumonia that got her, finally. Sent her to the hospital. I was there with her for three days, in a pitiful gray room. She talked to me. Rambled. She was weak. The doctors gave up on her. She called out for my father, who'd been dead for twenty years. She told me she saw angels. But sometimes she seemed almost lucid. She asked me once to bring her her shoes. She wanted to get out of that place. She kept asking me, more and more insistently. She begged. But where could I have taken her?

Kate read through the message and wondered what he wanted from her. Sympathy?

Her thumbs hovered over the screen of her phone, but she didn't respond to him.

He had more to say though. One last thing.

What I'm trying to tell you— My mother lived a long life. She didn't die before her time. That's the best we can hope for, any of us. You need to learn this, Kate. It's going to happen, no matter what we do.

We can't escape it. I learned it in that hospital room. We are all going to die, raving.

The white moth flew away from her and she stood alone by the grave. A minute passed, then two, and the three dots did not reappear. Kate put her phone away and took a last look around. The place where she stood was exposed to the sun, but most of the cemetery was shaded by old trees.

He could be hiding anywhere among them.

Before she left, she walked down to the blue sedan. There was no one inside. But beyond it, beside a weathered gravestone, knelt an old woman planting flowers. Kate waved to her, and she waved back.

Now, lying in bed with the wind blowing outside her window, Kate reads those messages from the day of the funeral again. She never deleted them.

She showed them to Vera Landen back then, and Landen shared them with the FBI. They put a tap on Kate's cellphone, but there were no more messages from Merkury, and they gave up on it after a few weeks.

The phone Merkury used was acquired from a department store in a small town in Tennessee. It was a cheap pay-as-you-go model, purchased with cash, and was never used to contact any other number.

An FBI profiler speculated that Merkury had no children of his own but wished that he did, and had therefore formed an attachment to Kate.

It's as good an explanation as any.

For a time, Kate held on to the idea that Merkury might have driven the white van that caused the accident that killed her mother. When her father got out of the hospital, she pressed him to remember more about it, but he could never tell her anything, and there were no other witnesses.

She came to accept that she would never know for sure.

But if she's honest with herself, she has to admit that she believes what Merkury told her. She has believed it for a long time.

It wasn't me.

The world is full of misfortunes.

21

That night is a restless one, but when Kate finally finds sleep again she's out for a long time. On Saturday at noon, she's awakened by the noise of a vacuum cleaner and Bruce Springsteen's "Born to Run."

Her father is cleaning the house. She goes to the living room and finds him gliding the vacuum over the floor in time with the beat of the drums. He's singing along. Badly.

When he sees her in the doorway, he calls out to her over the racket: "Good morning! You missed breakfast. Crack an egg, fry some bacon. It's a gorgeous day! Get outside!"

She leaves him there and scrambles two eggs and skips the bacon. Takes her plate and a cup of coffee out on the porch, but the music is practically rattling the windows. Her father is singing along to "Thunder Road" now.

She retreats from the porch to one of Lee Tennick's camp chairs by the RV.

Her father was right about the day. It's fifty-five degrees and the sun's out.

Kate puts her feet up on Tennick's milk crate and digs into her eggs, but she can't help thinking about Jenny Wyler and Bryan Cayhill.

When her plate and cup are empty, she uses her phone to run a Google search on Bryan's father. She knew he was rich, but now she learns he has a hedge fund, Cayhill Asset Management, based in Connecticut. There's a phone number on the company's website, but when she calls she gets no answer.

She raps on the door of the RV, waits, raps some more, and eventually Tennick comes out yawning, looking as if he just got dressed.

"I need a phone number for Martin Cayhill," Kate says.

Tennick blinks at her. "Yeah?"

"The police would have to have one, right?"

He thinks about it. "Yeah."

"And you have a friend in the department . . ."

He scratches his stomach, catching on. "I'll make a call."

Kate arrives in New Canaan, Connecticut, at twilight, after a drive of more than two hundred miles. When she comes to Martin Cayhill's street, she realizes she was expecting some kind of massive compound, walled and gated, patrolled by dogs and suited men with handheld radios.

What she sees is a big house, five thousand square feet at a guess, with a big terraced yard to go with it. There's a fence and a gate, but no guards, just an intercom and a CCTV camera. She rolls down her window, presses a button, and says, "Hello?" There's a click and the gate swings open.

The driveway is paved with gray cobblestones and runs up in a gentle curve to the house. Kate gets out of her car and follows a bluestone walkway flanked by two ornamental cherry trees. Mrs. Cayhill is waiting for her at the front door.

"Welcome," she says. "We haven't been introduced. I'm Nicole. Martin is in the library."

Kate thinks, Of course there's a library.

She tries not to gawk at the foyer, which rises to a dizzying height and features a massive chandelier of black steel and glowing Edison bulbs. The same black steel makes up the risers and railings of the staircase that leads to the second floor. The stair treads are great slabs of stained hickory.

The library, though, is on the ground floor, down a wood-paneled hall. Mrs. Cayhill leads the way. There's a fire burning in a stone fireplace and three walls of built-in bookshelves. There's a desk across one corner, facing into the room, a brown leather sofa with two matching armchairs, and a mahogany coffee table.

Martin Cayhill rises from the sofa to greet Kate. He gives her a short tour of the room, finishing with the family photographs that fill the mantel above the fireplace—mostly shots of Bryan at various ages. Nicole Cayhill slips away and returns with a tray that holds a thermal pitcher and mugs. She pours them each a mug of hot chocolate.

The Cayhills sit together on the sofa, Kate in one of the chairs.

Mr. Cayhill says, "You were cryptic on the phone."

"I know," says Kate.

"You found out something about Bryan."

"Possibly. The problem is I'm not sure what I found."

Mr. Cayhill smiles. Kate takes it as encouragement.

"Bryan had a friend," she says. "A young woman who worked at the college. Whether they were more than friends, I don't know. I think they were. The young woman—she left home a few weeks before Bryan was killed. She left without telling her father or most of her friends."

"And you think she was involved with Bryan," Mr. Cayhill says. "Romantically."

"I can't be sure. She says she wasn't. But I've been in the house where she used to live with her father. I found this in her room."

Kate brings the diamond earring out of her handbag and passes it to Martin Cayhill.

"I think Bryan might have given it to her," she says. "I asked her about it, but she wouldn't give me a straight answer."

Mr. Cayhill hands the earring to his wife.

"This young woman," he says. "What's her name?"

"Jenny Wyler."

Mr. Cayhill's face is hard to read, and Kate isn't sure he recognized the earring. But she's positive that he's heard Jenny Wyler's name before. Mrs. Cayhill has too.

"You know about her," Kate says.

Mr. Cayhill reaches for his mug of hot chocolate. He holds it in front of him with two hands. After a time he says, "I've told you how I feel about my family's privacy."

"Yes, you have."

"So I need to know what your motives are. Are you here as someone writing a book?"

"I'm here as someone who wants to understand Bryan and what happened to him."

It's the right thing to say, and Kate means it. She watches Mr. Cayhill struggling with something. He wants to talk about his son, that's plain, but he doesn't know if he should.

"I'd like to trust you," he says. "But what I could tell you . . . it could never appear in print."

"It won't."

Martin Cayhill looks to his wife, and she gives him the tiniest toss of her head. As if to say it's up to him if he wants to spill family secrets.

Kate watches him make his decision. It plays out in a series of small movements: setting his mug down on the coffee table, adjusting his watch on his wrist, smoothing the front of his white dress shirt. Then he's ready to begin.

"I believe I told you Bryan's mother died when he was a young child," he says. "It was breast cancer that took her. Bryan was seven when the doctors gave her the diagnosis, and though we did our best to shield him from it, we couldn't hide what was happening. He witnessed her fight and her slow fading away. He had just turned nine when she passed.

"I saw the change in him after. It went through phases. First he withdrew, barely spoke, didn't want to eat. Then he started acting out: talking back to his teachers at school, getting into fights at recess. Thankfully the fighting didn't last, but there were other things as he grew older. Smoking cigarettes, stealing bottles from my liquor cabinet. I sent him to a therapist and I thought things were improving. In a sense they were. The smoking and drinking stopped.

"Then I met Nicole and we got engaged. Bryan thought I was trying to replace his mother. He was in high school at that point and spent a year neglecting his work. It was his way of protesting.

"That phase passed too. He was always a smart kid and I smoothed things over with his school so he wasn't held back. Maybe I shouldn't have.

"In any case, time went by and Bryan got interested in football. He made the varsity team in his senior year. He applied to colleges and was accepted at Seagate. But his acting out never went away. I started noticing things going missing: cash from my wallet, small items from around the house. Vases, knickknacks. Cuff links and a silver money clip I inherited from my father. Bryan didn't take them to sell them. He never wanted for anything. I always gave him spending money. I believe he took them to get my attention."

Mr. Cayhill shrugs. "Small things, as I said. Not worth bothering over. But at the end of last year Bryan came home for Christmas break. He was here for two weeks. And in early January I discovered that his mother's jewelry had gone missing.

"It was a valuable collection, everything I had given her over all the years since we first met. I kept it in a box in the safe in my office upstairs. And one day I saw it was gone. I phoned Bryan at Seagate and told him. He said it was a shame, but it was all insured, right? I didn't press him about it. After all, I didn't know for sure he was responsible."

Mrs. Cayhill has been quiet all this time, but now she pats her husband's knee and says gently, "We knew."

The diamond earring is on the coffee table. Martin Cayhill bends forward and picks it up.

"This is one of a pair I gave to Bryan's mother while we were dating. If he gave it to Jenny Wyler, she must have meant something to him. That makes me glad."

He turns his face away from Kate, and she thinks he's working to hold back tears. When he turns back, his eyes are dry.

"There's more to tell," Kate says to him.

He nods.

"About Jenny Wyler," she says. "You've heard of her before today. Have you met her?"

Mr. Cayhill takes a deep breath before continuing. "Bryan brought her here at the beginning of September, about a week after he returned to Seagate for the fall semester. He told us a story: she was pregnant, and he was the father, and they weren't going to get married but he wanted to do right by her. I don't know if it was true."

"She didn't look pregnant," Mrs. Cayhill says.

"They told us she was about three and a half months along," says Mr. Cayhill. "Which would mean he got her pregnant at the end of the spring semester. If they were telling the truth. Of course it could have been a lie. Another example of Bryan acting out—taking money from my wallet, but on a larger scale."

"You gave them money?" Kate asks.

"Ten thousand that day," Mr. Cayhill says. "Plus a promise of three thousand a month to be deposited in Miss Wyler's bank account. Doesn't seem like enough to raise a baby. But it's what they asked for. I didn't haggle over the amount. I wanted Bryan to understand that I would give him what he needed from me. I would hold back nothing." He looks at Kate with sad eyes. "Maybe you think I was trying to buy his love."

"No."

He spends a moment in silence, one hand closed around the earring, the other resting on the arm of the sofa.

Then: "You said you've spoken to Jenny."

"I saw her last night," Kate says. "If she's pregnant, she's still not showing."

The sadness in Martin Cayhill's eyes deepens as the implication sinks in. It's another thing he has to let go of: the idea that his son might have had a child.

Kate tries to offer him comfort. "I don't know if Bryan was dating Jenny, but I believe they were good friends. She was someone he could talk to. About you. About his mother. I think he asked you for money because he wanted to do something good for her, and I think the money helped her leave a situation where she wasn't happy."

Mr. Cayhill listens and nods once as if he's grateful. "She's welcome to it then." He opens his hand and looks down at the diamond earring. "I wonder if Bryan gave her all of his mother's jewelry and not just this. We looked for the jewelry in his house in Alexander, but we didn't find it."

Kate thinks of the sapphire earrings Jenny was wearing the night before.

"It's possible," she says. "I don't know."

Mr. Cayhill gazes at the fireplace for a time, lost in thought.

"His mother would have wanted him to have the jewelry anyway," he says. "So he was free to do with it what he liked." He turns back to Kate. "If you see Jenny again, ask her to come visit us, would you? And tell her that if she needs anything, she can call us."

22

Kate spends the night at the Cayhills' house. They insist. They don't want her making the long drive home in the dark.

The room they give her is on the second floor and has its own full bath. There are towels laid out for her, a toothbrush, toothpaste. Shampoo and conditioner. A bottle of spring water on the bedside table. The sheets on the bed are soft and smell of lilacs.

It's warm and the light of the bedside lamp has a yellow tinge that lends the room an unnatural feeling. Kate opens the window a crack and turns the lock on the knob of the hallway door. She undresses and gets under the covers and tries to settle in.

When she was sixteen her parents took her on a trip to see the Grand Canyon. They all slept in the same hotel room, her parents in one of the double beds, Kate in the other, and one night she woke to see a figure sitting at the foot of her bed.

A girl with dark hair and pale skin, dressed in a white blouse and a gray skirt.

Melissa Cornelle.

She didn't speak, or even look at Kate. And when Kate closed her eyes and opened them again, she was gone.

Kate has never seen her since, but sometimes it feels like she might. Like tonight.

A night-light would help, but the room doesn't have one.

Kate flicks off the lamp and takes her chances in the dark.

In the morning the Cayhills feed her French toast and send her on her way with a small cooler full of sandwiches and bottled water. She crosses into New York State, stops for gas, and drives north on the Thruway.

When she comes to the exit she needs to take to return to Alexander, she passes it by.

Around two in the afternoon, after more than four hours on the road, she leaves the Thruway and drives through the countryside among the foothills of the Adirondack Mountains. Her stopping point is Westernville, on the shore of Delta Lake. Population 832.

The road she wants is easy to find. There's a billboard just before the turn. Sometimes it advertises used cars. Today it's a white field and the words THIS SPACE FOR RENT.

The house is the same as she remembers. Maybe the metal roof is a bit rustier, the green paint on the clapboards a little more faded by the sun. The driveway has a strip of grass growing down its middle. The front door is decorated with a bronze silhouette of a rooster.

Kate doesn't knock. She walks around to the backyard instead. And sees a white-haired lady wearing an apron over a flowered dress. She's standing at a plastic patio table, carving a pumpkin into a jack-o'-lantern.

She's Alice Cornelle, Melissa's mother.

"Katy!" she says.

She lays her knife down, comes around the table, and enfolds Kate in a hug. Alice is in her late sixties, a heavy woman but full of energy.

She squeezes Kate, rubs her back, then draws away and holds her by the shoulders.

"Let me have a look at you," she says.

Kate takes the opportunity to do the same. Alice's face has a few more wrinkles than she remembers, but her eyes are as bright as always and she has the same toothy smile.

"Pretty as ever," she says to Kate. "What has it been? Two years?"

"I think you're right."

"Well, sit down and tell me the news."

Kate was fourteen the first time she heard from Alice Cornelle, more than three years after Melissa's death. A letter came in the mail on a day in late summer, and Kate's mother opened it and read it first before passing it along.

"She seems like a nice lady. But you don't have to answer it if you don't want to."

The letter read as if Alice and Kate were old friends. It was full of the mundane details of Alice's life and the goings-on in her family. She worked at the local library and her husband drove a delivery truck. There was only one line about Melissa, mentioning how much Alice missed her. There were many lines devoted to Melissa's older sister and younger brother.

Kate wrote a short reply in the same vein, talking about the house where they were living, her father's job, and things they'd done over the summer.

Alice sent more letters after that, often with many months in between. Kate didn't always answer, but after she turned eighteen she accepted an invitation from Alice to visit, making the drive from Ohio to upstate New York on her own.

Alice in person was the same as in her letters, a woman devoted to her family. Melissa's sister and brother were both married by then, and both had young children. Kate met them all at a family barbecue on a

Saturday afternoon. They were happy and welcoming. No one asked her to talk about the night Melissa died.

Since then, Kate has made a handful of other visits. Alice always asks her the same things: how her father is doing, if she's seeing anyone, when she's going to get married and start a family of her own. The last question gets delivered playfully, and Kate always deflects it by asking after Alice's grandchildren.

It's the same this time, and Alice is excited to talk about her new grandson, born five months ago. He's her seventh grandchild.

"Maybe the last," she says. "Sally tells me she's done, and Tim and his wife say the same. But I can always hope, can't I?"

"Yes you can," says Kate.

There's a lull in the conversation and the two of them sit looking into the yard. Alice has sheets drying on a clothesline. There's a squirrel foraging around an old tree stump.

Alice folds her hands over her stomach and says, "She would have turned forty this year." She's talking about Melissa, of course. "Sometimes I like to think she's out in the world living her life. Not thinking about us. Doing her own thing. That would be all right with me."

Kate likes the idea. Every now and then she imagines that her mother isn't really gone, that she's only moved away and might come back.

One idea slides into another, and an image of Jenny Wyler comes into Kate's mind. The girl who left her father's house to live her own life. Kate finds herself telling Alice about the Wylers: about Samuel Wyler asking her to look for his daughter, and what happened when she did. Which leads her to talk about Bryan Cayhill too, and her trip to see Bryan's parents.

"Those poor people," Alice says. "I've been following the news about their boy. I've been praying for them." She reaches for Kate's hand. "You've got yourself all caught up in it."

Kate looks away from her. "My agent wants me to write about it, but I don't know if I should."

"You'll make the right decision," Alice says.

"She wants me to write about all of them. Melissa too." Kate forces herself to meet Alice's eyes. There's nothing but kindness in them. "I wouldn't do it without your blessing. I'd never do anything that would hurt you."

The kindness doesn't waver. "My dear girl, you should do whatever is best for you. I trust you." She squeezes Kate's hand and they sit together watching the sheets on the line sway gently in the wind.

After a while Kate stands. "I should go."

"Nonsense," Alice says. "Stay for dinner."

Kate holds firm. "I need to get back. But next time . . ."

Alice pushes herself up from her chair and walks with Kate to her car. They embrace again before Kate climbs in behind the wheel. Alice stands with her hand on the car door as if she's going to shut it, but before she does, she says:

"The girl, Jenny—you haven't spoken to her father since you found her?"

"No."

"What are you going to tell him?"

Kate hesitates. "I don't know. I think she would rather I didn't tell him anything. She doesn't want him to know where she is."

Alice leans closer. There's an intensity in her expression that Kate has never seen before.

"That man has got to be sick with worry," Alice says. "You have to tell him you've seen his daughter and she's safe. Even if you leave him in the dark about the rest."

The drive from Westernville to Alexander takes Kate along the shore of Delta Lake and through a city called Rome. From there it's a straight shot on a two-lane road that runs south past a prison and a series of little towns: Vernon Center, Knoxboro, Augusta, Solsville.

She's south of Solsville when her cellphone rings. She has it charging on the passenger seat and she can see the call is from her father. She lets it go to voicemail.

Less than a mile on, as she's rolling through the town of Madison, she hears the ping of a text. She looks down at the screen to read it.

Talk to me, it says.

It's not from her father. It's from Devin Falko.

Another ping: I'm worried about you.

"Are you sick with worry though?" she says aloud.

She's had her radio tuned to a rock station, but it's turning staticky. She switches it off, slows down, pulls into the parking lot of a funeral home.

Sick with worry. That's what Alice said about Jenny Wyler's father. He had to be sick with worry about his daughter.

But was he?

Kate gave Samuel Wyler her cellphone number when they talked on Tuesday. Now it's Sunday and he hasn't called her. Not for a progress report, not for anything.

He's not acting like someone who's worried.

She tries calling him now, in the lot with the engine idling. Gets no answer. She leaves a message asking him to return the call.

Maybe he's a patient man. Maybe he doesn't want to bother her. Maybe.

It's a puzzle.

Kate gets back on the road under a gray sky. There's only six miles to go, and it takes her less than ten minutes. But it's enough time to begin to doubt herself, to wonder if she made a mistake.

On Bird River Road, when her father's house comes into view, she has the sinking feeling she should never have gone searching for Jenny Wyler.

23

There are three cars in the driveway: her father's Volvo, Lee Tennick's Civic, and a cruiser with the markings of the Alexander police department. Kate parks on the grass to avoid blocking anyone in.

Vera Landen is talking with Tennick in front of his RV. Kate's father is observing from the porch of the house.

Kate's arrival disrupts things. Chief Landen spots her and comes striding toward her. Kate gets out of her car and waits.

"Where have you been?" Landen says.

"What's going on?" Kate counters.

"I hardly know where to begin," Landen says. "But I think we should talk at the station. Maybe then you'll take me seriously."

She grips Kate by the arm and starts to lead her toward the cruiser, but before they reach it, Kate's father steps down from the porch.

"Vera," he says. "You can talk to her here. Or not at all."

His voice is stern and Landen stops. She looks grim. The two of them stare each other down, arguing without using any words. Landen is the one who relents.

"Fine," she says.

They end up talking in the house. Kate's father has made coffee, and Landen pours some for herself and goes looking in a cupboard for sugar. By the time she sits down at the kitchen table she seems to have her anger under control.

She's dressed more formally than usual, in a dress shirt, blazer, and slacks. The clothes are crisp, but she looks tired.

"Are you going to tell me what happened?" Kate asks her. "Or will I have to assume the worst?"

"I'm curious," Landen says, stirring her coffee with a spoon. "What would the worst be?"

"Something happened to Jenny Wyler."

Landen arches her eyebrows. "That's interesting. When's the last time you saw Jenny?"

"Friday night."

"And you haven't spoken to her since? You don't know where she is?"

"Is she missing?"

Landen sips her coffee before she answers. "There was a break-in at Jenny's apartment in Syracuse. Or I should say, the apartment where she was staying. It was rented in the name of one of Diana Perez's friends. You've met Miss Perez."

"Yes."

"The break-in happened a little before one a.m. Saturday morning. It was Jenny's father, Samuel Wyler. He kicked the door in. Jenny was there with a young man, Ian Gardner. Ian went to see what the commotion was about, and Jenny wasn't far behind him. I believe she stopped to put her shirt back on. That was the scene that confronted Mr. Wyler: his daughter and a boy coming out of a bedroom. He came to his own conclusions about what they'd been up to. Do you know what kind of man Mr. Wyler is?"

"I have an idea," Kate says.

"He went into a rage, and Ian took the brunt of it. The boy suffered a broken arm. A shattered knee. He took several blows to the face. Lost some teeth. He's looking rough right now."

"Oh my god."

"Jenny tried to get in between them and got a black eye for her trouble. One of the neighbors called 911. Fortunately. When the police arrived, they found Mr. Wyler trying to force Jenny into his car."

"But they stopped him."

Landen nods.

Kate can feel herself shaking. She wants to get out of this room, away from Landen. It takes an effort of will to stay in her chair.

"He came to see me," Kate says. "Wanted me to look for his daughter."

Landen gives her another nod. "Tennick told me as much, just now."

"I thought he was a grieving father. I didn't know what he would do. But I led him right to her, didn't I?"

"It seems that way," Landen says. "When you went to look for Jenny Friday night, did you tell Mr. Wyler you were going?"

"No."

"He must have followed you. I suspect that was his plan all along. He couldn't find her on his own, and he thought you might have better luck."

"What does he say?" Kate asks. "Have you questioned him?"

"The Syracuse police have him in custody. He's not talking. They took statements from Jenny and Ian. Ian was the one who told them you had been asking questions about Bryan Cayhill. That's why they contacted me. They thought there might be some connection to Bryan's murder."

Kate can still feel herself shaking. She gets up from the table and runs a glass of water from the tap. Takes a long drink.

Sitting down again, she says, "Is there a connection?"

Vera Landen regards her coolly from across the table. "A connection between Samuel Wyler and the murder of Bryan Cayhill?"

"It's not as wild as it sounds," Kate says. "Wyler found Ian with his daughter and gave Ian a beating. If he found out Bryan was sleeping with Jenny, is it crazy to think he might have killed him?"

"Was Bryan sleeping with Jenny?"

Kate shrugs. "She told me they were just friends. But her father might have *thought* they were sleeping together—"

Landen slams her open palm on the table. "Just stop," she says. "You don't know what you're doing. Samuel Wyler isn't a murderer. He's not Merkury. He's an overprotective father with a violent temper. He approached me weeks ago when his daughter left home. He wanted me to find her. I turned him away because it looked to me like a nineteen-year-old girl striking out on her own, tired of dealing with her father's bullshit. Which is exactly what it was. If you had come to me, I could have told you. If you had informed me that Jenny knew Bryan Cayhill, I would have sought her out and talked to her. Now I can't."

"Why not?" Kate asks.

"Because she's run off again. No one seems to know where. I imagine she's afraid. Afraid of what will happen if her father gets let out on bail. Which he very well might." Landen brings her palm down on the table again, gently this time. Her voice takes on a quiet intensity. "You need to stop screwing around," she says. "I'm serious. Before you cause more damage."

24

When Kate was eleven, after Melissa Cornelle, her parents took her to see a doctor named Andrea Walker. "She's a psychologist," Kate's mother said. "Someone people go to when they've been through a bad experience and they need to talk about it."

Kate went to four or five appointments, and she remembers bits and pieces of them. She remembers Dr. Walker smiling at her and trying to get to know her, asking about her favorite things. What kind of food she liked, what TV shows, what movies.

She remembers telling Dr. Walker about the night she found Melissa— not the real version, but the nice, clean version where the killer spoke three words to her and she said nothing to him at all.

"Do you know what trauma is?" the doctor asked. "It's a reaction we have, an emotional reaction, to an event like the one you went through. The thing to understand is that however you feel when you think about what happened—if you're sad or afraid or nervous—these things are normal, and we can find ways to deal with them. How does that sound?"

"Okay," Kate said.

"So can you tell me how you feel when you think about that night?"

Kate remembers the doctor waiting for her to answer, how quiet it was in the office. She remembers how soft her own voice sounded.

"Sometimes I feel like I need to get away from myself."

"Thank you for telling me," Dr. Walker said. "This is something we can talk about. Why do you feel you need to get away?"

"I don't know."

"It's okay to say it, whatever it is. Sometimes it's hard to deal with problems we have, and we feel it would be easier to run away. Could that be what you're feeling?"

"I guess."

"Are there other reasons we might want to get away from ourselves?"

Kate remembers a wave of anxiety passing through her, because she was edging a little too close to the truth. But sometimes you have to be daring.

"If we feel ashamed?" she said.

The doctor nodded. "Sometimes if something terrible happens to another person, but not to us, we can feel guilty or ashamed," she said. "But you're not responsible for what happened to Melissa. In a way, the two of you went through an ordeal together, and you're still here and she's not, but that's not your fault. It doesn't make you a bad person."

These words are etched into Kate's mind, because they marked the moment when, however briefly, her anxiety gave way to respect. Dr. Walker was clever. She had guessed the truth—that deep down Kate believed she was a bad person.

Of course, it wasn't just something she believed. She *was* a bad person. If the doctor knew everything, she would have to agree.

Would a good person have talked to the man who killed Melissa Cornelle?

Would a good person have touched Melissa's hair when he told her to?

And why would he have left Kate alive, if she wasn't a bad person like him?

"I need to ask you something," Dr. Walker said. "This feeling that you need to get away from yourself. How often does it come to you?"

This was a question not so different from the others, but to Kate it seemed as if the mood of their discussion had gotten darker. They had been talking about important things. Serious things. But now they were touching on something dire, something grave.

The true answer was *Often. All the time.*

But Kate said, "I don't know."

Dr. Walker nodded again. "What would it be like to get away from yourself?" she asked.

Kate couldn't think of a good answer. This was what she was trying to figure out. How to do it—how to get away.

"Whatever the truth is, you don't have to be afraid to tell me," Dr. Walker said. "Do you ever think about hurting yourself?"

She said it mildly, and her expression was normal and calm. But Kate knew that people could lie with their faces, and sometimes they didn't use the words they really meant. Dr. Walker didn't mean "hurting." She was asking Kate if she ever thought about killing herself.

Which meant Dr. Walker wasn't so clever after all. Because whatever "getting away" meant, it wasn't the same as killing yourself. That was obvious.

This was when Kate understood that Dr. Walker wouldn't be able to help her.

She would have to figure things out on her own.

Kate's bedroom in her father's house is twelve feet by fourteen. She retreats there after Vera Landen has finished questioning her and gone away.

It's eight o'clock by then, and her father starts cooking a late dinner. When it's ready—she can smell it—he knocks on her door and asks if she wants to come out and eat. But this room is all she can manage. Even twelve by fourteen is too big. Kate wants to move the walls in closer and do away with the door altogether.

When she doesn't give him an answer, her father leaves and comes back with a plate for her. He knocks again, waits an interval, comes in and puts the plate on the desk. It's roasted tilapia and rice pilaf.

But he's not just delivering food. He has something to say.

"This, what you're doing, it isn't good for you."

Kate is sitting up in bed. Lying down would be a complete surrender.

"You know I like having you here," her father says. "But with everything going on, I think it might be better if you go back. To Ohio. Get some distance. Figure out what you want to do. Write another book, sure. But not about this. You're too close to it. I worry you're going to get hurt."

He's standing by the desk with his hands on his hips. She sits with a pillow between her back and the headboard and considers how best to get him to leave.

"I'm fine, Dad," she says.

It's not the words that do the trick, it's the cold tone she puts into her voice.

He sighs and goes out, leaving the door of the bedroom open. She listens to him walking away, his footsteps on the hardwood floor.

The open door is wrong. Kate bears it for a minute or two, then slides off the bed and crosses the room to close it.

She picks up the plate her father left her. Cuts off a piece of fish with her fork and tastes it. A small piece. Enough to know it's good and she doesn't want to eat it.

Her phone pings in her pocket. A text from Lee Tennick.

She'll be all right, it says. Let's think positive.

He's talking about Jenny Wyler.

Kate taps out a reply: Maybe. Either way I fucked up.

The way I remember it, there were two of us. We both fucked up.

Which is valiant, but untrue. Chasing after Jenny was Kate's doing. No way around it.

She swipes her screen and finds her text thread with Devin. There's nothing new from him. Just his last message: I'm worried about you.

He's probably in his room at the Seagate Inn. She's not going there. She shouldn't go anywhere. She should stay here and suffer.

You can't get away from yourself.

Dr. Walker told her that, in their last session together, before Kate refused to go anymore.

"The good news is, you don't have to," the doctor added. "You can learn to get along with yourself instead."

It sounded profound, and she seemed pleased to have come up with it.

Kate wanted to smack her in the face.

Maybe you can't get away from yourself. But you can try.

Sunday night. Kate lies down in her clothes on top of the covers. She closes her eyes, but she doesn't fall asleep. At some point she gives up and stares at the white ceiling.

She makes it to ten o'clock, but then she can't keep still anymore.

She takes a breath and holds it—her mother's trick for getting out of bed. The pressure builds up inside her. When it's too much she lets it burst out and just like that she's on her feet.

Her coat is hung over the back of her desk chair. She puts it on. Puts on her shoes. Then she slips the latch of the casement window, swings it open, and climbs out.

There's no doubt about her destination, but she takes her time getting there. She does some thinking along the way.

She can picture Jenny Wyler, the way she looked when they spoke in the lobby of the Hotel Skyler. She seemed happy living on her own, away from her father.

And where was she now? No one knew. That's what Landen said. Jenny was on the run. Afraid.

Where would she go? What would happen to her?

Kate has a powerful imagination. Walking along in the dark beside the stream, it's easy for her to assume the worst. It's easy to picture Jenny lying dead somewhere. Like Melissa Cornelle.

There's an unsettling moment, when Kate sees the silhouette of the oak tree in the distance, when she thinks she'll find Jenny there on the ground.

It's only her imagination, of course. When she reaches the tree, the ground is empty. Nothing but fallen leaves, and the limb that split off from the trunk.

Kate remembers coming back here once when she was eleven, the night before her family moved away from Alexander. She had to sneak out in the dark, because her mother watched her closely during the day. But she couldn't keep watch all the time. Everyone has to sleep.

There was nothing to see here then, only a leftover twist of yellow crime-scene tape to mark what had happened.

Kate remembers that night. Lying down on her back under the tree. Like Melissa. With her arms stretched out.

Thinking about what it would be like to be dead.

Thinking about *him* and the kind way he spoke to her.

You're very brave.

She remembers facing the truth about herself. That it was her idea to kneel down by Melissa's body. Her idea to touch Melissa's skin. He didn't make her do those things.

And she didn't mind talking to him. She wanted to. She liked it.

Lying on the ground that night, she realized she could never tell anyone the truth. What would they think of her?

Tonight Kate doesn't get down on the ground. She stands by the stream listening to the current. The moon is waning, but it's still three-quarters full, and bright enough to see by.

She can see some things very clearly.

She was careless when she agreed to help Samuel Wyler. Her carelessness cost Ian Gardner a beating and Jenny Wyler a black eye. And it might have cost Jenny more if the police hadn't shown up when they did.

It still might cost her much more—if her father is set free, if he finds her again.

Kate is responsible for this. She has to face it. She knows things she didn't know when she was a child.

One of them is this: The first step in getting away from yourself is acknowledging your own nature. Accepting your guilt.

The night air is cold on her face. She can hear the stream flowing steadily. Her body is tired from the driving she did today. She should return to the house and try to sleep.

There's nothing here, no comfort to be found.

She stays anyway.

Hard to say how much time passes. Maybe the rhythm of the current hypnotizes her. But the next thing she's aware of is the crackle of footsteps in the leaves. And a voice.

"You're brave," it says.

25

Kate knows the voice, but she spins around to see.

It's Devin Falko.

A chill runs over the back of her neck, colder than the night air.

"Why did you say that to me?"

His brow furrows in confusion. "I don't get it. I said you were brave."

"Why?"

"Because you're out here. At this place, in the dark, by yourself."

He steps closer to her and she instinctively steps back.

"Are you screwing with me?" she says. She can feel her heart racing.

He starts to move closer again and she holds her palm out to ward him off.

"Don't."

"What's wrong?" he asks.

"Why are you here?"

"You've been dodging my messages. I told you I was worried about you."

"How did you find this spot? Have you been here before?"

He spreads his arms out. "Kate, you've told me the story. How you came out here that night. I followed the stream. It wasn't hard."

Her heart rate isn't slowing. She wants to get away from him, but if she backs up any farther she'll be in the water.

"Look," he says. "I went to the house. Your father let me in. He went to your room to call you and realized you weren't there. You left the window unlocked. He figured you'd be here. I mean, where would you go? He was going to come and look for you himself, but I told him I'd do it."

Devin's face in the moonlight is pleasant and his voice is the voice of reason. Kate doesn't trust any of it. He's standing five feet away from her, but it's too close. She makes a shooing gesture and he steps back.

"You shouldn't be here," she says.

"Why?" he asks her.

"It's presumptuous."

"Presumptuous?"

"I don't want you here."

"Kate, what's this about? What's going on?"

She realizes there's been something building up in her for days. Maybe it's why her heart is going crazy in her chest.

She can't hold things in any longer.

"*You lied to me*," she says. Her voice is not especially loud, but it's fierce.

Again Devin looks confused. "About what?"

"Shouldn't be hard for you to figure out. How many lies have you told me?"

"Kate—"

"About *her*. Melissa. You taught here at Seagate when she was a student."

There's a flash of something in his eyes. It looks a lot like anger.

"Where did you hear that?" he asks.

"From the chief of police—Vera Landen. Is that what's important, where I heard it?"

Devin bows his head and smooths his fingers through his hair. When he's done, the anger is gone from him. He's all sweet reasonableness again.

"Listen to me," he says. "I didn't tell you because it was meaningless. A coincidence. And I knew you would have a hard time seeing it that way. In retrospect, I can see that keeping it from you was wrong."

"Oh, can you? What else have you kept from me?"

He's slow to reply and there's a subtle change in his posture. A lowering of his shoulders. He's the injured party now, the one who's been put-upon.

"There's nothing else, Kate."

"Are you sure? Because in *retrospect* I have questions. Like how did we meet?"

He looks at her sidelong. "You know how we met. It was after your book came out, at one of your readings."

"In Columbus," she says. "Where I lived. How did you end up there?"

"I had a teaching job there, until I quit and opened my practice. You know this."

"How did you end up at my reading?"

"I saw a write-up in the paper when I was looking for something to do that night. What do you think, Kate? Do you think I arranged my life in order to meet you? Do you know how paranoid that sounds?"

There are things about Devin Falko that have always irritated Kate. One of them is the condescending tone he sometimes falls into. Another is when he uses words like "paranoid."

"Don't act like I'm crazy," she says.

He lets out a sigh. "Here we go."

"What does that mean—'here we go'?"

"It means you have certain habits, Kate. When someone challenges you, you get defensive. You accuse them of thinking you're crazy."

"I guess you've got me figured out," she says. "How about we talk about you—"

He points a finger at her. "This is another thing you do. Go on the attack."

Condescending. But Kate doesn't let him put her off. If he wants to call it an attack, she'll attack.

"You're seventeen years older than me," she says. "What does that say about you? How much did you know about me before we met? Did you know about the eleven-year-old girl who found the body? Is that who you wanted to meet when you came to my reading? Were you thinking about her when you asked me out for a drink?"

Devin shakes his head. "You were twenty-five when we met, Kate. You weren't a child."

"You didn't think about that girl at all?" she says. "No, not you. Because you're healthy and normal."

Another head shake. "I'm not going to be drawn into this, Kate. This drama."

She steps forward until she's close enough to touch him.

"You're so, so normal."

She looks into his eyes and pushes up his shirt sleeve. Traces a finger over the scars on his arm.

"Stop it," he says.

"What about Melissa? She was younger than you too. Not by seventeen years, but still. Did you have her in one of your classes? Did she come to your office to talk about her grades? She was beautiful. And you, the handsome young professor."

"This isn't real, this tale you're spinning," Devin says. "I didn't know her."

"Are you sure? Is that what Chief Landen's going to find out when she looks into it?"

"Why would she—"

Kate is watching Devin's face in the moonlight. He's putting things together.

"Oh god, does she think I'm *him*? Is that what she told you? Does everything with you come back to Merkury?" He takes Kate by the wrist, but gently. "Is that what you think of me, that I'm a murderer?"

Sadness and disappointment in his eyes. The feelings could be genuine. Or not.

"I have to admit, I didn't see this one coming," he says. "I knew you had trust issues, but this—"

When she hears "trust issues," she wants to hit him. She tries to pull away, but he keeps hold of her wrist.

"I'm not him, Kate. I'm a man who loves you. That's all."

She makes a fist with her left hand and pounds his chest with the side of it. Tears her other arm away from him. She puts some space between them again, her footsteps stirring up the leaves on the ground.

"You're right about one thing," she says. "I don't trust you. I don't want to be out here with you. You should go back. Back to the inn, and then back to Ohio. I don't want to see you anymore. There's no reason for you to stay here."

She doesn't know what to expect from him: rage or pleading or indifference. He goes with acceptance.

"If that's what you want, Kate," he says. "But at least let me walk you back. I don't like you being out here alone."

She stays where she is. "I don't want to walk with you. I'm fine out here on my own. I'm *brave*, remember?"

Maybe the word means something to him. Maybe he's a liar. Maybe he's the killer she talked to when she was eleven. But if he is, he doesn't show it. There's nothing to read in his face, unless it's sorrow.

He turns away from her.

Kate stands with the tree at her back and watches him, a figure receding into the dark.

After a while she loses him in shadows. He could be waiting for her out there. She thinks about cutting through the woods and making for the road. Returning to the house that way.

But she's brave.

She gives him ten minutes and sets out. The stream is there to guide her. The grass is taller than when she was a child, and the stars above seem brighter. She carries on and comes to the place where the ground slopes up. The flagstone path is the same as ever. It leads her to her father's backyard.

She walks around to the front of the house. Devin's car is not in the driveway. She steps onto the porch and finds the front door unlocked. Her father is in the kitchen puttering around, wiping down the counters.

"Devin was here," he says. "Did he find you?"

"He found me," Kate says. "I'd rather you didn't let him in the house again."

Her father nods without interrupting his work, and she leaves him there and heads to her room. She closes the door behind her, but she doesn't take off her coat or her shoes.

Sitting on the edge of the bed, she scuffs a heel over the floorboards.

"Who do you think you're kidding?" she whispers to herself.

Every nerve in her body is lit up bright like the stars. There's a buzzing in her skin like an electrical current. Her heart is beating slower than it was in the woods, but faster than it should.

She won't sleep, not like this. She can scarcely sit still.

She needs to get away from herself, and she knows how. No one ever told her, but she figured it out. It's simple: you think of something self-destructive you could do, and then you do it.

Sometimes it's difficult to come up with something, but not tonight. She knows just the thing.

Bouncing up from the bed, Kate checks her pockets for her keys and phone.

The casement window is waiting.

She goes out into the dark and skirts around the house to her car. Turns the key in the ignition and drives.

* * *

Devin Falko has his shirt sleeve rolled up and his knife in his hand.

He did what Kate wanted: walked back to the house, got in his car, rumbled down the driveway to Bird River Road. He turned left and made for downtown Alexander. Drove two miles before he turned back.

So not exactly what Kate wanted.

Now he's parked on the shoulder of the road east of the house. His car's engine and lights are off. He's holding tight to the knife, but he hasn't unfolded it yet. There's still time to stop and try something else.

The windows are all up. He could scream and no one would hear him. But screaming won't be enough. He knows it won't.

Things are slipping. It might have been a mistake to go see Kate tonight. It was obviously a mistake to see her in that place, which is so freighted with meaning for her. Over the years Devin has seen many versions of her, but none quite like the one he saw tonight.

This one was almost a stranger.

Or then again, no. This one was a version of Kate who saw *him* as a stranger.

Devin slips the folded knife into his shirt pocket. He opens the driver's door and steps out. The road is empty. He pushes the door shut and moves around to the passenger side. Leans against the fender. There are trees out there in the dark, on the far side of an open field.

He turns to look at the moon in the southern sky. He studies it, the mottled surface. All those imperfections, those are mountains and craters and plains of solid lava. You'd need a telescope to see them properly, but it's a wonder you can see them at all across all that distance.

The world is a wondrous place. Full of beauty.

It's almost enough to make you think that things will work themselves out.

And that you don't have to slice your skin open with a sharp object.

Devin laughs at the thought, there by the roadside.

This is part of it. Part of the ritual. Pretending that you might not do it.

He rubs the thumb of his right hand over the scars on his other arm. Feels the ridges, the random pattern. All those straight lines intersecting.

He takes the knife from his pocket and folds out the black steel blade. Thinks of Kate and what he wanted and what he's lost.

He lays the blade against his skin. Lightly. This is part of it too.

There's no rush.

A long, shallow stroke is what you want. The fine edge drawn across the skin. You do it right, it barely hurts. It's not so much about the pain.

He waits on the cusp, under the steady moon.

And he's ready.

Now.

26

Devin adjusts his grip on the handle of the knife and glides it across his skin like a bow on the strings of a violin.

A red seam opens in his arm.

He feels the sharp intake of his own breath.

You do it once, you want to do it again. And he does.

The sweetness is impossible to describe. The relief.

You are not lost.

She is not lost.

You can recover from this. You can get everything back.

She left before, and she came back to you.

You need to handle her right. That's always been true.

You've already started. You didn't argue with her tonight. She told you she wanted you to go, and you went. That was good.

You told her what you needed to tell her.

I'm a man who loves you.

That reached her.

It must have reached her.

You can still get what you want.

Devin pulls the blade across his skin one more time, and that's enough. No need to overdo it.

There are tissues in the car. He gets back in and wipes the knife clean. Folds it and lays it on the passenger seat. There's blood seeping from his arm. He lays a tissue over the cuts and leaves it there.

He starts the car and rolls down his window. The air smells clean. He tips his head back and closes his eyes.

He's tired. He could almost sleep right here.

The rasp of another engine starting stirs him and his eyes come open automatically. He has a good view of Kate's father's house, roughly two hundred yards distant. There's a car moving in the driveway, and he watches it swing its back end around and aim itself toward the road.

There's a light on a pole at the end of the driveway, so he can see the car plainly when it turns left and heads west. Away from him.

It's Kate's car.

Too soon to talk to her again. She needs time to cool off. But he's curious about where she's going so late.

Snap decision. Curiosity wins out.

He switches on his headlights and follows her.

She turns south at the first stop sign she comes to, as if her destination is downtown Alexander. Devin's hopes rise, thinking she might be bound for the Seagate Inn, going to see him. He knows her moods and how they can change.

But when she reaches downtown she passes the inn. The stoplights are blinking amber at this hour. She rolls through them, still southbound, passing the campus and the stadium and the hospital. The EMERGENCY sign is lit up bright over the ambulance bay, big white letters on a red background.

After the hospital she slows to make a turn, west on Hilton Road. In half a mile she turns again. There's a tennis court on the right, a clubhouse on the left. Then a series of gray two-story apartment buildings.

The second-floor apartments have balconies. Here's one with colored Christmas lights strung along its railing. College kids talking with red cups in their hands.

Kate finds a parking space and slots her car into it. Devin hangs back and watches.

Kate remembers the building from the last time she was here, but that was during the day. She expected it to be dead on a Sunday night, but there's techno music blaring from stereo speakers, and someone's grilling burgers on a patio. The glass doors at the front entrance are locked, but when she moves around to the side there's a steel door propped open with a concrete block.

Her footsteps ring on the metal stairs and there's an antiseptic smell in the air. At the top of the stairs another steel door opens into a long hallway. She remembers the number. Apartment 207.

Noise on the other side of the door: music and shouting and video-game gunfire. Kate knocks with her knuckles and then with the heel of her hand. Loud.

Thump, thump, thump, thump, thump.

The kid who comes to the door towers over her. He's wearing sweat-pants cut off at the knees and no shirt. He's got a tattoo of a wolf's head on one bicep and a gaming control in his hand.

He gives her a wide-eyed look and says, "Yeah?"

"I'm looking for Travis," she tells him.

He rounds back into the apartment and yells, "Travis!" Then returns to his spot on the sofa, where there's another one just like him. The two of them go back to their game, thumbs flying over the controls, blowing away enemy soldiers on the big screen in front of them.

Kate steps inside and goes searching. The first door she comes to is an empty bedroom, the second is a bathroom with towels over the shower rod and socks on the floor. Behind the third door she finds Travis Pollard at a desk typing on a laptop. He's facing away from her.

She picks up a pillow from his bed and tosses it at him. A square hit between the shoulder blades. He spins in his chair with a scowl on his face, but when he recognizes her, his expression softens. He pulls earbuds from his ears and gets up. He's wearing jeans and a blue dress shirt with all but one of the buttons undone.

"What are you doing?" Kate asks him.

It takes a moment for the question to register. Travis glances at the laptop and then back at her.

"Sociology paper," he says. "It's about mass media and ethnic stereotypes—"

Kate stops him with a raised hand. "I don't really care. Do you have some time for me?"

He's still trying to make sense of her sudden appearance. "Time?"

"Try to keep up. Do you have time. To spend. With me. Right now?"

"Sure," he says. "Like another interview?"

She moves closer and reaches out to trace her fingers from his Adam's apple down to his sternum. "Not an interview, Travis," she says.

You think of something self-destructive, and then you do it.

She watches the gleam come into his eyes. His slow-dawning smile. She feels his right hand when it finds her waist. His touch is overly familiar. Arrogant. He runs his palm up and down her side. Leans into her as if he's going to kiss her.

She pushes him back. "Not here, you idiot. Take me somewhere."

Devin sees Kate come around the side of the building. While she was inside, he moved his car to a parking spot where he can watch her without worrying too much about being seen.

He feels a twist in his stomach when he realizes she's not alone.

There's a college kid with her, tall, blond, obviously a jock. He's buttoning up his shirt as he walks behind her. Wearing a mischievous grin.

He gets into her car on the passenger side. She slides behind the wheel.

Devin places his hand over the knife on the seat beside him.

An unconscious gesture.

He gives them a head start out of the lot and follows.

She drives back to Main Street and turns north. There's the hospital again, with the EMERGENCY sign. There's the stadium and the gym and the campus. No one on the sidewalks. No traffic to wait for at the stoplights when they pass through downtown.

When they're far enough north, Main Street isn't Main Street anymore. It's Route 12B. There's a grocery store on the edge of town. A gas station with glaring white lights and a pickup parked at one of the pumps.

Then letters in red neon that spell out YOUR MOTEL and VACANCY.

The motel is a long, low building painted dark green. Kate turns into the lot and parks at the north end near the office.

Devin drives by without slowing.

A quarter mile on, he finds a feed store and pulls into the empty lot. He stops long enough to shift into park, but he knows what he's going to do. He's not staying here.

The tissue he put over his cuts is stuck to his arm, held there by his dried blood. He peels it away, wads it up, tosses it into the back seat.

He shifts into drive and gets back on 12B.

When he reaches the motel, he parks all the way down at the south end. There are four other cars and several empty spaces between his car and Kate's.

He can't see the office from here, but he sees Kate and the jock when they stroll along the front of the building and stop at one of the rooms in the middle. The jock has the keycard. He goes in first and Kate slips in after him and closes the door.

*　*　*

The room has a queen-size bed. Brown carpet on the floor. Walls covered in wood paneling. But it seems clean and doesn't smell of smoke.

Good enough, Kate thinks.

She drops her handbag on the chair by the door and lays her coat over it. Travis tosses the keycard onto one of the night tables and turns to face her. He's smiling. He's got the same arrogant gleam in his eye as he had at his apartment.

He reaches for her, grips her waist again.

"Can you behave?" she asks him. "This only works if you behave."

He starts unbuttoning her blouse. "Sure," he says.

She pushes his hands away. "I can undress myself. Why don't you take off your shirt."

She can tell he's not used to being told what to do, but he goes along. Makes a performance of it, working the buttons, pulling the shirt off one shoulder and then the other. His chest and abs are well defined. He tosses the shirt on the bed and stands still for a moment so she can admire him. He's no stranger to being admired.

But he's impatient. Eager to go on. He reaches for her.

"Wait," she says. "Get down on your knees."

Travis laughs at the idea, but when he sees that she's serious he does what he's told. It puts him beneath her, which is what she wants. She's looking down at him as she slips free of her blouse and her bra. She steps into him and kneads his shoulders as his lips find her stomach.

His mouth moves higher and his knuckles trail along her skin. His fingers dip inside the waistband of her jeans, but he doesn't try to pull them down, so he's capable of learning.

Kate moves her hands to his head and guides him to her breasts. Feels her nipples stiffen under his tongue, first one and then the other. She lets out a gasp. He takes it as an invitation to use his teeth.

She tangles the fingers of her right hand in his hair and pulls his head back firmly until he's looking up at her.

"You were right," she says. "What I saw when I was young, it messed me up. Do you want to see how it messed me up?"

He doesn't smirk but he doesn't take her seriously either.

"Sure," he says.

She pulls his head back farther to get his attention.

"Don't say 'Sure' to me. It's yes or it's no."

His blue eyes stare up at her. "Yes."

She can feel the same eagerness in him, but now it's mixed with uncertainty, curiosity.

"Good," she says. "You'll get what you want, believe me, but you'll get it on my terms. The main thing is, if I'm a little rough with you, that doesn't mean you get to be rough with me. Do you understand?"

"Yes."

She lets loose his hair and brings her palm down to his ear, his cheek, his neck.

"I think we'll get along then," she says.

27

Lee Tennick can't get to sleep on Sunday night.

He's thinking of Jenny Wyler and where she might be. And of Ian Gardner, who took a beating from her father.

But mostly he's thinking of Clay McKellar, who is gone beyond retrieving, who has family in Texas, a mother and a sister who are going to miss him for the rest of their lives.

Tennick wonders if there will ever be any justice for Clay. No one is focusing on him. He's an afterthought, a footnote to the murder of Bryan Cayhill. That's the way Vera Landen seems to be treating him. Tennick tried to talk to her about him today, in between answering her questions about Jenny and Ian. She seemed annoyed to hear Clay's name.

Landen still has the kid's cellphone and laptop computer. She's supposed to give them to Tennick so he can send them to Clay's mother. But all Landen would tell him today was that he would get them in due course.

Which was a polite way of telling him to fuck off.

There's probably nothing of use on the cellphone or the laptop, but Tennick would like to get his hands on them anyway. He has fantasies of searching through Clay's photos and finding an image of Merkury. Something grainy, taken at night, but just clear enough to make out . . .

It's not going to happen. But what Tennick does have are the things he collected from Clay's apartment, the personal stuff from his desk. He hasn't shipped those things to Texas yet. They're in the barn.

He goes out to get them. It's chilly and the only light in the Summerlin house is coming from an upstairs window. Kate's car is gone from the driveway.

Inside the barn door, there's a switch on the wall. It turns on a single bulb up in the rafters. Off to one side are stacked boxes destined for Goodwill, but the stuff Tennick wants is heaped in a wicker laundry basket on top of them.

He carries the basket into his RV and starts unloading it on his Formica table.

The first things to come out are three framed photographs: High-school Clay in a marching band uniform, his arms around two of his friends. Younger Clay sitting by a Christmas tree unwrapping a present, with a girl in footie pajamas who must be his sister. An older man and woman at a party—Clay's parents before his father died.

Under the photos are books and a pile of papers. Exams and essays. Tennick wonders if these are worth sending home to Clay's mother.

At the bottom of the pile he comes across a copy of the script for the film Clay was working on. *VICTIM/KILLER* by Lavana Khatri. Tennick is not going to send it to Mrs. McKellar, not with that title.

But maybe there's something here, something worth knowing. The margins are full of handwritten notes. Tennick folds back the title page and starts to read: FADE IN: EXTERIOR, SHACK IN THE WOODS – NIGHT . . .

* * *

Devin Falko resists for as long as he can.

He knows what he should do. Drive back to the Seagate Inn and stay there until the morning. Then get out of this town. It's simple. There's nothing to be gained by any other course of action.

He's not a lunatic. He's not going to burst into a motel room where his girlfriend is having sex with another man.

Is he?

No.

He has a measure of dignity.

But he can't make himself leave. Even though he knows he shouldn't talk to Kate tonight. He's not calm enough. He would say something he'd regret.

Still, he's not budging.

He's in his Lexus and he's got the knife. It's balanced on his leg with the blade unfolded.

His hands are on the steering wheel.

The neon light is burning. It's there when he turns his head and looks out his window:

YOUR MOTEL

And underneath:

VACANCY

The letters red like blood.

You can only put it off for so long.

Devin picks up the knife, turns his left arm over, and drags the blade across his skin.

"Oh my god," Travis Pollard says.

He's naked, lying on his back in the motel bed. Kate is on her knees, straddling him.

He's laughing and trying to catch his breath. He covers his eyes with his hands, then takes them away to look up at her.

"Do you do that all the time?" he asks.

The truth is, Kate has never done it before, not like this. She always held back with Devin. She was afraid to hurt him.

Travis is still laughing, with the occasional "Wow" thrown in.

The only light in the room is the bedside lamp, and in its glow Kate can see the marks of her hands on Travis's throat, especially where she pressed her fingers against his carotid arteries. She didn't know how he would take it. She thought he might fight her. And he did struggle at first, getting used to it. He wriggled side to side, arched his back. But he didn't try to push her off.

It was good to watch. His eyes were fixed on hers the whole time. Right up to the end when his eyelids began to flutter and it seemed like he would pass out. That's when she eased off.

She didn't want to kill him, after all.

She has read about it before, so she knows that the most pleasurable part is supposed to be when it stops. When the blood goes rushing back to the brain. Along with endorphins and dopamine and serotonin.

Makes you giddy, apparently. If you're the one having it done to you.

If you're the one doing it, there's a different kind of pleasure: Everything heightened. Brighter light, clearer sounds. A deeper sense of touch. Kate is incredibly aware of the motel sheets beneath her legs, the cool air of the room against her skin, Travis inside her.

"What do you want now?" he asks her. "We can do anything you want."

He's happy and full of life, and what she wants is to feel the weight of him on top of her. That's the thing she needs, to really get away from herself.

She still doesn't like him, but she seems to have knocked the swagger out of him, at least temporarily. It makes him easier to bear.

He's smiling up at her. "You want to do the same thing again, don't you?" he says. "We can do it again."

Kate lays a palm over his heart. It was pounding wildly before, but now it's settling down.

So why not?

They have nothing but time ahead of them. And she does want to do it again.

Devin has things under control.

There's blood trickling down his arm, but not a lot. He hasn't gone too far. He can stop if he wants to.

Maybe he should.

He pulls some tissues from the box on the passenger seat and wipes the blood from his arm. He uses another tissue to clean the knife.

Better.

Let's think about this rationally.

You're stressed-out.

Okay. But it's more than that, isn't it?

You're angry. You're allowed to be angry.

You tried to have a conversation with Kate, and she started throwing accusations around. Because she can't deal with conflict. Rather than handling things in a mature way, she ran off to a motel room with a college kid.

Anyone would be angry. It's a normal reaction.

I know it's tempting. You would like to go kick down that door. It would be satisfying. Beat up your rival—that's caveman stuff. It's primal.

You're not a caveman.

You're not.

The script is only sixteen pages. Lee Tennick reads through to the end, and there are no revelations. The notes written in the margins are mostly about lighting and sound, locations and props. Tennick isn't sure what he was hoping for. Maybe Clay McKellar's best guess about the identity of Merkury. But if Clay had any thoughts on the subject, he didn't jot them down here.

Tennick tosses the script aside. He's restless, and he thinks a beer might help him sleep, but he hasn't had one in five days. He takes a bottle from the fridge. Twists the cap off and smells the beer, but doesn't drink it. After a while he pours it down the sink.

His bed is in the back of the RV. He takes the script with him and lies down to leaf through it again. Most of the story is told visually, with very little dialogue. It begins with the female character, referred to only as Victim, in the moments after she has escaped from the shack. You see her standing in the woods, with a pair of handcuffs dangling from one wrist. Almost immediately it flashes back to a scene where she's inside, still being held captive. She's lying on the floor, hands cuffed behind her back, ankles bound. The sole source of light in the room is a candle on the workbench.

There's no one with her, except a mouse.

```
VICTIM watches the mouse crawl across the floor
    in front of her, its claws tapping on the con-
    crete. It comes to the inside of the closed
    door of the shack, as if it wants to go out.
    Rising up on its hind legs, it scratches at
    the door.

The perspective shifts and we're looking at
    VICTIM from behind. She's holding a broken
    piece of a plastic zip tie, using it as a
    shim to try to slip the ratchet of one of
    the handcuffs and free herself.

The door opens inward and the mouse scur-
    ries away. KILLER enters wearing worn-out
    clothes and black boots. He closes the door
    and, without saying anything to VICTIM, moves
```

```
to the workbench. He's occupied there, but
we're seeing him from behind. We can't tell
what he's doing.

The mouse comes back to the door. VICTIM
continues trying to open the cuffs. KILLER
hears the mouse scratching and turns around.
He walks to the door and watches the mouse.

    KILLER bends down, picks up the mouse, and
    stands straight again. He watches the mouse
    struggling in his hand before closing his
    fist around it and squeezing. He drops the
    dead mouse on the floor in front of VICTIM.

    KILLER crouches down by the door and looks at
    VICTIM curiously. Without taking his eyes
    off her, KILLER reaches out and scratches
    at the door with his fingernails, imitating
    the mouse.
```

It was a creepy scene when Tennick first read it, and it's creepier the second time around. It raises goosebumps on his arms.

He digs into his pocket for his phone and finds the voicemail message Clay McKellar left him a few hours before Clay died. He taps the screen to play it.

It's me. You said I should call if I needed to talk. Don't know if you meant it. It's . . . I don't know what time it is. I've got all the curtains closed, but I can see daylight peeking through. So this is not a midnight drunk dial . . . Can't be if it's not midnight, right? . . . This can't go on. I thought I'd get over it. 'You're being paranoid,' I said, but I don't know. I saw what I saw. You can't unsee something, right? . . . God, I'm tired. I think there's something wrong with me. Heard something scratching on the door. Did I open the door? No, I did not . . .

Tennick sits up in his bed. He remembers asking Clay's neighbor if her cat might have scratched on Clay's door. Remembers her saying, "Maybe it was a mouse."

Maybe it was. Or maybe it was Clay's imagination.

What if the voicemail reveals what was on Clay's mind the day he died?

What if it shows who he was afraid of?

Not the killer from the movie. The movie is fiction.

But what about the actor who played the killer?

Travis Pollard.

28

Kate can feel the sweat evaporating from her skin.

Her sweat and Travis's, both together. It's a nice sensation. She thought she would feel bad about this, but she feels fine.

It's good just to lie still, naked on the rumpled bed. Alone, because Travis went into the bathroom to take a shower.

Kate could almost spend the night here. But she suspects things might look different to her in the morning.

She listens to the shower running and slips out of bed and starts to gather her clothes. Travis's jeans are on the floor with hers. She tosses them onto the bed and a silver money clip falls out of his pocket. Thick with twenties and fifties. Rich kid.

It's funny. She almost felt guilty when she made him pay for the room.

She slides the money back into his pocket. Finds her bra and underwear. She's fully dressed and has her shoes on by the time Travis comes out of the bathroom with a towel wrapped around his waist.

"You're not leaving, are you?" he says.

"I think so," she tells him. "I'll drive you back to your apartment if you want."

He comes around to where she's standing at the foot of the bed. Traces his fingers along her forehead and into her hair.

"If you think so, that means you're not sure."

He leans down as if he's going to kiss her, but draws away at the last moment. Jumps onto the bed, playful, and says, "Come on. You should stay. We've got a thing going here."

"A thing?" Kate says.

"We're good together. You're edgy. I knew it the first time we talked."

"You said I was messed up."

He makes a dismissive gesture. "Bad choice of words. 'Edgy' sounds better. But we're the same. That's what I'm trying to tell you."

"You're edgy?" she says.

"I've had my moments."

"When?"

He pats the mattress beside him, and after a few seconds she joins him on the bed.

"I used to shoplift," he says. "When I was a kid."

"Oooh," she says.

"I stole DVDs, video games, clothes. Clothes are the easiest. All you have to do is put them on in the dressing room and walk out of the store. I had friends who were afraid to do it. But I don't have that in me."

"You don't have what? Fear?"

"Not in a situation like that," Travis says. "When I was twelve, one of our neighbors skipped town. Just took off one night with his family. I think they were about to be evicted. Their house was left unoccupied for a long time. My best friend and I decided to break in. We met there at midnight, but he chickened out. I went in by myself. Climbed through a window. It was strange. They had gone in a hurry, left a lot of stuff behind. Furniture, toys, books. One of the kids left her My Little Pony toothbrush. I stayed in there for an hour, just me and a flashlight. Never felt scared. Even when the cops came."

"The cops came?"

"I was up on the second floor. Heard someone pull into the driveway. My friend had run off home by then. I went to a window and saw it was a patrol car. There was only one cop, actually. I think they sent someone out there once in a while because they knew the house was empty. This guy barely got out of his car. I watched him smoke a cigarette, leaning against the trunk. He didn't even walk around the place. If he had, he might have noticed the window I'd broken. People are lazy."

Travis is lying with his hands behind his head. Just the towel around him. Perfectly relaxed. Kate isn't sure about the purpose of his story, unless it's to impress her.

Her cellphone rings and when she pulls it from her pocket she sees it's Lee Tennick. She lets it go to voicemail.

"Someone's calling you late," Travis says.

True. It's after one o'clock. Time to head home.

Kate is returning the phone to her pocket when she hears the ping of a text message.

Travis laughs. "Someone's persistent."

She almost doesn't read the text, but if it's Tennick again, maybe it's important.

She hauls the phone back out. It's Tennick.

I think Clay might have been afraid of Travis Pollard.

Kate frowns at the screen, and something prickles on the back of her neck. Not fear, but definitely a sense of unease.

"What's wrong?" Travis asks.

She sits up and swings her feet off the bed, facing away from him. She composes a one-word response: Why? Then hits the send button and starts in on a second message: I'm with him

But Travis is moving behind her. Too late she tries to stand, and he pulls her back onto the bed and twists around until he's on top of her. He grabs her phone and holds her down while he reads it, his arm across her throat.

"Kate," he says. "This is disappointing."

"Get off me," she says. "Or I'll scream."

And there it is, the smirk she remembers from the first time she met him.

"You did some screaming before," he says. "Have you forgotten already? I liked it, believe me. But nobody came running. So let's say no screaming. If you do, I'll put a pillow over your face."

Kate watches him tapping at her phone with his thumb, like he's deleting the message she started. Then he swipes at the screen, scrolling back through her earlier exchanges with Tennick.

"There's nothing else on there about you," she says. "I don't know why you're doing this. It's all a mistake."

Travis powers off the phone and tosses it aside. Holds her arms down on the bed. Brings his face close to hers.

"I've been trying to figure you out," he says. "Ever since you showed up out of the blue tonight. What were you after?"

"You know what I was after."

His eyes are searching hers, and she can almost see the wheels turning behind them.

"No," he says. "I'd like to believe this was just about sex. But I can't really afford to be wrong, can I? You know something."

"I don't."

"Yeah, you do. I was almost convinced you were clueless, until your friend sent you that message. Lee. You can't tell me *he* doesn't know anything. He thinks I killed Clay."

"That's not what the message said."

"But it's what he thinks. Otherwise why would it matter if Clay was afraid of me? Do you think I killed him?"

"No," Kate says.

Travis laughs. "You need to get better at lying. This playing dumb, it doesn't suit you. You're smart about people. Do you know when I first realized it?"

He pauses, waiting for her to answer. She shakes her head.

"It was when you asked me about Lavana's camera lens, if I was the one who moved it. I told you no, but that was a fib. I did move it. You were even right about the reason. It was so damn boring, making her movie. Waiting for her to get her camera set up, her lights. Everything had to be perfect. I had to find ways to entertain myself. Sometimes I'd blow a take on purpose, just to screw with her. She was always goofy when we worked in that shed. Talked about the energy in there. When I moved that lens, it spooked her. I swear to god, she thought it was spirits. Ghosts."

Kate can feel her arms going numb from the way he's holding them. She tries to pull them free.

"Travis—"

He relaxes his grip, but he's still not letting her up.

"The point is," he says, "I'm not buying this act you're putting on. You didn't come to me to play your little choking game and get laid. Let's be real. You need to start telling me the truth."

It's absurd how wrong he is, and under other circumstances Kate might laugh. But right now her mind is racing. She could scream, but he's right: there's no guarantee anyone would come. And fighting him seems futile. He's much stronger than she is.

Talking her way out seems to be her best chance. It's obvious now that he killed Clay McKellar. Otherwise he wouldn't have reacted so strongly to Tennick's message. But if she admits that she knows, how does that help her?

All it does is give him a reason to kill her.

But he already suspects that she knows. And he's asking her to tell him the truth.

What truth can she tell him?

There's nothing.

She doesn't even know why he killed Clay. They were friends, weren't they? They worked on Lavana Khatri's movie together.

And the three of them found Bryan Cayhill's body.

Does this have something to do with Bryan? She already considered the possibility that Travis killed Bryan and made it look as if Merkury had done it. But Tennick shot down that idea. Travis had an alibi. The others did too.

So it must be something else.

What motive would Travis have for killing Clay?

To silence him? About what?

To gain something from him? But what could Clay have had that Travis would want?

Kate remembers Clay's apartment and its thrift-store furniture. She can't imagine Clay having anything there worth taking. And Travis is a rich kid. Rich kids don't need to kill for money.

Kate feels Travis tightening his grip on her again. She's been silent for too long. He's getting impatient. Everything in her wants to push him away and break free, but he's in control. He could kill her and get away with it. And it wouldn't bother him. He wouldn't be haunted. That's what he said about finding Bryan's body.

I'm not gonna carry it around for the rest of my life.

I've seen death before.

Chickens torn apart by foxes.

Calves that were stillborn.

Travis grew up on a farm.

The thought makes Kate frown.

Is Travis rich?

Bryan Cayhill was, but is Travis?

Travis lives in an apartment with two roommates. And not a fancy apartment either.

But he's walking around with a clip full of cash in his pocket.

He wants to hear the truth from her.

Kate doesn't know everything, but suddenly some things are falling into place. She knows where to begin.

"Bryan Cayhill was a thief," she says. "I found out from his father. As far as I'm aware, his father is the only person he ever stole from. It started out with small things from around their home. Bryan took them and hid them away, and when he came to Seagate I guess he brought them with him. He kept them in the house his father bought for him in Alexander. On Summit Avenue, a few blocks from Clay McKellar's apartment."

Travis is staring down at her. She can tell from his eyes that she's on the right track.

"One of the things he stole was a money clip," she says. "The one that's in the pocket of your jeans."

"Have you been going through my pockets?" Travis asks her.

"Yes," Kate says. "But I saw the clip before, at your apartment, the first time we talked."

That's a lie. But it's a lie that could help her get out of this room.

"After Bryan died," she says, "you broke into his house. It was a bold thing to do but—how did you put it?—you don't have any fear in you."

She realizes now why he told her the story about breaking into his neighbor's house when he was twelve. He wanted to see how she would react, to suss out what she knew.

"How did you get into Bryan's house?" she asks him. "You went at night, I suppose. And the backyard has that tall privacy fence. Was there a window open on the second floor? Did you climb up onto the portico roof to reach it?"

Kate can feel Travis's fingers digging into her arms.

"How do you know?" he asks. "Did Clay tell you?"

"No. I've been to the house. That's how I would have gotten in. Was Clay there with you?"

She watches him try to decide how much to reveal.

"Clay was there," he says. "But not with me. I parked at the movie theater and walked to Bryan's house. To scope things out. Clay saw me and followed me. Bad luck. He was out for a walk. This was only a couple of days after we found Bryan by the pond, and I think Clay had trouble sleeping."

"You didn't notice him following you?"

Travis makes a sour face. "More bad luck," he says. "I was on the lookout for cars parked near the house. I thought the cops might be watching it. But there was nothing, and the house was dark when I got to it. I could tell there was no one in there. So I walked around to the back and went in the way you said."

"What did you think you would find inside?" Kate asks.

"I didn't really know," he says. "But I knew Bryan's family had money. I thought there could be some cash lying around. Once I was inside, it was like old times. I felt like exploring."

"You found more than cash," Kate says.

Travis looks down at her curiously. "What do you think I found?"

"Jewelry," Kate says. "A lot of it." Everything Bryan's father ever bought for his mother, she thinks—minus some earrings Bryan gave to Jenny Wyler. "Nothing cheap either," she says. "Bryan's father owns a hedge fund. He can afford the best."

She's right. She can read it in Travis's expression. She needs to be careful now, and she needs to keep their conversation going.

"Where did you find the jewelry?" she asks him.

There's a bitter edge in his voice when he answers. "It was in a backpack in Bryan's bedroom closet, if you can believe it."

"Rich people can afford to be careless," Kate says. "So you took the backpack and, what, climbed out through the window?"

Travis smiles. "I guess I could have. But it was easier to walk out the back door."

"Is that when Clay saw you?"

The smile leaves him, and Kate thinks he's going to keep the rest to himself. But in the end he's just a college kid and he's been holding on to a bad secret. That's hard, and lonely. He wants to tell her.

"Clay saw me when I came around to the front of the house. He was on the other side of the street. I think he'd been walking up and down the block, waiting for me to reappear. When we saw each other, he froze. I waved to him and crossed the street. I wasn't gonna run away. How would that have looked? My plan was to say I'd been visiting a friend, but the first words out of Clay's mouth were 'That's Bryan's house, isn't it?'"

"So what did you tell him?" Kate asks.

"I came up with a lie. I said Bryan had borrowed a jacket of mine and I needed it back. I didn't want to bother his family about it, so I thought I should just go in and get it."

"Clay must have wondered how you got in," Kate says.

"I told him I found the back door unlocked. I knew my story was weak, but I figured he had seen me go around to the back of the house empty-handed and come out with the backpack, and I could have had a jacket in the backpack. I hoped he would buy it."

"But he didn't."

"I wasn't sure. We walked back toward downtown together and he didn't have much to say. I left him in front of his building. But every time I saw him after that, he acted strange. Like he was half afraid of me. The day of Bryan's memorial, he wouldn't even look me in the eye. So the next day I figured I'd better talk to him."

"Did you go to his apartment?"

"I meant to. I was driving there and I spotted Clay on Main Street, walking south. I parked my car and followed him on foot. I wanted to get him alone. It's not the kind of thing you talk about in public. He walked past the campus and came to the trailhead and went into the woods. And I thought, Okay, this is good, we've been here lots of times to shoot Lavana's movie, so I can pretend I just happened to run into him. I caught up to him by the shed in the woods."

Travis pauses, and Kate wonders if she's going to have to prompt him. But after a few seconds he continues on his own.

"I had worked out what I wanted to say. I wasn't gonna tell him the truth, but I thought I needed to give him a better lie. I stuck with the part about going to Bryan's house to get my jacket, but I dropped the part about the door being unlocked. I told him about climbing in through the window. And I admitted that while I was in there I found some cash and took it, which was true. I said it was stupid, but it was done, and I couldn't take it back, and all I asked was that he not tell anyone he had seen me there, because I didn't want to get in trouble. I said I would give him half the money—eight hundred dollars—and we would both forget it ever happened."

"That was smart," Kate says.

"I thought so," says Travis.

"But Clay didn't go for it."

"No."

29

"Clay didn't want the money," Travis says. "He probably thought taking it would be wrong. But there was something else. He was scared. I think he had it in his head that I had killed Bryan. Which was stupid. As if I would kill him just so I could rob him. Who would do that?"

"No one," Kate says.

"Obviously. But that's what Clay thought. And he tried to run. I should have let him go, but I was worried about who he might talk to, what he might say."

"So you stopped him," Kate says.

There's a hint of sorrow in Travis's eyes.

"It was easy. Clay was smaller than me, and he wasn't fast. As soon as he tried to make a break for it, I grabbed him, threw him against the door of the shed. That scared him even more. I wanted him to calm down. So I stepped back. I wasn't worried that he would run again. If he did, I would catch him. But he didn't try."

"What did he do?"

"Something I didn't expect. He pulled the shed door open and ducked inside. He had spent time there, we both had, so he knew what was in there. When I went in after him, I saw he had a shovel in his hands. He swung it at me. He wasn't kidding around either. He was aiming for my head."

Kate can picture it, and Travis seems to be picturing it too. His voice sounds distant, detached.

"I don't think Clay had been in too many fights in his life," he says. "But I've been in a few. I dodged the first swing and grabbed on to the handle of the shovel before he could try for a second one. I wrestled it away from him. But he wouldn't quit. There were tools on the workbench and he went for one of them. A wrench. And I hit him with the shovel."

Travis flinches as if he's remembering the impact. "I meant to hit him with the flat part of the blade, but I think the edge caught him. He stumbled and went down on one knee. Put his hand to the back of his head, and when he pulled it away there was blood on it. I didn't think I hit him that hard. He should have been okay. But when he got up he swayed and staggered toward the door. I dropped the shovel. I meant to help him. Outside he fell, and got up again. Didn't seem to know where he was going. I chased him, if you can call it that, around the shed to the back. Caught him there. He tried to tear away from me and tripped. Ended up on the ground.

"I got down there with him, and he started yelling for me to get away. He wouldn't stop. I never decided to kill him. I wanted to shut him up. I had on a sweater over a T-shirt, and I took the sweater off and put it over his mouth. I told him to settle down, but he started thrashing around and I had to get on top of him. I kept pressing on the sweater and listened to his heels kicking at the ground. I thought someone might come by and hear, but nobody did."

With his story winding down, Travis is coming back to the present. His voice is stronger, more matter-of-fact.

"Afterward, I took the sweater away from his face. His eyes were open, but they weren't looking at me. I was going to cover him with a pile of leaves, but he reminded me of Bryan when we found him. Bryan's eyes were open too. And the shovel was in the shed. I broke the handle off from the blade and put it under Clay's shoulders and spread his arms out. I thought I would get some rope and come back, do the whole thing, hang him up in a tree. But by the time I walked to my car, I realized what a terrible idea that was. You don't want to push it. You want to quit while you're ahead."

"I think that was wise," Kate says. "The handle of the shovel was enough to point to Merkury. Something could have stopped him from finishing his ritual. That's what I thought when I saw Clay."

She's careful to sound neutral, nonjudgmental. It's the only way forward she can see, because she's in a dangerous place. On her back, like Clay, with Travis on top of her, pinning her down. And pillows within his reach.

"I don't blame you for what happened," she says. "I don't think you meant to do it."

"No?" he says.

"No. And you don't have to do it again. There's a difference between me and Clay. He wouldn't take the deal you offered him, but I will."

"Is that so?" Travis says. "You'll take eight hundred dollars? And you won't tell anyone what you know?"

He's testing her, Kate thinks. Eight hundred is not enough.

"I want half the jewelry too," she says. "That's good for both of us. If I take half, I can't turn you in without implicating myself."

He's looming over her with the gray ceiling above him. She watches a smile curl the corners of his mouth and then move to his eyes.

"There you are," he says. "That's why you came to me tonight, for the jewelry."

She nods without speaking.

"You knew about the jewelry because you've talked to Bryan's father."

"Yes."

"And you guessed that I had it because you saw the money clip. Something else Bryan stole."

"That's right."

"You saw the money clip the first time we talked."

This is the most dangerous part, Kate thinks. She's looking up at him, and though his grip on her arms has eased, the muscles of his shoulders and chest seem as tense as a snake coiled to strike.

She never saw the money clip that first time. They sat together on the balcony of his apartment and she didn't have an opportunity to go through his pockets. She remembers a table on the balcony. She could say she saw the clip there. But it would be a lie.

He's waiting for her to lie.

She lets out a long breath and decides to take a chance.

"I didn't see the money clip before," she says. "Not until tonight. The reason I came to you is because I felt like hell and I needed to get some relief. But we can still make a deal. Half the jewelry is fair."

It's the right decision, she thinks. Travis releases his hold on one of her arms and reaches out to trace his fingertips along her cheek.

"Do you think I can be forgiven for killing Clay?" he asks.

"Yes," she tells him.

"I'm not so sure," he says, rubbing his thumb across her lower lip. "The thing is, I didn't set out to do it, but it didn't bother me. Not even a little."

He's coiled. Like a snake. There's no time for her to react.

He snatches up a pillow and shoves it down onto her face.

30

He learned something from smothering Clay.

It takes longer than you imagine, and when you think it's done, it's not really done. People are tricky that way. They pass out before they die.

Travis smothers Kate until she passes out.

Then he's stuck with a series of problems to solve.

He needs to tie her. Here's the pillowcase from the pillow. There are seams along each side. With help from the jagged edge of his apartment key, he rips the seams apart. Now he has one long piece of fabric. Using the key again to get things started, he tears the fabric into three strips.

One to bind her ankles. Another to tie her hands behind her back. He takes one of the thin white washcloths from the bathroom and stuffs it in her mouth. Uses the third strip to secure it in place.

There's one problem solved.

Next up: getting her out of here.

He dresses while he's thinking. Underwear, socks, jeans, shirt. He picks up Kate's cellphone from the floor. Checks that he has his own.

Okay.

This is the riskiest part: getting her to the car. Someone might see.

That's why she's still alive.

If he's going to be caught, he'd rather be caught with an unconscious woman than with a dead one.

Kate's car is parked three or four spaces away. He needs to move it so it's right in front of the door. Won't take a minute. He finds her keys in her coat.

She's on her back on the bed. Travis holds his hand under her nose to confirm that she's breathing.

Good.

What else?

He unplugs the room phone from the wall and puts it on the high shelf of the closet. Then thinks twice and uses a hand towel from the bathroom to wipe down the phone and all the surfaces he and Kate might have touched.

He drops the towel and picks up Kate's coat and handbag from the chair. Stands with his back against the door.

Last chance to reconsider. He could untie her, let her walk out of here, give her half the jewelry, and trust her to keep quiet.

But he doesn't trust her. She's smart. Slick. He understood it as they were talking. She only wanted to get away. She would have said anything . . .

She could take half the jewelry and go straight to the police and turn him in.

Stick to the plan then. Move the car.

He's about to go out the door when he notices the motel keycard on the bedside table. He walks over and picks it up and slips it in his shirt pocket.

How embarrassing would that have been, if he went out and couldn't get back in?

Lucky, he thinks.

You dodged a bullet there.

* * *

Devin feels cold.

It's not from loss of blood. What he's lost doesn't amount to much.

It's because it's a cold damn night.

He has managed to stay in the car, which is a victory in itself. He's done it at the cost of a few slashes on his arm and a few minutes between each one.

All right, it's more than a few slashes.

But the time in between is what matters. It means he has discipline.

He spreads some clean tissues on the passenger seat and lays his knife on top of them. Reaches for the ignition, intending to start the engine and run the heater.

But before he does, he sees the door of the motel room open. He watches the college kid step out. Kate isn't with him. He's carrying a small bundle under his arm.

Is that Kate's coat?

The kid goes to her car and starts it. He backs it out of the space it's in, maneuvers it around, and backs it into the space in front of the door. He pops open the trunk and turns off the engine. Then he's out of the car, leaning into the trunk, lifting out a cardboard box.

Kate keeps jumper cables in there, window washer fluid, road flares, a first aid kit. Devin knows, because he has traveled with her.

The kid moves the box from the trunk to the back seat.

As if he's making room.

Kate is nowhere in sight.

Devin picks up his knife and steps out of his car. Slams the door.

The kid sees him. Stares at him over the top of Kate's car.

Devin squares his shoulders and straightens his back. Makes his voice deep and puts some threat into it.

"What the hell are you doing?" he says.

* * *

Kate wakes up with a spasm running through her like a cough.

But it's not a proper cough, because there's something in her mouth. Rough against her palate. It makes her panic. She can't breathe. Can't breathe.

Wait.

Her shoulders are hurting, her arms are bound beneath her. Her legs are tied. He's not here. Travis. Where is he?

Can't breathe—

Hold on. She *is* breathing, but not well. The thing in her mouth—she can't spit it out. She pushes at it with her tongue. Concentrates on drawing air in through her nose.

Better. She's not breathing deep, but it's deeper than before.

Travis—she can hear him coming out of the bathroom. She closes her eyes.

He's in the room with her, moving around. She doesn't dare look.

She tries to stay perfectly still.

After a time he opens the door, and the temperature of the room changes. Cold air coming in. When Kate hears the door shut, she opens her eyes. He's gone.

She bends her knees. Scoots along the bed. Her legs go over the edge and she rolls up until she's standing on the floor. Feet tight together. Hard to keep her balance.

A car starts up outside.

Kate looks across the room at the door. She could get to it. She could open it. But it's the middle of the night. No one's going to be out there.

Except Travis. He's out there.

Is he leaving? She doesn't think so. She thinks he's moving her car. Her phone is nowhere in sight. Her coat and her bag are gone too.

She thinks he's coming back for her.

And if he is, there's not much time.

The motel phone is gone from the night table. Kate looks down at her ankles. He used sheets to tie her. No. The sheets on the bed are intact.

A pillowcase.

Shouldn't be hard to cut through. But there's nothing to cut with.

She scans the room. What can she use?

Chair. TV. Framed picture on the wall.

If she could break the glass . . .

She has to get there first. Little hops. Careful, or she'll fall over. She comes to the wall but can't reach the frame with her hands behind her back. She tries nudging it with her shoulder. It doesn't move.

Is it bolted to the wall?

There must be something else. The lamp on the bedside table. She could break the bulb. But the glass in a lightbulb is thin and delicate. Too delicate.

There's the remote control for the TV. The alarm clock.

She hops over and picks up the TV remote. There's a little panel on the back you take off to change the batteries. She can feel it. A tiny catch. She releases it with her thumbnail.

She returns the remote to the table. Holds on to the little plastic panel.

If she can break the plastic, she'll have a sharp edge.

Outside, a voice calls out.

It's unexpected. Disorienting. It shouldn't be there.

It's Devin's voice.

"What the hell are you doing?" he says.

Goddamn homeless person, Travis thinks.

The guy's face is pale. His sleeves are rolled up and there's blood running down his left arm.

Shit. Is that a knife?

He's holding a knife.

"Where's Kate?" the guy says. "I want to see her, right now."

Not homeless then. Not some random dude. Which makes it worse. He's older, but looks to be in good shape. Apart from the bleeding.

Jesus. Why is he bleeding?

The guy goes to the door of the room and tries it, but of course it's locked.

"The keycard," he says. "Give it to me."

He's worked up. Angry.

Travis moves around to the trunk of the car but no closer.

"Calm down," he says. "Who are you?"

Makes the guy angrier. "Who are *you*, you twerp? Give me the key."

Travis stays where he is.

The guy comes at him. With the knife.

Travis has seen exactly one knife fight in his life. In a roadhouse bar in rural Vermont. Two bikers. One of them got his stomach cut open.

It taught Travis an important lesson. He doesn't want to be in a knife fight.

But here the guy comes. Aiming the knife straight out like it's a rapier. Like he's in a play. As he gets close, he draws it back as if he's going to slash Travis's neck.

The only thing Travis can think to do is go for his wrist. With both hands.

It's beautiful. Travis locks one hand around the guy's wrist, the other farther along the arm. Pushes the arm up. Spins a hundred and eighty degrees, so his back is against the guy's chest. Then slams the knife-hand down onto the right rear fender of Kate's car.

The guy keeps hold of the knife.

And brings his left arm up. The bloody one. Wraps it around Travis's neck.

Travis drives his head backward. Connects with the bridge of the guy's nose.

Hears a groan.

Travis slams the guy's knife-hand once more against the car. This time the knife goes flying.

Devin feels blood trickling from his nose and over his lip. There's a shock of pain in his right hand. But he's not out yet. He tightens his grip on the kid's neck, hoping to cut off his air. The kid releases his wrist and reaches back with one hand to strike at his face. With the other hand he grabs Devin's arm, attempting to ease the pressure on his neck.

Devin doesn't let up. He leans back, trying to lift the kid off the ground.

Travis lifts one foot up and braces it on the rear bumper of the car. He uses it to shove himself backward. The guy loses his balance, and both of them topple over.

Travis lands on top. Scrambles sideways to his hands and knees, and from there gets to his feet.

The guy is breathing hard on the ground, but he's not done. Travis retreats toward the trunk of the car. Lets him get up.

He puts up his fists like a brawler. But Travis just waits for him.

He charges, as Travis knew he would.

Travis dodges to one side and lets momentum carry the guy forward. Shoves him as he goes by, to help him along. The trunk is open. The guy scrapes his head on the lid of it.

Travis takes hold of the guy's shirt collar and yanks him back. Then pushes him forward again. And slams the lid of the trunk down onto his shoulder blades.

The guy tries to haul himself out. The next time Travis slams the lid down, it hits the back of the guy's neck.

The third time, it smashes into his skull.

Travis looks around for the knife. There it is on the concrete. Moonlight glinting off the silver handle. He picks it up.

The guy is dazed, but he's bracing himself with his arms against the rear bumper of the car. Trying to rise.

Travis pushes him down and grabs his hair. Draws the blade across his throat.

31

Kate hoped it would be easier, cutting through her bonds.

She managed to break the plastic panel from the remote control. It has a sharp point on it now. It's no good for slicing, but she can poke it through the fabric, maybe open up a hole that she can tear wider. But it's difficult. She can't see what she's doing. She has to go by feel.

She doesn't know what's going on outside. She could move to the window, shift the heavy curtains, and look, but there's no time to be a spectator. She has to free herself if she can.

She blocks out everything else, concentrates on working the point of the plastic cover through the fabric. She misses the click of the lock, but she sees the door to the room swinging open.

She wants it to be Devin.

It's Travis.

He looks at her coolly, as if he's not surprised to find her on her feet. He holds himself with a serenity that seems out of place.

Kate almost doesn't notice the blood on his hands.

He makes his way around the bed toward her. She has time to slip the plastic panel into one of the pockets of her jeans.

He pushes her onto the mattress.

Then he goes around the bed again, into the bathroom. She hears water running.

She slides off the bed as quickly as she can. Onto her feet. Hops for the door.

She almost makes it.

Travis comes out of the bathroom with a towel, drying his hands. When he sees her, he smiles faintly and shakes his head.

He picks her up and carries her on his shoulder. Uses the towel to wipe the door handle. Opens the door, goes out, pulls it shut behind him.

Kate feels a cold wind. Her car is there. She doesn't see Devin.

She thinks Travis is going to put her in the trunk.

He dumps her on the back seat.

Travis cruises slow and easy out of the parking lot of the motel.

He surveys the place in his rearview mirror. There's no one outside. No curious guests coming out to gawk. No diligent employees.

Travis saw only one person on duty when he went into the office to pay for the room. A fat old woman watching a TV mounted on the wall. She seemed sleepy. She might not have heard anything. Or if she did, she might not have taken an interest.

Kate waited in the car when he went into the office. It's possible no one saw her here at all.

Apart from the guy in the trunk.

Lee Tennick reads through the scene from the movie again—the one where the killer scratches on the door of the shack—and wonders if he's making something out of nothing.

It struck him as too much of a coincidence: that Clay McKellar, who worked on the movie, would leave him a message about something scratching on his door. But the more Tennick thinks about it, the more it seems it might have been just that. A coincidence.

He almost lets it go. The hour is late, and he's tired. But when you spend your days researching unsolved crimes and talking about them on a podcast, you develop a dark imagination.

When Tennick sent his text to Kate—I think Clay might have been afraid of Travis Pollard—she replied almost immediately: Why? But she started to type another message. Tennick could see those three little dots floating on the screen of his phone.

Kate's second message never came through. The dots disappeared.

Tennick sent a follow-up text, explaining about the scene in the movie script. And received no reply. He called Kate and left a voice message, asking her to get back to him.

She hasn't returned the call.

Now he sends her another text:

This is probably silly, but I'm worried about you. Tell me you're okay.

He watches the screen.

Nothing.

Kate's car is not in the driveway.

Devin Falko was here earlier. Vera Landen floated the idea that Devin could be Merkury.

A dark imagination. It's a curse.

Tennick calls the Seagate Inn and asks to be connected to Devin's room.

The clerk tries and informs him that there's no answer.

She sounds young and bored. He asks her if she could go up and knock on Devin's door. She's reluctant to leave the front desk, but Tennick can be charming when he wants to, and persuasive.

She goes up and knocks. Calls him back to say that no one came to the door.

Tennick thanks her and makes one more call. He tracked down Travis

Pollard's number after Bryan Cayhill died, along with the numbers of the others who found the body. He phones Travis now and listens to the ringing on the line. The call goes to voicemail.

What is he supposed to say? *Are you a murderer?*

He ends the call without leaving a message.

It's creeping on toward two a.m. Kate isn't his wife, or his sister. It's not his place to worry if she doesn't answer her phone at this hour. It's not his responsibility to go out searching for her in the night.

But she's his friend. Maybe she wouldn't agree, but she is.

Tennick takes his keys from the hook by the door and heads out.

Travis Pollard is unafraid.

He's handling things rationally. Driving at the speed limit. Radio off. He needs to think. Make plans.

Kate is lying across the back seat, where he put her. She turned onto her side to face forward. She wants to be able to see him, he supposes.

The cardboard box from the trunk is up front with him now, on the passenger seat. There's a smear of blood on it from when he moved it after the fight. But no one's going to see the blood, just as no one's going to see Kate tied up in the back. Travis won't be driving through town. He's not worried about the police pulling him over.

He doesn't have far to go.

Kate is still working on freeing her hands.

She slipped the plastic panel from the remote out of her pocket as they were driving away from the motel. She's been digging the sharp point of it into the fabric that's around her wrists, and she's made a hole that her thumb can fit through. But it's not enough. She needs to make the hole bigger.

And she needs to keep her movements small, so Travis won't notice.

At the same time, she's working on the gag in her mouth. It's a half-assed thing: a strip of pillowcase holding in a rag. If she opens her mouth wide, there's a gap above the strip. She uses her tongue to try to push the rag past her front teeth and through the gap.

She gets a tail of it out and keeps going. When half the rag is out she tries to speak.

"Where's Devin?" she says.

It comes out garbled, but it's enough to get Travis's attention. He glances over his shoulder at her and sees what she's done. She thinks he'll either get angry or ignore her, but he surprises her. Returning his eyes to the road, he reaches back between the seats. She bends herself toward him. He grabs the end of the rag and pulls it free.

The strip of pillowcase remains, but the breath she draws is glorious.

"Where's Devin?" she asks again.

It still doesn't come out clear, but Travis understands her.

"Was that his name?" he says. "Devin?"

"What did you do?"

"He came at me with a knife, so I had to kill him."

It's what Kate feared, but hearing it makes it real. A wave of anguish rolls over her. She presses her face against the car seat. She doesn't want Travis to see her cry.

She feels herself sobbing. Makes an effort to be still.

"Where are we going?" she asks.

There's no reply at first. Just the car gliding along through the night, Travis's hands steady on the wheel.

Then he says: "We're almost there. We're going to the pond."

When Lee Tennick drives out, he's thinking of the night he and Kate went looking for Clay McKellar. Another Sunday night. Only a week ago.

They started out optimistic, thinking they might find Clay walking around in downtown Alexander or on the Seagate campus. Then they considered drearier possibilities.

Weatherstone Pond, where Bryan Cayhill had been found.

The shed in the woods.

This time, the optimistic route seems counterproductive. Tennick is operating on the assumption that something has gone wrong. If he's mistaken, he and Kate can laugh about it tomorrow. But if he's right . . .

He decides to check the dreary places first.

Weatherstone Pond is closer.

He makes his way north and west to Portage Road. The headlights of his Civic shine through a mist of rain in the air. He turns on the wipers. A deer on the roadside flashes by. Tennick comes to the turnoff he wants, the small parking lot bordered by railroad ties. The Civic rolls over the gravel.

Empty. No other cars here.

Tennick stands at the top of the slope and looks down. Even in the dark he can make out the oak tree, the pond. There's no movement.

But he's here. He might as well look closer.

He brings a flashlight from his glove compartment. Goes all the way to the edge of the pond. Circles the oak. The old crime-scene tape is trailing on the ground. There's no indication anyone's been here.

Back up the slope to his car. He's feeling good. He's probably wrong about all of this.

But he'll drive south and check the shed in the woods anyway.

"This isn't the pond," Kate says.

She's sitting up in the back seat on the passenger side. Working the sharp point of the plastic through the fabric around her wrists. The hole is bigger now. She thinks she's close.

Travis took her down a road she didn't recognize and turned onto a rutted lane overgrown with weeds.

"It is," Travis says. "It's Weatherstone Pond. A different part. We found Bryan on the eastern shore. This is the western shore. We came here once, me and Clay. Scouting locations for Lavana's movie. There's a wooden dock this side that runs along the shoreline. A place you could tie a canoe. We never filmed here though."

Tiny specks of rain cover the windshield. Travis switches on the wipers. The lane they're on runs through a stand of trees and takes a slight turn to the left. When the shore of the pond comes into view, Travis stops the car and cuts the engine.

"You don't have to do this," Kate says.

"You don't know what I'm gonna do," he counters.

"Listen. Devin attacked you with a knife. That's what you said."

"Right."

"He's my boyfriend. We tell the police he followed us to the hotel, which he obviously did. He caught us together and he was jealous. He attacked you and you killed him in self-defense."

Travis adjusts the rearview mirror so he can look at her.

"And we leave out the part about me tying you up?" he says.

"Yes."

"And about Clay?"

"Clay too."

"Why would you agree to do that?"

Kate is hardly moving her hands at all, because she can't afford to have him realize what she's doing. But the hole in the fabric is growing.

"We already made a deal," she says. "You give me half of what you stole from Bryan Cayhill's house."

She sees his smile in profile, and in his eyes in the mirror.

"You're cute," he says.

Then he's out of the car and jogging around to her side. Kate conceals

the piece of plastic in her closed fist. When Travis opens the door beside
her, she tries to slide away from him. He grips her arm and pulls her back,
but he doesn't drag her from the car.

He belts her in.

Travis's first thought was to hang Kate in a tree, like one of Merkury's
victims.

It seemed like a natural solution. Believable. Because she had encountered Merkury years ago. But there are drawbacks. He would need a
wooden pole and rope. Where would he get these things in the middle
of the night without being noticed?

The pond seems like a better way. Travis is counting on the water to
wash everything clean, to eliminate evidence. And if he's lucky it will
conceal her, and Devin, at least for a few days. Maybe longer.

If he can get the car out far enough. If he can sink it below the surface.

He could try pushing the car into the water, but the slope of the
ground is gentle here. There won't be enough momentum. It's no good
if it gets hung up on the dock.

If he were in a movie, he would wedge a stick between the driver's seat
and the accelerator, then shift the car into gear and jump free. But he
wonders if that would work as well in real life as it does in the movies.
He's wary of any plan that involves jumping from a moving car.

Besides, the car might veer off course.

He needs to steer it.

He can see it in his mind. If he builds up the right amount of speed
and passes over the dock, the car should be carried out into the water.

He'll only have one chance to get it right.

He's a strong swimmer. He's not afraid.

Standing behind the car, he unbuttons his shirt. Kicks off his shoes.

*   *   *

Kate slips her thumbs through the hole she's made in the fabric. Her movement is limited, but she thinks she'll be able to tear through it.

The driver's door opens and she sees Travis climb in. Naked except for his boxer shorts.

He slides the key into the ignition and twists. The engine rumbles, loud. He engages his seatbelt and jams the gearshift into drive.

Crazy. She understands what he's doing. He's going to drive into the water.

The fabric is ripping apart, and then she feels it stop. She repositions her fingers and thumbs.

The headlights come on. The wipers sweep the mist from the windshield. Travis stomps the accelerator and the car jerks forward.

Kate is tearing at the fabric as they barrel down toward the pond. The water waits for them, gray-black and smooth as glass.

The car bounces over the uneven ground. Tall grass and brambles scrape against the undercarriage. The headlights shine on a wooden dock. Kate can distinguish the individual planks.

Travis lets out a whoop and the tires roll over the wood. The car is airborne for an instant before it hits the water.

Kate's head snaps forward. The seatbelt restrains her body. Knocks the breath out of her. Sends a searing pain through her chest.

There's a whip-crack sound as Travis's airbag deploys.

The car goes under the surface and bobs up again. It floats, wobbling front to back, side to side. There's already water coming in.

Travis fumbles at the catch of his seatbelt. The dashboard is still lit up. And the headlights. The wipers are still wiping.

Kate strains at the fabric binding her wrists.

Travis gets free of his seatbelt and lowers the two front windows. More water pours in. He twists around in his seat so he can go through the driver's window headfirst. Kate hears one of his hands slap the top of the car. His other is braced on the side mirror.

Then he's out through the window and gone.

The cabin is filling up fast, water rushing over the front seats and into the back. It's up to Kate's knees.

Kate makes a final effort to tear through her bonds.

And feels them break. Her hands are free.

The car is sinking under the surface. The water is up to her waist.

She finds the button of her seatbelt with her thumb and releases it.

The lights flicker and go out.

She feels the water rising to her chest, tries to stay calm. The strip of pillowcase Travis used to gag her is still tied around her mouth. She tugs it down below her chin.

Her legs feel leaden. She's still bound at the ankles. Her little sharp piece of plastic isn't going to help now. There's not enough time.

The car settles onto the bottom of the pond, and Kate tips her head up in the pocket of air that remains in the cabin. She takes a big breath before the water overwhelms her.

Then she's under.

The murky dark is terrifying. All she wants is to leave it.

Wait.

Easy now.

She pulls her upper body through the space between the front seats. Hovers in the water and feels for the cardboard box. It's wedged on its side between the passenger seat and the glove compartment. She struggles to pull it out.

She's close to giving up when it comes free.

She settles it on the passenger seat and runs her hands over the things inside it. Bottle of window washer fluid. Blanket. Jumper cables.

First aid kit.

It's a white plastic box—gray in the dark. Kate draws it out and opens the lid. Explores it mostly by touch. Roll of gauze. Paper tape. Packets of aspirin and antibiotic ointment. Tweezers. Latex gloves.

A small pair of scissors.

Kate tucks them in a pocket of her jeans. Maneuvers herself around and grabs the steering wheel.

Her lungs feel like they're going to burst.

She shifts the airbag out of her way, finds the opening of the driver's window, and pulls herself through. Then sets her feet against the door and pushes herself toward the surface.

Travis is trembling with adrenaline when he climbs out of the water onto the dock. He rolls onto his back and spreads his arms out, the planks hard and cold against his bare skin.

The moon hangs low in the southwestern sky, a blob of white behind a veil of wispy gray clouds.

Travis revels in the pounding of his heart, the rise and fall of his chest. He lets out a howl.

But there's no time for celebrating. He rises and crosses the dock to the shore, trailing wet footprints behind him. First thing to do: retrieve his clothes.

Then: He has Kate's phone—he'll need to get rid of it. And Devin's car is still at the motel. If it's found, people will wonder what Devin was doing there, and it's not something Travis wants them to wonder. He'll need to move it.

He's shivering cold, but the walk to the motel should warm him up. Four miles, maybe five. Might take him an hour and a half. He'll have time to think about where to move the car.

He reaches the place where he left his clothes. The rain, what little there was, has stopped. He picks up his jeans and pulls them on. Devin's keys are in his pocket.

Travis is facing the pond as he puts on his shirt, so he sees the moment when Kate comes up to the surface. He hears the splash of water, a burst of coughing, a series of gasps as she takes in air. He watches her smooth her hair out of her face. With her hands. Her no-longer-tied hands.

Son of a bitch.

She goes under again and he wonders what she's doing. But she's up ten seconds later, bobbing in the water. She scans around her as if she's trying to get her bearings. Catches sight of him across the distance.

And laughs.

He watches as she turns away and starts swimming for the far shore.

The scissors did their work. Kate's legs are free.

The water is bitter cold, and it's hard to judge the distance to the shore. She feels like she's making no progress. The freestyle stroke she's using keeps her face too much in the water. She needs to breathe.

She rotates onto her back and it's better, but still slow. Her arms are doing most of the work. Her shoes are making it hard to kick.

Looking at the sky, at the far, high layer of clouds, it's easy to believe she's floating in place. But she's moving. She can feel herself moving.

Travis pulls on his socks.

He's not going back into the water. If his memory serves him, he's close to the northern end of the pond. There's a trail that runs through dense woods in an arc. He walked it with Clay when they came here scouting locations. It will take him around to the eastern shore, where Kate is headed. He'll have to cover more distance than she will, but he can run faster than she can swim.

He steps into his shoes, ties the laces, heads toward the dock at a jog. Before he reaches the dock he swings north and picks up his pace. Runs past an old boathouse toward the woods. He's worried about finding the trail, but there it is, marked with a NO HUNTING sign nailed to a tree. It's a narrow, dark ribbon of dirt and sticks and dead leaves.

There are patches of mud that are hard to see in the dark, but the leaves provide traction and he keeps his footing. At one point the trail veers so close to the pond that it's covered with standing water, but the moonlight catches the surface and Travis sees it in time to jump over.

He clears the water but slips on the other side and stumbles forward, catching himself on his hands. It jars him, but he's okay. Nothing broken, nothing sprained. He picks himself up and wipes his muddy hands on his jeans.

And keeps going.

Kate is bleeding.

She leans against a tree and pulls the sock from her left foot. There's an ugly laceration on her heel.

Her shoe slipped off in the water, and it made more sense to go on than to hunt for it in the dark. When she drew close to the shore, she stood up to wade the rest of the way in, and she stepped on something—a sharp stone, she thinks, though it could have been glass. Tennick told her that college kids partied here. Some of them might have been careless with their bottles.

Her sock is torn, but she puts it back on. She hobbles farther away from the shore and into the woods. The pain in her foot is bearable, but she doesn't want to know how it would feel to run on it.

She looks back at the pond and listens. No movement. No splashing. Travis didn't try to swim after her. But she doesn't believe he gave up.

If she follows the shoreline south, she'll come eventually to the spot where Bryan Cayhill's body was found. If she walks east through the trees she should sooner or later reach Portage Road.

She's not sure how far her wounded foot will take her either way.

Limping on through the woods, she comes to a place where two logs are lying parallel to each other. A stretch of mud and leaves runs between them. The logs are marking the edges of a trail.

She follows it south for a few dozen feet, until her heel steps on something that makes her scream. She lifts it up, hopping on her right foot. She plucks the cap of an acorn from the wound.

A voice calls out. Not close, but not too far. Taunting.

"Kaaaaate!"

She lowers her foot and stands still. She won't be able to outrun him. The only weapon she has is the pair of scissors in her pocket.

She could move off the trail and try to hide.

She spots a fallen branch on the ground, long and straight.

The size of a good walking stick.

Broken to a sharp point on one end.

Travis speeds along the trail in the direction the scream came from.

Devin's knife is in his pocket. Travis draws it out and unfolds it. Running with a knife, not the smartest thing. But it's not so muddy here. He isn't worried.

He's in a zone, flying along, heart pumping. The air he's breathing tastes sweet. He doesn't feel the cold.

He says her name again—"Kaaaaate!"—but not as loud. It's for him to hear as much as it is for her.

He passes between two fallen logs and sails around a bend in the path. And up ahead of him, Kate steps out from behind a tree.

Holding a stick.

Kate had it pictured in her mind, but it's not quite like the scene from Lavana's movie.

There he is, shirt unbuttoned, arms pumping. Dumb look of surprise on his face. She plants the blunt end of the stick on the ground. There's not really time to aim the pointed end.

Travis swerves at the last second anyway. The point tears a gash along his right side below his ribs.

Kate tries to keep her hold on the stick. Travis knocks her down as he goes by.

She lands hard on her back but he lands hard too. Rolling onto her elbow, she sees him sprawled facedown on the trail, his arms splayed.

She gets to her knees, and he tries to push himself up. He lets out a plaintive sound that's too high-pitched to be a moan. His hand goes to his side and comes away smeared with blood.

Kate rises to her feet, feels a stab of pain in her wounded heel.

Travis is crawling.

She didn't register the knife before, but he had one. It's in the dirt in front of him. He reaches for it.

The stick was broken in two by the impact. Kate picks up the longer half, takes three limping steps, and slams it against the wound in Travis's side.

This time he moans.

She drops onto him, straddling his back.

His fingers close around the handle of the knife, and he twists around to stab at her.

She raises the stick and brings it down on the side of his head.

32

Lee Tennick is driving home after checking the shed in the woods when he receives a call from his cop friend, Ralph Beckham.

"Got something big."

"What?" Tennick says warily.

"Homicide."

Tennick slows and pulls off onto the shoulder of the road.

"Please tell me it's not Kate Summerlin."

"Holy shit," Beckham says. "How did you know?"

Tennick closes his eyes and leans his head against the window beside him.

"Do they know who killed her?" he asks. "Was it Travis Pollard?"

"I guess you already heard about this," Beckham says. "I thought I was giving you a scoop. But whoever told you must've got it garbled. He didn't kill her. She killed him."

Kate changes out of her wet clothes and into the dry ones her father brought her.

He was the first one she called when she found her phone in Travis's pocket. Her second call was to 911. They advised her to stay where she was, but she paid them no mind. She took one of Travis's shoes to replace her lost one and walked to the gravel lot on Portage Road.

She was sitting on a railroad tie when the first police car arrived. Her father showed up three minutes later, with Vera Landen following close behind.

Landen is mellower than usual. Almost kind. Maybe it's the late hour. She applies a temporary bandage to the wound on Kate's heel. Brings out a blanket from her car and holds it up so Kate can have some privacy while she changes.

Then the two of them sit in the car and Kate gives her a rough outline of what happened and tells her where to find Travis's body. Kate didn't mention Devin on the 911 call, but she does now. Chief Landen sends two of her officers around to the other side of the pond.

An ambulance arrives with no fanfare, no sirens blaring, and Lee Tennick turns up around the same time. The cops let him into the lot, but they don't let him near her. She sees him standing out in the cold, talking to her father. He waves to her, and she waves back.

He's still there when the EMTs carry the body on a stretcher up the hill. Travis has a sheet over him. It makes him look small.

Landen needs to go over everything in fine detail, but first she drives Kate to the ER, where a young resident tends to her heel properly. Afterward, they talk in Landen's office at the station. One of Landen's sergeants, a bald cop named Dietrich, sits off to the side taking notes. Kate's clothes, bagged as evidence, are on a table by the window. The pieces of the stick she used on Travis are there as well, along with his knife and, in a smaller bag, Kate's scissors.

Kate lays out the whole story, and Landen listens with few interruptions. When Kate describes what happened with Travis at the motel, she doesn't shy away from the sex or the choking, and Landen's face betrays no reaction.

When they come to the end, Landen has questions. She gets up from her desk and stands over the two halves of the stick on the table.

"You hit him in the head—" she says. "How many times?"

"Three," Kate says.

"Three times. And he stopped moving."

"Yes."

"But he was still alive."

Kate nods. "I could hear him breathing."

"Was he unconscious?"

Some questions aren't really questions. This one is a warning. Kate realizes that Landen is trying to guide her.

"I had no way of knowing if he was unconscious. He might have been faking."

"So you were afraid of him," Landen says. "You still considered him a threat."

"That's right. I was in fear for my life. He had already tried to drown me. I thought he might get up and attack me again."

Landen picks up the evidence bag that holds the scissors.

"That's when you used these," she says.

She sits behind her desk again and lays the bag on the blotter. The blades of the scissors are stained with blood.

Kate doesn't remember taking the scissors from her pocket. But she remembers holding them tight in her fist. Squeezing them until her palm hurt. Jabbing them into Travis's neck.

"How many times did you stab him?" Landen asks.

"I can't answer that. I didn't count."

She stabbed him until it seemed like enough. She must have hit an artery, because there was a lot of blood. It spurted into the air, onto her hand and her arm. She washed it off later in the water of the pond.

But first she stood over Travis's dead body. His blood was black in the moonlight. It darkened his blond hair, and streaks of it covered his chin. His eyes were open but hidden in shadows.

He wasn't beautiful. Not like Melissa Cornelle.

Kate left him as he lay.

She feels an ache in her heel where the doctor stitched her cut, and in her chest where the seatbelt dug into her, and in her shoulders from the strain of having her hands tied behind her back. But she doesn't feel anything for Travis Pollard.

Landen is holding the bag with the scissors up to the light. Contemplating them.

"I guess you were lucky to have these," she says.

She tosses the bag carelessly onto the desk.

"That's enough for tonight. Why don't you go home."

The next two days bring a bustle of activity.

The police arrange to have Kate's car hauled out of the pond. She isn't there to see, but she hears about it from Lee Tennick. He tells her about the cops who pored over the room she shared with Travis at Your Motel, and about the search of Travis's apartment, which turned up the jewelry stolen from Bryan Cayhill's house.

"About a million dollars' worth," Tennick says.

It's Tuesday and the sun has been down for more than an hour. Tennick has a fire going. Kate is in one of his camp chairs with a blanket wrapped around her. There's a platter on the milk crate between them: fried chicken and salt potatoes that her father made.

Out on Bird River Road, a car drives by slowly. It's not the first one, and probably not the last. Rubberneckers, Kate thinks. Like people slowing down to get a better look at an accident. They want to see the woman who got abducted. And got away.

Tennick must have noticed the car too.

"It won't last," he says.

But it might. A news van came by in the afternoon, from the CBS affiliate in Syracuse. Kate stayed in the house, and it went away. There was a different one on Monday, and she suspects there will be another tomorrow.

"You should have a lawyer," Tennick says.

"That's what my father said."

"He's right."

"He's getting one. I can't deal with it."

"If you put out a statement, it might placate the news people. I could help you."

Kate hugs the blanket closer around her. "I bet that would get you a lot of hits for your blog."

It sounds flippant, even to her own ears, and she regrets it immediately. She can see the hurt in his eyes.

"I meant I could help you write it," Tennick says.

She turns away from him and stares at the fire. "I know. I'm sorry, Lee."

He takes a chicken leg from the platter and bites into it, and Kate listens to him chewing. Her body aches and she's tired and she wants to hide somewhere, preferably a place where she never met Travis Pollard. Or Merkury.

She falls asleep at eleven that night, and wakes at three a.m. The wind rattles her bedroom window. She tries to remember her mother sitting on the edge of her bed. She closes her eyes and imagines her mother's hand resting over her heart. She thinks of her mother's trick for getting up when you don't want to: holding your breath until you can't any longer.

"I did it," she says aloud. "I held my breath."

But there's no one to hear.

She drifts along on the edge of sleep and time passes slow. She keeps her phone by her pillow so she can be sure it's passing at all. It's 3:49, and the next time she checks it's 4:33. Then 5:02. At some point she slips over the edge.

And wakes to a crash at 6:27. She sits up quickly and hears the rev of a car's engine receding. And her father's footsteps on the second floor. He comes pounding down the staircase and she meets him at the bottom, but he rushes into the kitchen ahead of her and switches on the light. The broken window is the first thing Kate notices. The curtains are billowing. There's glass on the floor, and a brick. A red brick with black writing on it: *KILLER*.

Her father, in a sweatshirt and flannel pajama bottoms, whips open the front door and runs out. Tennick is in the driveway in his bathrobe.

"Gray SUV," he says. "Couldn't see who it was. I got the plate."

Tennick goes back into his RV to fetch his phone and call the police. Kate finds a broom in the front closet to sweep the glass, but when her father comes in, he tells her to leave it. She stands in the doorway of the kitchen holding the broom and it feels light, insubstantial. She lets go of it and it clatters to the floor.

Her father puts his arm around her and pulls her close. She rests her head on his shoulder and realizes she's crying.

"My sweet, sweet girl," he says. "This should not have happened to you."

"I can't—" she says.

He holds on to her, strokes her hair.

"I can't stay here."

She doesn't even try to get back to sleep.

At ten a.m. she meets with the lawyer her father found, a distinguished man in his sixties, silver-haired and sharply dressed. The meeting lasts well into the afternoon, and he seems upbeat and confident.

Her father drives to the police station afterward. She stays in the car while he goes in and talks to Vera Landen. He comes out with Kate's coat and handbag. They're in rough shape from the time they spent in the pond, but her driver's license and credit cards are fine.

By six o'clock Kate has rented a car and packed for the trip to Ohio. The drive to her uncle's cabin will take nine hours or more. She hopes to make it at least halfway before she has to stop for the night.

She says her goodbyes to her father and Tennick, but there's one last thing to do before she leaves town. She hasn't forgotten about Jenny Wyler.

She drives to the Seagate campus and parks her rental in the visitors' lot. Then walks to the dining hall and talks her way past the kid who's scanning student IDs. The dinner rush is underway.

She spots Diana Perez clearing trays and wiping down tables. The girl looks irritated when she sees her.

"I'm working," she says.

"I only need a minute," says Kate. "I'd like to know if you've been in touch with Jenny."

Diana glares at her. "Even if I had, why would I tell you?"

"I'd like to help her if I can."

"You didn't help her the last time you went looking for her. In fact, it seems like you're kind of dangerous to be around."

Kate lets that pass and pulls a folded paper from her pocket: a page from her notebook where she's written her cellphone number. She holds it out.

"If you hear from Jenny and she needs a place to stay, or anything, tell her she can call me."

Diana makes no move to take the paper.

"Please," Kate says.

The girl shakes her head, but reaches for the note with two fingers, as if she's touching something unclean. She tucks it in the pocket of her apron.

Kate thanks her and walks away. The people around her have gone quiet and she can't help thinking there are eyes on her. She keeps her head down, and by the time she reaches the exit, the feeling has faded. The regular din of conversation has resumed.

Outside the sky is a darkening blue. Kate is wearing an old coat her father gave her. She left her own coat behind at the house. She doesn't think she'll want to wear it again.

When she crosses Main Street there's no traffic for as far as she can see. She comes to the visitors' lot and looks back, and there are squares of light in random patterns in the windows of the dorms and globes of light like beacons at the top of the Hill.

She walks along a row of cars with shadows in between them, a lone arc lamp buzzing above her, and it's tempting to believe that she's departing from the real world and entering something else. A lesser place, grim and desolate and empty.

33

SIX WEEKS LATER

On the eighth of December, Vera Landen is in a room at the Holiday Inn in Columbus, Ohio.

She fears she might be turning into a cliché: the obsessed detective. She brought pictures of the Merkury victims with her, twelve of them, from Melissa Cornelle to Bryan Cayhill. It's almost midnight, and she's sitting cross-legged on one of the room's two double beds, her laptop in front of her, the photos laid out in the shape of a fan. She's typing notes on her conversations with friends and colleagues of Devin Falko.

She spent hours back home in New York going over Falko's credit card statements and travel history, looking for anything that might place him in proximity to the Merkury killings. Airline reservations. Gas station and hotel charges. There's no correlation she can find. Which is suggestive, but not conclusive: Falko might have avoided flying altogether, and paid cash for gas and lodging.

Hence this trip to Columbus. Landen has been here for two days, and she has managed to eliminate Falko as a suspect in the murder of Bryan

Cayhill. There are multiple witnesses who can place Falko in Columbus, at a friend's bachelor party, on the night Bryan was killed.

What's more, Landen found a secretary in the psychology department at Ohio State University who helped her comb through records of Falko's time as a professor there. His attendance at a departmental conference, where he delivered one of the lectures, rules him out as a suspect in another of the Merkury killings.

Landen is confident now that Devin Falko was not Merkury.

This is progress. Of a sort.

She debated taking this trip at all. She's doing it at her own expense, and in theory she shouldn't have to. Merkury has taken victims in multiple jurisdictions, and law enforcement officers in those places have been working together for years to identify and capture him. Their efforts are coordinated by an FBI agent named Dan Gonzalez, based out of the field office in Albany.

Landen phoned him weeks ago to ask if he could contact someone at the FBI's Columbus field office and persuade them to look into Devin Falko's background. Gonzalez said he would, but then a month went by without a word from him.

When she followed up, he was vague. Said he was working on it. She got the sense that he was skeptical of the whole idea of investigating Falko.

"You might get just as far by waiting," he said.

"How's that?" Landen asked.

"Falko's dead. So if there's another Merkury killing, it wasn't him. And if there's not . . ." Gonzalez let the thought trail off.

"So we wait and see?" Landen said.

"No, no. We'll go through the motions. If we don't, who will?"

It was a cynical thing to say, but Landen took something from it. Even if the FBI field office in Columbus agreed to do as she asked, they might only go through the motions. Now that Landen has done the work herself, she's satisfied that it was done right.

She closes her laptop. Stacks the twelve victim photos and slides them into a folder. She moves everything to the spare double bed with her suitcase. Tomorrow she drives home.

She'll make a detour first. She's been keeping tabs on Kate Summerlin and knows that she's staying in the small house outside Bradner where she found her before. It's worth stopping there, Landen thinks, even though it will add about an hour to her trip.

Kate Summerlin interests her. Landen cares about the girl, as exasperating as she is. And she would like to know how Kate is feeling in the aftermath of killing Travis Pollard.

The obvious thing to do would be to ask her.

But she wonders if Kate would give her the truth.

Kate has gotten into the habit of going for walks in the morning, and it's dawning on her that where she's living now is not so different from where she was before.

Start with Alexander in upstate New York. Take away the college and drive out into the country. Subtract the hills and the curves. Make the roads run flat and straight, north to south, east to west. Make them intersect at perfect right angles.

And there you are: Bradner, Ohio.

The view from Holcomb Road, northwest of Bradner, is either woods or fields. In early December the trees have lost their leaves and the fields have all been harvested. It's a landscape of browns and grays. And blue for the sky. The sun's out.

Kate is wearing the coat her father gave her and a pair of hiking boots that were a gift from her uncle. She keeps her hands in her pockets and moves at an easy pace. The wound on her foot has healed nicely, but it's still tender.

She walks on the north side of the road, two miles east, then crosses to the south side and heads back.

Her cellphone is in the inside pocket of her coat. Sometimes she forgets to carry it at all. Early on, she got calls from reporters wanting to talk about Travis Pollard. She left them unanswered and deleted the voicemails. Eventually the calls stopped.

Often on these walks Kate plays music on her phone. For a while she listened to old episodes of Lee Tennick's podcast. This morning she's listening to nothing but her footsteps. She resists the temptation to count them. There's nothing much out here to mark time or distance. There are few houses and little traffic. Some days Kate finishes her walk without seeing a car.

Not today. She hears one over her shoulder, getting closer. But it doesn't pass. It pulls up parallel to her and keeps pace. A familiar blue SUV. Driven by Vera Landen.

"I thought that must be you," Landen says.

"What are you doing here?" Kate asks her.

"I wanted to talk," Landen says. "Get in. It won't take long."

She stops the car. Kate stands still for a moment to demonstrate that she has a choice in the matter. Then crosses the road and gets in on the passenger side.

"You look good," Landen says.

When Kate doesn't answer, she adds:

"I've been on the road since seven this morning. Came here from Columbus."

Kate keeps quiet and Landen starts driving again.

"I understand they had a church service last month. For Devin. I guess his parents are religious. I don't suppose you went."

"No," Kate says.

"People I talked to said it was nice."

They come to the driveway of the house where Kate is staying. Landen drives past it.

"There's something I wanted to tell you in person," she says. "I've been looking into things and I cleared him. Devin wasn't Merkury."

Kate watches the road ahead. "That's nice."

"I know this is late in coming," Landen says. "Maybe I shouldn't have shared my suspicions about him with you. If I had it to do over . . ."

She lets the thought dangle. Kate has had time to consider what might have happened if Landen hadn't planted the idea in her head that Devin might be Merkury. And if Kate herself hadn't let it take root. Her final conversation with Devin would have played out differently. She wouldn't have gone to see Travis. Devin would be alive.

He died because of her.

It's not something she wants to dwell on.

"It already happened," she says to Landen. "There are no do-overs."

The woman nods and comes to a stop sign and makes a right turn. Drives with one hand on the wheel. They cruise along without talking for a minute or two, then Landen brings up something Kate has tried to forget about.

"That time you thought Merkury had been in your father's house. How sure are you?"

Kate was certain then. But it seems like long ago.

"Pretty sure," she says.

"I got the lab results back on the steak knife. The one you thought he moved. They found no fingerprints or DNA."

"He never leaves prints or DNA," Kate says.

Vera Landen makes no comment. She comes to another intersection and turns left this time. They pass by a teenager riding a four-wheeler through a field, stirring up a trail of dust.

"How are you handling things?" Landen asks.

There's a gentleness in her voice that Kate doesn't especially like.

"Are you trying to be my friend, Chief Landen?"

The woman presses on, undiscouraged. "You went through something. And you left town suddenly. I wondered how you were doing."

"I like it out here," Kate says. "No one talks to me about Travis, and no one throws bricks through my windows."

She sounds angry. She's aware of it. Some of her anger is about the brick, and about the word written on it: *KILLER*. Some of it has been in her a long time, bubbling under the surface. Devin told her once that she was angry at her mother. For dying.

Kate got mad at him for saying it, which he told her only proved his point.

But the brick, the broken window, she's working on letting that go. There's no mystery about it. The culprit was identified easily, based on the license plate number Lee Tennick saw. The car belonged to Matthew Pollard, Travis's older brother. Kate's father declined to press charges, and Kate agreed. She figured Matthew was entitled to one brick.

There was talk of a civil suit from Travis's family, for wrongful death. But Kate's lawyer tells her nothing has been filed. And so far, the district attorney has brought no criminal charges against her. Kate doesn't bring any of this up with Landen. She would rather not think about these possibilities. They don't seem real.

Landen comes to another intersection and makes another turn. She's quiet, and Kate thinks their conversation has come to an end.

But no.

"It's no small thing, killing someone," Landen says. "You don't want to keep it all in. You might find it's too much to deal with alone."

Kate wants to say she's fine and Landen is being presumptuous. She can feel a little bit of the anger inside her boiling over.

"What do *you* know about it?" she asks Landen. "How many people have *you* killed?"

The woman's face betrays no reaction. Her answer, when it comes, is formal and dignified.

"None," she says. "But I know people who have. And I am possessed of imagination and empathy."

They pass the rest of the drive without talking. Another ten minutes on the back roads of northwest Ohio. Maybe Landen is trying to think of something more to say, or maybe she likes the scenery. They make their way back to Holcomb Road, and Landen turns into the driveway. Takes Kate all the way to the house. It's clad in the same worn-out vinyl siding, but there's fresh white paint on all the trim and new shingles on the roof.

"You've been working," Landen says.

"My uncle did a lot of it."

"Do you think you'll stay here?"

"I don't know," Kate says, stepping out of the car. "For now."

She walks toward the house without saying goodbye. Before she reaches the door, Landen powers down the driver's-side window of the SUV and calls to her.

"I meant to ask you about Jenny Wyler."

"What about her?"

"The last time we talked, she was in the wind," Landen says. "I'm wondering if you've heard from her."

"No."

"Well, if you do, let me know. I hope she's all right."

Landen raises the window, swings the SUV around, and heads out. Kate stands on the front step until she's out of sight, then goes inside.

The interior of the house has undergone some renovations as well. It's a work in progress. The wood floors have been sanded and stained a rich syrupy color and finished with polyurethane so they gleam. The windows have new curtains and the walls a new coat of paint. The old ratty sofa and armchair have been replaced.

Jenny Wyler is lying on the new sofa, reading a book.

"You took a long walk," she says. "Who were you talking to?"

Kate hangs her coat on a hook by the door. "The fuzz."

"The what?"

"The po-po," Kate says. "A lady copper from back east."

"You're weird."

"I know."

"You didn't tell her I was here."

"Of course not."

"Cool," Jenny says, closing her book. "You want breakfast? I'll make bacon."

Kate got a call from Jenny about a week after Halloween. The girl was stranded in Harrisburg, Pennsylvania, where she'd been staying at a youth hostel, afraid to go back to her apartment in Syracuse. Her car had never been in good shape, and it had finally crapped out on her.

Diana Perez had offered to pick her up, but she didn't want to stay with Diana.

"He knows where she lives," Jenny explained.

She was referring to her father. By then, he had been released on bail to await trial for the break-in and the assault on Ian Gardner.

"You can come here," Kate said.

"Where's here?"

"Ohio. The middle of nowhere."

"I don't know," Jenny said.

"It's up to you."

There was a long stretch when neither of them said anything. Kate thought the girl might have hung up.

Finally Jenny said: "The thing is, I need someone I can trust. Are you someone I can trust?"

"Yes," Kate told her. "I promise."

Jenny bought a Greyhound ticket to Toledo, and Kate picked her up at the bus station. The only luggage she had was a backpack. She was more subdued than Kate remembered. Warier. Said nothing at all on the drive back to Bradner, and very little for the rest of the evening.

Three days went by before Jenny talked about what had happened at her apartment in Syracuse. How frightened she was of her father. Seeing him punch Ian over and over. The way he wouldn't let up, even when Ian was down on the floor, even when she begged him to stop. She had always known that her father had violence in him, but she had never seen it come out the way it did that night.

"I never want to see him like that again," she said.

She had stayed in Syracuse long enough to give a statement to the police and to visit Ian in his hospital room. But as soon as she could, she gathered some things from her apartment and drove south to Binghamton. From there she spent two weeks drifting, not knowing where to go, sometimes sleeping in her car. Just wanting a place where she could be on her own, without worrying that her father might find her.

"You've found it," Kate told her. "You're safe."

The next day Jenny seemed better, and since then they've settled into a routine together. Kate worried that the house would be too small for both of them, but Jenny has proved easy to get along with. She likes to cook. She cleans up after herself. And she's taken a strong interest in working on the renovations.

The plan is to redo the kitchen next. Take up the cheap linoleum from the floor and replace it with ceramic tile. Put in new cabinets and countertops, a new sink, maybe even a dishwasher. Jenny has been watching YouTube videos on her phone, learning about plumbing and tiling.

Kate's uncle is paying for everything. Jim Rafferty has a real estate business to run, but he's been checking up on Kate every few days, driving down from his home in Perrysburg, half an hour away. He did the repairs on the roof himself, beginning on the weekend after Kate returned here—even though he could have easily afforded to hire someone to do the work.

It wasn't about the roof, of course. Kate isn't naive. Uncle Jim thinks she needs looking after. You kill one college kid, and suddenly everybody's worried.

She played her part: steadying the ladder when he climbed it, passing tools up to him, clearing away the old shingles after he scraped them off. Trying to show him she was okay. The work took days, and after it was finished they celebrated by cooking burgers on a charcoal grill in the backyard. They ate them off paper plates on a weathered picnic table under a sycamore tree.

"Your grandfather was a carpenter," Kate's uncle said. "He grew up in this house and inherited it from his parents. Could never bear to part with it. He used to insist on bringing us here every summer, your mother and me. Your grandmother indulged him. I think she would have liked someplace finer to go on vacation."

Kate had heard this before, but she didn't interrupt him.

"Your mother and I, we liked it here," he said. "We would get ourselves lost in the woods. Or we'd walk into town and hang around with the local kids. Your mother could make friends with anybody.

"She was a bit of a tomboy. Only a year younger than me. She wanted to do everything I did." He looked up at the sycamore. "We used to climb this tree, walk out on that limb there like it was a tightrope. Gave your grandmother fits when she saw us. I fell one summer and broke my leg. They had to drive me to the hospital in Bowling Green. The following year, your mother did the same. She was in a cast for weeks. But when we came here the next summer, she got back up in the tree."

Kate's uncle gave her a kindly smile from across the picnic table, and she understood he was trying to offer her something: a lesson about resilience after a misfortune. She was grateful that he didn't make it explicit.

He had one more thing to add.

"Your grandfather left me this place when he died. But it belonged to your mother as much as to me. Which means it's yours. You're not a guest here. You're home. You can stay as long as you want."

34

On Friday the tenth of December, Kate comes in from her morning walk to find that Jenny has acquired a Christmas tree.

It's a sturdy pine sapling, four feet high, and Jenny has it in a corner of the sitting room in an old tin washbasin she's using as a planter.

"I found it in the woods," she says. "Didn't seem right to cut it down, so I dug it up instead."

In the afternoon they drive into Bradner and pick up ornaments and garlands and a string of Christmas lights. Kate has a used Mazda she bought from a dealer in Toledo. Her uncle loaned her the money. She plans to pay him back when the insurance claim on her old car comes through.

They decorate Jenny's sapling with the garlands and ornaments, but the lights seem like overkill. They hang them around the frame of the front door instead. Kate hasn't shopped for presents, but she finds things to put under the tree. Her father has been sending her care packages—pasta and jars of sauce, basmati rice, cans of soup and peaches—as if he thinks she has no access to groceries.

He's been forwarding packages too: from Martin and Nicole Cayhill, from Alice Cornelle. Alice sent homemade cookies and brownies. The

Cayhills sent crackers and preserves and summer sausage, cocoa mix and bottles of wine.

Jenny makes chicken stir-fry for dinner, and afterward they light a fire in the woodstove in the sitting room. They read and drink hot cocoa. Jenny shops for kitchen cabinets on her phone, finds some with Shaker-style doors. She shows them to Kate.

Says, "I bet Uncle Jim will buy us these if we ask him."

Around eleven Jenny goes to bed. Kate moves her armchair closer to the fire and dozes. An hour goes by. The fire dies down. She sits up and reaches for her cocoa, but it's gone cold.

She takes her mug to the kitchen and leaves it in the sink. Confirms that the back door is locked. Then the front door.

Jenny is asleep in the bedroom, curled up on her side like a child. There's only the one double bed and they've been sharing it, though it didn't start out that way. For the first week, Jenny slept on the sofa, but one night when it rained and thundered, she came in and climbed under the covers with Kate.

Kate likes the company. She imagines this might be what it's like to have a sister.

But now she's awake. She leaves Jenny sleeping and returns to the sitting room. Picks up a pen and a notebook from the bookshelf. The notebook has a brown leather cover. It reminds her of the ones her mother used for journaling.

It's another gift from her uncle.

Kate settles in on the sofa, opens the notebook, and writes a single line.

I'm afraid I don't have anything to say.

Other lines follow:

I need to write a book, but I haven't written a thing.

I could say I lost something that night at the pond, but that's wrong. I lost it before. Direction. Purpose. If I ever had it.

Who are you saying this to? Who is this for?

But Kate knows. It's for her mother. If her mother is anywhere, she's here. Not in the house in Alexander. Not in any of the places they lived before or after.

In two weeks it will be Christmas Eve. I miss you. It's not fair what you did. Leaving.

But I'm not mad at you.

I need you.

I need

The pen goes still on the page. Kate doesn't know what she needs.

Before she figures it out, there's a ping on her cellphone.

It's on the floor next to an outlet, charging. She unplugs it and brings it back to the sofa.

There's a text from a number she doesn't recognize.

Kate

And three dots floating underneath. More to come.

I'm sorry.

There's a tiny part of her that's filled with hope, that believes in the possibility of miracles. But the rest of her knows. Her mother is not in a place where she can send text messages.

I should have contacted you sooner. I didn't know if you would want to hear from me. But please believe me: I've been thinking about you, and I'm sorry you had to do what you did.

Kate makes no reply. She watches the three dots, and more comes through.

I know what you're left with at a time like this. The burden. I would take it away from you if I could. I would bear it myself.

More:

I wish I had known. About young Mr. Pollard. I would have visited him. He would not have troubled you.

It would have been a novelty for me—doing it to someone who deserved it.

The point is: I am already lost. But not you.

You are a good person. Untarnished. Incapable of being tarnished.

I have been in the wrong. For years and years. But you are in the right.

You need to hear this. You need to know it.

Kate tosses her phone away, onto the seat of the armchair. She lies back on the sofa and covers her face with her hands. She can feel tears on her cheeks. She opens her mouth to let out a wail, but there's no sound.

Her body shudders.

He's an affront. She wants to kill him.

With the stick she used on Travis.

With the scissors.

With her hands.

She sits up and reaches for the notebook. Turns to a blank page and writes:

I hate you.

It's too mild. But all she can do is repeat it.

Hate you.

Hate you.

The words look ugly. They don't belong here. Not in the same place where she was writing to her mother.

Kate tears the page from the notebook and brings it to the woodstove. Opens the cast-iron door.

The fire is out, but the coals are still hot.

When she puts the page in, it blackens and smokes and curls.

Her phone pings again.

She crosses to the chair and snatches it up. She's ready to smash it on the floor.

She wants no more from him.

But the new text is from Lee Tennick.

It says: Jenny Wyler's father is dead.

35

The Wyler house in Earlville looks bleak in the fading of the day.

Lee Tennick was here last night, and it was livelier then: police cruisers all along the street, a van from the county morgue, curious neighbors gathering on the sidewalks, bundled in their winter coats.

Ralph Beckham tipped Tennick off about the killing. Beckham was on the scene with Vera Landen, helping out the local cops. There hadn't been a homicide in Earlville in more than thirty years.

Tennick talked his way into one of the next-door neighbors' yards. He was able to snap a few pictures when they brought Samuel Wyler's body out the back door on a gurney and rolled it around front to the coroner's van. He got some good images of the cops and the crowd as well.

Today there's a hush over the neighborhood. Tennick sets up his tripod on the sidewalk in front of the house so his camera can capture the whole length of the building. The lawn is overgrown and dotted with dead leaves. There are two painted milk cans, one on either side of the front door. Sky blue. Tennick likes the symmetry, and the pop of color.

He stays for half an hour and takes a series of shots as the dusk descends.

* * *

Kate and Jenny leave Bradner at eight a.m. on Saturday and arrive in Alexander, New York, at five thirty in the evening.

Kate's father has a roast in the oven, carrots and potatoes to go with it. The three of them share a somber dinner, and afterward Jenny wants to drive to her father's house in Earlville. Kate convinces her it can wait. They watch television together until Jenny starts to look sleepy, then Kate takes her up to the spare bedroom on the second floor and helps her settle in.

Kate's bedroom downstairs looks just as she left it, though the sheets and blankets smell freshly laundered. She's tired from the long drive, but she's not ready to sleep.

She finds Tennick in his RV, and they sit across from each other at his Formica table.

"I've missed you," he says, and it sounds like he means it.

His hair is longer and his face appears drawn, as if he's lost weight. Kate realizes she's missed him too, but she's not going to get all sentimental.

"Tell me what you know," she says.

She got the barest of details from him last night: that Samuel Wyler had been found dead in his home and that it was a homicide. But since then he's had time to find out more.

He doesn't disappoint her.

"Wyler's neighbor got a dog last week," he begins. "A mutt from the pound. Day before yesterday it started acting strange every time she let it out. It went to the fence between her yard and Wyler's, and it yapped and whined. She didn't worry too much about it. But yesterday she left the dog out a long time, and it dug under the fence. She found it on Wyler's back steps, sniffing at the door.

"The neighbor hadn't seen Wyler in a couple of days. When she knocked he didn't answer, and when she tried to look through the windows she saw that all the curtains were closed. So she tried the knob of the back door and it was unlocked. She opened it and saw Wyler's body lying on the kitchen floor."

"How did he die?" Kate asks.

"Blunt-force trauma," Tennick says. "Somebody slammed his head against the floor. But before that, they used a Taser on him and beat him up. He fought back. There were signs of a struggle in the house."

"Do they have a suspect?"

"It could have been a robbery gone wrong," Tennick says. "Wyler's wallet and car are missing. But the police are looking at Ian Gardner. Their theory is it was payback for the beating Wyler gave Ian in Syracuse. Or maybe Jenny asked him to do it, because she wanted her father out of her life for good."

"Do you buy that?" Kate asks.

"You tell me."

"Jenny didn't ask him. She was afraid of her father, but she didn't want him dead."

"I guess you know her better than I do," Tennick says. "How did she wind up with you anyway?"

"She called me," Kate says. "She needed a place to stay."

Tennick gives her a long appraising look.

"What does that make you now? Her guardian?"

Kate doesn't answer him. But it's a valid question. Her plan was simply to bring Jenny home and return by herself to Ohio. But now she's not sure.

The girl is alone. Kate feels some responsibility for her.

"It still could have been Ian," Tennick says. "Maybe he came up with the idea himself. Maybe he thought he was doing Jenny a favor."

It's plausible, Kate thinks. Just barely. But she doesn't believe it. She had many hours, during the long drive from Ohio, to consider who might have killed Samuel Wyler.

"It wasn't Ian," she says. "It was Merkury."

*   *   *

It's not easy, convincing Vera Landen.

Kate calls her Sunday morning and they meet at the station downtown. Their conversation is a stilted one, because Landen doesn't want to reveal details of the crime scene, and Kate doesn't want to admit that she already knows some of the details. She doesn't want to make trouble for Tennick—or for his source.

It's obvious, though, that the murder doesn't fit Merkury's M.O.

"Wyler was found at home," Landen says. "Not hung in a tree. And—how shall I put this?—there was a certain brutality to the crime, a crudeness that's not characteristic of Merkury."

These facts are hard to argue with, but Kate has evidence to back up her view: Merkury's text messages from Friday night.

Kate is reluctant to reveal them, but there doesn't seem to be an alternative. And she has one piece of consolation: the messages are a monologue. She never responded to him.

She shows Landen the entire thread, but there are a few crucial lines.

I know what you're left with at a time like this. The burden. I would take it away from you if I could. I would bear it myself.

I wish I had known. About young Mr. Pollard. I would have visited him. He would not have troubled you.

It would have been a novelty for me—doing it to someone who deserved it.

"He feels bad about me having to kill Travis," Kate tells Landen. "Killing Samuel Wyler was his way of doing something nice for me."

"So Wyler deserved it?" Landen says.

"A case could be made," says Kate.

"But why would Merkury think so? Are you suggesting he knew Wyler?"

"He could have known what Wyler did—the break-in and the rest. It made the news in Syracuse."

"Fine," Landen says. "Suppose he knew about Wyler. How is killing Wyler doing something nice for you? Wouldn't it be doing something for Jenny? How does Merkury connect her to you?"

This is the part that bothers Kate the most. It suggests that Merkury might be observing her more closely than she ever suspected. But there's an alternative.

"I put up flyers with Jenny's name and picture on them. And my name too. I posted them around the Seagate campus and in Earlville. He might have seen one."

Landen nods, but she looks like she has doubts. She keeps Kate in her office for an hour asking questions, trying to poke holes in her theory. The next day, Monday, Kate has to go over everything again with the Earlville police. They talk to Jenny as well.

On Tuesday morning Jenny schedules an appointment at a funeral home. Kate drives her there and sits with her while she makes arrangements for her father. It's hard to judge how the girl is doing. When Kate told her that she thought Merkury was the one who killed her father, Jenny took the news silently, and she hasn't wanted to talk about it since.

As for the arrangements, Jenny keeps things simple. There will be no casket, no viewing. Her father's body will be cremated. There'll be a church service and then a brief ceremony at a local cemetery, where the remains will be buried beside her mother's grave. The only question is the timing. The funeral director promises to make a call to the county coroner, to find out when the body will be released.

In the afternoon, Jenny wants to rest. She's still staying with Kate, though she has mostly abandoned the guest bedroom upstairs. She's gotten into the habit of sharing Kate's bed like she did at the cabin. Around three o'clock Kate looks in and finds her sleeping soundly.

Kate takes the opportunity to drive to the Wyler house in Earlville. She lets herself in with the key from under the milk can. The police have finished processing the scene—she confirmed it with Landen—but what's left behind is a fair amount of disarray.

Signs of a struggle, Tennick said.

There's a broken lamp in the living room, along with a good-sized dent in the wall behind the sofa. An end table has been knocked over, leaving framed photographs scattered across the carpet. There's dried blood on the tiled floor of the kitchen. Not as much as Kate would have expected.

She finds rubber gloves, sponges, and a bucket in the cabinet under the sink. She mixes dish soap and hot water and cleans up as well as she can. The hardest part is the grout between the tiles. She scrubs it with an old toothbrush until the stains are almost undetectable.

On Wednesday morning it snows. Big flakes drifting through the sky. It's the fifteenth of December.

Kate is back in the Wyler house, and this time Jenny is with her. When they first came in, Jenny moved through the rooms tentatively, touching the doorways as she passed through them, as if to reaffirm that the house was real. But now she seems at ease.

They open some windows to let in fresh air, but after a time they close them again and run the furnace to warm things up. Jenny takes a transistor radio from one of the kitchen cabinets and finds an FM station playing Christmas songs.

"I want a stereo," she says. "I don't know why we never had a stereo."

The snow tapers off and Jenny sits at the table going through her father's mail, separating out the bills she'll need to pay. Kate sits with her and helps her make a list of other things she'll need to do. She should call the minister at her father's church and ask him to perform the funeral service. She should get the word out to friends of her father's who may want to attend. Relatives too. She has an aunt in Chicago, another in Phoenix, various cousins. She wants to write an obituary to run in the newspaper.

By the early afternoon, things seem under control. There are plans in place at least. Kate makes a run to a restaurant on Main Street and picks up Philly cheesesteak sandwiches. When she returns, the radio is playing a cover of "Baby, It's Cold Outside."

Jenny is napping on the long gray sofa in the living room. Lying on her side, brown hair falling across her cheek. Beautiful. Peaceful.

Kate unwraps one of the sandwiches and eats it cross-legged on the carpet, watching over her. Sunlight comes through the front windows. Outside, the snow is already starting to melt. Jenny wakes, turns onto her back, yawns, and sits up.

"That smells good," she says.

"There's one for you," Kate says. "But maybe we should take it with us."

Jenny smiles. "Where are we going?"

"My father's house. You've had a rough few days. You shouldn't push too hard. We can come back here tomorrow."

Jenny looks around the room. "I thought I might stay here."

"All right," Kate says. "I can stay with you."

Jenny scoots down onto the floor with her. Touches her knee.

"You're sweet. But I think I need to get used to it. Him being gone."

There's a sadness in her that Kate recognizes. It doesn't matter what her relationship was like with her father. She's lost something she'll never get back.

"You don't have to be alone," Kate says.

"I do, eventually," Jenny says. "Might as well be now."

As she drives away from Jenny's house, Kate is in a melancholy mood. She's thinking about fate and possibilities and why things happen the way they do.

She has often wondered what her life would have been like if she had never climbed out her window the night Melissa Cornelle died, if she had never encountered Merkury. Would she have been a happier person, more carefree? Or if the white van hadn't run her parents off the road, if her mother was still alive. Without the weight of that grief, would Kate have written more, would she be further along in her career?

You can play the game both ways, she thinks. Suppose Samuel Wyler had never come to her wanting to find his daughter. She never would have met Jenny. That's something she wouldn't want to have missed out on. A good thing that came into her life.

It's only a seven-mile drive north to Alexander, and it goes smoothly. The roads are clear in spite of the earlier snow. There's an alternate history where Kate gets stuck behind a school bus after leaving Jenny's house, or where she encounters an accident on Route 12B, a jackknifed semi-truck delaying traffic.

But these things don't happen. She breezes past the hospital and the college, and the lights downtown are green for her. There's the police station and the Seagate Inn. Then another mile and she passes the grocery store on the edge of town. The Sunoco station.

Coming up on the right: Your Motel.

Kate can't help looking as she goes by. There are a handful of cars in the parking lot. One of them is a Volvo.

It looks like her father's.

She doesn't have to slow or turn around or go back. But she does.

Rolling through the motel lot, she gets a close look at the Volvo.

No mistake. It's her father's.

She parks at the far end of the long building. Without realizing it, she's in the same spot where Devin parked the night he followed her here.

Her father's Volvo is in front of one of the rooms. Not the room she shared with Travis, but only one door down.

Kate remembers when she and Tennick drove past Vera Landen's house and saw her father's car. She hasn't given much thought to the idea that her father is sleeping with Landen. She certainly never asked him about it.

But why would they need to come here? Landen lives alone.

Kate sits in the car with the heat running.

Girl detective, she thinks to herself. What do you imagine you're going to find out?

She takes out her phone and types a text message to her father.

Where are you?

She stares at the words, wondering what he'll say, what lie he'll tell. As she's about to hit send, she catches a glimpse of movement out of the corner of her eye. It's a door opening. She turns to see her father emerging from his motel room. Navy blue slacks, white shirt. Jacket and tie. The way he dresses when he teaches class.

The woman who steps out of the room behind him is not Vera Landen.

She's young. A student. Wearing heels, a skirt, a sweater. An overcoat, unbuttoned.

She has dark hair and pale skin.

Like Melissa Cornelle.

36

Kate has considered the possibility that her memory of the night she found Melissa's body is unreliable.

Devin brought it up once.

"It could have been your father, Kate. The man who was there that night. You never saw him."

"I heard his voice," she said.

"The mind has its defenses. If you can't bear to remember something, you can alter the details. You can make yourself believe you heard someone else's voice . . . As far as that goes, you might have seen your father that night and made yourself forget."

"I never turned around," she said.

"Are you sure? Maybe it's easier to believe you never turned around."

But Kate was unconvinced. Her memory was all she had. It had to be real. How could she doubt it?

And if it was real, the logic is simple.

She was eleven years old when she heard Merkury's voice, and if she heard it again today, she probably wouldn't recognize it. Would you recognize someone's voice if you only talked to them once eighteen years ago?

But Kate knows her father's voice, and she knew it when she was eleven. She knew then that it wasn't him. So she knows it now.

Otherwise, the world makes no sense. Anything goes.

It's not worth thinking about.

But here she is, thinking about it.

They're twenty feet away from her—her father and the young woman. Kate sits motionless in her car, hoping her father doesn't look her way.

But he does.

His only reaction is a flicker of pain that passes over his face. As if he's been poked with a needle. It's there and it's gone.

He doesn't break stride. He and the young woman get into the Volvo and drive away from the motel. Kate watches them go in her rearview mirror.

She doesn't follow them. She doesn't trust herself to drive.

She caught the flu once in college, and about three days in she started feeling dizzy. She let herself fall into bed and her dorm room slowly spun around her. No matter what she did, she couldn't get it to stop.

This is like that.

Her reality is taking a slow turn around her.

What did she see?

Her father coming out of a motel room with a student. So let's be real. Her father is having sex with a student. That's what people do in motel rooms in the middle of the day.

If it's happening now, it could have happened back then.

Kate was twelve when she first became aware of the rumor that her father had been sleeping with Melissa Cornelle. She found it on an amateurish true-crime website, reported as fact—with a link to Lee Tennick's blog. Tennick was more circumspect about it. He implied it, came right up to the edge of saying it, and let his readers draw their own conclusions.

When Kate was thirteen, she asked her father about it. He told her not to believe stories she read online. "People tell lies," he said. "It's the easiest thing in the world."

She trusted him.

It's possible she was right to trust him.

Seeing him today with a student—it proves nothing about what happened eighteen years ago.

He might never have slept with Melissa.

Or if he did, it doesn't mean he killed her.

But Kate needs to know, one way or the other.

She gets herself under control. Looks around her and wills the world to hold steady.

The motel recedes from her as she backs her car out of the parking space. She gets turned around and onto 12B. A mile north, she makes a right onto Bird River Road. Puts the lowering sun behind her.

The road rises and falls. The driveway of her father's house is wet with melting snow. Tennick's car is parked by the RV. Her father's Volvo is not here.

When Kate enters the house, she knows it's empty. She climbs the stairs to the second floor and imagines she can feel the steps bending beneath her feet. The door to her father's bedroom is ajar. She can glimpse the foot of the bed. The window.

She pushes the door with her fingertips and hears the slow creak of the hinges as it opens wide. There's a bureau against the wall opposite the window. An heirloom from her mother's family. Kate remembers it being here when she was a child, and in every house they lived in.

Back then, the top was cluttered with her mother's hairbrushes and makeup. Now it's piled with papers and books. *Slaughterhouse-Five*, *For Whom the Bell Tolls*, *Ethan Frome*, *Native Son*.

The bureau has six drawers, and Kate opens each of them. Her mother used to keep her journals here. All those notebooks with brown leather covers. But Kate finds folded bedsheets and blankets, her father's pants and sweaters.

The shelf in the closet yields nothing better. There's a space heater and an electric fan. A collection of board games.

The last place Kate tries is under the bed. There's eight inches of space and the floor is thick with dust. She finds a pair of forgotten shoes and a long plastic bin with a white lid.

She pulls the bin out and brings it up onto the bed to open it. There are keepsakes from her childhood on top: report cards and drawings and watercolors. And underneath them, seven notebooks.

If Kate's father had an affair with Melissa Cornelle, her mother might have known, or suspected. And if she did, she would have written about it.

Sitting on the bed, Kate opens one of the notebooks and sees her mother's handwriting. Graceful cursive letters in blue ink: *Kate had a fever this morning and a sore throat, and I worked myself into thinking she had the mumps. Pediatrician laughed at me. "What you've got is a girl with a cold," he said.*

Kate looks at the date on the entry. It's too early. Five years before Melissa died. She glances through the other notebooks and finds one that starts in the fall when she was ten.

There's a sheet of green construction paper folded in half between two of the pages. Kate opens the journal there, sets the paper aside, and scans the entries.

One of them is a single sentence:

He's doing it again.

It's dated November sixteenth.

Three days later, on the nineteenth, there's this:

Tried to talk to him and he lied to my face. Unbelievable.

Kate reads on, but the next few days are about preparations for Thanksgiving.

She's still reading when her father arrives home. She hears the Volvo approaching, the engine cutting off. Downstairs the front door opens.

Her father calls out: "Kate?"

The sheet of green paper is beside her on the bed. She picks it up to mark her place in the journal. But curiosity makes her unfold it.

It's a diagram of the solar system drawn with colored pencils. She doesn't remember it, but it's obviously something she drew in elementary school. There's her name at the top: *Katy Summerlin.* The planets are laid out in order, starting with the farthest from the sun. Each one labeled:

Pluto
Neptune
Uranus
Saturn
Jupater
Mars
Earth
Venus
Merkury

37

Kate stands up from the bed. The green paper falls from her hand and glides down to the floor.

Her father appears in the doorway. He left his jacket downstairs. He still has his tie on.

"I'm sorry," he says. "About what you saw at the motel."

Kate needs a moment to find her voice, and when she does it sounds strangely hollow.

"Are you?" she asks.

"I am. Did you follow me there?"

She shakes her head. "I happened to pass by."

"Well, I'm embarrassed. A girl shouldn't have to know about her father's love life."

"Is that what it is? Love?"

Her father's cheeks blush. "Maybe we shouldn't talk about this. Is there any chance we could forget it happened?"

"No."

"I guess not," her father says, leaning against the doorframe. "Okay. Her name is Emily. She was in my fiction writing seminar last spring.

She's not in any of my classes now. She's twenty-one. It's all consensual. I've seen her a few times."

"I thought you were seeing Vera Landen," Kate says.

There it is again: the pained look she saw at the motel.

"Vera's not always the warmest person," her father says.

He's got his hands in his pockets and his shoulders are hunched. Like he's trying not to squirm.

"Is that the way Mom was too?" Kate asks. "Not the warmest person?"

Her father sighs and takes his hands from his pockets to rub his face. The colors in the room are dim. The sky is gray outside the window.

"Is this what we're going to do?" he says. "Talk about all my sins?"

"So it's true, about Melissa," Kate says. "And Mom knew."

He smooths his tie over the front of his shirt and stands straighter. Clears his throat. He's Arthur Summerlin the college professor, lecturing.

"Marriages are complicated, Katy."

"Don't call me that."

"They are. You don't know. Your mother and I were young when we got married. Inexperienced. We were compatible in most ways. But you can't know how things are going to go when you start out—"

"You slept with Melissa. Are you trying to justify it?"

"I'm trying to explain—"

"So explain to me how she died," Kate says. "I don't want to hear the rest."

Her father holds himself still, draws in a slow breath through his nose, lets it out.

"Melissa was murdered by a lunatic who went on to kill eleven more people," he says. "Is that where we are? Is that who you think I am?"

"You haven't denied it yet."

He raises his right hand as if he's swearing an oath.

"Kate, I deny it."

The green paper is on the floor between them. Kate picks it up, unfolds it, offers it to him.

"It's right here," she says. "*Merkury*. With a *k*. Why are you lying to me?"

She watches him scan the paper. Sees sadness in his eyes.

"I didn't know your mother kept this." He gazes past her at the bed and seems to notice the bin and the notebooks for the first time. "I never had the heart to look through all that stuff."

"That's all you have to say?"

She's watching him, and she sees his posture change. Like he's been carrying something heavy and the strength is running out of him. He steels himself for one final effort.

"You need to let this go," he says. "I never killed anyone. I had no reason to kill Melissa. And if I were going to kill her, why would I leave her body less than a mile away from my own house? What sense would that make?"

"But this," Kate says, pointing to the paper. "Am I supposed to ignore this?"

"It's a child's drawing, Kate. Tear it up. Burn it. Put it in a frame on the wall. I don't care what you do with it. But don't press me anymore. I'm saying this for your sake."

He's holding the paper out to her with one hand, but the other is braced on the doorframe. His energy is spent.

"I can't forget this, Dad," she says. "You have to tell me."

He makes no move. Says nothing.

"It can't be worse than what I'm thinking," she says.

He closes his eyes.

"Believe me, Katy. It can."

38

"It was Mom," Kate says.

She's sitting on the bed again. Her father is in a chair by the window. The green paper is on the windowsill.

"You shouldn't blame her," he says. "It was my fault. Melissa wasn't the first time I cheated. Before her— Do you remember when we lived in Buffalo?"

Kate does. She remembers the winters, when the wind blew the snow in drifts against their house.

"I had a student at the university there," her father says. "Julia. She was a brilliant writer. Not that that justifies anything. She was ten years younger than me. It didn't seem like very much. We had a fling. I guess I was careless. One of your mother's friends saw us together."

"She told Mom?"

"No. She came to me. Threatened to tell your mother unless I told her myself. So I did, and it was awful. The way your mother looked at me. It made me understand what I'd done. The betrayal. I knelt at her feet. Put my head in her lap and cried like a baby. I promised I would end it. Swore I would never do it again."

"But you did," Kate says.

"I tried not to. But when I met Melissa . . . She was beautiful, obviously. And she admired me."

He bows his head. He was never a tall man, but sitting by the window he seems shrunken. His hair is more gray than black, and it's thinning at the crown. This is the first time Kate has thought of him as frail.

"You'll think I'm vain," he says. "But a man likes to be admired. And it was easy with Melissa. Natural. I didn't have to pursue her. She came to me."

His head comes up and he flicks a hand through the air. "I should have resisted. I knew it would hurt your mother if she found out. So I tried to be careful. When I saw Melissa, it was always in the evening in my office on campus. There were no restaurant dinners, no rendezvous out of town. Melissa knew we had to be discreet. She knew how to behave in front of other people.

"But your mother had suspicions. I was spending more time in my office. She asked me what was going on—if I was straying. That's how she put it. I told her no. 'Don't make a fool of me,' she said. I told her I wouldn't. I never meant to."

"How did she find out?" Kate asks.

"She came to campus to visit me one night, and as she arrived at Corwin Hall she saw Melissa leaving. She stopped and had a conversation with her. It could have been by chance, but I think your mother came around on more than one night. She was trying to catch me. After she talked to Melissa, she came up to my office and told me she had met the most charming girl. Even then, I didn't admit anything. I said I was Melissa's adviser and I'd been giving her notes on one of her manuscripts."

"But Mom didn't believe you."

"No. I knew she didn't. But I made a mistake, because she didn't seem angry. Or hurt, the way she had before. We didn't talk about it. I thought we had come to an understanding, and as long as I didn't flaunt it or embarrass her, she would look the other way.

"That's how things stood for weeks. Your mother changed, but I didn't see it. I was distracted. She withdrew a part of herself. She was still devoted to you, Kate. But not to me. I only recognized it after."

Arthur Summerlin stares at the floor for a moment, then looks up.

"I need you to know that she never meant for you to be involved," he says. "She wanted to be out of town when it happened, so she arranged a visit to Ohio to see your uncle. She wanted to take you with her. But I insisted that you stay here. I thought I was doing something positive. Stepping up to look after you, so your mother could enjoy some time on her own. She never imagined what would happen, that you would find the body. If she knew—I promise you she wouldn't have done it."

"But what did she do?" Kate asks. "Who was the man I spoke to by the stream that night?"

"Someone she hired," her father says. "I don't know his name. I don't think she knew his name."

"She paid someone to kill your mistress. And she admitted it to you?"

"Not in so many words. But I knew. When I saw Melissa's body that night, when you woke me up and brought me there, I knew it wasn't random, it wasn't a coincidence. And when I saw that word, *Merkury*, written on her . . ."

His voice falters, but then he goes on. "I knew it was your mother sending me a message." He picks up the green paper from the windowsill. "I remember the day you brought this home from school. You were eight, maybe nine. That night, after you went to bed, your mother showed this to me and joked about it: 'She gets her spelling from your side of the family.' It was a memory of a time when your mother and I were happy. She was reminding me of what I had ruined."

Kate stands up from the bed, restless. "If you knew," she says, "how could you stay with her? How could you go on . . ."

"As if nothing had happened? It wasn't an easy decision. I thought of going to the police, but I couldn't see how it would help. It would have made things worse. I was in sorry shape, struggling to hold things together. You were struggling too. You needed your mother. I couldn't take her away from you."

Her father runs a hand over his brow and through his hair.

"As time passed, things went back to normal," he says. "Your mother wasn't an evil person. She was my wife, and we got on with our life together. Since we never talked about it, I could almost believe she hadn't done it."

Kate paces across the room to the bureau. She can see herself reflected in the mirror, her father in the background.

"But if you never talked about it, how could you be sure?" she asks. "What if it wasn't her? What if it was random after all?"

Her father smiles and holds up the green paper. "Katy, a few minutes ago you were showing me this and insisting it couldn't be a coincidence."

"It's hard to understand though. Regular people don't hire killers. How would she know how to go about it? How would she pay for it?"

Her father folds the paper and returns it to the windowsill.

"Maybe that's enough," he says. "Maybe it's better if you don't dig any deeper."

"What are you not telling me?"

"I'm serious. You've heard enough."

There's a plea in his eyes, but Kate is unpersuaded.

"We've come this far," she says, turning to look at him directly. "I want to hear it all."

He stares out the window, and what color is left in his face drains away. She watches it go. When he speaks again, his voice is flat.

"Your mother didn't find a killer on her own. Your uncle helped her."

"Uncle Jim?" Kate says.

"That was plain to me from the start, as soon as I thought about it. Because you're right: your mother wouldn't know who to call to have someone killed. But your uncle . . . Well, he makes his money in real estate. And he's not helping his neighbors sell their houses—he's handling big transactions, commercial developments. In that kind of business, you come into contact with some shady characters. And he's always been a smooth operator. He can talk to anyone. People tell him things."

"You think Uncle Jim knows hitmen?"

"I think he knows a guy who knows a guy who can put you in touch with a hitman."

"You're guessing about this," Kate says.

Her father gets up from his chair and picks up the lamp from the nightstand by the bed. He turns it over and peels off the felt on the bottom. In the hollow at the base of the lamp, there's a miniature cassette tape in a plastic case.

"I'm not guessing, Kate," he says.

He has a pocket-sized cassette recorder in one of the drawers of the nightstand, but the batteries are dead. There are fresh ones downstairs in a cupboard. They end up listening to the tape at the kitchen table.

"I recorded this a few weeks after your mother died," Kate's father says. "I've kept it ever since. I was always afraid I might be accused of killing Melissa, and I wanted to be able to defend myself."

He slips the tape into the player. "When I recorded this, I was home from the hospital, still recovering from the crash. Your uncle drove to Oberlin on a Saturday. He had paid for your mother's gravestone and it had just been installed. He wanted to see it and lay some flowers on her grave.

"I invited him to come by the house after. I had some photographs of your mother's, from when they were kids. I told him I wanted him to have them."

Her father presses the play button on the cassette recorder. There's nothing at first, then Kate can hear voices that sound like they're in another room.

Her father: *I've got them for you in here.*
Her uncle: *I need to head back.*
Her father: *Stay a minute. Sit. We'll have a drink.*

The voices are clearer now.

Her uncle: *I'm driving, Art.*
Her father: *One drink.*

There are murky sounds on the tape. Maybe chairs being pulled out.
A bottle and glasses being set on a table.

Her father: *What did you think? I thought they did a nice job with
    the stone.*
Her uncle: *Yeah.*
Her father: *It was generous of you. I'm grateful.*
Her uncle: *Don't thank me. She was my sister.*

There's a silence that drags on for several seconds.

Her father: *You never liked me much, did you?*
Her uncle: *That's not true.*
Her father: *Come on. If we can't be honest now—*
Her uncle: *It's not. I liked you fine, in the beginning. My parents
    didn't think much of you. They pegged you as a dreamer who
    wouldn't amount to anything. I stuck up for you.*
Her father: *Really?*
Her uncle: *Because I thought you made Susan happy. That's what
    mattered.*
Her father: *I guess that didn't last.*
Her uncle: *No.*
Her father: *I tried.*

Her uncle: *That's not the impression I got.*

Her father: *I did. I tried to make her happy.*

Her uncle: *You tried to make yourself happy. But it's none of my business now. You're free, aren't you? You can fuck as many coeds as you like.*

Her father: *There we go. Now we're talking plainly.*

Her uncle: *Did I offend you, Art? I know I'm not wrong. It's smooth sailing for you now.*

Her father: *You're right. It'll be safer now. It was a little dangerous before.*

Her uncle: *Dangerous?*

Her father: *For the coeds.*

There's a pause.

Her uncle: *I don't have any idea what you're talking about.*

Her father: *Sure you do. We both know what happened to Melissa Cornelle.*

Another pause.

Her uncle: *Let me see that.*

Her father: *Why?*

"My phone was facedown on the table," Kate's father explains.

Her uncle: *Unlock it.*

Her father: *For god's sake.*

"He wanted to check and see if I was recording him. Once he did, he turned off the phone, just to be sure. But the cassette recorder was on the counter right next to us, hidden in a cereal box."

Her father: *Are you satisfied?*
Her uncle: *What do you want me to say?*
Her father: *I want you to acknowledge what happened.*
Her uncle: *What do you think happened?*
Her father: *Susan had Melissa killed, and you helped her.*
Her uncle: *How did I help?*
Her father: *You put her in touch with the killer.*
Her uncle: *Because I hobnob with killers all the time.*
Her father: *You would only need to know how to get in touch with one.*

Another pause, longer this time.

Her uncle: *Stand up.*
Her father: *What for?*
Her uncle: *Unbutton your shirt.*

"He's checking me for a wire now," Kate's father says.

Her father: *Is that good? Can I button up?*
Her uncle: *Do what you want.*
Her father: *I'm wondering about you, Jim. How you justified it to yourself. Helping my wife find someone to kill an innocent girl.*
Her uncle: *I didn't do that.*
Her father: *Oh, come on. Susan wouldn't have had a clue—*
Her uncle: *She didn't tell me the target was a girl. She said the target was you.*

Kate gasps and looks across at her father. He's rubbing a hand over his mouth, unfazed.

Her uncle: *You didn't know that part. Yeah, she wanted you dead. I tried to talk her out of it. Tried to convince her to divorce you.*

But that wasn't enough. I don't think you realize how angry Susan was, how badly you hurt her. She thought if you got divorced, you'd wind up marrying some younger woman. She wasn't going to be replaced. She wore me down, and I gave her the money she needed. Thirty thousand dollars. That's what I was willing to pay to see you gone.

Her father: *What changed her mind? Why was Melissa the one—*

Her uncle: *I wondered the same thing. It was about Kate. When it came down to it, Susan couldn't bear the thought of Kate losing her father. She decided you might be salvageable. If she did away with your side piece, maybe you'd get the message. It made me sick, that the Cornelle girl had to pay the price. I don't believe you were worth saving.*

Kate's father reaches over and presses the stop button on the cassette recorder. The two of them sit for a time in the suddenly quiet house.

"Do you think he was telling the truth?" Kate says at last.

"About what?" her father asks.

"About Mom wanting to have you killed."

Her father runs his tongue across his teeth. "Why would he lie about that?"

"Maybe he was trying to hurt you."

"Maybe he was."

Kate has the uneasy feeling that she's missing something. Her father is staring down at his hands on the table.

"It doesn't bother you," she says.

"What?"

"That Mom thought about hiring someone to kill you. It didn't bother you when you were talking to Uncle Jim either. You didn't react when he told you."

"You're making something out of nothing," her father says. But he's still staring down. He won't look at her.

"Did you already know?" she asks.

He finally looks up. "Of course not."

"You knew. Why are you lying? What are you keeping from me?"

He doesn't say anything. He seems to draw into himself, and Kate is once again struck by his frailty. But it doesn't make her feel sorry for him. It makes her angry.

"I want the truth," she says. "If you're going to keep it from me, I swear I'll leave right now and never come back. I'll never speak to you again."

Her father winces as if he's been stung. But he still doesn't answer.

She puts the question to him once more: "Did you know that Mom thought about having you killed?"

She watches his face. Sees the struggle that plays out there, and the moment when he surrenders.

"I didn't know until your uncle told me," he says. "But I wasn't surprised. This is hard for me to say to you, Katy, but I didn't stop straying after what happened to Melissa Cornelle. I mean I did stop, for years. But there was a girl at Oberlin. The same story. She admired me. I couldn't resist. By then, your mother and I, we were still married but it was only a routine we went through. So I didn't think it would matter . . . On the night your mother died, she told me she knew about the girl, she had known for weeks. She couldn't believe I had done it again. That's why . . ."

Her father trails off, his breath uneven. His hands come up to cover his eyes. Kate wants to fill in the rest: *That's why your mother was distracted. That's why she swerved when the white van cut us off.*

But her father finds his voice and lets her have the truth.

"There was no van that night, Katy. Your mother drove off the road on purpose. She was aiming for that tree. I wasn't supposed to survive. She meant to kill us both."

39

Arthur Summerlin has never been a religious man, but when he was young his parents took him to church. As a child who loved language, he paid attention to the Bible readings and the sermons.

At the moment, there's a particular line running through his head: *The thing which I greatly feared is come upon me.*

He's sitting alone at the table with the cassette recorder in front of him. Kate has gone away.

He withheld the truth from her for years and told himself that he was doing it for her benefit. He didn't want her to think ill of her mother. He knew he was protecting himself too, keeping his own transgressions hidden away, but his primary motive was a righteous one.

It was bad enough that Kate lost her mother. She shouldn't have to lose her image of her mother too. But now she has.

The thing which I greatly feared . . .

He can't forget the hollow look in Kate's eyes when he told her the truth about how her mother died. The weight that settled onto her. She carried it with her when she left the house.

He watched her go and wanted to ask her if she was coming back, but he was afraid of what her answer would be.

Instead he picked up the cassette recorder and called after her, "What do you want me to do with this?"

"You know what you need to do," she told him.

She's right. He knows.

He needs to turn the cassette tape over to Vera Landen.

There's no excuse for holding on to it any longer. Is he supposed to try to preserve his dead wife's reputation? Or his own? Should he care about what people think? Kate is the only one whose opinion matters. So the damage is already done.

Though maybe not all the damage.

Arthur has an awkward conversation ahead of him with Vera. He lied to her eighteen years ago when she asked him about his relationship with Melissa Cornelle. He said Melissa was one of his students and nothing more. Vera believed him.

She won't like finding out that he deceived her.

The fact that he's been sleeping with her for the past two years will make it worse. She's bound to wonder about his motives.

His motives were pure, more or less. After his wife's death, when he accepted a position at Seagate College and moved back to Alexander, he was lonely. Vera Landen was an attractive, accomplished woman. Those were the main reasons he pursued her.

But if he's honest, he has to acknowledge that the first time he asked her out for a drink was something of a test. He was curious about whether she had any inkling of the truth about Melissa's death, and he judged that if she suspected he was involved in any way, she would turn down his invitation. When she said yes, he felt safe. Comfortable.

That's over now. He'll have to feel uncomfortable for a while.

No sense in putting it off. He locks up the house and gets his Volvo out of the garage. Vera's place is less than five miles away. He drives there with the cassette recorder on the passenger seat. Such a small, fragile thing.

He's tempted to take the cassette out and pull the tape free—unspool it foot by foot, yard by yard. He wouldn't even need to stop the car. He could toss the whole mess out the window and be done with it.

He resists the temptation. The lights are on at Vera's house. She's home. He parks by the porch and sits for a moment before getting out. She opens her front door as he's climbing the steps.

"Arthur," she says, surprised to see him.

He holds up the cassette recorder.

"There's something you need to hear."

Kate drives for an hour after leaving her father's house, wandering around on the back roads before returning to Route 12B and heading south.

She ends up in Earlville and parks on the street in front of the Wyler house. She retrieves the spare key from under the milk can, but thinks better of using it. She doesn't want to scare Jenny. She knocks instead.

Jenny has been cleaning. The carpets have been vacuumed, the kitchen floor mopped. The counters and the sink gleam. She takes a break and makes a batch of microwave popcorn. Kate sits with her on the sofa and tells her about seeing her father at the motel and what happened after. Everything pours out of her in a rush: about her father's infidelity and what her mother chose to do about it and how her uncle helped.

When she comes to the end, Jenny says, "That's fucked-up."

It is. Undeniably. And among the many fucked-up things about it is that it has forced Kate to reconsider her assumptions about Merkury.

Learning that he's a hired killer has had the strange effect of humanizing him. He's not someone who kills compulsively. He has reasons.

She is just beginning to think about the implications of this.

Most importantly: It seems plain that each of Merkury's victims died because someone wanted them dead and was willing to pay.

Including Bryan Cayhill.

Which raises the obvious question: Who wanted Bryan dead? He was a troubled kid, especially after he lost his mother. But his father was devoted to him, willing to give him anything to prove his love.

Maybe that was the problem.

How did Martin Cayhill's second wife feel about his devotion to his son? What if Nicole Cayhill saw Bryan as a rival? Could she have wanted him dead?

Suppose she did, and she hired Merkury to handle the job. Nicole seems like a pleasant, kind person, and it's hard for Kate to picture her as someone who would hire a killer. But no harder than picturing her own mother that way.

Whether it was Nicole who had Bryan killed or someone else, Martin Cayhill deserves to know the truth about Merkury. But Kate wonders if it's her place to tell him. Maybe this is a time to proceed with caution. The fact is, the thought of doing anything at all feels overwhelming. What she really wants is to sleep and to forget. To seal away what she learned today about her mother.

She drifts off on the sofa with her head on Jenny's lap, and when her cellphone pings she doesn't hear it. The message is a brief one from her father.

I went to see Vera. It's done.

40

Eight days later, on the twenty-third of December, there's snow falling in Alexander.

Vera Landen is working at home, in the spare bedroom she has set up as an office. She's at her desk with a big mug of coffee, sitting with her feet up and her chair tipped back. Her house is old, and the radiators are pouring out heat, and the window by her desk is fogged with condensation. She reaches over and wipes it clear, revealing a view of spruce trees on a nearby hill. They stand out sharply against the evening sky.

The fog returns slowly to the window, and the shapes of the trees blur. Until Landen wipes the window clear again. Then they're back. It's like magic.

Much the same has happened with the Merkury case. The glass has been wiped clear. Now there's a whole new view.

It's easy for Landen to see how wrong she was—how wrong everyone was—to think of Merkury as a serial killer. And how much more sense it makes to see him as a killer for hire.

Consider his victims: men and women, young and old, no common thread tying them together. Because he wasn't choosing them.

Consider his signature on the bodies—*MERKURY*. With a *K* instead of a *C*. Landen went through a period when she thought it might be the key to breaking the case. She consulted linguists who told her that Merkury might have ethnic ties to Poland or Belarus. Because in those countries the name of the planet closest to the sun is spelled with a *K*.

All the while, *MERKURY* was based on a child's misspelling. Because Susan Summerlin wanted to send her husband a message. Wanted him to know that she was responsible for the death of his mistress.

Landen went down another blind alley with the killer's ritual: the ropes and the poles and the trees. She has pages of notes from FBI profilers: musings about religious iconography, crucifixion imagery. All those bodies hanging with their arms outstretched. But now the deep symbolism of the Merkury murders looks contrived—like someone's idea of what a serial killer would do.

Maybe the ritual was Susan Summerlin's idea, or maybe the killer improvised it himself. Either way, he used it twelve times over a span of eighteen years. Landen's guess is that his victims number far more than twelve—that the Merkury persona was a suit he could put on or take off at will. It wouldn't always be useful. It meant extra work and extra risk. But it might be worthwhile sometimes, to set the police on the wrong track, to make them chase after a phantom.

As she sits at her desk sipping her coffee, Vera Landen feels alert and alive. Now that she knows Merkury's secret, she believes there's a real chance of catching him.

When Arthur Summerlin came to her and played her the recording that implicated his brother-in-law, he was meek and apologetic. He obviously expected her to feel betrayed. And it's true that withholding the tape from her and lying to her was a betrayal. She should be angry, but she isn't, because she hasn't been thinking about Arthur. She's been too busy.

She drove to the FBI field office in Albany and shared the tape with her contact there, Dan Gonzalez. Since then they've had long discussions about how to proceed. All the Merkury killings will need to be looked at with fresh eyes, and Gonzalez is working to make that happen.

In the meantime, it's tempting to move quickly against Arthur's brother-in-law, James Rafferty, for the role he played in Melissa Cornelle's death, but the Cornelle case is almost two decades old. Rafferty knew how to contact Merkury once, but that doesn't mean he would be of any help in tracking down Merkury today, even if the tape recording could be used to leverage his cooperation.

The Bryan Cayhill murder, on the other hand, is less than three months old.

Landen believes the best chance of capturing Merkury lies in discovering who hired him to kill Bryan.

The day after Arthur turned over the tape, Kate Summerlin came to Landen with a theory: that Nicole Cayhill might have wanted to get rid of her stepson. And as much as Landen disapproved of the girl playing detective, she found herself in agreement. It made sense.

Martin Cayhill is a wealthy man, and any money he might lavish on his son, any inheritance he might pass on, would mean less for Nicole.

In the days since she spoke to Kate, Landen has been looking closely at Nicole Cayhill—an easy thing to do in the age of social media. Nicole has a Facebook page and an Instagram account, both of them public.

She has more than six hundred Facebook friends, but a far smaller number that she interacts with frequently. One of them in particular has drawn Landen's attention.

Sheryl Minasyan.

Nicole and Sheryl went to Bryn Mawr College together, graduating in the same year. They often meet in New York City for dinners and Broadway shows. For the past several years they have gone on vacation together for a week in January, traveling to various locations, always someplace warm: Aruba, Valparaíso, Buenos Aires, Puerto Madryn.

Nicole's Instagram is full of pictures of the pair of them. Martin Cayhill is nowhere to be seen.

For this coming January, the destination is Rio de Janeiro. Sheryl is counting down the days on her Facebook page.

Sheryl's profile lists her as single, but Landen has looked back through the woman's timeline and learned that she was married once. To an investment banker who was a decade older.

Aaron Minasyan.

Now deceased.

Landen gathered the details from news reports and condolence messages posted to Sheryl's timeline. Aaron Minasyan died in the spring five years ago, at the age of forty-eight. He'd been hiking alone in the Catskills and had fallen to his death. A tragic accident. Seemingly.

There's nothing to say otherwise in the public accounts, but Landen wants to know for sure. If Nicole Cayhill hired a hitman to kill her stepson, someone must have put her in touch with the killer. What if it was her friend Sheryl, who used the same killer to take out her husband?

Aaron Minasyan died in Greene County, and Landen has tried contacting the county sheriff, a man named Lloyd Ollinger. She has left messages, but Ollinger hasn't returned her calls.

She tries again and gets the man's voicemail. Leaves another message asking for a callback. Her phone rings around ten minutes later.

"You're working late," Ollinger says.

"Thanks for getting back to me," says Landen.

"I meant to call sooner, but it's a busy time. With Christmas coming—"

"No problem, Sheriff. I could use some help with a death in your jurisdiction. Aaron Minasyan."

"So you said. I didn't recognize the name at first. Had to dig out the file. I have to wonder why you're taking such an interest in a hiking accident."

"It could be related to another case. Are you sure it was an accident?"

Ollinger is silent for a moment before he answers.

"I have to admit I had some doubts at the time. But my wife is always telling me I have a suspicious nature."

"What made you suspicious?" Landen asks.

"Wasn't any one thing," Ollinger says. "But Aaron Minasyan was in good shape. He was an experienced hiker by all accounts, and the trail he was on wasn't a difficult one. It's called Giant Ledge, and there are actually five rock ledges along the trail. People stand on those ledges and take pictures all the time, and even the inexperienced ones manage not to fall off."

"But Aaron fell. Had he been drinking?"

"The M.E. found no alcohol or drugs in his system. And no one saw him fall. So what can you say? You ever heard of the high-places phenomenon?"

Landen has, but she lets Ollinger explain.

"Some people, when they stand in a high place looking down, they feel the urge to jump. I've read that it's really the body's way of telling you you're in danger and it's time to step back from the edge. But on very rare occasions, people let the urge take them. They jump. I wondered if that might have happened here. Or if it might have been a straightforward suicide, something Aaron planned to do all along."

"Was there any reason to think he was suicidal?" Landen asks.

"No. People I talked to thought he was happy. Successful in his career. No money problems." Ollinger pauses. "Of course that's another thing you wonder about. The money. You know Aaron Minasyan had a younger wife. Sheryl."

"Yes."

"And no children, so Sheryl inherited everything. Aaron had a life insurance policy too, with her as the beneficiary. But that had been in place for years. Lots of people have insurance, right?"

"Sure."

"You always have to suspect the wife," Ollinger says. "But you need more than a hunch. I didn't have anything solid to go on."

"But you had a hunch."

For a few seconds the line is quiet. Then Ollinger says: "Look. I'll tell you what I had. We tried to interview everyone who'd been on the trail that day. A lot of work, and we didn't get much return for our effort. Except for one thing: a few people reported seeing someone walking back along the trail that afternoon—it would have been after Aaron fell. A white male in sunglasses and a baseball cap. Dressed in jeans and a gray T-shirt, carrying a water bottle. Thing is, we were never able to track the guy down."

"Can you give me more of a description? Height, weight?"

"Five ten, or six feet. Medium build. Dark hair or dirty blond. In his thirties or as old as fifty. You know how eyewitnesses can be. Not much to go on, and no one actually saw him with Aaron, so what can you make of it? I would have felt better if Aaron's wife had been hiking with him. Maybe they're standing together on a ledge and she gets the idea to give him a little push. That would be clean and simple. But he was there alone. I got the sense he was one of those people who are looking to find themselves, or find God, or whatever you hope to find out in nature . . . Maybe he just fell. Accidents happen."

Maybe, Landen thinks. But the man in the sunglasses—

Could have been nobody. Or it could have been Merkury.

"You must have interviewed Sheryl Minasyan," Landen says to Ollinger. "What did you think of her?"

"She was what you would expect," Ollinger says. "Distraught. Grieving. If she was faking . . . What can I tell you? Nothing seemed off. That's why I let it go. Do you think I did the wrong thing?"

"I don't know. I'm trying to figure this out. Where was she, do you remember? The day her husband died?"

"In Manhattan. That's where they lived. Sheryl went out shopping that afternoon with a friend."

Landen takes her feet down off her desk. "What was the friend's name?"

"Let me check the file." Empty static on the line, and the sound of papers rustling. "Here it is: Nicole. Nicole Cayhill."

41

Kate spends Christmas Eve at Jenny Wyler's house.

They've re-created the scene from the house in Ohio, with colored lights hanging around the frame of the front door and a live pine tree—a sapling Jenny dug up from somewhere because she didn't want a tree that had been cut down.

The house is warm and smells of freshly baked apple pie, and through the kitchen window Kate can see snow falling in the backyard. The flakes hang in the air and move sideways on the wind at a slow, dreamy pace, as if they're reluctant to reach the ground.

Kate wants to go out there and hurry them along. She feels like she's in limbo, waiting for something to happen.

She's been sticking close to Jenny, especially at night. Ever since her father revealed the truth about Merkury, the threat of him seems more real. He's no more dangerous than he was before, but Kate feels as if he is.

Jenny seems to share the same feeling. She has changed the locks on her doors and installed extra deadbolts. And she sleeps with a gun under her bed now—an old shotgun her father used to keep in a closet.

Some nights Kate and Jenny stay at Kate's father's house, and there it's a different story. Arthur Summerlin doesn't believe in having guns around, so instead he bought a Louisville Slugger and keeps it at his bedside. He gave Kate a canister of pepper mace. She carries it with her everywhere she goes.

She's careful about keeping her bedroom window locked too. It's easy to imagine Merkury climbing through it. Even though, as far as she knows, he's never been inside her father's house.

She thought he had been. The incident with the mysterious moving steak knife convinced her that he had come in through her window and wandered around. But her father disabused her of the notion. He admitted that he was the one who had moved the knife.

"I'm sorry, Kate," he told her. "I didn't think it was healthy for you, staying around here, dwelling on Merkury. And I'll say it: I didn't want you digging too deep. I never wanted you to find out the truth about your mother. I thought if I made you believe he had been in the house, it would spook you. I hoped you would go back to Ohio."

He asked her to forgive him, for everything. Kate hasn't done it yet. She's not sure she will. For now, it's a silent negotiation. They're figuring out how to act around each other. Her father seems eager to please her. He's been cooking even more than usual. Tonight it was baked salmon with a maple glaze and roasted asparagus. He made enough for Jenny too, and Kate wrapped up her plate and Jenny's and brought them over. They've finished now and Jenny has taken the apple pie out of the oven, but it needs to cool.

"Gives us time to open presents," Jenny says.

She wants Kate to open hers first. It's brightly wrapped and beribboned, topped with a red bow. When Kate tears through the paper, she finds a drawing of a bluebird, matted and framed. It's rendered in colored pencil and the detail is almost photographic.

"You drew this?" Kate says. "It's beautiful."

Jenny's cheeks flush pink. "The tail feathers aren't right."

"They look right to me," Kate says. "Seriously, I feel lame now. I got you a sweater."

Later on they eat pie and Jenny brings out a Scrabble board. They play two games, winning one apiece. Kate's phone pings a few times with Christmas messages, mostly from friends in Ohio. There's one from Lee Tennick that comes in around midnight: *Merry Christmas, Kate!* It's accompanied by a snowman emoji.

Things have been strained between them for the past few days. Kate never told him about her father's revelations, never let him hear the tape recording her father made. Tennick found out anyway, from his friend in the Alexander police department. But it hurt his feelings that Kate didn't confide in him.

"What did you think?" he said. "That I'd blab about it on my podcast? I wouldn't."

Which is half true. He might not blab about it now, but the story will make it onto his podcast eventually. Kate can see no way to avoid it. The truth will come out. Lee Tennick won't be the only one telling it.

For now though, the only thing to do is wait. Kate got a Christmas card from Martin and Nicole Cayhill, and she sent them one in return. Keeping up appearances. She wants to tell Martin Cayhill that his wife might have had his son killed. She can't.

Vera Landen made her swear she wouldn't talk to anyone about what she knows.

She got a tin of homemade Christmas cookies in the mail from Alice Cornelle. She sent a handwritten thank-you note back. Sooner or later, Alice will learn the real story of her daughter's death: that Kate's mother arranged for Melissa to be killed.

Kate knows she should be the one to tell her, though she doubts she has the strength to do it. In any case, she can't. Not yet. She can't run the risk of the truth becoming public. It would compromise the Merkury investigation.

At midnight the snow is still falling. Kate watches it through the kitchen window and marvels at it: drifting down with an infinite patience. Looking for all the world as if it might never stop.

At midnight Vera Landen is in her office at the station house. She should go home, but she has no one to go home to. Arthur Summerlin has tried calling her several times, but if he thinks they're getting back together he's delusional. Tonight she's focused on what's ahead. She's planning, strategizing. Figuring out how she's going to handle the interrogation of Nicole Cayhill.

If it were up to her, she would do it sooner rather than later. But Dan Gonzalez at the FBI will make the ultimate decision about when to pay a visit to the Cayhills. He'll be accompanying her. Landen spoke to him about it this morning.

"What if we went tomorrow?" she said.

"Tomorrow's Christmas," said Gonzalez.

"That could work in our favor. Catch her off guard."

"We're not doing it on Christmas."

They end up doing it during the nothing week between Christmas and New Year's Eve. On the twenty-ninth of December, Landen drives to New Canaan, Connecticut. Dan Gonzalez meets her in the parking lot of a diner, and they go on together to the Cayhill house. It's eight in the evening when they arrive at the gate.

At the very same time, Sheriff Lloyd Ollinger and one of Gonzalez's colleagues are calling on Nicole's friend Sheryl Minasyan at her Manhattan apartment.

Landen presses the button on the intercom and looks into the Cayhills' CCTV camera. There's a buzzing sound and the gate swings open.

When they reach the house, Gonzalez hangs back and Landen is the first one up the steps. She knocks on the door. Martin Cayhill lets them into the grand foyer, greets them under the black chandelier. Nicole Cayhill is coming down the staircase.

Landen studies her face, and it might be her imagination, but she thinks Nicole looks anxious.

"Is this about Bryan?" Martin Cayhill asks. "Have you learned something new?"

"Yes," Landen says. "We have."

42

On New Year's Eve, Kate is at her father's house. Jenny is in Syracuse with Diana Perez, celebrating at Faegan's Pub.

"You could come," she said, before Diana arrived to pick her up.

"Not my crowd," Kate told her.

"I don't feel right leaving you alone."

"Don't be silly. Go. Have fun."

"I could stay here," Jenny says, but even though she tries to hide it, Kate can sense the reluctance in her voice.

"Is Ian Gardner going to be there tonight?" Kate asks.

Jenny smiles. "He's supposed to be."

"Then you're not staying here. Go."

A few minutes before midnight Kate is reading in her room, trying to stay awake. There's a ping from her cellphone. A text from Lee Tennick.

I've got news.

She texts him back: Happy New Year, Lee.

Big news, his next message says. About M.

She replies: I think you're overestimating how much I want to hear about M.

He sends her a frown emoji. Then: Suit yourself.

A minute passes before she hears another ping.

Pretty big news though.

Kate tosses her book aside, puts on her coat and shoes, and walks out to the RV. When she taps on the door it opens immediately, as if Tennick has been standing there waiting.

"Come on in," he says. "I made hot chocolate."

She barely has time to sit before he starts in on his story.

"Nicole Cayhill confessed. She hired Merkury to kill Bryan." Tennick's voice is higher than usual. He's excited. "That's the headline," he says. "Now you need the background."

He tells her about Nicole's friend, Sheryl Minasyan, who had a husband who died in a hiking accident—and about Vera Landen's theory that it wasn't really an accident.

"Landen's working with the FBI. They've been planning things for a while, and two nights ago they made their move. They interviewed Nicole and Sheryl separately and played them off against each other. Offered each of them a deal, but only if they were the first one to talk. Sheryl asked for a lawyer straight off, but Nicole hemmed and hawed. 'This is crazy. I don't know what you're talking about.' Martin Cayhill defended her at first, until Landen took him aside and filled him in about the evidence that Merkury is a killer for hire and not just some lunatic. Landen played him your father's tape. That turned Cayhill around. He was looking at his wife in a whole new light. Told her he would pay for a lawyer if she cooperated. But if not he would cut her off."

"What did Nicole tell them?" Kate asks. "Does she know Merkury's name?"

"No, but she told them how she contacted him—through a site on the dark web—and how the payment worked. Nicole doesn't have money of her own, but Martin let her handle the household finances. She was skimming for years, making cash withdrawals from their joint account. A few hundred dollars every week. It worked out to a small fraction of their monthly expenses. Martin never noticed. Nicole put the money into personal accounts he didn't know about."

"Are you saying she planned for years to have Bryan killed?"

"Maybe. But that wasn't her only goal. She helped out her friend first. Sheryl Minasyan arranged her husband's hiking accident, but Nicole fronted her the money. Transferred sixty thousand dollars to a numbered offshore account—I guess Merkury's price has gone up over the years. Once her husband was dead, Sheryl collected his insurance and paid Nicole back."

Tennick has been talking fast. He pauses to stir his hot chocolate.

"Where does that leave things?" Kate asks. "Dark web sites and off-shore accounts— Is Landen any closer now to finding Merkury?"

"Well, she's not going to find the man's name or address. But think about it: if you know how to contact him, all you need to do is hire him to kill someone and arrest him when he shows up to do the job."

"Really?" Kate says. "Is that what Landen's going to do?"

Tennick smiles, as if he's finally gotten to the best part.

"She doesn't have to. Nicole Cayhill already did. Her plans didn't end with killing Bryan. She already arranged a hit on her husband."

When Kate returns to the house it's after one a.m. Her father has gone up to his room. Jenny is still out, but she has a key of her own, so Kate locks up, brushes her teeth, and goes to bed. She lies awake staring at the frost on her casement window and falls asleep with the image of it in her mind.

The window is in her dream.

In the real world the frost is limited to the bottom four panes of glass, but in the dream it covers all sixteen of them. In three of the panes, someone has traced letters in the frost: a *K*, an *A*, and a *T*. While she watches, an *E* appears on another pane. Whoever's drawing it is on the other side of the glass.

In the dream Kate rises from her bed and works the latch of the window. She opens it six inches, expecting a rush of cold air, but she gets nothing—neither the rush nor the cold.

She opens it more and sees her mother standing outside. She looks the same as Kate remembers, except for her hair. She used to dye it, but now it's turned gray.

"Come inside," Kate says.

Her mother looks unhappy. "I can't."

"I'll come out then."

"We can't do that either," her mother says. "This will have to be enough."

Kate tries to reach through the open space, but her hand ends up on the windowsill. She doesn't try again.

"I've missed you," Kate says.

"I know, but you're angry with me too."

"I'm not."

"Don't lie. You don't have to spare me."

Kate would like to object, but she can't. She *is* angry.

"Poor Kate," her mother says. "I told you before. You deserved better parents."

"I would have settled for the ones I had. You didn't have to go."

Her mother crosses her arms over her chest as if she's cold.

"I put up with a lot," she says. "Don't judge me too harshly."

Kate tries to say *I don't judge you*, but the words don't come out.

"I have to go," her mother says.

Kate wants to stop her. Tries to lift her hand from the windowsill. It doesn't move.

"It's too cold," her mother says.

"I can't feel it."

"It was always too cold. I never liked it."

"Are you sure you can't come in?"

"Poor Kate. You'll be all right. I don't think they're going to catch him."

Half awake, half asleep, Kate feels her legs twitch. She stops breathing, then opens her mouth to take in air.

In the dream she says, "You know about that?"

"Even if they do catch him, he probably won't squeal on you," her mother says. "He won't tell them about the secrets you kept."

"I don't care if he tells," Kate says.

Her mother smiles, and without Kate touching it the window starts to close. She tears her hand free of the sill and tries to stop it, but it's heavy. Whatever's moving it is too strong—

Kate snaps awake and tries to swing her feet off the bed, but her legs are tangled in the covers. She's not alone. Sometime in the night Jenny came home and climbed into bed with her. There's an instant when Kate is sure that something terrible has happened, that she'll reach over to find Jenny's skin cold, but then the girl shifts around to look at her.

"Did you have a bad dream?"

"No," Kate says. "Go back to sleep."

She feels Jenny settle in again. Tries to settle in herself, turning her pillow over, pulling the blanket onto her shoulders. The alarm clock by the bed reads 5:41. The window is closed; the latch is in place. There are no letters written on the glass.

Kate lies awake, thinking about the last part of her dream. It's an interesting question—what he'll tell them if they catch him. In the dark before morning, the whole idea seems unreal.

Merkury getting caught.

Tennick seemed optimistic about it.

"It's supposed to happen soon," he told her before she left his RV. "Merkury is supposed to kill Martin Cayhill at his house in New Canaan. Nicole arranged for it to be done while she's away, on vacation in Rio with Sheryl Minasyan. It's perfect, because they vacation together every year, always in January. The idea is for it to look like a break-in, a robbery

that turned violent. So Landen and the FBI are going to let it happen—
only Martin won't be there. And Nicole and Sheryl won't be in Rio,
obviously. The FBI isn't going to let them leave the country."

"You know a lot about what they're planning," Kate said.

Tennick smiled. "It pays to have friends. Ralph Beckham sat in that
chair you're in and laid it all out for me. All it cost me was a couple of
beers. Beckham is supposed to be there when it happens. He'll be going
to New Canaan with Landen to represent the Alexander P.D. They'll
be part of the team that stakes out the Cayhill house. The one thing
Beckham didn't tell me was when it would happen. My sense is that the
FBI has a timeframe, maybe even an exact date, but it's need-to-know,
and Beckham doesn't need to know yet."

"When he knows, is he going to tell you?" Kate asked.

"He says he won't, but I'm still working on him."

"I don't like the sound of this, Lee. You're not gonna go there, are
you?"

"That's not the question."

"What's the question?"

"Are we gonna go there?"

At four a.m. on the first day of the new year, the killer known as Merkury
is in the company of a lovely woman: blond, late thirties, with radiant
skin and hips that flare out from a slender waist.

He's in her bed, and she's lying on her side facing away from him, half
covered by a linen sheet. He slips his hand under the linen and runs it
over the curve of her hip.

"What are you doing, sugar?" she asks him, her voice lazy and contented.

"Admiring you," he says.

Her laugh is lazy too.

They've gotten together five or six times over the course of many
weeks, always at her apartment. When they met, she was the one who

made the first move. It happens more than you would think. He has an easy way about him, and the kind of looks that women find both attractive and unthreatening.

When he rises from the bed she doesn't say anything. She might be asleep or only resting her eyes.

He moves through her apartment in the dark. Though he's accustomed to being in other people's homes, there's always something thrilling about it. He feels a sense of power.

In her kitchen, he touches her coat where it lies over the back of a chair. His is on another chair. There are photos of children on her refrigerator. Her nieces and nephews. She had cancer when she was younger, and it left her unable to have children of her own.

The things people will tell you.

Turning away from the pictures, he allows a fantasy to unfold in his mind. What if he stayed here? What if they lived together? She could cook meals and he would wash the dishes afterward and take out the trash. He thinks she would be agreeable and even-tempered. There's a playfulness in their relationship that he enjoys.

But she doesn't even know his name. When she asked, he gave her one he made up on the spot. He can't remember what it was, and she might not either. She always calls him "sugar."

He returns to the bedroom and stands over her. She's definitely asleep. He bends to kiss her brow. It's time to make his exit.

Gathering his clothes, he dresses quietly and leaves her.

As he drives away from her apartment he feels energized. It's a clear night and the trees along Main Street in Alexander are still strung with holiday lights, lending the place a magical air.

He doesn't live here—in fact, he rarely stays long in any one place. But he has spent time here and he likes the town. It has a wholesome feel. It reminds him of where he grew up.

He drives north past the police station. The sidewalks downtown are empty. New Year's Eve revelers have made their way home. He has the night to himself.

There is nowhere he needs to be, and his only plan is to find a hotel room a fair distance from here, maybe somewhere along the New York Thruway. But he can't help making the turn onto Bird River Road and cruising by the Summerlin house.

He smiles when he sees that the porch light is on. You could take that as an invitation, a sign of welcome, if you wanted. For a moment he slows down.

Then the house is gone in the dark behind him.

There's one other spot on this road that he knows: a turnoff onto a wide track that runs a little way into the woods before giving out. It's where he parked the night he killed Melissa Cornelle.

He's tempted to stop there and take a walk through the woods to the oak tree by the stream. The scene of the crime.

He resists the temptation. He doesn't need to see that place again. He remembers it well.

He scouted it beforehand. The main thing was the tree. It had to have a limb strong enough to support the weight of the body. He picked out the oak the day before and left the wooden pole he planned to use hidden in the underbrush nearby.

One less thing to carry when the time came.

He planned it out as well as he could: a rented van, a burlap sack, zip ties, rope, black ribbon, a red marker. The abduction went as he hoped it would. He had observed Melissa enough to know she was prone to late-night walks around her neighborhood.

He found a place where he could conceal himself and see when she left her apartment. He had parked the van at a convenient spot along the route she took. Melissa walked out her front door around 12:45 and he followed her on foot, waiting for the right moment. When it came, he was on her before she realized what was happening. Got the burlap sack over her head and forced her into the back of the van. Used the zip ties to bind her wrists and ankles.

Drove her out to Bird River Road.

She pleaded with him the whole way, tried to bargain. It wasn't easy to hear, but he told her there was nothing he could do for her.

In the van, parked on the track in the woods, he pulled the sack from her head, folded it, and pressed it down over her nose and mouth. Eventually she stopped struggling.

From there it came down to logistics: moving the body and the other things he needed. He knew he would have to make two trips. The body went first, and when he reached the oak tree he laid Melissa on the ground and took off her shoes. Cut the zip ties from her ankles and her wrists. He retrieved the wooden pole from its hiding place and laid it underneath her shoulders.

He had cut six lengths of thin rope and stowed them in his coat pockets. He used them to tie Melissa's arms to the pole, three on either side. From another pocket he drew the red marker and wrote *MERKURY* on the girl's stomach. That was for the client, the woman who was paying him for this. He had no idea what it meant.

The black ribbon he tied around the girl's neck was his own little touch. Something for the police to puzzle over. It signified nothing. When it was in place, he picked up the girl's shoes and stood in the moonlight listening to the stream, looking over his handiwork.

He was satisfied.

One final step: hanging her in the tree. For that he needed a much longer, thicker piece of rope. He went to the van to get it, and when he returned he found Kate Summerlin kneeling in the grass by the body.

He didn't know her name, of course. She was just a child in the woods at night. Not a part of the plan, but sometimes you have to adapt.

He was used to adapting.

Melissa Cornelle would come to be known as Merkury's first victim. But she wasn't *his* first victim. This wasn't his first time.

"Don't turn around," he said to Kate.

It's a fascinating question—what he would have done if she had disobeyed him. He has convinced himself over the years that he wouldn't have killed her, but part of him realizes he might be flattering himself. He has killed for less cause.

Fortunately, the question remains a hypothetical. She didn't turn.

What she did was charm him.

He remembers bits of their conversation. How at ease Kate seemed— though she must have been afraid. He remembers her openness, her curiosity.

"What's her name?" she asked him.

"Melissa."

"Is she dead?"

No panic in her voice.

"I'm afraid she is," he said.

"How did it happen?"

"Someone smothered her."

"Did you see who it was?"

A question only an innocent would ask.

"We don't have to tiptoe around it," he told her.

"Did you smother her?" she asked.

"Yes."

"Why?"

He couldn't answer that one, but he liked her for asking. It showed courage and sensitivity. She was trying to understand.

She was not his daughter. He had no right to be proud of her. But in that moment he was.

Though he never asked her name that night, he made a point of learning it after. And as time passed, he kept track of her. It seemed important. He had become attached to her, in his own way. He wanted her to have a good life.

Whatever his faults, he is not without feeling.

In the intervening years, he has read the accounts of his crimes. He knows that Kate has never told the whole story of the night Melissa Cornelle died—or if she did, the details never made it into any of the news stories.

It's possible she kept everything to herself.

Sometimes he wonders if Kate even remembers what really happened. He would understand if she didn't. She was only a child.

The truth is, he hopes that she has forgotten.

He remembers.

Melissa wasn't the first person he killed, but she was the first he smothered. Sometimes it takes practice to get things right.

That night, under the oak, he thought he was done. He was ready to walk away.

"I'm leaving now," he said to Kate. "Don't turn. Don't look. I'm trusting you."

And right then, Melissa stirred and opened her eyes.

43

When the time comes, Lee Tennick is ready.

He's had a bag packed since the first of January. The gas tank of his Civic is full. The oil level is good. Plenty of air in the tires.

He's been checking in regularly with Ralph Beckham, hoping to find out when he's going to New Canaan, when the Merkury stakeout is going to happen. But Beckham has suddenly turned conscientious about his job. Last time they spoke, he said: "I can't help you, Lee. Operational security. Once it's over, I'll tell you anything you want."

But Tennick wants to be there. This is history, after all.

So he keeps an eye on Beckham as much as he can, without being too obvious about it. He catches a break on January twentieth. At eight o'clock, Tennick is in Ptolemy's Pub on Main Street—and Beckham isn't.

His absence raises a red flag. Ptolemy's is his regular haunt.

Beckham's friend Tracey is tending bar. She tells Tennick he hasn't been in.

A few minutes later, when Tennick drives past Beckham's house, the man's car is in the driveway. Lights are on in the living room.

Does Tennick stop and park down the street? Does he walk back for a closer look?

Yes he does.

It's a ranch-style house with big front windows. The curtains in the living room are partway open. Beckham and his wife are sitting together watching television.

There are patches of snow on the lawn. Tennick avoids them when he walks around to the backyard. Finds another window with a gap between the curtains. He peers through and sees a bedroom with a duffel bag on the king-size bed.

Someone's been packing.

On the way back to his car, Tennick takes another look through the front window. Beckham is still there, relaxing with his wife on a Thursday evening. Like a man who knows he's got a big day ahead of him tomorrow.

On Friday afternoon, Jenny Wyler drives from Earlville to Alexander. In her new car.

It's a used car, if you want to be a stickler about it: a Nissan Versa with fifty thousand miles on it. But she bought it last week, so it's new.

She got a sweet deal from one of Diana Perez's friends. Paid cash. Martin Cayhill has been as good as his word, depositing three thousand dollars a month into her checking account. It might not last, but as long as it does, Jenny is in no hurry to find a job.

At Seagate College, the students are back for the new semester. Jenny sees them on the sidewalks as she drives by. Half of them aren't wearing coats.

The scene makes her think of her father. He wouldn't approve. It's one of the things he was strict about: *Always dress for the weather, Jenny.* And she does, though it doesn't always work. She caught a cold a week ago. She's still getting over it.

At the intersection of Broad Street and Main, she stops for a red light. On her left is the Odeon Theater, advertising THE LADY FROM SHANG-HAI on its marquee.

Underneath, smaller letters spell out: VICTIM/KILLER: A SHORT FILM BY LAVANA KHATRI.

Kate has told her about it. They're supposed to see it together tonight.

The light changes and Jenny drives on. She's been worried about Kate ever since the beginning of the year, ever since Kate confided in her about the plan to catch Merkury—and about Lee Tennick wanting to be there.

Jenny hasn't had much to do with Tennick, but her impression is he's kind of an oddball.

And a bad influence.

Don't go looking for trouble, her father would have said.

As Jenny approaches the Summerlin house, she has an uneasy feeling. She half expects to find Kate's car gone from the driveway, but it's there. Tennick's is too. Jenny parks and lets herself into the house without knocking. Kate's father is in the kitchen. He waves as she walks by. The door to Kate's room is open, and Kate is standing by the bed.

Tossing clothes into an overnight bag.

Kate didn't plan to go, not at first.

She tried to talk Tennick out of it on New Year's Eve.

"What's the point?" she asked him.

"If the FBI brings in Merkury, that's a huge story," he said. "I need to cover it."

"You could cover it from here."

"Not as well."

"If you think they're gonna let you interview him, you're an idiot."

"I don't—"

"Then what? You're gonna get pictures?"

"Why not? I'm a journalist."

Kate almost laughed, but caught herself. Tennick saw it anyway and understood. Gave her his wounded look.

"You don't have to go with me," he said.

"I'm not going," she told him. "You shouldn't either, Lee."

But she's had time to think about it since. She has lain awake at night more than once thinking: You know you're going. You have to. It's all been leading up to this. You can't hide from it.

Then last night she got a text from Tennick: It's happening tomorrow. I plan to leave around 3:00.

Okay, she replied.

It's ten minutes to three when Jenny shows up in her doorway.

"Where are you going?" Jenny asks.

"Out of town," Kate says. "I won't be gone long."

"Where out of town?"

"To see a friend."

"What friend?"

"Don't worry. I'll be back soon."

Jenny steps up to the bed. Dumps the clothes from Kate's bag.

"What are you doing?" Kate says.

Jenny tosses the bag on the floor. "You can't go."

"No?"

"No. Because we're going to the movies. You promised."

"We'll do it another time."

"There won't be another time."

"Jenny—"

"Tell me why it's so important to you."

"I can't."

"Because it's not."

But it is, Kate thinks. She can't explain why. It would sound ridiculous. She thinks she needs to be there. It's an obligation. It's her responsibility.

She's afraid if she's not there, they won't catch him.

"I can't tell you why," she says. "But I have to go."

Jenny shrugs. "Fine. I'll go with you."

"No. Don't even think about it."

"If you go, I go," Jenny says, crossing her arms. "I don't see how you can object. It's not gonna be dangerous, right?"

Kate's phone pings with a message from Tennick: Time to head out. Are you coming?

She picks up her bag from the floor and says to Jenny, "I can't argue about this."

"That's good," the girl says. "I don't want to argue. But if you go, I'm going. If I can't ride with you, I'll follow you. My car's right outside."

She's steady as stone, her eyes defiant. Kate feels her own resolve fading. Merkury might be her responsibility, but he's not Jenny's.

Tennick's message is waiting. Kate taps out a reply:

Sorry. You're on your own.

Kate doesn't want to admit it, but she feels relieved.

The afternoon turns brighter. Literally. The sun comes out from behind the clouds. Her father puts on music, another one of his Bruce Springsteen albums. Jenny drags Kate outside and starts scooping up some of the snow that's left on the ground, making snowballs. They throw them at the side of the barn and the door of Tennick's RV.

Later they walk down to the stream, though not as far as the oak. The setting sun casts an orange glow over the western sky.

Kate's father fries pork chops for dinner and serves them with roasted sweet potatoes and a green bean salad. After the dishes are cleared away, he brings out a deck of cards. The three of them play a few games of rummy.

Around seven fifteen they retire to the living room. *Groundhog Day* is streaming on Netflix, and Jenny hasn't seen it. They put it on. Jenny was sniffling on their walk outside, and Kate knows she's had a cold. By the time Bill Murray starts to learn piano, she's looking tired. But she stays sitting up, shoulder to shoulder with Kate on the couch, as if she's afraid Kate might give her the slip.

It's after eight thirty when Jenny lies down. Kate's father has gone upstairs. Andie MacDowell is making her bid at the bachelor auction. Three hundred thirty-nine dollars and eighty-eight cents.

Jenny holds out a bit longer—curled up on her side with her feet touching Kate's thigh—but by ten minutes to nine she's asleep. Kate lowers the volume of the television and listens to her breathing for a while. Then inches forward on the couch and gets up slowly.

Jenny doesn't wake.

Lavana Khatri's student film is playing at the Odeon at nine o'clock, followed by *The Lady from Shanghai*. The show is unlikely to start exactly at nine. Kate could still make it there.

Or she could drive to New Canaan and meet up with Tennick. It's a long way to go, and she would arrive in the middle of the night.

But if Merkury shows up to kill Martin Cayhill, the middle of the night is probably when he'll do it.

44

At nine o'clock on Friday night, Lee Tennick is freezing.

He turns on the engine of his Civic and runs the heater. He can't decide which is more conspicuous: sitting at the side of the road with the engine off or with the engine on. So he's been alternating between the two.

The main problem is that the houses in the Cayhills' neighborhood are spread out, with big yards, and they all have garages, so no one parks on the street. Tennick can't get close to the Cayhills' house without sticking out like a sore thumb.

So he planted himself near the western end of the Cayhills' street. With the zoom lens on his camera, he can see the house. There are a few windows showing light. Beyond that, there's no activity he can detect.

There might not be any for hours.

Tennick bought a large takeout coffee from a shop about a mile away, but it's already gone. And he has already eaten a sandwich from the cooler in the back seat.

He keeps his camera within easy reach, and whenever a car comes by—which is rarely—he holds his phone up to his ear so he'll look like someone who has pulled over to make a call.

And he waits.

At nine o'clock on Friday night, Martin Cayhill is drinking Kentucky bourbon.

At least that's what he's supposed to be doing. Vera Landen doesn't know what he's actually doing. Cayhill is holed up in a hotel room in Stamford, and he can drink whatever he wants. His wife is in a separate room at the same hotel. They're being watched over by a couple of local cops.

What Landen knows is this: Nicole Cayhill told Merkury that her husband had a habit of coming home at the end of the week and drinking his cares away, and that after his son's death, his habit only intensified. So Friday night would be a good time to do the deed.

Nicole filled Merkury in on other things too, like the layout of the house and the type of alarm system installed in it. Tonight the alarm is set. Landen suggested setting it, and Dan Gonzalez agreed. If they make things too easy for Merkury, he might sense that something is amiss.

And presumably the killer knows how to disable an alarm.

They want him to enter the house. When he does, if he does, he'll be met by six heavily armed men—a tactical team made up of personnel from the FBI and the Connecticut State Police.

One of them is a passable match for Martin Cayhill in terms of build and appearance. He drove Cayhill's car from Cayhill's office to the house around seven p.m. The rest of the team has been in the house since the early afternoon.

Landen doesn't know if Merkury has been watching the house, but she's betting he hasn't been watching it all day.

The whole operation is a gamble, if you think about it. Still, Landen feels fortunate in one respect. The Cayhills have only two close neighbors. The land across the road from them is a nature preserve.

The neighbors to the west are a retired three-star general and his wife. When the FBI approached them about using their house as a base for an important law enforcement operation, they were happy to cooperate. They're staying at the home of one of their children.

The neighbors to the east are a neurosurgeon and an architect. They were told they would need to leave their house while the utility company performed repairs on a nearby pipeline—and were provided with a check to compensate them for the inconvenience.

Which means the house to the east is unoccupied, and the house to the west is where the FBI has set up its command center. Special Agent Gonzalez is in charge of the operation, and Landen is pleased that he hasn't tried to sideline her. She's right there with him, along with one of her sergeants, Ralph Beckham, and three other agents from the FBI.

From the master bedroom on the second floor, they have an excellent view of the Cayhill house and its grounds. Their best guess is that Merkury will approach the house from the back, but he could also cut through the nature preserve across the street, so Gonzalez has people watching in both directions, taking turns, equipped with night-vision binoculars and thermal-imaging cameras.

Around nine forty-five, Landen is taking a turn watching the Cayhills' backyard when Ralph Beckham comes in and taps her on the shoulder.

"I've got something," Beckham says. He doesn't look happy about it.

Landen follows him to the other side of the house, to a bedroom with windows facing both south and west.

Beckham says: "I've been concentrating on the south window, scanning the tree line of the nature preserve. And in my defense, you can't see it from there. But then I went to this window . . ."

He hands Landen a thermal camera and points out the west window. Landen uses the camera to scan along the road. Far off, near the end, there's an orange mass. A car. The driver behind the wheel shows up as a blotch of red.

Landen moves the camera aside and the car just about vanishes. If she squints, she can make it out.

While she's watching, its running lights come on, as if the driver has started the engine.

The headlights remain dark. The car doesn't move.

"I don't know how long it's been there," Beckham says. "I'm sorry."

Landen nods once to acknowledge the apology. "If it's Merkury, what's he doing there?" she says, handing the thermal camera back. "I guess it could be somebody stranded. Car trouble."

"I don't think so," Beckham says.

He looks even unhappier than before.

"I think I know who it is," he says.

Lee Tennick is reconsidering his options.

If the FBI captures Merkury tonight, they'll probably do it in the Cayhill house, or in the yard. It's bound to happen fast. Then they'll want to get him away from here as quickly as they can. They'll have a vehicle ready to transport him.

Tennick won't see anything. Not from his current position. Maybe, if he's ready with his camera, he'll get a shot of a van driving by.

He needs to be closer, and it's impossible.

Unless—

He opens Google Maps on his phone. There's the nature preserve off to his right. He switches to satellite view.

If he drives around to the south, there's a place he could leave his car.

He could cross through the preserve on foot. And watch the Cayhill house from the woods across the road.

And freeze.

But sometimes that's the price of being a journalist.

Tennick sets his phone aside and is ready to put the car into gear when he spots a vehicle leaving the driveway of one of the Cayhills' neighbors. It turns toward him and he watches as the headlights get closer and closer.

When it passes, he can see that it's a black SUV. He watches its taillights in his side mirror. There's a stop sign where the road comes to an end at a T intersection. The SUV's brake lights flare as it comes to a stop.

A passenger gets out. The SUV moves on, making a left turn.

As Tennick watches in his mirrors, the passenger jogs across the road and approaches the Civic from the rear.

Tennick moves his camera from the seat beside him and unlocks the doors.

Vera Landen climbs in and says, "What the hell are you doing?"

The FBI has a sweet setup in the Cayhills' neighbors' house.

Tennick would be in heaven, except that Landen won't let him have his camera or his recording equipment or even his phone. They're all locked in his car, which is in the neighbors' garage out of sight. Landen is holding his keys.

Tennick is banished to the first floor, where he can't see much of anything. The Cayhills' perimeter fence is blocking his view. He's under instructions to make himself invisible.

"I don't want to see you, I don't want to hear you," Landen told him. "The only reason you're here is that I can't trust you out there. If you get in our way I'll make sure you're charged with obstruction. I might do it anyway. You, and your friend too."

She's referring to Beckham. Even though Tennick tried to explain that Beckham didn't tell him this was happening tonight, that he came here without Beckham knowing.

"I'll want to hear exactly what he told you, but not now," Landen said. "For now, shut up."

So Tennick lingers downstairs in the living room. The curtains are closed and there are table lamps switched on and CNN is playing on the wall-mounted television with the sound muted. To someone passing by, it would look as if the owners were at home.

Tennick gets bored very quickly.

He toughs it out until around twenty minutes to eleven. Then wanders into the kitchen. The big stainless-steel refrigerator has two doors, and on one of them the homeowners have left a note for the FBI: *Help yourself to anything inside.*

When Tennick opens the door he sees deli trays of cold cuts and cheese like you might bring to a party. On the counter are bags of kaiser rolls. He finds lettuce and mayonnaise and gourmet mustard and sets about making sandwiches.

He carries a platter of them upstairs and makes room for it on a console table in the hallway. One of the agents passing by gives him a look. But takes a sandwich.

Leaning against the wall at the top of the stairs, Tennick can hear Landen and the others talking occasionally in low voices in one of the bedrooms.

Beckham passes through the hall once and glares at him. But no one tells him to leave.

Tennick is still there at ten minutes after eleven when Landen says: "Wait. What's this now?"

Landen looks out through one of the east-facing windows. The lights are off in the bedroom, so she's not worried that Merkury will spot her.

A car has pulled up to the gate of the Cayhill property. It's a beater with a sign on top displaying the logo for Domino's pizza. Landen doesn't need night vision or a thermal camera to see it. There are lights on either side of the gate.

She and Gonzalez are in radio contact with the tactical team in the

Cayhill house. Landen picks up the handset and presses the transmit button.

"Can you see the vehicle out front?"

The leader of the team replies: "We've got it on the CCTV."

"What does the driver look like?"

"Too young. Can't be more than twenty-five."

"Any passengers?"

"Negative. But I can't see into the back seat. Could be someone there. Or in the trunk."

"Understood."

"Are we opening the gate?" the team leader asks.

Landen looks over at Dan Gonzalez. "What do you think?"

"I don't get the game here," Gonzalez says. "Is this supposed to be Merkury's way in? He's counting on Cayhill to accept delivery of a pizza he didn't order? Does that make sense to you?"

"No," Landen says. "Maybe it's a diversion? He wants Cayhill focused on the gate while he approaches from another direction?"

Gonzalez shrugs.

Landen hits the transmit button on the radio. "Tell the driver you didn't order a pizza. Use the intercom. Don't open the gate."

"Roger that," the team leader says.

"I want to talk to that driver," Gonzalez says to one of the other agents. "See if you can pick him up, but follow him for a while first. Let him get out of the neighborhood."

The man nods and heads out.

Watching through the window, Landen sees the Domino's car backing away from the Cayhills' gate and into the street. From there it drives west. She observes it until it passes out of view.

Gonzalez is scanning the Cayhills' backyard with night-vision binoculars.

"Anything?" Landen asks him.

"Nothing."

The front yard is illuminated by landscape lights that follow the curve of the cobblestone driveway. Landen spots something moving on the lawn, but it's small: a skunk making its slow way through the grass.

As Landen watches it, she sees a flash of yellow in her peripheral vision. Another car has pulled up to the gate.

It's a taxi.

She gets on the radio. "We've got a second vehicle. You see it?"

"Affirmative . . . Driver is an Asian female. Are we letting her in?"

"No, we're not," Landen says. "Same as before. Send her away. And stay alert for Merkury attempting to enter the house from the backyard."

She looks over at Gonzalez, who shakes his head.

"I don't think this is meant to be a diversion," he says.

Landen doesn't either. She thinks they've been made.

She thinks Merkury is fucking with them.

When a third car shows up—another pizza delivery, Papa John's this time—she's sure.

Tennick is still at the top of the stairs when Vera Landen charges out into the hall.

Angry.

She doesn't look surprised to see Tennick there.

"What did you do?"

Tennick shrinks away from her. "Nothing."

"Who did you talk to?"

"No one. I don't even have my phone."

"I mean before tonight," Landen says.

Tennick talked to Kate, but he's not going to say so.

"I swear, I didn't talk to anyone."

Landen grips his arm and leans in close, studying his eyes. Then turns away in disgust.

"You didn't have to," she says. "He probably saw you parked down the road."

Tennick gets banished downstairs again.

He can hear Landen and the others moving around on the second floor. He can only guess at what they're doing—whether they're still on alert for Merkury or winding down the operation.

He sees the Domino's delivery guy brought in and taken upstairs to be questioned. A short time later, they let the guy go and bring in the taxi driver.

Around the same time, Ralph Beckham comes down to the living room and drops into a chair across from Tennick.

"When did you park yourself down the street?" he asks.

"A little before eight," Tennick tells him.

"Looks like you're off the hook then. The Domino's pizza order was placed online in the afternoon, scheduled for delivery at eleven. The taxi and the second pizza delivery were probably arranged the same way. So the operation was blown before you got here. You really didn't talk to anybody else?"

Tennick sticks with his lie. "No."

"Maybe it was one of the others," Beckham says, gesturing vaguely at the second floor. "But I think I'm screwed anyway. I shouldn't have talked to you at all. That's on me."

He's slouching in his chair, looking miserable. There's something weighing on him, Tennick thinks. Something he's holding back.

"What else is on you, Ralph?" Tennick asks. "What did you do?"

Beckham answers with silence and a shake of his head.

"You did something," Tennick says softly. "Who else did you talk to?"

No reply. Tennick waits. Images flicker on the muted television. Beckham's face is half in shadow. Eventually he looks to his right and to his left, as if he's making sure that they're alone.

Then he says: "Tracey."

Tracey is Beckham's friend, one of the bartenders at Ptolemy's.

"What did you tell her?" Tennick asks.

Beckham sits up in his chair, leans forward, and points a finger at the floor.

"Nothing about this," he says, his voice barely above a whisper. "But back in December, when Arthur Summerlin turned over that cassette tape, when we found out that Merkury was a hired gun and not a serial killer—I told her about that."

He spreads his hands and lets Tennick work out the implications. If Merkury discovered that the police and the FBI were on to him, he would know he couldn't come here to kill Martin Cayhill without risk of being caught.

"I don't see how he could have found out though," Beckham says. "It's not like anyone overheard us. It was after hours at the bar, and Tracey and I were alone. And she's a sweet woman. I mean, who would she have told?"

45

Tracey Medved tries to look on the bright side of things. Like this:

It's a cold, dark Friday night in Alexander, New York, but little by little the days are getting longer.

She's tending bar at the age of thirty-eight, but at least it's a nice bar in a college town and the tips are good.

The guy she works for—the college kids call him Ptolemy, but his real name is Gerald—is contentedly married to a dude named Rick. So Tracey doesn't have to worry about him making inappropriate demands. And he lets her take breaks, every shift, even when it's busy.

Tracey is on a break now, in the parking lot behind the wheel of her Camry, smoking a joint. A few flakes of snow are starting to fall, but she has the heater on, so they melt when they hit her windshield.

She has eight minutes left on her break, and about two hours to go on her shift. No one's waiting for her at home.

But on the bright side—

There's a guy she's been seeing on and off. Older, and not exactly relationship material, but he treats her well and they have a good time. He's hard to get a handle on. She never knows when he'll turn up. You think you won't see him, and then he surprises you.

Like right now.

A car pulls into the space to the left of her, and when she looks over it's him. Big smile and he's making a come-hither gesture. She flashes him a smile back and kills the engine of the Camry. Stubs out her joint in the mint tin on the dash that she's been using as an ashtray.

She steps out of her car into the cold, opens his passenger door, and slides in next to him. He's got the heater running. He's looking good: black jeans, black shirt, black leather jacket.

"Well hello, sugar," she says.

He looks her over without a word, then leans in for a kiss. She does the same. She closes her eyes and feels the fingers of his right hand tangle in her hair.

Feels a needle slide into her neck.

Merkury pushes the plunger on the syringe and watches Tracey's eyes snap open wide.

She attempts to pull away from him, but he has her by the hair. He draws the needle out and puts his left arm around her and holds her close.

She tries to talk but her voice is weak and she only gets out three words.

"What did you—"

It happens fast. Her heart races and she can't get her breath, but there's a last bit of struggle in her, fiercer than he expected. She almost wrenches herself away from him.

Then it's over and he feels the spirit go out of her. He caps the syringe and puts it in his pocket. Moves her gently so she's sitting up in the passenger seat, head against the headrest. Her face is turned toward him, her eyes half closed.

He wants to close them all the way. He thinks she would look beautiful.

He feels terrible.

He has a sense of fairness, and he knows that her only sin was that he saw her one night tending bar and talking in a friendly way with one of the local cops.

Not really a sin at all.

He's grateful to her for telling him what the cops were thinking and what evidence they had. In an ideal world, he would have let her live. But in the real world, she would have been able to identify him. He doesn't like to leave loose ends.

He lays two fingers on her wrist to make sure there's no pulse. Reaches for her seatbelt and secures it around her to hold her in place.

There's more to do.

First, a bit of a drive.

Out of the parking lot and onto Main Street. Downtown Alexander is a charming scene, sidewalks and storefronts, specks of snow floating down. Merkury passes the police station and continues south, stopping for a red light. Other men might worry, but he knows how little attention people pay to what's around them. Anyone glancing at his car will think Tracey is asleep.

He rolls along, watching his speed, coming to the Seagate campus. The Hill looms up on his left. A trio of students cross the street up ahead and he brakes for them. One of them waves, laughing. Careless. Then they're gone and he's moving again, past the dorms and the stadium. The trailhead is hard to see from the street, but he scouted it out earlier, in the daylight. He slows and pulls off into a parking area that's little more than a patch of ground: dirt and grass and a sprinkling of snow. Big enough for maybe three cars.

His is the only one here.

There are no lights. He made sure of it before. He's far enough back from the street that no one passing will see him. Still, he pulls the car around so the passenger door is facing toward the woods. Cuts the engine.

This is the dicey part, moving the body. He has always found it useful not to think too much about it. He takes his time, slipping out of his leather jacket and stowing it in the back seat. Putting on a pair of gloves. He moves around to Tracey's side of the car and opens her door, unclips the seatbelt. Gets one arm around her back and the other under her thighs. Hauls her out and maneuvers her until she's slung over his left shoulder. He worked a few construction jobs when he was young. He used to carry sacks of cement this way.

She weighs more than a sack of cement, but he doesn't have to carry her far. He follows the trail into the woods, his eyes adjusting to the darkness. Fifty or sixty feet on, he sees his destination: the shed where Clay McKellar's body was found. He had nothing to do with Clay's death, but the building suits his purpose.

The police will know how to find it.

Someone made an effort to secure the door, but all they managed was a latch and a padlock. Merkury loosened the screws on the latch earlier. He gives the door a solid kick, and it swings inward.

He carries Tracey through the doorway and considers putting her on the concrete floor, but it strikes him as cruel. He lays her on the workbench instead.

He's sweating from the exertion, and the winter air feels pleasant on his skin. But there's no time to appreciate it. He's not done.

Outside again, he jogs along the path until he reaches his car. There's a thin film of snow on the trunk. He opens it up and does a quick inventory, even though he knows what he has: a Glock 19 in a clip-on holster, a black ski mask, a Kevlar vest, two jerry cans of gasoline.

He pulls out one of the jerry cans and closes the trunk.

He heads into the woods again at a brisk walk, the can bumping against his thigh. He reaches the shed and slips inside. Unscrews the cap from the can and sloshes gas over the back wall. It runs down the plywood and onto the floor.

He drops the can, picks up a rag from under the workbench, tosses the rag into the pool of gas. Tugs the glove from his right hand and stuffs it in his back pocket.

His matches are in the pocket of his shirt.

One is enough. He strikes it on the side of the box and tosses it onto the rag.

The flames crawl across the floor and up the wall.

Merkury backs out of the shed, leaving the door ajar. He pictures the police coming here. Finding this. It should keep them occupied.

He brought along a burner phone. He takes it out as he's walking back to his car. Dials 911.

"What's your emergency?" the operator asks.

Merkury puts some fear into his voice.

"I was walking in the woods," he says. "And . . . oh my god—"

"Where are you, sir?"

"There's a trail, south of campus. And kind of a shack in the woods. I think it's where they found that boy who got killed. Clay something."

"Is that where you are now?"

"I looked in—in the shack—the door was open. I wish I hadn't. There's a woman in there. She's dead."

"I'm sending help, sir. Can you stay there?"

"I'm outside. It doesn't feel right. Wait—"

He takes the phone away from his ear for a few seconds, then brings it back.

"Sir? Are you still there?"

"Sorry," he says. "I heard a noise. I think there's someone else here."

He lowers the phone again and listens to the operator calling for him—"Sir? Sir?"—but now he's at his car and he thumbs the button to end the call.

He brushes snow from the windows before he gets in. Drops the phone on the passenger seat. Turns the key in the ignition. When he puts the car in gear the tires spin for a moment on the wet ground, but then they gain traction and he's moving, back onto Main Street and heading north.

The Seagate campus comes into view and he sees the lights of a police cruiser in the distance. He drifts over to the side of the road to let it pass. Another one follows less than half a minute later.

He lets it pass as well and watches it recede in his side mirror. Then he pulls away from the curb and drives on toward downtown Alexander. Toward the police station.

When Kate Summerlin walks out of the Odeon Theater, it's getting close to midnight.

She arrived a little after nine o'clock, as the theater manager was introducing Lavana Khatri, who said a few words before the lights went down and they played her film. Kate had seen some of it already, bits of the beginning and the end, but most of it was new and she found herself swept along by the story.

Travis Pollard's scenes had been reshot with a different actor. The new guy wasn't bad, Kate thought, but in her opinion Travis made a better killer.

The theater was filled with students from the college, and when the film ended they gave it a standing ovation. Lavana took the stage and answered questions for half an hour. Kate watched it all from a seat in the back row.

Lavana must have noticed her there, because after the Q and A, the girl sought her out and invited her to a party. "Some friends and I are getting together to celebrate," she said. "In the common room at my dorm. I hope you can come."

It was the first time they had spoken since Travis died.

"I get it if you don't want to," Lavana said. "But I've been wanting to see you. So you'd be welcome."

She sounded earnest and Kate almost said yes, but a party in a dorm was the last place she wanted to be.

"Maybe we could meet up another time," Kate said. "I'm going to stay and watch *The Lady from Shanghai*."

After an intermission, the theater went dark again and the movie began to play, a classic film noir in black and white. Kate thought she had seen it before, and the early scenes seemed familiar, but there were long stretches in the middle she didn't remember at all. Then the climax came around—a shoot-out in a carnival hall of mirrors—and she was back in familiar territory. Her one regret was that it went by quickly. She wished she could rewind it.

As she steps out of the Odeon, she has that scene and its aftermath running through her mind. Mirror-glass shattering as the femme fatale played by Rita Hayworth fires at her older husband and he fires at her. Both of them falling, fatally wounded. Rita Hayworth crawling along the floor, saying she's afraid and doesn't want to die. Orson Welles as her lover, walking away from her, knowing he can't save her.

Welles in a final voice-over, talking about how stupid he's been.

Everybody is somebody's fool.

Kate finds her car in the lot behind the theater and wipes a dusting of snow from the windshield.

She drives out onto Main Street and turns north.

The downtown shops are closed at this hour. The movie theater and the bars are the only businesses still open. There's an old Ford parked at the curb in front of the police station. Kate almost passes it by.

It's Samuel Wyler's car, the one he was driving the day he came to her and asked her to find Jenny. Kate recognizes the scrape in the paint along the driver's side.

It's the car that was stolen by Wyler's killer.

Merkury.

Kate is halfway down the block when she pulls over. She gets out of her car without turning off the engine. She stands in the street with snow falling around her, letting the truth sink in.

Merkury is here. At the police station.

She doesn't know why, but it can't be for any good purpose. It's not as if he's turning himself in.

And she's here. Not by chance. No. There's a reason.

He is her responsibility.

She crosses the street slowly, pausing in the middle to let a truck go by. Its driver honks his horn at her. The sound seems muted, the way it would if she were hearing it underwater. Kate reaches the doors of the police station and draws one of them open. The fluorescent lights in the lobby glare unnaturally.

The sergeant's desk is off to the right, unattended. It's not really a desk at all, but a long, high counter. Kate makes her way around one end of it, fearing what she might find on the other side. But there's only an empty stool. No blood. No body.

The one sign of trouble is a puddle of coffee on the tiled floor, along with the pieces of a broken mug.

Below the counter there are drawers, and one of them is half open. Kate pulls it out further, not sure of what she's looking for. Maybe a gun. She could use something. All she has is the pepper mace her father gave her. It's in her coat pocket.

There's no gun in the drawer, only papers. Forms. She tries some of the other drawers, but they're filled with files and office supplies. The only thing that stands out is a pair of scissors.

Better than nothing. She takes them with her.

The station has been eerily silent, but when Kate comes out from around the counter she hears a distant sound: maybe a door closing. It's coming from somewhere in the depths of the building. There's a hallway off the lobby that leads back there. She approaches it, finds it empty. The first door she comes to opens into an interrogation room, the one where they put her the night she and Tennick and Lavana Khatri found Clay McKellar's body in the woods.

The room is empty.

The second door leads to a big office space. Four desks, all of them deserted.

Behind the third door is another interrogation room. With a cop lying on the floor.

He's in his fifties. Bald. Kate recognizes him as the sergeant who sat in when Vera Landen interviewed her the night Travis died. Sergeant Dietrich.

He's handcuffed to a leg of the table in the center of the room. The table is bolted to the floor.

Kate tucks the scissors she's been carrying into the right-hand pocket of her coat and kneels by the sergeant. His eyes are closed, but they open when she touches his shoulder. At first he's unfocused, and then he recognizes her and a look of confusion comes over him.

"What are you doing here?"

Without waiting for an answer he tries to sit up. The effort makes him wince in pain.

"How bad are you hurt?" she asks him. The only damage she can see is a bloody lip.

"He did a number on me," Sergeant Dietrich says. "I think it was Merkury." His left hand, the one that's not cuffed, touches his side gingerly. "He broke some ribs. Stomped on my ankle after I was down . . . Kicked the back of my head—"

"We need to get you out of here," Kate tells him. Then leans her weight against the table to test its strength. It doesn't budge.

"Won't get anywhere that way," the sergeant says, looking at the cuff around his wrist. "We need a key."

"I'll get one," says Kate. "Tell me where."

Dietrich smiles crookedly. His eyes are turning glassy. He seems to be fading. "I'd let you use mine, but he took it. And there's no one else here."

"No one?" Kate asks.

"They all left. On an emergency call . . ." He looks around absently. "Try the desks. Across the hall. You might find a key."

Kate is reluctant to leave him, concerned about the shape he's in. But there's no choice. She jumps up and crosses through the hallway to the room with four desks. By the time she reaches it she has her phone out. She dials 911 and the operator comes on almost immediately.

"What's your emergency?"

Kate moves to the nearest desk and starts opening drawers.

"There's been an assault," she says. "On a police officer."

"What's your location?"

"I'm at the police station in Alexander. You need to send an ambulance." She moves to another desk and opens the center drawer. No keys.

"I'm sorry," the operator says. "Could you repeat that location?"

"The Alexander police station," Kate says. "I know how it sounds. There are no police here, except for one, and he's badly wounded. The man who assaulted him could still be in the building. Send whoever you can."

She taps the screen with her thumb to end the call, slips the phone into her pocket, and steps around to the next desk. The search goes faster with two hands, but she finds nothing. No spare handcuff key left behind. She tries the last desk with the same result.

She taps her knuckles on the desktop. Scans the room in frustration. And smells smoke.

An alarm goes off, as if on cue. From somewhere overhead a stern mechanical voice says: "*Fire . . . Fire . . . Fire . . .*"

Kate moves to the doorway, wary, and then into the hall. There's no smoke that she can see, but the smell is stronger. It's coming from further down, deeper in the building.

Vera Landen's office is down there.

Other doorways too.

As Kate is deciding what to do, Merkury steps through one of them and into the hallway.

He's all in black, wearing a bulletproof vest, and his face is covered by a ski mask. But she knows who he is.

She's frozen in place.

He's not.

He's coming toward her, and when her mind registers that fact she fumbles in her coat pocket. Her canister of mace is there. And the scissors she found.

She decides the mace is the better way to go, but by the time it's clear of her pocket, Merkury is already on her. Before she can spray him, he reaches out with a black-gloved hand and snatches the canister away.

His other hand holds a semiautomatic pistol.

She's looking into his eyes, transfixed, when he brings the pistol up and slams the barrel against her temple.

46

Kate hears voices.

Some of them are faint and distant and some are whisper-close. Some are speaking English, though she has trouble making out the words. The throbbing pain in her head doesn't help. Others are using a language she doesn't understand.

At first, all the voices are talking over one another, but most of them drop away. Finally there's only one left.

It's Travis Pollard's.

Kate opens her eyes and sees him looking down at her, a starry sky above him.

"I told you," he says. "I knew it all along. We're the same."

She doesn't reply. She's on her back with a hard surface underneath her, and it feels like he's holding her down.

"We've got a thing going," Travis says. "I knew we would end up in the same place."

He reaches for her neck and she tries to slide away from him, but she can't move.

She blinks awake and she's looking at the sky, but there are no stars that she can see, only snow drifting down in the light of a streetlamp. The pain in her head is still there.

She sits up slowly and realizes she's on the sidewalk outside the police station. She's not alone. There's a woman lying beside her, an older lady dressed for a night out, in knee-high boots and a dark wool overcoat and a thick gray scarf that looks like cashmere. She's unconscious.

Kate shakes her shoulder until she comes awake.

The woman stares up at her and says: "You're bleeding."

"So are you," Kate tells her.

The woman touches the side of her head and her fingers come away tipped with blood.

"I saw a man with a mask on," she says. "I didn't make him up, did I?"

"No," Kate says. "He's real."

"He was carrying you. I tried to stop him and he struck me."

She seems astonished at the idea.

Kate doesn't respond. She's looking around. Merkury's car is gone. She breathes in through her nose.

The woman with the cashmere scarf does the same.

"Do you smell smoke?" she asks.

"I need to get up," Kate says.

It's easier than she expects. The ground sways a little, but mostly it holds steady. She makes for the entrance of the police station and realizes that the woman with the scarf is trailing behind her.

"Is there a fire?" the woman says.

"Yes."

"Then it's not wise to go in, is it?"

"I have to," Kate says, reaching for the glass doors. "Call it in, would you?"

She passes into the lobby of the station without waiting for a reply. Inside, the smell of smoke is much stronger. Tendrils of it drag themselves across the ceiling. There are strobe lights flashing high on the walls. The mechanical voice from before is repeating its mantra: "*Fire . . . Fire . . . Fire . . .*"

Kate circles around the end of the sergeant's desk and rifles through the drawers again. She doesn't remember seeing a handcuff key before, but she wasn't looking for one. She thinks she might get lucky the second time around.

She doesn't.

Slamming the last drawer shut, she races through the lobby toward the hallway. The smoke is thicker there. She has to crouch to stay under it. She comes to the interrogation room where she left Sergeant Dietrich, fearing she'll find him passed out or dead, but somehow he has roused himself. He's sitting up, straining at the leg of the table, trying to use it as leverage to loosen the bolts from the floor.

"Hold on," she tells him. She doesn't stop.

The next room she comes to is filled with file cabinets. No desks to search. She leaves it behind and presses on to the far end of the hallway. On her left there's a closed gray metal door. The source of the smoke. It's seeping out from under the door. Rising up from there.

Kate can feel the heat coming off the metal even without touching it.

She dodges to the other side of the hall and through the open door of Vera Landen's office. There's a haze of smoke in the air, the worst of it hovering up by the ceiling. Kate stays as low as she can, but her eyes are watering. She's coughing.

Landen's desk is a heavy thing of dark-stained wood, with a center drawer and two more on the right-hand side. The center drawer is a disorganized mess: stray papers, loose change, scotch tape, rubber bands. No keys. The second drawer Kate tries is more of the same. The third—the bottom one on the right—is locked.

Kate spits out a curse word that turns into a sputtering cough. Desperate, she lifts up the blotter on the desk to look underneath, finds nothing, throws the blotter aside. She picks up Landen's inbox, turns it over, lets it fall to the floor. There's a plain white mug that holds pencils and pens. She spills them out over the desktop.

A small silver key comes out with them.

It's not a handcuff key, but Kate tries it in the lock of the bottom drawer and it turns.

She yanks out the drawer and the first thing she sees is a black revolver with a wooden grip. She grabs it and opens the cylinder.

It's loaded.

"That'll do," she says aloud.

She closes the cylinder and rushes out into the hallway. Moves in a crouch with the smoke stinging her eyes. The walls seem to withdraw from her and then come closer again. She lets out a jagged cough, and another, and another. And reaches the doorway of the interrogation room.

Stumbles through. Still coughing.

"Jesus," Sergeant Dietrich says. "You should get out of here. Leave me."

Kate holds up the revolver.

His eyes widen. "Where'd you find that?"

"Does it matter?" she asks.

He sits on the floor and leans away from the table, pulling the handcuff chain taut.

Kate gets down there with him and thumbs back the hammer of the gun. When she takes aim, the muzzle is two inches from the chain.

"Closer," Dietrich says.

She moves it closer, shaking a little, trying to suppress a cough. Dietrich turns his face away, looks nervous.

"Don't worry," she tells him. "I saw this done in a movie once."

The gun jumps in her hand when she fires, and the sound of the shot rings through the room. The chain snaps and Dietrich falls backward, groaning when he hits the floor, clutching at his wounded ribs.

"Are you okay?" Kate asks.

He nods and rolls sideways onto his elbow, trying to rise. Kate scrambles up, slides the revolver into her pocket, and helps him. He hops toward the door, favoring his left ankle. She keeps him steady.

The smoke is thicker in the hall, but it thins as they reach the lobby. The woman with the cashmere scarf is waiting outside the glass doors. She draws one open and Kate pushes the other, leading Sergeant Dietrich out into clean air.

Breathing it in, coughing, and breathing again.

There's a small crowd gathered on the sidewalk. A couple of college kids step in to help with Dietrich, getting on either side of him, guiding him down the block, away from the station house. Kate follows them.

They ease him down in front of an antique store, sitting him with his back against a brick wall. Kate crouches beside him and he offers her a wan smile. Takes her hand and squeezes it.

"You did good," he says.

He thanks her and says he owes her one, but her mind is on something else.

The fire.

Why did Merkury set it?

What was the purpose?

"The room across from Landen's office," she says. "What is it?"

Sergeant Dietrich's expression turns serious. "That's the evidence room."

"That's where he started the fire," Kate says.

"That's what I figured," Dietrich says, nodding. "He came here for the tape your father made. I told him it's not here. Which is true. The chief turned it over to the FBI. I guess he thought I might be lying."

Kate feels a tightening in her chest, a tremor of anxiety. She stands and turns away from Dietrich. Drifts toward the street. The woman with the cashmere scarf is there and takes her by the arm.

"Don't go far now," Dietrich says. "People will want to talk to you."

But Kate barely hears him. She's thinking about Merkury and the tape. He wanted it, and he didn't get it. What will he do now?

The tape is important, but it means little on its own. It's only valuable if her father can testify about when it was made and under what circumstances.

It's only valuable if he's alive.

"Are you all right, dear?" the woman with the scarf asks.

"No," Kate says.

Merkury is going to go after her father. He could be on his way to the house right now.

Around her, the night is alive with sounds. People calling out to each other. Sirens, drawing closer. Kate sees the lights of a fire truck coming up Main Street.

She breaks away from the woman with the scarf. Remembers the revolver and pats her coat pocket to make sure it's still there. Walks into the street.

A car swerves to avoid her, the driver slamming on the brakes.

Kate walks on without a pause. The sirens are louder now. She slips her cellphone from her pocket. Her car's engine is still running. The cabin is warm when she slides behind the wheel. The wipers are moving rhythmically across the windshield.

She calls her father as she pulls away from the curb. Main Street is black with melted snow. The phone seems to ring endlessly, and she's about to give up and try Jenny when her father finally answers.

Arthur Summerlin fell asleep reading Dostoyevsky.

His ringing phone wakes him. He rolls onto his side and rubs his face. Reaches for the phone and knocks it off the nightstand onto the floor.

When he looks over the side of the bed he can't see it. He throws off the covers and sits up. It's chilly in the room, and he's wearing only boxer shorts and socks.

He has to get down on his knees and reach under the bed to retrieve the phone.

"Hello, Kate," he says.

"Thank god," she says. "You need to get out of the house. Is Jenny still there?"

She sounds frantic.

"I don't know," he tells her. "I'm in my room. What's wrong?"

"Merkury," she says. "He could already be there."

"Why would he—"

"There's no time. You need to get out."

"Well, I'm putting on pants first. If I die, it'll be with dignity."

"Dad—"

He drops the phone on the bed. His pants are on the chair by the window. He gets them on. His shirt too. He leaves it unbuttoned.

He calls out, "Jenny!" and when she doesn't answer he calls her again.

His Louisville Slugger is leaning against the wall. He picks it up, and then the phone.

Kate is still on the line. "Dad?" she says.

"I don't think Jenny's here," he says. "Maybe she went home."

"She was asleep on the couch when I left."

He walks out of his room with the baseball bat. Feels the cold of the floor through his socks. He shuffles down the hall and gets to the top of the stairs.

Jenny Wyler is standing at the bottom looking up. Merkury is with her, all in black with a ski mask covering his face. Holding a gun to her head.

On the phone, Kate says: "Dad, what's going on?"

Merkury drapes a set of handcuffs over the railing at the bottom of the stairs.

"Leave the bat, Mr. Summerlin," he says. "And come on down here."

47

The roads are slick with snow. Kate takes the turn onto Bird River Road too fast, spins around, almost ends up in a ditch.

The car stalls, and when she turns the key to restart the engine, the ignition grinds and grinds. She panics. Turns it again. The engine roars to life.

She races up the hill and down the other side. Speeds along the curves as fast as she dares. When she comes to her father's driveway she takes the turn slow.

Merkury's car is there. Jenny's too.

Kate parks her car behind Jenny's and steps out in the freezing air. She feels it on her face. On her temple where he hit her.

She sees bootprints in the snow going around the side of the house, but nothing on the steps of the porch. She bounds up to the front door and finds it locked. Uses her key to get in.

The overhead light is on in the kitchen. Its glow spills out into the entryway. It's more than enough to show Kate what she needs to see.

A patch of blood on the hardwood floor.

Drops of blood on the stairs.

A stick of wood painted white—one of the balusters broken off from the stairway railing.

The baluster is lying in the open doorway of the living room.

No light in there, except what's filtering in from the kitchen.

Kate stands in the doorway, bracing a hand against either side of the doorframe.

The couch and the coffee table have been moved aside to clear a space in the middle of the room. There on the floor, Jenny is lying on her back, her face turned to the side, her arms spread out.

Like Melissa Cornelle.

Merkury comes down the stairs as quietly as he can. It's cold. The front door is open. Kate stands sobbing in the doorway of the living room.

He stops near the bottom of the stairs and says, "Don't turn around."

She lifts her head, but she doesn't turn.

He descends the last steps and closes the front door.

"Where's my father?" Kate says.

Merkury leans against the newel post at the bottom of the stairs.

"I put him in his bed. I didn't want you to see him down here. Not like that."

"What difference does it make where I see him?"

Merkury's mask is itching his face. He pulls it up to his forehead.

"I didn't mean to kill him," he says. "I want you to know that."

"You didn't mean—"

"I wanted to threaten him. I couldn't have him testifying against your uncle. That would put me at risk. You understand that, don't you?"

She doesn't answer him.

"It's hard to threaten people," Merkury says. "You have to be sure they take you seriously. I told him I would kill you if he testified. He swore he wouldn't, but I had to make sure. So I cuffed him to the stairway and made him watch me kill the girl."

Kate leans forward in the living room doorway. He can hear her crying.

After a time she wipes the tears from her face and says, "She was my friend."

"Would it have been better if I brought some other girl? I didn't have time to plan, and she was here. I thought I could use her to make the point I needed to make. But I guess I was wrong. Your father didn't like watching. He pleaded with me, and when that didn't work he tore the baluster from the railing and came at me with it. I had to shoot him."

"You didn't have to," Kate says.

Merkury pulls his mask into place again. "Maybe. But what he did was irrational. Brave, but irrational. You can't count on someone like that to keep their word."

In the doorway, Kate stares at Jenny's body. The girl's face is gray in the dim light. There's a pillow from the couch lying on the floor beside her. It's what Merkury must have used to smother her.

"I'm brave," Kate says. "Does that mean you can't count on me?"

Merkury steps closer to her. She can hear it. She can feel it.

"No," he says. "I trust you."

"So you're not going to kill me?"

"You know I wouldn't do that."

Kate slides her right hand down along the doorframe, closer to the pocket of her coat.

"Let me clarify that," Merkury says. "I wouldn't do it unless you forced me to."

He's very close to her now. She wonders if he has his gun out. She wonders if she could draw hers and spin around—

She feels his fingers in her hair. Ungloved.

Is that his gun hand?

She closes her eyes, tries to work up her courage.

And hears a voice speak her name.

"Kate?"

48

It's Jenny.

When Kate opens her eyes, she sees the girl moving. Sees her head come up from the floor. Watches her sit up. There's something dreamlike about it, everything happening gradually, as if the world has been dialed down to half speed.

Kate feels herself falling forward. She's not in the doorway anymore. She's on her knees beside Jenny, holding the girl in her arms. She can feel the warmth of Jenny's cheek against her own. She can hear herself laughing with joy and relief.

But Jenny is trembling. "I can see him, Kate," she says. Fearful, confused. "He tried to kill me. He's right there. Can you see him?"

Kate turns to see Merkury in the doorway, with the light from the kitchen behind him. He's putting his glove back on. His pistol is holstered on his hip.

He turns toward the front door and walks out of her sight.

She faces Jenny again.

"Listen," Kate says. "I need you to run. Go out the back door. Whatever you do, don't follow me."

"Where are you going?" Jenny asks.

"I'll be fine. Don't worry about me. But you have to run."

Kate kisses the girl on the forehead and gets to her feet. The revolver from Vera Landen's desk is in her pocket. She has it in her hand by the time she walks out the front door. She draws the hammer back with her thumb as she's climbing down the porch steps.

Merkury is almost to his car.

Kate raises the gun and fires a shot into the air.

He stops.

He's got the ski mask pulled up. She can see the back of his neck. It's pale against the black of his bulletproof vest.

"Turn around," she says.

"It's over, Kate," he tells her. "I've done what I needed to. We can both walk away from this."

"Not you," she says. "Get down on your knees."

He brings his hands up from his sides, but he's not surrendering. He pulls the mask down over his face and turns around.

Kate has the gun aimed at his head. "I told you. On your knees."

"I know what you're thinking about right now," he says. "I know why you're upset."

She steps forward until she's about fifteen feet away from him. She doesn't want to be any closer.

"I know it's not just about your father," he says. "That's a big part of it, but there's the other thing too."

Snow is falling all around her, but her face feels hot.

"Shut up," she says.

He points at the house. "What happened in there, some people would say it's a miracle. Your friend is alive. That's a win. Take the win and be happy. Forget about the other one."

There's a searing pain in Kate's head, and it's not from when he hit her.

"I swear to god," she says. "I will shoot you."

"I don't think so. It's not so easy, unless you've had practice. And you have to want it."

"What makes you think I don't want it?"

"I know you," he says.

She can't read his face behind the mask, but there's a gentleness in his voice. She recognizes it. It's unmistakable. Even after eighteen years.

"Don't misunderstand me," he says. "I don't claim to know everything. But about this one thing— Nobody else knows, do they?"

The gun feels heavy in Kate's hand. She can't bring herself to answer him.

"You don't have to be afraid of me," he says. "I want to help you. You and I, we can share the big secret. Sometimes they wake up."

The trigger is hard and cold against her finger. "I will kill you—"

"I'm not the one you're angry with. Or not the only one. But I promise you, Kate, of the two of us, I'm the only one who deserves it. You are innocent. Someone needs to tell you. If there's no one else to do it, let it be me. Let me absolve you."

The weight of the revolver drags her hand down, but she raises it up again. She feels fresh tears in her eyes, feels them roll down her cheeks. By the time they reach her chin, they're cold.

"I hate you," she says.

He nods and takes a step back toward his car.

"I have to leave now, Kate."

Before he can turn, she shifts her aim and shoots at the car's front tire. The first bullet strikes the hubcap. The second finds its mark. They're both startlingly loud. The tire starts to deflate.

"That was a stupid thing to do," Merkury says.

He's reaching for the gun on his hip. Kate aims for his head again but fires too quickly. The bullet strikes the vest and knocks him back against the car. She pulls the trigger once more, but it's a wild shot. It misses him entirely.

He gets his gun clear of its holster and fires twice. Kate feels the first bullet strike her right leg above the knee. The second tears into her left shoulder. The impacts throw her off-balance, but she recovers. She doesn't fall.

The revolver is empty. Useless now. She feels it slip free of her fingers and drop to the ground. She reaches under her coat to touch her wounded shoulder. Draws her hand out again and stares at her red palm.

"You shot me," she says.

Merkury lowers his gun to his side. Holsters it.

"You shot first."

Kate stares at him. The snow falling between them makes him seem unreal.

"I don't feel right," she says. "Am I going to die?"

"No," he says. "I wouldn't let that happen."

He sounds so solemn. It makes her smile. She steps forward, wondering if the leg he shot will carry her. It does. She takes more steps. They're smooth, like she's gliding through the snow. Covering the last of the distance, she staggers. But he catches her.

There's a hardness to him, but that's the vest he's wearing. The way he's holding her is tender. Both arms around her. He's rubbing her back. She lets herself lean into him.

He's taller than she is. She can feel his cheek against the top of her head. Rough—because the mask is between them. He reaches up and pulls it off. Rubs his cheek against her hair.

"Do you promise I won't die?" she asks him.

"My brave girl," he says. "I promise."

Her right hand slides into her coat pocket. The scissors are still there, the ones she picked up at the police station. She grips the handles tight.

His fingertips weave through her hair to touch the back of her neck. Gloveless.

She lets him have a few more seconds, then begins to pull away.

He lets her go.

She's looking in his eyes when she stabs the scissors into the side of his neck.

There's no scream. Only shock. His mouth falling open and a wild-eyed look.

Kate feels the heat of his blood on her hand. Twists the scissors and pulls them free.

"I'm not your girl," she says.

He shoves her away before she can stab him again. She stumbles back, falls in the snow. Struggles to rise. Her left arm isn't working as it should. Her wounded shoulder feels numb. Her wounded leg is stiff and slow to move.

Merkury has fallen back against the side of his car. One hand on his neck, the other on the grip of his gun. His mouth twists and a low sound comes out of him. Something like a growl. He wrenches his gun from his holster. Heaves himself away from the car and stands straight.

Kate gets to her feet at last. The pain in her leg makes her whole body tremble. She keeps hold of the scissors, as if they might protect her. Merkury raises his gun. She hobbles backward toward the house to put some distance between them.

He fires two shots, and she flinches at the sound of them, but neither one hits her. One of them shatters a window behind her.

Another shot, and she's still moving backward. She slips in the snow and lands hard on her back. Her shoulder throbs and her wounded leg won't move. Merkury is walking toward her, one ponderous step at a time, as if he's trudging up a steep hill.

With each step he fires a shot. The bullets strike the ground around her.

Kate lost the scissors when she fell. She thinks she ought to search for them. Or try to stand up. Or something. But she's tired. And cold. It's easier to keep still. Merkury is close now. She watches him sway and then stand firm. He straightens his arm and aims his gun at her. The muzzle is a dark, moving void. It sweeps past her and then comes back.

He pulls the trigger and she feels the bullet graze her ear.

He shifts his weight from one foot to the other. The muzzle of the gun traces a drunken pattern in the air. His left hand clutches at his neck, blood pulsing between his fingers.

Kate watches snowflakes falling down through the air. She feels one melt against her cheek.

There's a flutter in her chest that seems too fast for a heartbeat.

Her vision blurs. Against the snow, Merkury is a black shadow.

Last thing she remembers is the shadow dissolving into nothing.

49

SPRING

"I've been thinking about lies," Lee Tennick says. "About deception. About camouflage."

He's alone in his RV, talking into a microphone.

"In nature there are predators that use camouflage to make themselves more effective killers. The leopard's spots are meant to help it blend into the grasslands and forests where it hunts. The white fur of the polar bear makes it nearly invisible against a background of ice and snow.

"Some human predators rely on camouflage too. For years, the Merkury killer staged his crimes to look like something they weren't: the work of a disturbed mind, the result of pathology and compulsion. In this way, he was able to hide the true motives for his murders."

Tennick can hear himself in the headphones he's wearing. He's not impressed. This monologue seemed fine on the page, but now that he's reading it out loud, it sounds stiff and pretentious.

It makes no difference. He doesn't have to include any of this in his podcast.

He keeps the recorder rolling.

"This is the last episode in my ten-part series on the Merkury killings. It covers the events that took place earlier this year, on a night in late January, in the small town of Alexander, New York. This one is personal to me, because when I'm not on the road, Alexander is where I make my home. I've been inside the police station that Merkury set on fire. And as for the Summerlin house—where he carried out his final attacks on that night—I see it each time I walk out my front door."

Tennick stops to take a drink of water, then leans into the microphone again.

"Those of you who have been following this series will no doubt have one question at the forefront of your minds. Rather than keeping you in suspense, I'll answer it right now. Over the course of this episode you'll be hearing from many people who have insights into what happened here in Alexander, but you won't be hearing from Kate Summerlin. Her story is her own, and if she chooses to tell it, she'll do it in her own time."

The Summerlin house has a mailbox at the end of the driveway. Jenny Wyler walks out there at dusk and finds a thick stack of envelopes.

She sorts through them, standing by the road. Mostly junk, a few bills, two letters.

Walking back to the house, she stops at the place where she always stops: the little patch of ground where she found Kate lying in the snow.

Jenny didn't run that night, even though Kate asked her to. She saw the blood on the floor in the entryway of the house and followed the trail of it up the stairs. She found Kate's father in his room, laid out on his bed, dead of a gunshot wound to the chest.

She left him there and went to the guest bedroom at the front of the house. There she stood at the window and watched the scene unfold in the driveway. She saw Kate shot twice by Merkury, saw her stagger forward into his arms.

Jenny couldn't hear what they said to each other, but she saw Merkury take off his mask.

It looked like he was trying to comfort Kate.

There was nothing Jenny could do, not even call for help. Merkury had taken her phone, and Mr. Summerlin's. She could only watch—as Kate stabbed Merkury in the neck and retreated, as he advanced on her with his gun.

In the end he stood over her aiming down, so close that he couldn't possibly miss. Then he turned away, took three steps toward his car, and fell headlong into the snow.

Things moved quickly after that, and Jenny's recollection of the rest of the night is sketchy and impressionistic. She remembers running from the guest room, down the stairs, out into the cold.

She remembers kneeling beside Kate.

Kate opening her eyes and saying, "Please don't leave me here."

She remembers speeding on the slick roads in her car, with Kate lying across the back seat. Coming to the chaotic scene around the police station downtown. Fire trucks on Main Street blocking her path.

Cutting through side streets to make her way around.

Having to slow down by the college, because students were walking in the road. A surreal moment when the campus looked as pretty as a scene in a snow globe.

Then reaching the hospital. Honking her horn outside the emergency room. Nurses running out with a gurney.

Jenny spent the night in the ER waiting room. Fell asleep in a chair at some point. Got woken up by a doctor who told her Kate would be okay, and later by a cop who wanted to take her statement about the shooting.

"Shootings," Jenny told him.

"What's that?"

"More than one. Plus a stabbing."

She told him what happened, with as much detail as she could recall, but without any commentary. There were things she didn't understand, like the way Merkury held Kate after he shot her, as if he cared about her. Whatever that was, it was Kate's business.

She and Kate haven't discussed it since. The way Jenny sees it, if Kate wants to talk about it, she will.

Until then, Jenny has been spending as much time as she can at the Summerlin house, looking after things. Cooking meals, making sure the grass gets mowed and the bills get paid.

She drops the mail on the kitchen table. Except for the two letters.

They're both addressed by hand, from the same person. Alice Cornelle.

Melissa Cornelle's mother.

One is for Kate, the other for Jenny.

Jenny slides hers into her pocket. She'll read it later.

She has an idea of what it will say. It's the second letter Alice Cornelle has written to her. The first arrived a few weeks after the night Merkury tried to kill her. *Dear Jenny*, it began. *I hope you won't mind hearing from a stranger. I'd like to tell you about my daughter . . .*

The letter rambled on from there, but in a kindly, charming way—Alice writing about the child she lost and the children she still had with her. She wished Jenny a happy and blessed life, and ended with a P.S. *Don't feel you have to reply to this. It's enough for me to know you're out there in the world.*

But Jenny sent a reply. It seemed only right. She'll reply to this new letter too.

She taps the letter addressed to Kate against the edge of the kitchen table. Walks through the house to Kate's room and knocks softly on her door. Hears nothing from inside.

She eases the door open and sees Kate sleeping on her bed, her laptop beside her. She's been writing something lately, though Jenny doesn't know what it is.

She leaves Kate's letter on her desk and goes out, drawing the door shut behind her.

*   *   *

Kate is awake.

She lies still for a minute after Jenny is gone, then gets up from the bed.

There's a distant ache in her leg where Merkury shot her. She's been waiting for it to go away. Maybe it never will. The bullet chipped off a bit of her femur. "You'll be fine," one of the doctors told her. "Though you may be able to predict the weather."

The wound in her shoulder was trickier. Kate went through two surgeries to repair the damage. She's still in physical therapy, but she's getting so she can move her arm the way she used to. Just about.

She has scars now. Sometimes she looks at them in the mirror to remind herself of how she's been altered.

The house has been altered as well. Even though the blood has been washed away and the staircase repaired and everything returned to its place, it feels different, because her father is gone.

She had him buried in a cemetery nearby, not with her mother in Ohio. She judged that they didn't need to be together.

Jenny was at her side at the funeral, and in the days before and after. Lee Tennick too. Vera Landen put in an appearance. Kate didn't speak to her at the cemetery. Landen had already visited her at the hospital.

"Gunpowder and sweat," Kate said, when she woke up to find Landen sitting at her bedside.

Landen looked confused, and concerned.

"That's what Merkury smelled like," Kate said. "I want to say smoke too. But the smell of smoke was mostly on me."

Landen had many questions for her that day. Kate told her what Merkury said about her father, about why he killed him. She gave Landen an abbreviated account of what happened when she followed Merkury out into the driveway, when he shot her and she stabbed him. She left out almost all of the dialogue.

Kate feels a little bad about not telling Landen everything. The woman was kind to her and didn't press her too much about the details of her story.

"It's lucky that Merkury let you get close to him," Landen said. "That he let you lean on him after you were shot."

"I guess so," said Kate.

"As if he regretted hurting you."

"Maybe."

"I'll tell you something else—and this is strictly off the record. Merkury's gun had two bullets left in it when it was recovered. It's strange that he didn't use them."

"He was losing a lot of blood at the end," Kate said.

Landen nodded. "Maybe that's it. Maybe he was just too far gone."

The following day, Landen came to see her again. By then she knew Merkury's real name.

"Charles Peterson," she said.

"Really?" said Kate. It seemed too ordinary.

"We ran his fingerprints," Landen said. "He had no criminal record, but he served in the army when he was young, so his prints were in the military database. Charles Christopher Peterson, if you want to be precise. You'll be interested in this: he grew up in Ohio and worked for a while as a security consultant for a company your uncle did business with."

Kate remembered the doubt she had felt when her father told her that her uncle had been involved in setting up Melissa Cornelle's murder.

You think Uncle Jim knows hitmen? she'd asked him.

I think he knows a guy who knows a guy who can put you in touch with a hitman.

"It goes a long way toward explaining why Merkury was so eager to get his hands on that tape your father made," Landen said. "And why he went after your father when he couldn't get the tape. He told you the plain truth: he needed to be sure your father never testified against your uncle—"

"Because that would have put him at risk," Kate said. "Do you think my uncle knew Merkury's name? Do you think they met face-to-face?"

Landen shrugged. "I don't know for certain. Your uncle has hired a lawyer. He's not talking."

It was a lot to absorb, and it raised other questions in Kate's mind. One in particular.

"Do you think my mother met Merkury?" she asked.

Landen couldn't give her an answer.

Standing in her bedroom, Kate looks around for what's changed.

She knows something has, because Jenny came in, and she must have had a reason.

It's growing dark outside, and the only light Kate has is what's coming from under the door and from her laptop screen. All the corners of the room are charcoal gray.

She switches on her desk lamp and sees it: a letter from Alice Cornelle.

Kate hasn't spoken to Alice since the fall. In the interim, Alice has learned about Kate's father's affair with Melissa, and she knows that Kate's mother arranged to have Melissa killed. Landen was the one who told her.

Kate brings Alice's letter to the bed and sits with it for a while.

Opens it eventually.

She skims through to the end, knowing what she'll find there. It's the same sentiment Alice expressed in her last letter, in virtually the same words.

I know how you must be hurting. I hope you'll come for a visit soon. You will always be welcome here. You are precious to me, and I would never blame you for the sins of your parents.

Kate knows that she means it.

She could drive there tomorrow, to the town where Alice lives, and find her in the yard in the sunshine, hanging laundry up to dry. Alice would embrace her the way she always does. And if Kate tried to tell her she was sorry, Alice would say there's nothing to be sorry for.

But Alice doesn't know. She thinks she does, but she doesn't.

She's not in on the big secret.

Sometimes they wake up.

Kate has forgotten it many times herself. But now and again she remembers. On that night in January, when Merkury slid his fingers into her hair, when Jenny woke up and said her name out loud—

Kate?

—it came back to her:

The *other* night. By the stream. Under the oak tree.

The thing that happened when Kate was eleven.

50

Moonlight.

The wind whispering through the leaves of the oak.

Kate kneeling in the grass, looking down at the body of Melissa Cornelle.

Merkury standing behind her.

"You can touch her," he said. "There's no harm in it."

Kate touched the girl's skin, and it wasn't cold.

"Touch her hair," Merkury said.

Kate leaned forward and brushed aside the locks of hair that had fallen over Melissa's face. For an instant she thought she would see the girl's eyes staring at her, but they were closed. She drew her hand away.

"This seems wrong," she said.

"Which part?" Merkury asked her.

"All of it. I thought she was alive when I saw her at first. She shouldn't be dead."

"That's true," Merkury said, and he delivered his speech about death: "She was talking and moving around just a while ago. Now she's gone. All the same elements are here. Flesh and blood and bone. But it's not the same. It shouldn't be so easy for the life to go out of someone. It shouldn't be possible, but it is."

His voice was so gentle. Kate convinced herself she wasn't afraid of him.

"You're very brave," he said to her. And touched her—put his fingers in her hair.

"I'm leaving now," he said.

That's when Melissa moved.

The movement started in her legs. Her left knee came up and her left foot dragged along the ground. Then the same on the right. She was lying with her arms outspread and her head tipped to one side, her cheek resting on fallen leaves. She opened her eyes and looked up.

At the tree.

At Kate.

At *him*.

Fear took hold of her. Kate could see it in her face.

Melissa tried to move her arms, but they were bound to the wooden pole.

She fixed her eyes on Kate's.

"Help me."

Kate was stunned for a moment, then bent forward to untie her.

Merkury pulled her back.

"No," he said. His voice wasn't gentle anymore.

"You have to let her go," Kate said.

"That's not the way this works."

"But you have to."

Merkury got his hands under Kate's armpits and pulled her up onto her feet.

Melissa called out to her, desperate. "Please. Please help me."

"It isn't fair," Kate said. "She's okay. You have to let her go."

Merkury's hands were on Kate's upper arms now and his grip was firm. His fingers dug into her. It hurt.

"This is over," he said to her. "It's already done. You need to go. Back where you came from."

Melissa managed to sit up, dug her heels in, pushed herself backward along the ground. The wooden pole got hung up against the trunk of the oak tree.

Her eyes stayed locked on Kate's. "You can't leave me here."

"It's not fair," Kate said, struggling against Merkury, reaching for Melissa. But Merkury held her back.

Kate can still feel the struggle now, with her whole body, if she lets herself. She can hear Melissa crying. Pleading. She can feel herself fighting to break free from Merkury. An eleven-year-old against a grown man. She can hear herself trying to argue with him. Using whole sentences at first, and then just two words.

"No fair . . . No fair . . . No fair . . ."

Merkury held on to her firmly. She kicked at his legs with her heels. He picked her up roughly, carried her away from the tree and Melissa. Put her down on the grass again.

"Go," he said. A sternness in his voice. Not like someone who was angry, but like someone who was trying not to get angry.

When Kate didn't move, he shoved her. She stumbled forward, down on one knee.

"Please don't go," Melissa said.

"Last chance," said Merkury. "Run. Don't make me do something I don't want to do."

Last chance.

Kate surrendered.

The worst part. The most shameful.

She didn't run, but she got up off her knee and took a step. And another. Her body numb and shaking. Both. She couldn't hear the water in the stream, and the ground in front of her seemed thick with shadows.

She wasn't aware of moving her legs, but something was moving them.

Melissa's voice behind her was faint and not quite real.

"Don't go. Don't leave me here with him."

Kate felt the wet grass under her bare feet, and she thought she might sink into the earth.

The last word she heard from Melissa was "Please."

"No fair," Kate says to herself, sitting on her bed with Alice Cornelle's letter.

She sounds a lot like that child of eleven.

By the time that girl got back to her house, some of the shadows had withdrawn. The stars were shining. She woke her father and told him she had found a dead girl in the woods. An awful, awful thing, but bearable.

The truth never left her entirely, but she locked it away.

She would lock it away again if she could. She's been writing about Merkury for weeks, and she has enough material on her laptop to fill many chapters. But none of it is about what really happened with Melissa. She can't bring herself to write that part down.

On some level, intellectually, Kate knows she's not to blame for Melissa's death. But sometimes she can't resist the thoughts that come to her. Sometimes she's certain she should have stayed and fought longer. Merkury didn't even threaten to kill her. Not explicitly.

Shouldn't she have held out until he did? Didn't she owe Melissa that much?

If she had stayed and turned around and looked him in the eye, could she have convinced him to change his mind?

Or if she had realized, when she first saw her, that Melissa wasn't dead, could they have both gotten away before Merkury came back?

Alice Cornelle's letter is an invitation: *I hope you'll come for a visit soon.*

Kate wants to go. She needs to go. Merkury wasn't wrong when he said she needed to be absolved. But she never wanted absolution from him. She wants it from Alice.

She thinks Alice would give it to her if she asked. But she would have to tell Alice the truth, and how much pain would the truth cause her?

Today is the twelfth of May, the anniversary of Melissa's death, which means Alice has had nineteen years to grieve and to heal.

Would it be fair to tell her the truth now and make her grieve all over again?

Kate doesn't think so.

One day soon, she'll take a drive and visit Alice, and they'll talk and take what comfort they can from one another, as they always have. But Kate will keep the big secret to herself. She won't ask Alice to relive her daughter's death.

She believes she can do without absolution.

Around ten o'clock, Kate opens the casement window in her room and climbs out into the backyard. She takes a few steps in the grass in her bare feet and looks up at the sky. There's no moon yet, but the stars are beautiful.

If she holds still and listens carefully, she can hear the stream off in the distance. She walks a little farther, toward the line of old trees at the edge of the yard. Now and again she can hear their branches creaking in the wind.

These night sounds have an otherworldly quality, and as she listens she has a sense of being watched.

She's had it before, more than once, since Merkury died. As if he's out there among the trees. As if she might never be rid of him.

She knows it's irrational. The day after she got out of the hospital, she went to see Vera Landon in the temporary police station that had been set up in an empty storefront downtown. Landen understood what she needed, left her waiting for a few minutes, and returned with a folder that held a single autopsy photo.

The photo showed his face clearly, along with the wound in his neck. When Kate saw it, she knew he was dead and it was over and he was never going to come back.

He's not here.

Kate walks out to the tree line in the dark. Maybe it's an act of defiance. Maybe she just wants to prove something to herself.

She's not afraid.

Not of the dark. Not of being alone. She has, in a sense, lived most of her life alone.

She turns back to look at the house. There's the familiar light of her bedroom window. And more light, coming through the window of the back door.

As she's watching, the door opens and Jenny comes out. She looks around, concerned.

Kate begins to walk toward her. Jenny sees her and waves.

They meet in the middle of the yard.

"Are you okay?" Jenny asks.

"Sure," says Kate.

Jenny's face is serious. "You can tell me, you know."

Kate smiles. "Tell you what?"

"Whatever it is," Jenny says, reaching out to touch her arm. "You can tell me anything."

There's no simple explanation for what happens next. It's many things together: the night sky, her father's absence, the wind in the grass. A touch and some words. It's ridiculous, Kate thinks. She took a bullet to the leg and stayed on her feet. This is what's going to bring her down?

She tries to brush it off. Tries to walk past Jenny toward the house. Finds herself walking into Jenny instead. Feels Jenny putting her arms around her.

"I can't," Kate says. And she's crying.

Jenny holds her up for a long while, then something breaks and Kate descends until she's kneeling on the ground. But she's not alone. Jenny goes down with her, the two of them on the lawn under the stars.

"I can't," Kate says again. "I can't."

Over and over.

But no matter how many times she says it, Jenny doesn't let go.

Acknowledgments

I'm grateful to my editor, Joe Brosnan, for taking on this book and help-ing me improve it in a multitude of ways. And to my agent, Victoria Skurnick, for her friendship and guidance over many years.

Thanks also to Morgan Entrekin, Jim Levine, Melissa Rowland, Miek Coccia, Courtney Paganelli, Timothy Wojcik, Julia Berner-Tobin, Jenny Choi, Mary Flower, Bill Weinberg, M. P. Klier, and Zoe Harris. And to my brother, Terry, and my sister, Michelle.

I would never have made it through the writing of this book without Liz Barrett and Deborah Berman. That is the plain and simple truth, and it's why I've dedicated it to them.

This novel is set in the fictional town of Alexander, New York, at an invented college called Seagate. Any resemblance to Hamilton, New York, and Colgate University is coincidental and can easily be explained away.